What people are saying about …

Talking to the Dead

"It isn't often that I get so hooked on the characters and story that I forget time and purpose. *Talking to the Dead* caught hold of my heart from page one. It takes a gifted and intuitive writer like Bonnie to bring humor into the middle of such a serious story. Call her the Jodi Picoult of Christian fiction! Beautifully done! I can't wait to read the next story she writes."

Francine Rivers, best-selling
author of *Redeeming Love*

"Rarely have I read a book that so completely captivated me. After reading the opening line on page one, I stayed up half the night to finish it. Bonnie Grove earns the title of master storyteller in *Talking to the Dead*. The tale of one woman's journey through grief, mental illness, and betrayal is uplifting and filled with hope. The description that fits best is hauntingly beautiful."

Ane Mulligan, editor, Novel Journey,
and Afictionado columnist

"In *Talking to the Dead,* Bonnie Grove takes readers on a vivid journey through the memories of a woman grieving for her late husband. We're drawn into Kate's life, gripped by the slowly unfolding drama that unravels her sometimes-painful past and, more importantly,

reveals the key to her future. A captivating, powerful story. I highly recommend it.

Virginia Smith, author of *Age before Beauty* and the Sister-to-Sister series

"*Talking to the Dead* will break your heart and put it back together, better than new. God bless Bonnie Grove for this riveting, insightful, unforgettable story! I couldn't put it down."

Kathleen Popa, author of *To Dance in the Desert* and *The Feast of Saint Bertie*

"Bonnie Grove's amazing novel takes the reader on a unique and compelling journey into loss and restoration; a blend of *The Pilot's Wife* and *Girl, Interrupted*. Well done."

Sharon K. Souza, author of *Lying on Sunday*

"*Talking to the Dead* is a deeply moving narrative about grief, sanity, love, betrayal, and hard-won redemption. Bonnie Grove entices, tortures, then salves her readers through gritty characters and pitch-perfect writing. I thought about this book long after I put it down, and it stays with me today. Highly recommended."

Mary E. DeMuth, author of *Watching the Tree Limbs* and *Daisy Chain*

"*Talking to the Dead* is a shirk-your-duties kind of book. You'll read it to the neglect of laundry and cooking and bring it with you to read in the car at stoplights. With a story that unfolds in the most surprising ways and a protagonist so true-to-life you feel like you should be praying for her, *Talking to the Dead* delves deep into the recesses of grief, anger, and most importantly, redemption. Bonnie Grove has set the bar high with this one. I can't wait to read her next book."

Alison Strobel, author of *Violette*
Between and *Worlds Collide*

"With tightly woven prose that is achingly real and skillfully rendered, Bonnie Grove has crafted a deeply moving story of grief, betrayal, and redemption. Grove's engaging, authentic style is resonant, and her words linger long after you've set the book down."

Susan Meissner, author of *The Shape of Mercy*

"In *Talking to the Dead,* Bonnie Grove masterfully takes you on an authentic journey through grief and recovery with a twist, and leaves you wishing for more."

Debbie Fuller Thomas, author of *Tuesday*
Night at the Blue Moon and *Raising Rain*

"Bonnie Grove has a remarkable gift not only for can't-put-the-book-down storytelling, but she also takes on big, weighty issues—betrayal, grief, wrenching regrets—and handles them with compassion, humor, and ultimately, hope."

Joy Jordan-Lake, author *Blue Hole Back*
Home and *Why Jesus Makes Me Nervous*

"Masterfully written, *Talking to the Dead* thrusts you into the murky world of grief. Despite the deep subject, Bonnie Grove handles the topic with a light hand as we sojourn with a woman who questions her sanity while viewing life with a quirky sense of awareness. With a bittersweet blending of grief and grace, *Talking to the Dead* leaves you feeling fully satisfied."

Megan DiMaria, author of *Out of Her Hands* and *Searching for Spice*

"Bonnie Grove's debut novel is one to savor, brimming with an addictive story, characters you come to love, and a perfect dollop of humor. Good gravy, is it good: I'm talking stay-up-later-than-your-early-morning-permits good. Dear reader, you are in for a treat."

Kimberly Stuart, author of *Act Two*

"Bonnie Grove's *Talking to the Dead* is a disturbing yet redemptive spiral through complicated grief. You can't help but cheer for her heroine as she emerges from her chrysalis of pain a stronger, wiser woman, ready to soar. Christian fiction lovers will relish this tale."

Claudia Mair Burney, author of *Zora and Nicky* and *Wounded*

TALKING TO THE DEAD

TALKING TO THE DEAD

a novel

BONNIE GROVE

David C Cook®

transforming lives together

TALKING TO THE DEAD
Published by David C. Cook
4050 Lee Vance View
Colorado Springs, CO 80918 U.S.A.

David C. Cook Distribution Canada
55 Woodslee Avenue, Paris, Ontario, Canada N3L 3E5

David C. Cook U.K., Kingsway Communications
Eastbourne, East Sussex BN23 6NT, England

David C. Cook and the graphic circle C logo
are registered trademarks of Cook Communications Ministries.

This story is a work of fiction. All characters and events are the product of the author's
imagination. Any resemblance to any person, living or dead, is coincidental.

LCCN 2009924471
ISBN 978-1-4347-6641-0
eISBN 978-1-4347-0034-6

© 2009 Bonnie Grove
Published in association with the Books & Such Literary Agency
52 Mission Circle, Suite 122, PMB 170
Santa Rosa, CA 95409-5370
www.booksandsuch.biz

The Team: Susan Tjaden, Nicci Hubert, Jaci Schneider, and Evelin Roncketti
Cover/Interior Design: Amy Kiechlin
Cover Photo: Getty Images, Stone Collection, Felipe Dupouy

Printed in the United States of America
First Edition 2009

1 2 3 4 5 6 7 8 9 10

032709

For Steve, Benjamin, Heather—
We're in this together
and
For Gordon—Who helped me see

ACKNOWLEDGMENTS

Books are collaborative efforts. Forget the notion of the cloistered writer alone with her thoughts, the romantic myth of isolated keyboard clacking in a mountain cabin. Oh, certainly there is the writing, the idea that belongs wholly to the author (as much as any idea can belong to anyone)—but that alone creates only a manuscript. It takes much more to make a book. Here are the people it took to make this one.

My gratitude to the extraordinary team at David C. Cook—Dave Grove, for his enthusiastic love for his job. Deb Templemeyer, who took the time to care about what happened to the manuscript. Susan Tjaden, who has been a champion of this book from the beginning, and a joy to know and work with. You've brought joy to the journey. My thanks and admiration to Don Pape: You are the guy an author dreams of having in her corner, a man of integrity. I don't know where I'd be without Wendy Lawton of Books & Such Literary Agency. Wendy, you are a standout in this industry, a champion. And what would this book be without editor Nicci Jordan Hubert? Wrestler of words, grappler of paragraphs, grasper of concepts—it's my great pleasure to know and work with you. It is obvious you do what you do for one simple reason: love. For readers, for authors, for art.

I owe so much to Isabelle Vouve, my dear friend who faithfully read every word and offered so much more than her "eagle eyes," but gave her heart. I love you, Belle. And thanks to Debi Knutson, the friend who walked with me in the valley, and walks with me still. Much love. I'm grateful for the prayers of the people in our church home—they helped more than can be expressed.

Thanks to my family, my mom and dad who have rejoiced with each giddy step, prayed every day, and have turned into first-class booksellers. Great smooches and hugs to my children Benjamin and Heather, too young to understand what all the fuss was about. They are my heart. And my thanks to Steve, my favorite person. You're the one who made all of it possible. Forever and a day.

1

Kevin was dead and the people in my house wouldn't go home. They mingled after the funeral, eating sandwiches, drinking tea, and speaking in muffled tones. I didn't feel grateful for their presence. I felt exactly nothing.

Funerals exist so we can close doors we'd rather leave open. But where did we get the idea that the best approach to facing death is to eat Bundt cake?

I refused to pick at dainties and sip hot drinks. Instead I wandered into the backyard.

I knew if I turned my head I'd see my mother's back as she guarded the patio doors. Mom would let no one pass. As a recent widow herself, she knew my need to stare into my loss alone.

I sat on the porch swing and closed my eyes, letting the June sun warm my bare arms. Instead of closing the door on my pain, I wanted it to swing from its hinges so the searing winds of grief could scorch my face and body. Maybe I hoped to die from exposure.

Kevin had been dead three hours before I had arrived at the hospital. A long time for my husband to be dead without me knowing. He was so altered, so permanently changed without my being aware.

I had stood in the emergency room, surrounded by faded blue cotton curtains, looking at the naked remains of my husband while nurses talked in hushed tones around me. A sheet covered Kevin from his hips to his knees. Tubes, which had either carried something into or away from his body, hung disconnected and useless from his arms. The twisted remains of what I assumed to be some sort of breathing mask lay on the floor. "What happened?" I said in a whisper so faint I knew no one could hear. Maybe I never said it at all. A short doctor with a pronounced lisp and quiet manner told me Kevin's heart killed him. He used difficult phrases; medical terms I didn't know, couldn't understand. He called it an *episode* and said it was massive. When he said the word *massive*, spit flew from his mouth, landing on my jacket's lapel. We had both stared at it.

When my mother and sister, Heather, arrived at the hospital, they gazed speechlessly at Kevin for a time, and then took me home. Heather had whispered with the doctor, their heads close together, before taking a firm hold on my arm and walking me out to her car. We drove in silence to my house. The three of us sat around my kitchen table looking at each other.

Several times my mother opened her mouth to speak, but nothing came out. Our words had turned to cotton, thick and dry. We couldn't work them out of our throats. I had no words for my abandonment. Like everything I knew to be true had slipped out the back door when I wasn't looking.

"What happened?" I said again. This time I knew I had said it out loud. My voice echoed back to me off the kitchen table.

"Remember how John Ritter died? His heart, remember?" This

from Heather, my younger, smarter sister. Kevin had died a celebrity's death.

From the moment I had received the call from the hospital until now, slumped on the backyard swing, I had allowed other people to make all of my bereavement decisions. My mother and mother-in-law chose the casket and placed the obituary in the paper. Kevin's boss at the bank, Donna Walsh, arranged for the funeral parlor and even called the pastor from the church that Kevin had attended until he was sixteen to come and speak. Heather silently held my hand through it all. I didn't feel grateful for their help.

I sat on the porch swing, and my right foot rocked on the grass, pushing and pulling the swing. My head hurt. I tipped it back and rested it on the cold, inflexible metal that made up the frame for the swing. It dug into my skull. I invited the pain. I sat with it, supped with it.

I opened my eyes and looked up into the early June sky. The clouds were an unmade bed. Layers of white moved rumpled and languid past the azure heavens. Their shapes morphed and faded before my eyes. A Pegasus with the face of a dog; a veiled woman fleeing; a villain; an elf. The shapes were strange and unreliable, like dreams. A monster, a baby—I wanted to reach up to touch its soft, wrinkled face. I was too tired. Everything was gone, lost, emptied out.

I had arrived home from the hospital empty-handed. No Kevin. No car—we left it in the hospital parking lot for my sister to pick up later. "No condition to drive," my mother had said. She meant me.

Empty-handed. The thought, incomplete and vague, crept closer to consciousness. *There should have been something.* I should have brought his things home with me. Where were his clothes? His wallet? Watch? Somehow they'd fled the scene.

"How far could they have gotten?" I said to myself. Without realizing it, I had stood and walked to the patio doors. "Mom?" I said as I walked into the house.

She turned quickly, but said nothing. My mother didn't just understand what was happening to me. She knew. She knew it like the ticking of a clock, the wind through the windows, like everything a person gets used to in life. It had only been eight months since Dad died. She knew there was little to be said. Little that should be said. Once, after Dad's funeral, she looked at Heather and me and said, "Don't talk. Everyone has said enough words to last for eternity."

I noticed how tall and straight she stood in her black dress and sensible shoes. How long must the dead be buried before you can stand straight again? "What happened to Kevin's stuff?" Mom glanced around as if checking to see if a guest had made off with the silverware.

I swallowed hard and clarified. "At the hospital. He was naked." A picture of him lying motionless, breathless on the white sheets filled my mind. "They never gave me his things. His, whatever, belongings. Effects."

"I don't know, Kate," she said. Like it didn't matter. Like I should stop thinking about it. I moved past her, careful not to touch her, and went in search of my sister.

Heather sat on my secondhand couch in my living room, a two-seater with the pattern of autumn leaves. She held an empty cup and a napkin, dark crumbs tumbling off onto the carpet. Her long brown hair, usually left down, was pulled up into a bun. She looked pretty and sad. She saw me coming, her brown eyes widening in recognition. Recognition that she should do something. Meet my needs, help me, make time stand still. She quickly ended the conversation she was having with Kevin's boss and met me in the middle of the living room.

"Hey," she said, touching my arm. I took a small step back, avoiding her warm fingers.

"Where would his stuff go?" I blurted out. Heather's eyebrows snapped together in confusion. "Kevin's things," I said. "They never gave me his things. I want to go and get them. Will you come?"

Heather stood very still for a moment, straight-backed like she was made of wood, then relaxed. "You mean at the hospital. Right, Kate? Kevin's things at the hospital?"

Tears welled in my eyes. "There was nothing. You were there. When we left, they never gave me anything of his." I realized I was trembling.

Heather bit her lower lip and looked into my eyes. "Let me do that for you. I'll call the hospital—" I stood on my tiptoes and opened my mouth. "I'll go," she corrected before I could say anything. "I'll go and ask around. I'll get his stuff and bring it here."

"I need his things."

Heather cupped my elbow with her hand. "You need to lie down. Let me get you upstairs, and as soon as you're settled, I'll go to the hospital and find out what happened to Kevin's clothes, okay?"

Fatigue filled the small spaces between my bones. "Okay." She led me upstairs. I crawled under the covers as Heather closed the door, blocking the sounds of the people below.

2

It was dark when I half woke. I wasn't alone in the bedroom. I could see nothing in the darkness, but I could feel Kevin standing by the door. My heart beat out a staccato rhythm, but my body remained loose and limp. I opened my mouth, but found I had no voice. The words I formed fell back into my throat. His presence seemed to move from the doorway to the end of the bed. Whatever his intent, I was powerless to either resist or comply. I blinked in the darkness, tears forming at the corners of my eyes.

"Go back to sleep. Everything is fine," Kevin said, his voice low and commanding.

Everything wasn't fine. He was dead and I was alone and none of this was supposed to happen. I rolled onto my side and sobbed as the darkness overtook me.

I awoke with a start. I heard a noise, rumbling and deep, like a man's voice. I strained my ears, but heard nothing more. The sun peered in around the blinds. Kevin's clothes were at the bottom of my bed, neatly folded.

I grabbed the clothes and buried my face in their folds. They smelled of citrus, as if recently laundered. I slipped on Kevin's blue-striped dress shirt. His belt lay coiled on top of his black slacks. I found his wallet in the back pocket and placed it on top of his dresser beside his wedding ring the funeral director had returned to me only two days before. Something was missing, but I couldn't think what. Another noise, this time like the scraping of a chair.

I headed downstairs. I went into the kitchen and was neither surprised nor alarmed to see Blair Winters sitting at the table. He looked up from the magazine he was reading and gave me a small "Hey." Blair held up the set of keys that Kevin had given him the day we moved in. "I let myself in." He pocketed them.

Blair Winters was Kevin's best man at our wedding and best friend in life. He was a pallbearer at Kevin's funeral and cried without restraint at the grave site.

They were an unlikely pair, Kevin and Blair. They had met at basketball tryouts their junior year of high school. Kevin was a serious guy who believed in hard work and dating one girl at a time. Blair was already on his way to becoming one of the most popular guys in high school. He had a rumpled, lazy look that drove girls crazy, which was fine with him.

When Blair left Greenfield for college, everyone in town said he'd never come back. They were wrong. The ink wasn't dry on his degree before he was back in town, much to the delight of his mother and the dismay of several coeds. He opened a small skateboard shop that dealt in exclusive, expensive parts. His mother had called his shop "a fine waste of an expensive degree."

I could still see the remnants of the playboy I knew in high school as I looked at Blair's face that morning. I noticed lines forming around his mouth, and a sadness that stretched over his face like a mask, but they did nothing to diminish his sex appeal. Even in my numb state I recognized his appeal. He looked like a man any woman would kiss. A coed, a mother, a nun.

I grabbed a box of cereal. "What are you up to?" I opened the fridge for the milk. I had to move two casserole dishes and a bowl of grapes in order to reach it. The entire town had cooked for me. I would be eating lasagna for years.

"Nothing," he said, tossing the magazine into the recycle bin by the back door. "I checked on you, but you were sleeping so I came down here."

"How long have you been here?"

He looked at his bare wrist. "Uh, it was pretty early when I got up. I couldn't sleep so I decided to go for a walk. I wandered around for a while and found myself in front of your guys' house. Your house." He pawed at his face with both hands. "I guess it was around three," he spoke into his palms.

"A.M.?" I asked stupidly.

"Yeah."

I shrugged and grabbed two bowls. Blair and I ate our cereal in silence.

"Do you want to know what his last words to me were?" Blair asked, breaking the stillness. He didn't look at me, just traced the maze on the back of the cereal box with his index finger.

"Yes."

"We were on the phone, the day before he … We'd been talking for about ten minutes; I was trying to help him with a problem he was having." He threw me a look I couldn't read, and then went back to the maze. "It was just some stuff at work he was trying to get straight. Anyway, at the end of our conversation, he said, 'You're a great friend, Blair. Like a brother.'" Blair's face trembled and crumbled. I thought he was crying, but when he spoke next his voice was calm. "Do you remember his last words to you? I mean, do you want to tell me?"

"No."

Kevin's last words to me? Did he kiss me good-bye before he drove off into his eternity? Did he call me from work to tell me he'd be home early—or late? Had he called on his cell phone, pounding his fist at red lights and telling me how he loved me? I didn't know. I couldn't remember.

Since Kevin died, I had tried to look into the days and weeks prior, but all I could see was a yawning, dark hole. My memories had been taken by blunt force. I wasn't sure when it happened, when my memories had slipped away. But looking at Blair's grief-doused face, I was certain they were gone.

Most of them, anyway. The dark hole, the abyss where my recent past resided, wasn't a complete void. Swirling in the midst of obscurity were pockets of light, like snapshots. Each one swam alone, unconnected to any other, unfettered. One of them, more a soundtrack than an image, played over again in my mind: Kevin saying, "Don't wait for me."

The statement taunted me like a bully. What did it mean? Whom was he speaking to? When had he said it? And when would I remember again? But even if I couldn't make sense of what he was saying, I played it over and over in my mind just to hear his voice.

Blair stared at me for a few moments, and, when it was clear

I would say no more, he got up from the table in a series of jerky movements that caused milk to spill from his bowl onto the table. "Sorry. I should go." He walked to the back door. I followed wordlessly. Blair kissed the top of my head, an easy place for him to reach. He was over six feet tall, I just over five foot four. "If you need me, I'm only a phone call away. Day or night, Kate. Okay?"

"Okay."

He reached for the knob and hesitated. He turned and looked into my eyes. "Seriously, Kate. Anything."

"I know."

When he was gone, I locked the back door and felt the emptiness of the house enfold me.

I left the dishes on the table and walked into the living room. Everything had been cleaned mercilessly. I could see no evidence of the funeral reception. It was as if it had never happened. I sat on the floor, my back to the two-seater sofa, and drew my knees up to my chest. Maybe it hadn't happened. Maybe it was a mistake. A divine clerical error.

Once, when I was at home unpacking my food after grocery shopping, I discovered a bag that didn't belong to me. I had stood in my kitchen wondering what I should do with four avocados, a package of condoms, and denture cleaner. Maybe that's what had happened this time. I'd picked up someone else's tragedy by mistake.

"The cereal is going to dry right onto those bowls," Kevin said from the kitchen.

"Who cares?" I said, lost in my wishful thinking.

"You hate it when the cereal is stuck to the sides of the bowl."

"Kevin?"

"I'm cold," he said.

"Where are you?"

My head felt light, a nebulous balloon floating above my body. I ran into the kitchen, catching my toe on a chair. "Kevin?" There was no one there.

The phone rang. I stood immobile, staring at it. My heart ricocheted off my breastbone as I reached for the receiver. I picked it up and pushed it to my ear. My lips parted. "Kevin?"

"Kate?" my mother said. "Are you there? I wanted to tell you that I left a turkey salad in the fridge for your lunch." I nodded, saying nothing. I hung up. It wasn't Kevin. He wasn't here. Hope and helplessness blended like oil and water in my stomach. *Of course Kevin's not here*, I thought. He's dead. No one talks to the dead.

3

I rambled through the main floor of my small house that night. Earlier the sunset had thrown prisms onto my walls, but now it was dark. The only light came from the streetlamp shining through the front window, turning my walls the color of muddy floors. Normal people were sleeping. But I wasn't normal, not anymore. Several times that night I stood at the bottom of the stairs that led to my bedroom. I gazed up into the darkness of the second-floor hallway, but I couldn't climb the stairs. Couldn't lift a foot to the first step. It was as if my desolation had multiplied the power of gravity. I was stuck.

My body was somnolent, but my restive mind barked out orders to keep moving, stay awake, stay watchful. I paced on rubbery legs, longing for unconsciousness. My mind, luminously awake, sewed blindfolds of anger and forged a strong rope of despair. Bound and helpless, I spoke: "Kevin?" Only the ticking of a clock responded. I picked up a cushion from the sofa and hugged it like a lost love. "Kevin, are you there?" I waited for an eternity. I closed my eyes and concentrated on trying to hear his voice. I listened until my head hurt. The silence whistled to me.

As the night advanced, my thoughts began to wander. I thought of Kevin, took inventory of him, touched him with my mind. His eyes, brown and sharp, taking in every detail around him. His hands, holding a pencil, flipping on a light switch, caressing my skin. His legs, thin but strong. My annual joke, spoken at the first sign of summer, when Kevin would tromp down the stairs wearing shorts for the first time in months: "Are those your legs, or are you riding a chicken?" His laugh, short bursts likes a gun firing. His scent: clean, earthy, masculine.

I thought of sleep—so close, yet so unattainable. I thought of turning on the TV. It would be a good distraction. The news maybe. I could find out what had happened in the world since Kevin died. See who else was persisting in the face of loss, pain, grief, and confusion. But the idea crushed me. I couldn't bear to share the planet's burden today. I thought of food—I hadn't eaten since breakfast. I thought of cereal bowls and Kevin talking to me about cereal bowls. I closed my eyes, reliving the moment. I knew his voice. I'd spent years mapping its cadence. It was the voice that said "I do," told me the Visa bill was overdue, and groaned my name in the middle of the night. I shivered in my warm living room. An ache, like a fist, sat in my belly. "Kevin?" Nothing.

Tears of frustration rolled fat and useless down my cheeks. What was I expecting? I hadn't anticipated hearing his voice in the first place. I hadn't asked God, or the universe, or my sainted aunt for this gift. Maybe he wouldn't speak again. Maybe it hadn't happened at all. A small voice whispered, "It did." I lowered myself to the floor and put the pillow behind my head. My eyes closed. Sleep came, not on a gentle breeze, but like a clout from the end of a club. I fell into its darkness thinking: *I understand nothing.*

❦

"You've gone and done it now," Kevin whispers in my ear. "You're stuck with me." He whirls me around the edges of the dance floor, doing his best imitation of a waltz. My white gown fans out behind me as we spin. I giggle, actually giggle, so unlike me, so removed from serious Kate, this giddy woman spinning in the arms of Kevin Davis. "Kate Davis," I say, rolling the name around my tongue. His hand is on the small of my back, pressing me close and all I want to do is run away with this man and make love to him until we are both exhausted and stupid. The thought sends volts of electricity flying through my body. Then I spot my mother, gesturing wildly at me, waving me in. She mouths words I can't make out. Then she holds up her hands in front of her face, pretending she's holding a camera, her index finger clicking wildly on the imaginary button. We're wanted for photographs.

I flick my wrist at her, but that only gets her more worked up. She begins to alternate between taking pretend pictures and waving me over in giant movements, as if she were a dockworker and I the Queen Mary.

"Mom wants us for a picture," I tell Kevin. Without missing a beat, he turns us toward where my parents are standing and cha-chas us over to them.

Mom grabs my wrist, nearly yanking my shoulder out of its socket. "Great-Uncle Jonah is leaving." She says this loudly, as if making a general announcement to the room, then she leans in and whispers, "Can't stay up one minute past nine for anything.

Not since the hernia operation. Grumpy old coot." She throws her arms up, "Uncle Jonah, I've found them. Stand there and I'll take your picture. No, there, against the wall. Just back up a few feet. Against the wall. Just move—oh never mind, that's fine."

Kevin and I stand on either side of my great-uncle Jonah and smile. Dad holds up the camera, ready to click. Great-Uncle Jonah looks down at his feet.

Mom waves her hands over her head. "Woo hoo! Look up here, Jonah. Woo hoo."

Uncle Jonah stares down at the floor.

Dad says, "Close enough." As he pushes on the button, Great-Uncle Jonah bends down and picks up a penny off the floor. He holds it up and smiles as if it were a Spanish doubloon. "Looky what I got here." He turns to me. "My lucky day. Where's my coat?" He toddles off down the hall and my mother holds her hands up on either side of her head and pretends to tear her hair out. Events make her nuts. She wants everything to be perfect.

Dad shakes his head at the camera. He looks up. "Hey, I need a dance with my girl." He holds his elbow out and I take his arm. "Sorry, sport," he says to Kevin. "She was mine first."

Kevin grins. "Yep. And she's mine now, but I'll let you borrow her."

Dad's face sort of freezes, a grin on his face that doesn't reach his eyes. He presses his arm close to his side, squeezing my hand between. He half leads, half drags me to the dance floor. The music is a fast rock song, but Dad pulls me into a waltz and we start making a box with our feet. "Happy?" he asks. He has to yell into my ear, the music is so loud.

*I stand on my tiptoes so my mouth can reach his ear. "Yes,"
I holler. "This is what I want."*

*Dad looks past me, over my shoulder, and I turn to follow
his gaze. Kevin is standing beside his best man, Blair Winters.
They're laughing; Blair holds a beer bottle and takes occasional
small sips from it. This is strange because I know Blair doesn't
much care for the taste of beer. I couldn't recall the last time I'd
seen him drink one.*

*There are five women surrounding Blair and Kevin, and
they are laughing. One of them snakes a hand across Blair's
shoulder and whispers into his ear. He nods and takes another
fast sip of beer, his eyes darting all over the room. Another girl
stands close to Kevin; she laughs at something he says. They look
like a beer commercial, two handsome men surrounded by a
bevy of chicks.*

*Blair's darting eyes rest on Dad and me on the dance floor.
I lift a hand off Dad's shoulder and wave. Blair holds up his
beer bottle and points a finger at me, his left hand tucked low
into the pocket of his tuxedo pants. The corners of his mouth
go up in a nearly-there smile, then he turns away. The woman
standing by Kevin puts her hand on his arm as she laughs and
laughs. In all the years I've known Kevin, I've never known
him to say anything that singularly hilarious. I try to drag my
dad closer to them, but he spins me around, so my back is to the
scene, his lips pressed together until they are white slits.*

*A moment later Kevin taps my father on the shoulder. "I
need my wife back." Dad hands me over to Kevin, his face
unreadable.*

I write "Kate Davis" with a flourish, but it doesn't match the name on my credit card and the hotel desk clerk, frumpy in her brown uniform and matching bellboy hat, frowns and tears up the paper. She shakes her head at me as if I were a naughty child caught picking my nose.

Kevin takes out his credit card and hands it to the clerk. She smiles, thrilled to do business with a reliable man who doesn't go around changing his name and creating unnecessary paperwork for underpaid hotel clerks forced to wear cutesy uniforms. Kevin smiles and winks at me as he signs the slip. He has a sort of "I'll take care of ya, baby" swagger in his manner as if at any moment he will doff a fedora and say, "This way, toots!"

I should be insulted. I should put my hands on my hips and remind him which century we live in and doesn't he know I can take care of myself and who does he think he is? But his slow smile and hooded eyes tell me he knows exactly who he is, and, in spite of myself, I feel something very close to swooning. I may hate myself in the morning, but for now, I'm all Jell-O legs and heart palpitations.

The desk clerk, seemingly as charmed as I am, falls all over herself, "Yes, Mr. Davis, thank you, Mr. Davis, ring if you need anything, Mr. Davis." Kevin puts his arm around me and says, "Got all I need right here." And I beam like a seventeenth-century Cinderella.

Kevin is handsome in a smooth-faced way. His wide-set brown eyes and clipped brown hair give him the look of a *trustworthy son, but his tall, muscular frame and broad shoulders give him a movie star feeling. Everywhere we go, people smile at him.*

Our porter is also wearing a bellboy hat that, in combination with his huge ears and mildly bucktoothed smile, makes him look like a performing monkey. He wheels our luggage to the elevator and pushes the Up button. I snuggle Kevin's arm and sigh. I'm with Kevin in paradise. Okay, it's not paradise; it's Niagara Falls, the tackiest place on earth—home of heart-shaped beds, Ripley's Believe It or Not! Museum, and more neon signs than should ever be assembled in one place—but for me, it's perfect.

In our room Monkey Boy stands by the door and clears his throat. Kevin hands him money, but I can't see how much because Kevin's back blocks my view. I throw myself on the bed, which is disappointingly firm, and I hear the door close. Kevin stands at the bottom of the bed and smiles down at me. He jumps onto the bed and scoops me up into his arms and kisses me until I forget my name, Davis or no Davis.

He pulls away, coming up for breath, but instead of loosening clothing or, at the very least, kicking off his shoes, he gazes out the patio doors at a cloudless sky. "This place is fantastic." He pulls me up so I can look out too. It really is something, but watching through the all-weather windows is much like seeing it on TV with the volume off. Kevin lets out a sigh. "Let's travel the world together, Kate. You and me."

I fiddle with the buttons on his shirt. I don't answer because I know he's just dreaming, just excited to be here, miles from home, cozying up to waterfalls. He's talking the talk of a romantic, but he doesn't mean it. We both know our plans. The ones we made together huddled in the backseat of his not-so-classic, two-door Monte Carlo, motor running, and risking asphyxiation for the chance to be alone for just an hour or so. We both want the same things from life: to live in Greenfield, to have four children, and own a house large enough for all of us to be comfortable. He rolls me onto my back and makes a low growling sound in the back of his throat and now none of it matters anyway. Not the dreams, not the house, not the children, not the cloudless sky.

4

The back door opened and closed. The sun poured into the living room. I didn't move from my position, lying on the floor. It didn't matter much who was entering my house. I recognized my mother's sensible brown shoes as she walked into the room and stopped a few feet from where I lay.

"Napping?" she said.

"Uh, yeah, sort of. What time is it?" I asked, pushing myself up into a sitting position. Her arms were filled with books.

"Three fifteen," my mother said.

"Oh man."

"I brought you some books," she said. "I'm not saying you have to read them. I just thought they might be, uh, useful. Helpful." She bent and placed the stack on the floor beside me. I picked up the top one. *Finding Your Way after Your Spouse Dies.*

Your way to what? I thought.

I eyed the rest of the stack with apathetic suspicion.

She gestured to them. "Just a thought. No pressure." She straightened and her eyes swept over the room. I followed her gaze. Pillows from the sofa and a cotton blanket lay limp and crumpled on the floor. A pair of jeans and Kevin's blue dress shirt mingled with the socks I had taken off last night. A bowl of congealed yogurt sat beside a half-eaten apple on the coffee table. The debris of despondence. I realized, too, the house smelled musty. The smell that hits you when you come home after being away for a week. It must have been obvious to her that I had been camped out on my living room floor since the funeral, more than a week ago. I offered no explanation.

My mother pressed her lips into a thin white line. I fingered a copy of *Getting to the Other Side of Grief* and felt a chasm open between me and my mother. Like we were castaways on separate islands, waving to each other from our beaches but unable to swim the distance to connect. I wondered what she was thinking. What she knew that she couldn't tell me, that I'd have to find out on my own. I raked a hand through my greasy hair.

I suddenly envied my mother. Sure, she'd lost her husband, but she'd had the luxury of time with him. Forty-three years. Kevin and I had five years. She'd raised her children with her husband by her side. My arms were empty, my womb unattended. Self-pity writhed in my chest, pushing upward until it burned my eyes. I pushed the stack of books away with my big toe.

"Do you need anything?" she said.

Everything. "No. Nothing."

She nudged the books toward me with her brown suede mules. "If you decide to look at them, start with these two." She bent over and grabbed *Experiencing Grief* and *The Heart of Grief.* "They're library books."

Alone again, I pushed the pile of books as far as I could reach. The books Mom had read after Dad died. It looked as though she had surrounded herself with books. Fortified herself against her emptying future.

Dad. I hadn't thought of him since before the hospital called to tell me about Kevin. Dad was sixty when he died. He had just up and died. That is what Mom said, "How could he just up and die?" Like it was his fault. In a way it was.

Dad's death turned him into a newspaper headline: "Man drowns trying to save boy." It was the kind of story that makes you give up reading. Right when you get to the part that tells you how both the seven-year-old boy and his would-be rescuer were swept downriver, fated to die in each other's arms.

He didn't know the kid. He and my mother had been walking by the river. He had heard the calls for help, saw the hand reaching out of the water and the brown head of hair going under. He left my mom standing on the riverbank, gaping in fear and unbelief, and threw himself into the river. And died.

Sitting on the laminate flooring in my living room, I shuddered at the suddenness of life. Regret and sorrow bodychecked each other in my mind. A part of me wanted to call Mom, tell her I would read the books, all of them, and any others she had. To ask her how she was doing. To tell her I remembered what she had lost. To step out of the container of grief surrounding me and … and what? What did I think I could do for her? For anyone?

We'd been close once. We used to call each other for no reason, just to touch base. She would pop into the Wee Book Inn bookstore, where I'd worked until a few weeks before Kevin died. She'd browse the shelves and wait for my break so she could buy me coffee. But Dad's death had put a wedge between us. In her grief she stopped calling, stopped coming by the store, and I hadn't known what to do about it, what to say. Now I understood there was little that could be said to a woman whose only desire was to see once more the face of the man she married.

I rolled onto my hands and knees and crawled to the bookcase that held my photo albums, gripped with the sudden need to see my father's face. I selected an old one that was filled with pictures of my parents, many of them in black and white. I was searching for one particular picture, one with Dad, at Christmas, a long time ago. I turned to the page and studied the photo. He wasn't looking at the camera, but off to one side at something or someone beyond the frame of the picture. His mouth was wide open in an exaggerated expression of celebration. He held his left arm up above his head, his right arm wrapped around his torso. His body was at an odd angle, his right foot high off the floor.

He'd been dancing when the picture was taken. He looked alive. Invincible. My heart contracted. Like trying to give birth to pain—to get it out of my body somehow. The album slipped from my hands and I lay down on the floor exhausted.

"Kate," Kevin's voice came from above me. "The day we told your dad we were getting married, his face turned purple. I thought he was going to have a stroke."

I was sure I was dreaming. The scene flickered behind my eyelids.

"But he hugged us and yelled, 'Wonderful!'" There was a chuckle in his voice. "You wore that red dress," he said.

"Red," I mumbled.

"Go to sleep, Kate."

"I am asleep," I told him.

5

"The church is going to hell in a handbasket," Margaret Cunynghame said. She'd said the same thing about the democratic process, her great-uncle Murray, and the quality of produce at the Green Market.

Kevin had been dead for over three weeks when Maggie, as she preferred to be called, phoned to inform me she was coming over "for a good visit."

The church she spoke of was Greenfield Community Church, of which she was a member "in good standing." She'd been sitting in my living room occupying our orange wingback chair for the past half hour.

"I have no idea," Maggie said, "why on earth they want to paint pictures of Noah's ark all over the hallways. Animals and that sort of thing. What's that got to do with anything?" Her eyes were large with the question. Maggie spoke in a loud and careful manner one would use if addressing the UN. Every word evenly parceled out.

I knew little about Noah's ark or Greenfield Community Church, so I gave a small shrug in response. Maggie was, literally, a colorful woman. While you could not determine her age with any kind of precision (more than sixty, less than one hundred), she wore clothes that could rightly be described as "too young." Today she swathed her ample figure in a flowing, sateen shirt as yellow and bright as optimism. She paired the shirt with fuchsia polyester pants. Beside her chair sat a broad-brimmed hat the color of mulch. She resembled a giant tropical flower.

I cleared my throat. She gave me a knowing smile and said, "Kate, my pet, I've been prattering on, but now I must get to the point of my visit." She leaned forward and spoke in conspiratorial tones. "Do you know my story? My life story? Who I was before I came here? How I got here?"

Maggie had a vague friendship with my mother as they had been bumping into each other all over town for years. At the grocery store, the dentist, the town fair. Maggie had also been an infrequent customer at the bookstore. She bought romance novels in paperback and always required change from the "need a penny, leave a penny" bowl. I recalled that Maggie had attended my father's funeral swathed head to toe in black (the only time I had seen her without color) and had patted my mother's arm after the casket was lowered into the ground. I supposed it was possible that she had attended Kevin's funeral as well, but I couldn't recall seeing her either at the funeral parlor or my home after the interment service.

I gave Maggie a slim smile. "You're pretty well known around here, so I've heard some of the stories."

Maggie leaned back in her chair, offered the ceiling an expansive grin, and launched into her story. "I was married once. As far as I know, I'm still married. But my husband is gone. 'Long gone,' as they say in the ballparks.

"My husband took his leave of me ... but not by his choice." She paused and waggled her eyebrows at me. "I'm an American, but my husband and I lived 'across the pond,' as they say. Jeremy Cunynghame was a good man, ethical and virtuous. But some men hated him for it. One man in particular was out to destroy him. He told lies about Jeremy. I don't know what they were because Jeremy forbade me to read the papers or listen to the radio.

"One morning, very early, I awoke to find him packing a suitcase." She stopped, seemingly out of breath, and looked around. "Have you any water, dear? This story always wears me out."

When I returned with a glass of water, she took it without comment and drank deeply.

"I begged him to stay. I told him that we could face anything together. Come what may!" She dropped her chin to her chest and peered up at me. "That may seem dramatic, but be certain, it was a dramatic moment." She smoothed the blinding yellow shirt over her belly.

"He wouldn't listen," she said, her voice dipped so low she could have been attempting a James Earl Jones impersonation. "I asked him if he was in danger. He said only if he stayed. He said he'd return when it was safe to do so.

"I'm afraid I made a scene. Bawled and brayed like a donkey. Can you imagine?"

I shook my head. I preferred not to.

"When I asked him how long he would be gone, he just looked at me, like this." Maggie opened her eyes wide and stuck out her chin, and let the corners of her mouth droop low, a Buster Keaton lookalike. "When I begged him—begged, mind you—to let me come

too, he shoved me back onto the bed and said it was impossible."
She sipped at her water. "The weeks went by with no word from my
husband. Then months." She gave a minuscule shrug. "Then years."
She sat back in her chair, a faraway look in her eyes. I sat waiting too,
it seemed, for Jeremy's return.

She rested her head on the back of the chair and closed her eyes.
"After three years of waiting for my husband to return, two thoughts
occurred to me. One, he was not coming back. Two, I was a wealthy
woman. And three … I said three thoughts, right? And three, I
needed to stop moping around and get out of there."

"Wealthy?" I repeated. I had heard of Maggie's local philan-
thropy, but no one seemed to know the origin of her prosperity.

Maggie flapped her hand in a dismissive gesture. "Wealthy, yes.
I made my money the old-fashioned way." She flashed me a toothy
grin. "I inherited it."

Maggie had boarded up her grand home overseas, hopped a
plane, and landed into her new life in Greenfield. She had bought the
first house the realtor showed her. "It was on Apple Tree Lane. Who
wouldn't want to live on Apple Tree Lane?" She promptly went about
securing her place in the social circles of Greenfield County. Maggie
was a big and colorful fish in a small gray pond. She held strong opin-
ions and seemed to feel obligated to share them with everyone. With
her loud dress and louder voice, some town folks said she was not to
be taken seriously. But seriously was exactly the way Maggie wanted
to be taken. She joined the Greenfield Community Church choir, the
Chamber of Commerce, and the Ladies of Our Glorious Flag Quilting
Group.

"That's a great story, Mrs. Cunynghame," I said when she was done. And it was, but it gave me no clues as to why she was in my house.

"Kate," she said, "you and I have a great deal in common. We have both lost the husbands we adored." She hesitated. "Differently, I suppose. Yours died. You lost him, but you also know where he is. Mine, well, I good and lost him, didn't I? I couldn't find him if I looked. But never mind that. We're both facing the world alone; that is the point I'm making. I want to help you."

"Mrs. Cunynghame, thank you for wanting to help, but—"

"Stop calling me that. Call me Maggie," she said with a smile.

"There is really nothing that you can do … Maggie," I said.

"Nonsense, Kate. There is a great deal I can do. You require advice from someone who knows what's what and what's not."

"I appreciate your wanting to help. But I have my sister. And my mother."

"Your mother!" Maggie's voice rose to impossible volumes. "Love a duck, child, your poor mother. Sharp on the heels of her loss she has to bury another family member. Tossed with grief, she is. Her burden is too great, sweetie, to be able to take on yours as well." She was right. Mom was tossed with grief. How many books had she read trying to put her pieces back together?

My eyes drifted to at the pile of books on the floor. Maggie followed my gaze and I could see her eyes move back and forth as she read the titles. She turned her head sharply down and to the left in order to read the title of the bottom book. She mouthed the words *I Wasn't Ready to Say Good-bye*. She straightened her head and gave me a glittering smile. "Have you read any of them?"

I shook my head, shrugged, and shook my head again.

"The problem with self-help books is you first need to be in a place where you can help yourself," Maggie said.

I opened my mouth and waited for something to come out of it. Nothing did, so I closed it again.

"Do you know what I love about Greenfield?" she asked.

"Huh? Uh, I don't know."

"I love almost everything about it. It is a wonderful place to live. Especially when a body is healthy and life is good. Small towns. Can't beat them. But look at you. A beautiful young woman loses her handsome husband; it's a terrible shame, a real tragedy." She leaned forward in her chair. "How long have you been sitting here like this?" She threw her arms out, taking in the whole room. "Sleeping on the floor. Yes, I clearly see. It's all right, honey, I don't judge you. I understand more than you know. How long?"

Against my will my eyes filled with tears. I blinked rapidly for a moment. "Since the funeral. I slept upstairs the first night, but I've been down here ever since."

"You only go upstairs to change clothes?" she said, eyeing the jeans, socks, and shirts strewn on the floor.

"No. I don't go up there at all. I just use the clothes that were already in the laundry room, down here."

"I see," Maggie said. "I'm not trying to pry, child, but, how long has it been since you took a bar of soap to your skin?"

"I … I … don't … go upstairs."

"I understand. It's been weeks. Do you get many visitors?"

"Just my mom and sister." For some reason I didn't mention Blair.

"Just family. It's shameful how a whole town can show up for the funeral then disappear for the grief. You aren't going to find what you need here, child. You need to be in the city for what you need."

"I don't understand."

"I am advising you to get yourself to the city and find a good counselor. Someone you trust that you can talk to and work through some of this. Something you won't find in this small town." She waved both hands at the room.

"Oh well, I don't think I need—"

"My darling girl, you're in no position to even begin to know what you need. I'm here to tell you that you have two options."

"Maggie," I said. "Mrs. Cunynghame—" I corrected. She barely knew me, yet here she was giving me advice I hadn't asked for.

"Option one. Sit here in your living room until you decide to either live or die. Heaven knows how long it takes to make a decision like that. Could be years for all we know."

"Yes, but—"

"Option two. Decide you may as well start getting better so you don't get any worse. And it can get worse, dear child. I assure you, it can get a whole lot worse."

I wondered if I should tell her about Kevin's voice. No, I told myself. I couldn't talk about that. She'd think I was crazy. She already thought I was crazy.

Maggie stood up and headed for the door. "I need to go. But think about what I said. I have some names and addresses for you. Counselors you could try."

I cocked my head to one side. "Try?"

"You have to try them on, like clothes at a store. It's not one size fits all. You have to meet with each one until you find the one you like and feel you can trust." Maggie pulled the door open and stepped outside. I got up and followed her, stopping on the threshold. I felt the wind on my face for the first time in weeks. Its freshness, the joy of it, caught me by surprise. Maggie turned to face me. I watched her make a short study of my features. My dirty jeans and white T-shirt hung on my frame. My greasy hair flapped like strips of bacon in the wind.

"Kate, beautiful Kate," Maggie said. "Go have a long shower. You'll be surprised how some hot water and soap can make a body feel human again."

Maggie climbed into her electric yellow Mustang, and I watched, reluctant to close the door on the wind.

6

I pushed Maggie's words to the back burner of my mind the moment she left. I had other things to concern myself with. Standing at the door watching Maggie, I noticed my mailbox was filled with flyers, pamphlets, fast food coupons, and important letters. Three with the return address of the company that held Kevin's insurance policies. *Oh man.*

The third one informed me that, like Maggie, I was now a wealthy woman. It seems that when a husband dies at work, his widow cashes in. The sum on the page was big enough to, at any other time, make me happy. Giddy even. I felt numb.

I sat at the kitchen table and squinted at the fine print. I was entitled to grand sums of money, but I had to work for it. There were forms to be filled out, boxes to be checked, and information to be relayed. The last letter contained a list of duties I was required to perform before the insurance company could "release the funds." Like the money was a wild animal, caged, penned up for my safety.

I filled in as much information as I could but soon realized I'd need to make a trip to the bank where Kevin had worked. He had a safe-deposit box there containing mortgage, insurance, investment, and other important papers. I sighed. The idea of going down to the bank, the place where he had died, filled me with dread.

I reached for the phone and dialed. It rang five times before I realized I'd dialed Kevin's direct line. No one would be there to answer it.

I was about to hang up when I heard a sharp, "Hello?"

"Uh, hi," I squeaked.

"Who's this?" the voice demanded.

"I'm sorry. I just dialed the number without thinking. Out of habit, I guess. I'm … I'm sorry,"

"Kate? Is that you?"

"Huh? Yes, it's Kate Davis."

"Kate, this is Donna. I was walking by Kevin's office and I heard his phone ringing. Is there something I can do for you?"

Unwanted tears filled my eyes. I jabbed at them with an impatient finger. "Yes, please. I'm not sure who I should talk to."

"Whatever it is you need, I will help you."

I felt a cup of relief spill over in my stomach. "Thank you."

"I'm happy to do it," she said.

"I've been looking at the forms from the insurance company—"

I heard her take a sharp breath. "You haven't sent those back yet?" She sounded startled.

I shrank in my skin. "No. I just looked at them today."

"Today?" she said louder, almost annoyed. "Sorry, I didn't mean to raise my voice. It's just that, normally, we recommend these matters are attended to within a few days of the … passing. It's a sad fact, but when someone dies, the first thing the survivor should do is call the insurance company and visit the bank."

"Visit the bank? Why?"

"To unfreeze accounts, show proof of the will, gain access to funds, investments, clear debts, change over ownership of accounts and safe-deposit boxes, that sort of thing," she said sounding more like a banker now than a friend.

"Deposit box. Actually that's why I'm calling. Kevin has … had … a safe-deposit box," I said.

Donna was quiet for a long moment. In the silence I felt fatigue fill my body like an oil spill. I slumped in my chair, my eyes threatening to close.

"Is the box in your name too?"

I tipped my head back until it met the back of the chair. "I don't think so. I'm pretty sure it's just in Kevin's name." He had told me he was renting a box, but I had no compulsion to add my name to it. He was in charge of those things.

I heard a soft tapping sound, like fingernails drumming on a table. "Things are crazy at the bank right now. Since we lost Kevin, it's been chaos. I wouldn't want you to walk into the middle of this." She hummed tunelessly for a moment. "I'll pull a few strings and get the paperwork done and unfreeze Kevin's accounts for you. That way you can access the funds."

I had no idea Kevin's accounts were frozen in the first place. I briefly wondered how our bills were getting paid. I brushed the thought aside with an impatient wave of my hand.

"That would be a big help," I said.

"Good. It will take a few days for me to get it all sorted out. I'll call you if I need you for anything."

I hung up and put my head down on the table. A tiny thought

swirled. *What about the safe-deposit box? What about the insurance forms? Did we talk about that?* I let out a groan. I tried to replay the conversation, but it just sloshed around my brain. I reached for the phone again.

"There are copies in the den," Kevin said.

I froze, hand midair. My throat constricted. "Copies," I said. A thousand tiny needles pushed at my scalp and rushed down my body.

Kevin said, "I keep copies of everything in the desk in the den."

"Kevin?" Fear swept through my gut. *This is crazy.*

I waited for him to speak again. I stood very still for a moment, listening hard. "In the den," I repeated.

"Copies of everything in the middle drawer on the right-hand side." His voice was calm, conversational. I wasn't hearing him in my head, rather out loud, as if he were just in the next room, calling to me.

I jumped up and went into the living room. Nothing.

Finally I went down the hall to the den and found the papers in the desk, just as Kevin had said.

I wrap the gift in deep-blue paper, the most masculine-looking paper I could find. I don't bother with a bow or string because whenever Kevin sees a bow on a gift he wrinkles his nose, pulls it off, and says, "What's this for?" before tossing it over his shoulder. He was a man's man. No frilly stuff for him.

It's our third anniversary and that means leather. Twenty-fifth wedding anniversary is silver, fifty is gold, but third is leather, and I've bought the perfect gift. Plus I've made reservations at the Tower, an expensive restaurant with a medieval name that makes the best grilled salmon with dill reduction sauce in the world. It completely blows our meager budget, but I don't care. Kevin is worth it. And with all the hours he's been putting in at work lately, he needs a break. We both need a break.

I rip off a last bit of tape and press it to a ragged bit of paper in one of the corners. It looks terrible, like it was wrapped by a five-year-old. But tonight I'm too happy to care what it looks like.

I hear his car in the drive and scoop up the gift, hiding it behind my back while I position myself in front of the door. He opens the door, sees me, and smiles. "Whatcha got behind your back?"

I smile and roll my eyes. "Not telling."

"Then I guess I'm not telling either," he says, holding up a brightly wrapped parcel with a gold bow on top. I make a playful grab for it, but Kevin holds it over his head, well out of my reach. "Happy anniversary." He easily takes the gift from me and puts both of them on the kitchen table. "Presents later. I'm hungry."

At the restaurant he orders wine, then changes the order to champagne. "Leave the bottle," he tells the smiling waiter.

I eye the champagne, wondering how much it costs, but I hold my tongue. Not tonight. Tonight we won't talk about money or budgets or saving for a bigger house. I raise my glass. "To us. And to our future."

Kevin clinks his glass against mine. "Here, here." He takes a long gulp of champagne while I sip mine. He pours himself another. "It's going to be a great future, Kate. Things are starting to look up for us."

Up? I didn't know they had been looking down.

Kevin slurps up the last of his drink and reaches for the bottle. "You know how unhappy I've been in the loans department." His hand wobbles as he pours, and some champagne dribbles down the side of his glass. He picks it up and licks the side from bottom to top. "Can't waste it."

"Maybe you should hold off until our food comes."

He points a finger at me. "There's only so far a guy can go in the loans department, you know. There's a ceiling." He holds his hand over his head in an imitation of a ceiling. I can't help but laugh. "I hate ceilings, but"—he holds up a finger as if to shush me, even though I haven't said a word—"the new acquisitions manager called me to her office today and we had a long talk." He drags out the word "long," holding the O and stretching it to ridiculous lengths. "She says I'm in the wrong department. She says she's been watching me and sees my overlooked potential." He takes a deep pull on his champagne. "I have overlooked potential," he says, slurring.

A flutter of excitement rises in my chest. "I've always thought so, babe. So what does this mean for you?"

"It means," he says, plunking his elbow down hard on the table. "You're looking at the new assistant to the acquisitions manager. And you know what that means."

"No, what does—"

"It means a couple of years of effort and I'm a veep."

"A veep?"

He swings his glass wide, nearly swiping a passing waiter. "A VP, my clueless wife. A vice president."

I grab his hand across the table, ecstatic. "Kevin, that's wonderful news. I'm so proud of you." My head is instantly filled with what this could mean for us. Maybe we can buy a larger home sooner than we expected. A five-bedroom would be perfect. Our two-bedroom just isn't enough, and we've put off starting our family because money is so tight, but with this news ... "We can have a baby now," I blurt out. "We don't have to wait anymore."

Kevin's eyes cross briefly, then his eyebrows met in the middle of his forehead. "A baby?"

A giggle burbled up from inside of me. "Uh, yeah. With you on the fast track at work, we can have a baby now, and be able to buy a bigger house in just a couple of years. There's no need to wait anymore."

Our meals arrive, and Kevin stares at his as if he doesn't recognize it. Then he looks up, smiles, and winks. "Well, let's wait until after dinner, at least."

I kill the engine and car lights, and everything goes dark. The neighborhood is silent, sleeping. I try to help Kevin out of the car but he waves me off. "I'm not drunk, for the one hundredth time."

I unlock the door and flick on the lights we always forget to turn on when we leave. Two gifts snuggle on the kitchen table. I'd forgotten all about them.

Kevin comes in behind me and sees them too. "Oh yeah. Oh good. Let's open presents." He grabs the one he bought me and half runs, half stumbles up the stairs with it. "Let's open them up here."

I follow silently, not bothering to ask why. He'd been acting strangely ever since dinner. Talking loudly, drinking an entire bottle of champagne, then ordering a beer. I'd never known him to celebrate this way.

Kevin stands by his dresser, trying to light a candle. He strikes the match, nothing. Again. Nothing. A third time, sparks, then a fizzle, then nothing. He turns to me, holds out the matches, and I take them, lighting the match, then the other three candles perched on their individual holders. The dim glow flickers around the room. It feels peaceful, calming, sexy.

Kevin sits on the bed, cross-legged and bouncing lightly like a child. Strike sexy. He holds out his gift to me. "Three years of marriage. Three is leather." He grins. "You told me so."

I grin back and tug on a piece of tape, careful not to tear the brilliant red paper. Kevin leans over and snatches the gold bow from on top and puts it on his head. I laugh and pull off the wrapper. A white box, the kind you use to wrap the sweater you bought Grandma for Christmas. I throw him a toothy grin that I hope covers my disappointment. I don't want a grandma sweater. I pull the lid open and stare at the thing inside.

Kevin gets up on his knees and moves over to the end of the bed where I am standing. He peers into the box. "Try it on."

My stomach flops over. This is no grandma sweater; this is serious underwear for professionals. Did I say underwear? More like a contraption. It's black with a spattering of silver grommets and a few buckles tossed in for added flair.

Kevin rubs his hands together like a kid set loose in a candy store. "Just like you told me—leather."

I glance over at the gift I bought him. As if reading my mind, he turns and grabs it off the bed. "My turn," he says, ripping the masculine blue paper to shreds. He stares at his gift with unfocused eyes. "It's a book."

I nod. "A leather-bound book on the history of aviation."

"Cool," he says, placing the book on the floor beside the bed. He points at the leather thing in the box I'm holding. "Try it on."

I swallow the bile rising in my throat. "Uh, I'll put it on in the bathroom." I dash across the hall before his slightly drunken hands reach me. I close the bathroom door quietly and lean against it. I look at the offensive garment. Three years of marriage, and he'd never once hinted that he wanted this. It wasn't the sort of thing you put on to feel special or sexy. It was the sort of thing you put on and felt cheap. Disposable. Whorish. I had a drawer full of wonderful, soft, sexy things. I enjoyed wearing those. But this?

"Need help in there?" Kevin's voice called from the bedroom.

Help? I need an escape ladder. "No. Be right out." I close my eyes and chant, "I love my husband." I get undressed. I hold the offensive thing against my skin. "I love my husband."

It was dark by the time I finished filling out the insurance forms. My eyes stuck together when I blinked. I put the papers into a manila envelope and decided to walk to the mailbox, despite the late hour. A part of me was anxious to finalize the insurance settlement. It was a large amount of money. Guilt poked at my chest like a bully. You shouldn't care about money, it said. I grabbed my sweater and headed out the door.

When I returned home, I went to the kitchen, filled the kettle with water, set it on the stove, and went upstairs, taking them two at a time.

I hesitated at the top of the stairs. It felt strange to be up there. Like visiting a memory. I felt uncertain which way to turn. If I turned right, I would enter the bathroom. Left, I would be in the spare room. If I walked straight ahead, I would enter the bedroom Kevin and I had shared for the past five years. I turned right.

Avoiding my reflection, I twisted the water taps, stripped, and stepped into the shower. I stood still and bare under the flow of hot water. The bathroom filled with steam as I washed my hair and cleaned my body. Somewhere between the shampoo and the last scrape of the razor against my leg I began to feel, as Maggie had promised, human.

I stood in front of the mirror combing out my long brown hair, my right hand midstroke, when Kevin's voice came to me from the other side of the door. "Kettle's whistling."

"Okay!" I hollered back without thinking. I grabbed my robe off the back of the door and flew downstairs. I was in the kitchen, hand on the kettle, before my brain caught up with what had happened. I spun around and called, "Kevin?" I ran back up the stairs, stopping at the top. "Kevin," I called again. "I heard you. I hear you. Kevin, please," I said, my voice falling to a whisper. "Please. I hear you."

7

"You need to eat, Kate," Heather said. She was standing in my kitchen scraping casserole that was covered in a month's worth of mold into the garbage.

I sat useless at the table. I was spent from a week of filling in insurance forms and following the paper trail that ended with me being awarded a huge sum of money.

Heather had invited herself over and was now in the process of ridding my home of harmful bacteria by cleaning out the contents of my refrigerator. She put the dish in the sink and turned her attention back to the fridge. "I've never seen so much food stuffed into a refrigerator." She'd come by "just because," she said. But it was clear she was here to check up on me. Subtle is not Heather's middle name. She was always a flurry of activity. And I suspected that because she didn't have a boyfriend just then to lavish her attentions on, I became the object of her attentiveness.

I shrugged, "People keep bringing food over. I put it in the fridge."

"This is nuts," she said, her brown hair swinging across her back as she took stock of the chaos.

I sat on my hands. "Heather, do you remember, when we used to go swimming, how we'd stand on Dad's shoulders and jump into the water?"

Heather pulled out another dish—it looked like it used to be a dessert. She faced me. "Sure, he'd swim on the bottom of the pool until one of us could get our feet on his shoulders, then he'd stand straight up and we'd go flying," she smiled. "He seemed to never run out of air, waiting for us at the bottom of the pool."

Heather threw the dessert in the garbage and began rummaging through my cupboards in search of something. She was dressed in her version of casual, which meant wearing one piece of denim—in this case a bolero with tiny pockets on the front. The rest of her outfit consisted of matching tan linen. She looked gorgeous.

I ran a hand through my shoulder-length hair, and my finger snagged on a small knot. I pulled the brown strands apart while I spoke. "My favorite part was when he stood up. I never knew if my balance would hold. Then Dad would grab my ankles, stand up, and shoot me straight up out of the water. I felt like a rocket. Like a movie star."

"A movie star?" Heather asked, taking a break from her cleaning to look at me.

"Yeah. Special. That's how I picture it, you know. The way he died. I picture the boy standing on Dad's shoulders, Dad trying to stand up in the middle of the river and shoot that boy out of the water."

Heather spun away and started hunting through the cupboards again until she found the one that held all the Tupperware containers I had acquired as wedding gifts. They were shiny new. Every lid was accounted for. I'd barely used any of them. Kevin had been an eating machine, so there were rarely leftovers. She piled the containers and matching lids on the table in front of me. "We're going to divide this food up into single servings and freeze them." Heather was a force of nature when she decided to take charge. She turned the hot water tap, then grabbed a broom, sweeping while the sink filled.

I shrugged. The food didn't appeal to me. It had been brought here by sad-faced people who were so sorry they couldn't stay, but they really had to be going.

Heather rested the broom against the wall, turned the tap off, and then plunked the last of the containers on the table. She grabbed casserole dishes and bowls from the counter and plopped them in front of me. Compliant, I began transferring the contents in one of the bowls—raspberry Jell-O—into a single-serving plastic container.

"What was your favorite part?" I asked, balancing the wobbling goop onto a spoon. Something about the Jell-O seemed wrong.

She was bent over, head in the fridge. "Mine? Of swimming? Let me think."

"Can you freeze Jell-O?"

Heather spun around and marched to the table. "What? No. Oh for—here, give me that."

She took the Jell-O and handed me a dish filled with cabbage rolls. I began dropping them into plastic containers. I was pretty sure you could freeze cabbage rolls.

We worked silently for a time, me blopping food into small containers, and Heather scraping spoiled food into the garbage and washing the dishes. She turned and waved a spoon at me. "I liked everything about those times. Dad could be so much fun when he wanted to be. Swimming and summer vacations. Those are the times I remember Dad the most."

"The only times we ever saw him in shorts," I said.

We smiled at each other.

I snapped a lid on the container I'd just filled and added it to the stack beside me. I handed Heather the empty casserole dish and reached for another one. "What do you remember most about Kevin?"

Heather's smile faded. She turned back to the sink.

"Tell me," I said, looking down into the dish of lasagna. "I'd like to hear it."

Heather was quiet. Her hands busy.

I stared at my hands. Why won't she say something?

She came up behind me and put her arms around me. "I love you, Kate."

"I love you, too," I said, feeling uneasy. Why was she avoiding my question? Uncertainty crept up my spine and knocked on my skull.

"Your hair smells nice," she said.

"I just washed it." She really wasn't going to tell me. She was avoiding the question.

"I'm glad."

I nudged her arm. "Glad about what? That I washed my hair?"

"Yes," she said as she stood upright again. "That you washed your hair. I was getting worried about you. But I see you're getting better now."

I clenched the spoon. Better? What was that supposed to mean?

Did she think I was suffering some disease that I'd simply recover from? Just a bad case of Kevin-itis, should clear up in a few days. I felt my chest tighten as anger seeped in.

Heather returned to the sink and plunged her hands into the sudsy water, her back to me, talking over her shoulder. "You've been sleeping in the living room, and generally not taking care of yourself very well. It was freaking me out. But you look good. A bit pale, but still, you're obviously getting better."

I tried to concentrate on breathing as anger poured over me like a baptism. "I'm getting over it, you mean." I spoke through clenched teeth. Who was she to tell me what was normal and what wasn't? Who was she to be freaked out by what I did or didn't do? "That's what you mean, isn't it? I should be over it?"

Heather faced me, hands dripping. "No, I just mean that you're … showing signs of improvement."

I stood up so fast the chair tipped over. "Improvement?" I said, louder than I intended.

She shook her head, a mother hen explaining the facts of life. "Relax, Kate. There's no need to be upset. I'm paying you a compliment."

I pointed the spoon at her as if it were a switchblade. "Who asked you? Who asked you to come in here, take over my kitchen, and tell me how things ought to be? You don't know anything about what I'm going through."

Heather wiped the splatter of tomato sauce that hit her face when I flicked the spoon at her. "I'm only trying to help."

I glared at her, anger choking off my air supply. "You think I'm pathetic. That I need your help just to function."

She put out her hand like she was calling to a puppy. "No.

Kate, please, I didn't mean to offend you. I just meant I was happy—"

I cut her off. "You think you know better than I do how to grieve? How to be a widow? You think there are rules about what's normal and what's not?"

"No, of course not."

"Get out."

She stood motionless for a moment, perhaps waiting for me to change my mind, take it back, apologize. She glanced at the door, then back at me, a question in her eyes.

"GET OUT!"

Heather jumped at my shout. Her gaze fell to the spoon I was still pointing at her like a weapon. Without another word she opened the door and stepped outside.

I threw the spoon at the door. Unsatisfied, I picked up the casserole dish, half filled with lasagna, and hurled it. It shattered against the door, spraying food and glass everywhere. I picked up my chair and sat down hard, watching the tomato sauce bleed down the door like a hemorrhage. I put my head down and began to tap my forehead against the tabletop. A rhythm, a drumbeat, a mantra. After a few moments I picked up the phone and dialed. After four rings the answering machine picked up.

"Maggie," I said into the receiver, "I'd like the names of those counselors."

8

I bumped around the house for the next two days, wondering how to fill the time before my first therapy appointment. The thought of seeing a counselor made me nervous and self-conscious. And desperate. A part of me hoped for an easy answer, a mental-health silver bullet that would make my problems go away. Or at least explain to me what my problems were.

I made a list of everything I thought I should talk about. Kevin's sudden death. My father's death before that. Feelings of sadness. The strange and angry outburst at my sister. My hand hovered over the page, reluctant to write: "Hears voice of dead husband." *How crazy does that make me sound?* I looked around my living room, which had become my bedroom. *How crazy does this make me?* Do they measure on a sliding scale? Maybe they tally your behavior. Four behaviors and you're sane. Five and you're crazy.

I was too frightened to tally my behaviors.

I wrote out the answers to the questions I imagined a counselor would ask.

Age: 28.

Occupation: Housewife? *No.* Homemaker? *Nope.* Retired? *I thought about the amount of the insurance settlement.* Yeah, retired.

Marital status: Widow.

Reason for visit: See above.

Patient's ideal outcome from counseling sessions: Acquire ability to travel back in time.

I bit the end of my pencil. I had no idea what the counselor would ask me. I doodled in the margin, then wrote the only positive thing I could think of: washing my hair again—but then I crossed it out. How terrible was it that I didn't wash for three weeks? Even now, it wasn't as if I was making daily trips to the shower. I managed one trip in the past week. I pressed my fists into my temples and chanted, "Not crazy. Not crazy." I pictured Heather's pale face as she fled my kitchen. Something in her eyes. She had looked scared. Of me.

I tore the paper up and started a new sheet. I drew a chart with two columns and labeled them, filling in the blanks with my recent behavior.

Not Crazy	*Crazy*
Trouble sleeping	*Camping out on living room floor*
Mood swings	*Freaking out on sister and kicking her out of my house*
No interest in regular routine	*Forgetting to eat for days at a time, not showering—allowing leg hair to grow to braiding length*
Missing dead husband	*Hearing voice of dead hus—*

"Write down 'burns the toast,'" Kevin said.

My pen froze midword.

"You always burn the toast. It's a terrible habit."

Without moving I cast my eyes around the kitchen. I saw nothing, no one. My heart tapped out its fear. *This really is crazy.* Still, some strange part of me want to press on, to know what would happen if I tried to converse with him. "I don't burn it. You just like to eat raw toast."

I heard his laugh rumble through the air. I gasped. "Can I see you?" Silence.

Don't ask questions. "I'm the perfect housekeeper," I tried again.

"Tell the counselor you burn the toast, and you don't know how to fold socks," Kevin said.

What is this? I thought. Am I awake? Dreaming? Dead? I was afraid to move. "I miss you."

I waited. Nothing. I didn't know which was worse, hearing his voice or not hearing it. Which was crazier? Hearing the voice of your dead husband, or expecting to hear it?

I spread my hands out in front of me on the table. "I hear you talk to me about teakettles and burnt toast," I said. "You died and now you talk to me about socks."

"Everything is white."

"I don't know what you mean. What's white? Socks?"

Silence. Cold, frustrating, infuriating silence.

I blinked at the list I was writing and circled *crazy* with my pen. "I'm flat-out, stark-raving, bug-eyed crazy."

"Not crazy," Kevin said.

I looked at my chart. Should I feel better about my mental health because the voice of my dead husband assures me I'm not crazy? Somehow I did. Even dead, Kevin's opinion mattered more to me than my own.

It's the sort of place high school kids try to sneak into. Deafening music pulses like a heartbeat, the bass so loud it's impossible to hear the song itself. Heather and her new boyfriend, Paul, are on the dance floor, bouncing to the throb of noise. Kevin and I stand by a tall table with no chairs. Heather smiles and waves. I wave back.

Kevin pulls me close and bellows in my ear, "Let's go."

I shake my head no. He nods yes. I wish we'd learned sign language. I holler back, "We just got here."

He taps his watch. "Like, an hour ago." Then, just so I don't miss the point, he cups his hands over his ears.

I turn back to the dance floor and watch Heather and Paul. She has this cool-girl way of dancing; she can toss her head and swirl her hips all while looking like she doesn't really care. Paul is doing something strange with his hands. Balled into fists, he alternates between holding them close to his body and pushing them far out in front of him. He looks like a Rock 'em Sock 'em Robot boxer. We'd had dinner with them at the Tower, then Paul suggested this place. I turn to Kevin. "What do you think of Paul?"

Kevin tipped his glass back, dumping the last of the ice into his mouth. "I give it two weeks. Less if he keeps dancing like that."

My laughter is muted by the thumping music. I rifle through my purse until I find a pen. I grab his napkin and write, "Heather thinks he could be 'the one.'" After our meal Heather and I had gone to the ladies room together and taken far too long in there while Heather regaled me with Paul's many good qualities, starting with how punctual he is picking her up for dates. He was considerate and kind, she said. "Oh, and before our first date, he called me to ask what my favorite flowers were. Can you imagine?" She giggled at the memory. I couldn't help but like him too.

Kevin takes the pen. "Isn't that what she always thinks?"

I shrug and write back, "She's a romantic."

Kevin shakes his head. "She's codependent."

This bothers me more than it should. I've always considered myself a romantic too. Any girl who has read the complete works of Jane Austen before the age of fifteen has to be a romantic in the best sense of the word. Right? I gave Kevin a weak smile, but he's not looking at me. He's shaking his head at Heather and Paul on the dance floor. I'm suddenly offended. Heather is the nicest person I know, even if she is my sister. She's sweet and always thinks of others. How does that make her codependent? She and I used to sit on her bed and talk for hours about the men we would marry, making long lists of attributes we believed were critical to a man. I had always been amazed how alike she and I were. But I can't say any of this here, so I take the pen and write a lame, "No, she's not."

Kevin writes, "And he's a dork."

I give Kevin a look that says, "Huh?" And he points to Paul on the dance floor and raises an eyebrow. As if bad dancing summed up the character of a person.

I poke him with my elbow and write, "He's nice." I'm thinking about adding an exclamation mark, but Kevin grabs the napkin and crumples it in his hand. Heather and Paul have returned to the table. Paul's face glistens with sweat. Heather yells in my ear, "You guys aren't going to dance?"

I throw a glance at Kevin, who is gesturing to Paul in an attempt to communicate. "No."

Heather hollers into my ear, "Should we leave, then?"

I glance at Kevin. Paul is talking to him. Kevin nods, but doesn't look at Paul. I turn to Heather, "Yes, let's go." Heather grabs my arm and pulls me toward the exit, waving for Paul and Kevin to follow. She does a quick jog to the door, dragging me with her. We hit the cool summer-night air and the quiet is like a gift. The guys are several paces behind us. Heather squeezes my arm. "So?" She wants to know what I think of Paul. No, she wants to hear me say I think he's a dream man, the personification of all our long talks, that he's "the one." I look back; the guys are following, Paul is talking, gesturing in broad strokes, Kevin's hands are jammed into his front pockets, he nods now and again, his face a blank slate. Paul lets out a sharp laugh, a blowing "Ha!" and puts his hand on his stomach. He does look like a dork.

Heather whispers, "Isn't he fabulous?"

I pat her hand. "He seems … nice."

She pouts. "Just nice? That's all?"

"Yeah, that's all."

9

I sat in the small, stifling room and watched the counselor shift in his chair. First right, then left. He was a man of about fifty. He fidgeted constantly as I shook his hand and sat down.

He pursed his lips, tugged at his hair, crossed and then uncrossed his legs. "Tell me why you came to see me today."

I put my purse on the floor, smoothed my jeans with the palms of my hands, and crossed my legs. His jitters were catching. "I seem to be having trouble getting over the death of my husband, over a month ago."

Scooch, smile, pen click, frown.

I cleared my throat. "I haven't been myself."

Bum wiggle, foot shuffle, nod, nod, pen click. I wondered if his underwear had recently shifted, making sitting painful. Maybe it was the chair that was uncomfortable.

I watched him pull at his shirt. "Uh, some mood swings too."

He gave his pen three rapid clicks. "Mmmm, when did you first perceive the problem?"

Perceive? Like maybe I'd been crazy my whole life but just recently noticed. "Like I said, it started after my husband died."

He squirmed in his seat again. "I'm sorry to hear of your loss."

"You know what might help?" I asked.

His face brightened and he leaned forward in anticipation. "What?"

"Bigger chairs."

"Excuse me?"

I pointed to the chair he was sitting on. "If you got rid of that chair and replaced it with something bigger, maybe something with some extra padding, I bet it would be more comfortable." I was getting concerned for this man's health.

He jerked his head around, as if there might be an overstuffed chair lurking behind the draperies. I looked around too, taking in the details of his office for the first time. A battered desk made of particleboard sat at the far end of the room, piled high with file folders. Beside them sat an older-looking computer that hummed quietly, its green light blinking monotonously from its place on the monitor. It wasn't one of those sleek flat screens; it was fat and squat, taking up half of the desk. Above it was a small window that looked out to the brick wall of the neighboring building.

Aside from the two chairs we were occupying, there was a short, worn sofa pushed up against the concrete block wall. I knew without looking that behind me was an orange room divider—similar to one that could be found in a school class-room—that acted as a buffer between the space where we sat and the door. Nothing about the room spoke of good health, mental or otherwise.

"Once I found a really great swivel chair at a garage sale," I said. "I paid, like, five bucks for it."

He nodded gravely, as if I had just revealed important information about my psychological state. "Do you like to go to garage sales?"

"Oh sure," I said. "I helped a friend of mine furnish almost her entire house by buying things from garage sales. And you'd never know it. It looks great. Not like—" I waved my arm toward his shabby office. "Uh, what I mean is—"

"Not like this. Is that what you meant?" He glanced at his watch.

My hour was up.

∿౭✿౦∿

The next day, sitting at the kitchen table, I heard a tapping at the door. I looked up from the list I was writing. Blair's face, framed by the window, peered in.

"Your sister called me a couple of days ago, said you were cracking up," Blair hollered through the glass. I opened the door for him and he stepped inside. "You look fine to me."

"Thanks." I smiled and smoothed my freshly washed hair. I was even wearing a clean pair of jeans and a fresh shirt. I could pass for positively normal if no one looked too closely. I still hadn't gone into my bedroom, but I had enough clothes in the laundry to keep me going. I was washing them over and over so I didn't have to go into my room to get new ones. I was seriously considering running to the Shop 'n Save for underwear.

Blair smiled. "Want to talk about what happened with Heather?"

My mouth quivered, threatening to lead the rest of my face into a crying jag.

Blair put a hand on my arm. "I miss him too, Kate."

I glared down at my shoes, but I didn't push his hand away. "Please stop talking."

"Sure," he said. "No problem." He propped himself up against the counter and crossed his arms. His T-shirt rode up to reveal a sliver of taut skin. He looked big and lean and handsome. I noticed his jeans hitched just above his hip bone.

I looked away, feeling the heat rise in my face. "I'm angry."

Blair looked shocked and then his face went pale. "About what?" He suddenly wouldn't look at me. His eyes darted around the kitchen.

I gave him a questioning look, but he waved his hand in a "go on" gesture. "I don't know. I'm mad at my life, at the universe. I'm mad at Kevin," I said, startled by my own words, but they slid into place like truth.

He looked overly alert, eyes wide and intent, as if trying to interpret a language he had only passing knowledge of. "Mad at Kevin?"

"Yeah. For leaving me."

His mouth opened, then closed like a drowning fish. Finally he managed a strangled, "What?"

I held my hands out in an empty gesture. I didn't know how to explain. "I'm mad at him for dying and leaving me alone."

Blair let out a breath, like he'd been holding it. I supposed it *was* odd, maybe even improper, to be angry with my dead husband.

"Kate, he didn't mean to die," Blair said. "He didn't plan it. You can't be angry at him for it."

I cried. Big, sloppy sobs I couldn't hold back. Blair's arms went around me. He pressed me to his chest and held me there. I spilled snot and tears onto his shirt and spoke into his chest. "My whole life was entwined with Kevin's."

Blair moved his hands up and down my back. "I know. You guys were great."

I sniffed. "We were?"

Blair held me away from him. "Of course. You two were the storybook romance. Solid gold."

Gold? It occurred to me that Blair could fill in some of the missing pieces of my memory. "I quit my job at the bookstore …"

Blair narrowed his eyes into questioning slits. "Yeah. How come you sound like you're not sure?"

"I am sure. I mean … I just …" He pulled me to him again and made shushing noises. I knew I had quit my job, I was certain of that, but I couldn't remember actually quitting. Or why I quit. I loved books, and I loved working for the bookstore. What would have caused me to leave a job I loved? And why couldn't I remember? I pressed my eyebrows together. "I'm just tired. I know I'm not making sense. I'm sorry."

A soft rumble from somewhere deep in Blair's chest, the sound of mumbled understanding, of soothing empathy. I pulled away, but Blair caught my waist and wrapped his arms around me like metal bands. "You have nothing to be sorry for. You've been going through hell. You're allowed to not make sense." He tried to pull me closer, but I stood firm, pushing against his chest. He relaxed his arms and cocked his head to one side. "Let me help you, okay? Talk to me. I promise I'll just listen."

I nodded. I so badly wanted to talk to someone about what I had been going through, but it was difficult to find the right words. If he would be patient with me and just listen without interrupting, it would help. "I'm angry about everything and nothing. I don't even know if anger is the right word. I think I'm fine and then something sets me off, like Heather the other day." I recalled the red meat sauce oozing down the door and shuddered. "My feelings are right under the skin, right there, ready to come out at the slightest touch." I touched a finger to my forearm. "I want all of this to stop. And I want everything back that belongs to me."

"You mean Kevin?"

I nodded. "Kevin and everything else. He's gone and I can't remember what happened that day, what we said to one another. Or the day before, or the day before that. It's as if my memory is missing."

He cupped my chin with his hand and tipped my head up so our eyes met. "Don't push yourself, Kate. Losing Kevin was horrible. And sudden. Your mind hasn't had a chance to wrap itself around what's happened." Blair must have taken a few Intro to Psychology courses while he was away at college. His advice was shallow, but it did the trick. I felt a little better.

The soundtrack played in my mind again. Kevin saying, "Don't wait for me." I still couldn't connect to anything else. Just that, his voice, speaking to someone, maybe me, maybe not. Blair was right. My mind hadn't had time to absorb the shock. Eventually my memories would be restored. Maybe the next counselor could help me with that. I gave Blair a humorless smile. "You're right. I'll try to slow down."

Blair's gorgeous grin broke out all over his face. "Good. And while you're at it, stop freaking your sister out."

I thought about it for a second, then looked up with a small smile. "No promises."

10

Eliza Campbell's office was tucked away in a part of the city I wasn't familiar with, and I made three wrong turns searching for it. After Blair left, I had double-checked the address and driven to a massive Victorian-era home I had passed at least twice. I squinted at the building and sighed in frustration when I saw a teeny sign that read: *Whole Being Counseling.* I climbed out of my car and then up the wide stone stairs to the front door. The main floor lights were all out except for the porch and foyer. The entire place looked closed up for the day.

I turned the knob and was relieved to find it opened easily. In the foyer was a list of the names of the companies in the building. There were eight businesses set up in the house. Upstairs you could find both a massage therapist and a reflexologist. The main floor was home to a denturist, a tax accountant, and a Holistic Wellness Center, as well as a business calling itself the Success Sellers. I couldn't imagine what product they were offering. The basement level held the office of Eliza Campbell's private counseling practice and a taxidermist business called Live Again. I clumped down the stairs and made sure it was Eliza Campbell's office door I was opening.

I heard the faint sound of a bell ringing as I stepped into the waiting room. I knew it was the waiting room because there was a sign affixed to the wall that read, "This is the waiting room. Please take a seat."

I sat. I wondered if anyone knew I had arrived. I looked around. The room was small, the walls painted in muddy earth tones. The inner door, which, I presumed, led to Eliza Campbell's office, was bedecked with a hand-painted picture of a tree. Its swirling lines and drooping branches were green and brown, its flowers blue and orange. Two peacocks flanked the tree at the bottom while an array of other birds graced its branches. I had never seen a painting like it. On the table in front of me were current copies of *Psychology Today* and *Holistic Times*. A small black book lay beside the magazines. At first I thought it was a Bible, but when I picked it up, it turned out to be a book called the *Bhagavad Gita*. I stole a glance at the ornate door and thought about knocking. I reread the sign and waited.

I was wondering how to pronounce "Bhagavad" when the inner door opened and a woman poked her head in the room. "Kate Davis?" she said almost shyly. I nodded. "I'm Eliza Campbell. Come this way, please."

She led me into the inner office and seated herself in an over-sized chair that looked both chic and comfortable. She offered me my choice of either a similar chair, an arrangement of pillows on the floor, or a camel-colored couch, on which I was welcome to lie down if I first removed my shoes. I chose the pillows. I saw Eliza Campbell lift a long eyebrow at my choice, but she said nothing. I took a moment to get comfortable.

"Do you consider yourself a spiritual person, Kate?"

I blinked twice. Spiritual? Images flashed through my mind: an unkempt, dreadlock-wearing girl sharing a passionate embrace with an elm tree. A meditating Yogi defying gravity. A red-faced preacher hollering about hell and sin. I felt no connection to any of these images.

"I guess I'm ..." I stammered. "What I mean is ... I meant to be. I might be. Spiritual. I guess." I heaved my shoulders up and held out my palms in a *what can ya do* gesture.

Eliza Campbell looked spiritual. Like she could ascend to a higher plane of existence at any moment. Her dark eyes were framed by smoky eye shadow, making them appear deep set and large. Her mouth was wide and full. Her long brown hair was streaked with blonde and red, like she was trying on colors to decide which one she liked best. She wore loose-fitting clothes: billowing pants and a long, flowing blouse; a reformed sari, the color of dry mustard. Her face was calm and knowing. Although this was a counselor's office, I wouldn't have been surprised to see a crystal ball or deck of tarot cards among the artifacts that dotted the room. I didn't.

Eliza Campbell lifted a finger adorned by no less than three rings. A column of silver bracelets clacked together as she raised her arm. "What I hear you saying, Kate, is that you might be a spiritual person, but you aren't sure."

I nodded my quick agreement. That sounded pretty good. A spiritual wannabe had to be better than a no-show, right? I had attended Sunday school as a child, until I was about eight. But even sitting cross-legged among throw pillows on the floor of my counselor's office trying to think spiritual thoughts, I couldn't recall why I had started going, or what compelled me to stop.

"The reason I ask," Eliza Campbell said, "is because I take a spiritual approach to my counseling. By that I mean I see us all as interconnected beings. We are connected, not just to other humans, but to the earth, the universe, and the spiritual realm."

"Oh." I wondered if I should be taking notes. The only connection I had ever felt to the spiritual realm was watching zombie movies with my best friend, Tanya, in seventh grade. Scared us both spitless.

She waved her hand. "It sounds complicated, but it's not."

I picked up a pillow. "Interconnected. Right."

"I don't know your story, Kate, but I can see you are spiritually blocked."

"Blocked?"

"Closed off. Your spiritual taps are turned to the 'on' position, but nothing's coming through."

My spiritual pipes were plugged? This was news.

Eliza Campbell pointed at me. "Why are you hugging that throw pillow?"

"Pardon?" I unfolded my arms from around the pillow and held it at arm's length as if it had developed a rank odor. "I don't know."

"You are using the pillow as a shield, Kate."

"I am?" I supposed it wasn't a passion for polyester that had me embracing throw pillows. "Sorry." I put the pillow down.

"Don't apologize. I'm simply pointing it out to you. It's a sign of spiritual repression. One of several I've noticed since you first arrived."

"Repression. Right. I see," I mumbled, not looking up. Was there something I could do that was a sign of spiritual … whatever, unrepression? I felt vaguely defensive. Off balance. This wasn't the conversation I expected to have. Should I tell her how I prayed for my dead goldfish when it had been flushed when I was seven? How my sister and I would make fairy crowns from dried flowers and grant each other three wishes? Was that spiritual? Maybe I should hit her with the conversations I was having with my dead husband? That's not something that happens to spiritually repressed people, is it? Do spiritually plugged-up people talk to the dead?

"Tell me what brought you here to see me, Kate," Eliza Campbell said, interrupting my thoughts.

I felt unreasonably panicked. What had brought me here to see her? Serendipity? Colossal forces beyond my knowing? My car? All my reasons piled up behind the same giant cork that was plugging my spiritual access. I was sure there had to be an answer, somewhere in the universe. "I don't know what brought me here," I said. "Can I take a bathroom break?"

Again that long eyebrow arched. "I don't think you want a break, Kate. I think you want to end the session. Is that what you want?"

I thought for a moment, then said in a small voice, "Yes, please."

I spent the forty-five minutes it takes to drive from Eliza Campbell's office in the city back to Greenfield mentally yanking on my giant spiritual cork.

I hadn't even told Eliza Campbell about Kevin. His death. His voice. I couldn't. When she had asked me if I was spiritual, it was as if, somehow, a great crack had opened somewhere inside of me. I felt a sort of painful hope. There had been so much to think about. While I doubted it was her intention to get me defensive, her questions pushed me somehow.

Sure, I'd been embarrassed at first by the gaping void that was my past spiritual existence. But she assured me that I was a spiritual person, deep down. I just hadn't explored it yet. The proof of it was that I was there, talking to her. "There are no accidents," Eliza Campbell had said. "Everything happens for a purpose."

I took strange comfort in the thought. Perhaps it was enough to go on for now. It was as if simply talking about my utter lack of spiritual experience, calling it out caused a shift in the foundations of my thinking. I didn't have answers exactly, but just the idea of spiritual things—the fact of them, that they existed in the world—seemed to lighten my load, broaden my thinking. Maybe hearing Kevin's voice was, in fact, a spiritual thing. A spiritual experience on which I could build. Build what, I didn't know. But I felt, for the first time since Kevin died, that I could look up, look around. My spiritual cork was beginning to loosen.

I'm awake, but I keep my eyes closed and just feel. The warmth of the sheets against my skin, the comfort of the soft mattress. The sound of Kevin's breathing. I lie on my back and count back the days and weeks we've been married. More than three years, and it feels like five minutes.

I turn my head and open my eyes. Light from the street

pushes into the room through the cotton curtains and I look at Kevin's face, softened by sleep, in the dim shadows. The sheets are pulled down, exposing his bare chest to the cool night. I rest my hand there, the hair on his chest curls around my hand like an embrace.

I close my eyes and feel the rise and fall of his breath, the steady beat of his heart. Within moments my heartbeat matches his. I wonder how this could still feel so new, and I'm filled with beautiful longing. I inch closer, lay my head on his shoulder, fitting myself between his arm and torso. I press my length against his side. His arm goes around me, but he's asleep, unconsciously moving his body to fit with mine. The smell of him so familiar it's somehow a part of me. As I drift off I think, Mine.

11

When I arrived home from my appointment with Eliza Campbell, the last of the evening sun was spilling orange and blue onto the dark wood floor of my living room. It was late and I was hungry. I hadn't eaten before driving to the city for my appointment. In the kitchen, I opened and closed the doors of a few appliances, and within minutes I had a hot meal on the table. I offered up a silent thanks to microwave ovens and my sister's single-serving organizational skills.

I ate four cabbage rolls, a withered salad, and drank two glasses of water. It was more food than I'd eaten in the past week. Amazing how a full stomach can give a body a sense of bloated calm.

I filled the sink with warm, sudsy water and belched like a trucker, then set about washing the dirty dishes lined up on my counter. As I plunged both hands in, I found I was humming an old song from my childhood. From my maternal grandmother. My mother's favorite. I sang,

> "*Too-ra-loo-ra-loo-ral, Too-ra-loo-ra-li, Too-ra-loo-ra-loo-ral, hush now, don't you cry!*

"Too-ra-loo-ra-loo-ral, Too-ra-loo-ra-li, Too-ra-loo-ra-loo-ral, that's an Irish lullaby."

Water splashed onto the counter as I swayed to my own music. I'd been loosened somehow. The joints of my mind had been oiled by the idea of possibilities, that there were some, that they might be waiting for me.

Kevin's voice came on a breeze. "You used to sing that song while you were reading. I could never understand how you were able to read and sing at the same time."

I smiled down into the dishwater. Somehow I'd known he would speak. Maybe not right that moment, but just he would, sometime, speak to me again. It was as if I'd opened the door to an invited guest.

Eliza Campbell had said we are all connected. There was no reason for me to fear the man I was most connected with, was there? No reason to fear the connection that held us together. No reason to think all of this was crazy. Okay, it's not as if I was about to take an ad out in the *Sunday Times* announcing I was spending quality time with my deceased husband. But I was no longer thinking it was wrong, or crazy, or all in my head. Still, I didn't know how this worked. If only there was some sort of cosmic rule book, I thought.

I gazed down at the soapy water. "I am a multitasker by nature, Kevin." I made a slow turn on my tiptoes and faced the kitchen. There was no one there. I felt a fissure of disappointment. What was I expecting? That he would materialize before my eyes? I looked around the room, unsure of what to fix on. "You, on the other hand, have a one-track mind," I said to the microwave.

"Especially when it comes to you, babe," Kevin said. I heard the smile in his voice.

I thought of saying *I miss you,* but I remembered the last time I said that to him he had stopped talking. "You were very one-track-minded when it came to me, yes," I said to the cool, thin air.

"Sing to me, Kate."

In my kitchen, alone except for the remnants of Kevin, I sang,

> *"Me Mither sang a song to me, in tones so sweet and low.*
> *Just a simple little ditty, in her good ould Irish way,*
> *And I'd give the world if she could sing that song to me*
> *this day."*

Kevin's soft tenor joined in when I sang,

> *"Too-ra-loo-ra-loo-ral, Too-ra-loo-ra-li, Too-ra-loo-ra-loo-*
> *ral, hush now, don't you cry!*
> *"Too-ra-loo-ra-loo-ral, Too-ra-loo-ra-li, Too-ra-loo-ra-loo-*
> *ral, that's an Irish lullaby."*

I closed my eyes as I sang the final notes, a soft wave of comfort rolled over my body. I was smiling and crying at the same time. "That was nice."

I waited, but Kevin said nothing. I sensed somehow, inexplicably, that he wasn't gone. I only needed to say the right thing. Like turning a key, or flipping the correct switch in the fuse box.

I chewed the inside of my cheek, thinking. I couldn't ask him questions. He wouldn't, or couldn't answer anything. I supposed the rest of the rules would reveal themselves over time. I thought for a moment, conjuring a sentence I thought he might reply to. I spoke to the microwave. "You sing in the shower. Loud, hysterical opera."

Kevin said, "You love it."

I smiled. So far so good. "I do. You make up the craziest words."

Kevin bellowed out in comical operatic parody, "You gotta pizza pie! I wanna pizza pie! Oh no, it's for you, not I! Please share your pizza pie!"

I laughed. I could see him, standing in the steam-filled shower holding the loofah like a microphone, hollering over the rushing water. My mind clung to the image. Kevin. Naked. Steam billowing around him. Water and soap rushing down his torso. In an instant my body was flushed with desire so acute that it caused actual pain. I bent forward, sucker-punched by lust, trying to stave off its advance. I reached out, but my hands remained dry and empty. I wrapped my arms around myself and pretended they were his arms. I squeezed myself hard, waiting for the sweet ache to subside. My lips opened and closed, searching for a kiss that would never come. Loneliness filled my body like a million small stones.

12

Singing my mother's favorite song with Kevin in our kitchen reminded me that I hadn't spoken to her since the day she brought me the stack of books, over a month ago. She wouldn't contact me first, I felt sure. After Dad died, she made it clear to Heather and me that she would let us know when she was ready to talk, that she needed some space to adjust.

So the next morning I grabbed the keys to Kevin's car, and the stack of books I didn't read, and went to see her.

Standing in the kitchen of the house I'd grown up in, I held a small, heavy object that looked exactly like a flat brown rock. I looked at my mother. "What's this?"

She glanced at my hand. "It's a baking stone. It promotes even cooking."

"You just stick it in there with the bread or cake or whatever?"

"No, dear," she said. "First you have to heat it up in the oven. Then you put whatever you are baking on top of it."

I cocked my head to one side. Who was this woman who heated rocks? I couldn't imagine her doing this when I was growing up. "How long does it take?"

She folded, unfolded, and then refolded a dish towel. "It really shouldn't take more than forty-five minutes or so." She threw me a quick glance that seemed to say, "Please don't tell your dead father." Dad would have never understood his wife's desire to cook rocks. I could almost hear him sputtering, "Waste, that's what it is! Running the electric bill sky-high just to heat a rock. Ridiculous."

"It's good for pizza, too," she said, running her hand over the round, flat surface.

I put the stone down. "You like pizza now?"

"No."

I looked around the kitchen. I knew it like I knew my own childhood. But things weren't the same here. There were changes I'd failed to notice when I first came in. Changes since Dad died. Beside the baking stone sat a new recipe box with the words BITE ME stamped on the top. The artificial roses that had sat perennially on the kitchen table had been replaced with massive, living gladioli from the garden. The faded lace curtains had been replaced with cotton ones the color of butter. The wallpaper—a blue and purple riot of tiny flowers I had long ago stopped noticing—was now a clean wall of paint, a soft, hazy green that drifted before my eyes like a summer memory. My father's presence was nowhere to be seen. If he walked in now, he would look out of place.

"Are you cold, Kate?" my mother said.

My hands were running up and my arms, warming them in the already too warm kitchen. I dropped them to my side. "Is it going to get better?"

She took a long breath, and then let it out. She knew what I was talking about. "It's going to get different."

"I know life is different now, Mom. I meant—"

She raised a hand in a "shush, I'm talking" gesture. "I don't mean 'life is different.' I'm referring to the way you're feeling. About losing Kevin. About grief and loss and sadness. It changes." She stared down at the counter as if searching there for some lost secret. "It seems to me that feelings are the most unreliable things."

"I don't understand."

"I know. I don't mean to be vague." She took in a long breath. "When I lost your father, I felt like my life was over. Literally. That's what it felt like. But it wasn't true. My life wasn't over. It kept going. It keeps going." She shrugged one shoulder and turned away from me. "I feel differently today than I did in those first weeks after losing your father. I feel like my life has possibilities."

I traced a pattern on the countertop with my finger. Possibilities sounded better than questions and a memory filled with gaping holes. Better than a future that could not be fathomed or understood. "That's good, isn't it?"

She turned and looked at me for a long moment. "Is it? My feelings when your father died turned out to be wrong. My life wasn't over. Who's to say these new feelings will turn out to be right?"

"You mean—"

"I mean the one thing I've learned is that you can't trust your feelings."

"So what can you trust?"

"Kate, honey, I honestly have no idea."

Outside my mother's house, I sat in the car fiddling with the keys. I didn't want to go home. Being out, driving, seeing things other than my own four walls felt good.

I put the car in gear and pulled away from the curb. I was driving Kevin's brilliant-red Mazdaspeed3. I drove mindlessly for a few minutes, with no intended destination. The car maneuvered with little effort, cornering with only two fingers on the steering wheel. I felt vaguely dangerous. After a tight right-hand turn at the intersection of Drinkle and Magnolia, a smile pulled at my mouth.

"Come on!" Kevin bellows from the front door.

I hop on one foot, trying to pull my shoe on. Where's my purse?

"Let's go!" He's in the car now, window rolled down, thumping on the side panel with a fist, but he's grinning. "Put some hustle in it, babe."

I lock the front door and scurry to the car—my car, a green Ford Focus, perfect for bombing around town in. It may be my car, but Kevin is in the driver's seat. He honks as I walk past the hood, and I scream. "What did you do that for?" I say as I pull my seat belt on. He laughs and backs out of the driveway before I can get it buckled. I've never seen him like this, acting like a child on the way to the circus. I can feel the excitement from him, like waves. Suddenly I can't help but laugh too.

His right hand fumbles around near my leg, searching for the stick shift. He's used to driving a manual transmission. He grabs the lever that sticks out of the steering wheel column and rolls his eyes. "Automatic transmission," he mocks.

I cross my arms, pretending to be offended. "Technology exists to make driving simple. It should be utilized."

He pulls a fast right, one finger on the steering wheel. "That technology makes driving dull." He rubs his hands together above the wheel. Now he's steering with his left leg. "But this beauty we're going to pick up …" He lets out a slow whistle.

I smile at him. Not because we're on our way to pick up a new car, but because he's so happy about it. Happy? Try exuberant. Hands tapping to the beat of the song on the radio, head bobbing. He sings out an "uh-huh, uh-huh" along with the nearly incoherent words of the song. I feel the wind through my hair (both windows are down now) and the sun on my face as we speed through town toward the new-car dealership on the east side.

I reach across and squeeze his hand. He brings it to his lips and kisses it, a big, noisy smooch sound. "Mwah!" And tiny bubbles of contentment rise up from my stomach to my chest and fly from my mouth.

I giggle, not even sure what I'm so happy about.

I hadn't wanted this second car, didn't think we needed it. "What about our global footprint, or whatever it's called? Reduce, reuse, you know?" I had argued.

Kevin had just grinned and replied, "It's red and it has a sunroof."

I told him we couldn't afford it.

He smiled and said, "It's the price of success, babe. You have to look successful to be successful." I rolled my eyes at that bit of Tony Robbins advice, but he was convinced not only could we afford a new car, we couldn't afford not to get a new car.

"What about saving for a down payment on a bigger house?" I said.

He got very excited talking about home equity, and said, "Besides, when I'm a veep, I'll buy you three houses if you want."

At the dealership Kevin is out of the car before I can unlatch my seat belt. I wonder if they will raise the price of the car simply because they can see how eager he is. In his current state of emotion, they could probably charge him an additional five thousand dollars with ease. I hurry to catch up. This isn't difficult, because Kevin had suddenly slowed down, his giddy scuttle now a meandering slouch. I sidled up beside him. "Where's your bounce, Tigger?"

He stares at the doors, slowing until we are at a standstill in front of them. "Hang on." He turns and does a half jog to the show lot, me running behind him. He stops in front of a low, dark blue Audi, a serious car that looks like it might bite you if you stood too close. Kevin frowns at it, running a hand over his clean-shaven jaw. He lays two hands on the driver's window and leans in, peering at the interior. Pushing away, he glances at the building where Gary, our salesman, is no doubt watching the door, awaiting our arrival.

I tap Kevin's arm. "Hon, are you going to keep being weird, or are you going to go get your car?"

I scan the lot, but his brand-spanking-new Mazdaspeed3 is nowhere to be found. Probably in the garage getting its hubcaps polished or whatever they did just before handing over a new car. "Kev?"

"What do you think of this car?"

I point at the Audi. "This one? It looks like something my Great-Uncle Jonah would drive."

Kevin pulls his eyebrows in until they meet in the middle of his forehead. "Your Great-Uncle Jonah can't eat soup, never mind drive a car like this."

I shrug one shoulder. "If he could drive, this would be his car."

"Tony just picked one of these up," he mumbles. I don't know who Tony is, so I keep quiet.

I give his arm a tug. "It looks expensive. And the Mazda is expensive enough." He doesn't move. I give him my most alluring smile. "And it's red."

The corners of his mouth turn up, and he makes a snorty laugh through his nose. "Let's go." He scoops up my hand and he's happy again, walking with a jagged beat in his step. I glance back at the Audi, so stern and grumpy on the lot. It looks like a banker's car. Besides, the Mazda is a four-door, which will make it easier to get a baby seat in and out of.

Greenfield is a small town, which means that aimless driving has serious limits. I forced the Mazda into a too-sharp left turn and found the street was blocked by a farmer's field. End of the road. I fumbled with the stick shift and gave it a shove.

I looked at the black-and-white street sign. Apple Tree Lane. I'd never been down Maggie's street before. I hadn't intended to end up there. Still, I slowed the car and began studying the houses I passed. It didn't take long before I spotted a house that could only belong to Maggie. It was painted a painful shade of red and sported jaundice green shutters. The combination gave the house an odd aura. Like being sick at Christmastime. The sidewalk leading up to the house was bordered with deep purple delphiniums that stood at least five feet tall. As I drove past, I saw a riot of wildflowers growing along the front of the house. Bees and butterflies made equal time among the coneflowers, foxglove, and poppies.

I pushed my foot down on the accelerator while maneuvering the stick shift, but I forgot the clutch, and the gears made a horrible grinding sound. I looked down at the stick. I was in fourth gear. I glanced up, horrified to see I was speeding toward the fence that separated the road from the farmer's field at the end of the street. In a panic I pulled a fast U-turn and the car accelerated as it came out of the turn.

Dead ahead a Mustang made a slow approach into one of the driveways. I stood on the brakes. They screamed as my car slammed into the side of the Mustang. The air bag exploded in my face, pushing me back hard against the headrest. I felt a sharp pain in my neck. I pushed at the air bag, trying to move it out of the way so I could see what had happened. Out the windshield I saw the Mustang neatly folded around the front of the Mazdaspeed. I blinked stupidly at the scene out my window.

I saw the dark outline of the driver through the other car's shattered window. The driver sat motionless for a long moment, then leaned into the driver-side door and began rocking back and forth, pushing at it with a shoulder. *Must be stuck*, I thought.

The Mustang rocked back and forth, and then the door gave way and the driver emerged from the wreckage. *Maggie.*

She made slow but steady progress toward my car; her left leg seemed to jerk with each step. I scrambled for the door release, my hands shaking and weak. I pushed the door hard and it opened with a quick jerk. I fell into a tidy pile on the road.

I heard Maggie's voice say "Oh" as I hit the pavement. Then she was beside me, bending down and saying, "Are you all right, miss?"

From my position on the asphalt, I could see a line of blood running down Maggie's shoe. The blood started a small pool at her feet. There was a tear in her purple pants.

"Maggie, I'm so sorry."

At the sound of her name she jerked as if surprised. She bent and peered down at me. "Who—?" she began.

I turned my face up to her. I felt a sharp jab in the back of my neck.

"Kate! Are you hurt?"

I pushed at the ground, trying to stand up. Maggie held her hand out, but I waved it away. "I don't know. But you are," I pointed to her leg. Maggie looked down, saw the blood leaching out of her body, and let out a small noise that sounded like "Geep."

I stood, leaning hard against the ruined Mazda.

Maggie turned back toward her ruined car and hobbled toward it. "I have a cell phone in my purse."

"Let me get it. You stay still," I said as I lurched past her. Dizzy, I grabbed Maggie's purse out of her car. I closed my eyes and leaned on the roof of her mangled Mustang for a long moment as spots exploded behind my eyes. Finally I wobbled back to Maggie and handed over her purse. She pawed the contents in what seemed like slow motion. I felt a wave of nausea rise up into my rib cage. I sat down hard on the curb as Maggie spoke into the phone. Her face matched her lime green cell phone.

"They're on the way. Police, and the ambulance, too," Maggie said as she clicked the phone closed. She looked down at her leg again, then back at me. I was gently prodding the back of my neck with my right hand. I hit a tender spot and yelled out.

Maggie made a *tsk* sound. "I think we are headed for the hospital, dear."

I started to cry. "I hate hospitals."

13

I sat beside Maggie's bed in the hospital ER.

A young, solemn doctor had declared me healthy and "lucky." The pain in my neck and shoulders, caused by the force of the air bag throwing me back onto my seat and headrest, was muscular and would subside in a few days. He prescribed muscle relaxants with codeine.

I held Maggie's hand as we sat in silence, waiting for a doctor to come and stitch up her leg. Other than the cut, she'd suffered only bruises, mostly on the left side of her body. She would be sore, but fine. We were assured it would be a short wait until a doctor could come and put the needed stitches in Maggie's leg.

I rocked in my chair. "I'm so—"

Maggie threw me a hard look. She'd already told me to stop apologizing. She squeezed my hand and I squeezed back, hiding my apology in the soft pressure.

She leaned back against the pillows and closed her eyes. "It was a surprise, you know. To see it was you. Well," she gave a snorting laugh, "the whole thing was a terrible surprise. But to see it was you driving the car. You're the last person I expected to see lying in a heap on the road. In your living room, maybe. But not on the road."

I opened my mouth to reply but my attention was caught by the actions of a nurse across the corridor from us. She was standing in front of the nurse's desk, her hands full of clothing and a large plastic bag. I watched as she placed the bag on the desk and folded a pair of blue pants. She put the pants into the plastic bag, and then started folding what looked like a pair of boxer shorts. The hair raised up on the back of my neck as I watched the nurse carefully fold the articles of clothing and place them in the bag, which had the name "Zinik, Jaris" written across it in black, bold print.

I sprang up and half ran across the corridor toward the nurse. I heard Maggie call, "Kate, where are you going?"

I reached the nurse's station and grabbed the bag, but, in an amazing show of reflex, the nurse managed to hang on to it. She pulled hard and we did a fast tug-of-war. "What do you think you're doing?"

I let go. The nurse jerked and had to take a quick step backward to keep from falling.

I pointed. "What are you going to do with that?"

She stared down at the bag for a moment, then up at me with a look that said *dangerous person.* "Are you family?"

"Yes," I said. "I'm family. Not his family. Not Jaris Zini-whatever's family." I grabbed her arm. She pulled away, swinging her arm hard to the right. *She's scared of me.* "Please, I'm sorry. I'm not crazy. I'm not going to hurt you. I just need to know what you are going to do with that bag of clothes."

"What business is it of yours? I'm packaging them up for the family to take home."

"He died, didn't he?" I said, pointing to the name on the bag.

She crossed her arms, the bag flapping softly against her ribs. "I can't discuss this with you. You need to leave. Now."

"Please, I just need to know. My husband died two months ago, here, in this ER. When I left the hospital, they didn't give me anything." I gestured to her hands. "No bag of clothes. No nothing." I saw her face soften. It wasn't quite sympathy, but she wasn't going to holler for security ... yet. "My sister had to come back later to get his things."

The nurse pulled a frown. "That's unusual. But we're a busy hospital, and sometimes mistakes happen. We try hard to make sure the family members have all of the deceased's belongings before they leave the hospital."

"I'm missing his watch," I said. It was only after I had spoken the words I realized it was true. His watch. That's what had been missing from the pile of his belongings left on my bed the morning after his funeral.

The nurse patted Jaris's bag. "I have to go and give this to the family. If you like, you can talk to one of the nurses at the desk. Maybe one of them can help you." She walked away.

I looked at the nurses behind the desk. One was on the phone; two others had their backs turned to me, talking. I cleared my throat.

"Kate?" I heard Maggie call from across the hall.

I poked my head in the door. "You okay?"

"Yes, fine. I thought the doctor would be here by now. Good thing I'm not bleeding to death," she said with a small smile. She looked pale.

"I'll go see if I can find one." I left before she could protest.

I tapped the nurses' desk with my knuckle and smiled when the nurse, still on the phone, turned toward me. She leaned back in her chair and laughed into the receiver. The other two nurses were gone. I turned and searched the hallway until I spotted another nurse marching toward me. I hurried to her, stopping just in front of her.

"Excuse me, I—" She brushed past me, not breaking her fast pace. I trotted behind her. "I need to ask you a question."

"Yes?" She hustled down the hall, moving like she was in training for a triathlon. "What is it?"

I felt the effort of keeping pace with her in my lungs and aching muscles. When was the last time I'd gone for a walk? I was horribly out of shape. "I wanted to ask you what happens to people's clothing, belongings, that sort of thing." She was really moving fast.

"Lost and found is on the main floor, near the cafeteria." She said as she turned a corner.

I followed. "No, not lost things. I mean—"

The nurse came to a sudden stop and turned to face me. "Main floor. By the cafeteria." She spun and continued her one-person race.

I raised my chin and yelled to the ceiling. "I want my dead husband's watch!" I cupped my hand over my mouth, embarrassed.

The nurse reversed track and walked back to me, eyebrows pushed together, mouth hanging down in a loose frown. She looked thoughtful and annoyed. "What's his name?" she said.

"Kevin Davis," I said softly, trying to make up for my outburst.

"Fine, you go sit in the waiting room and I'll see what I can find."

"Actually I'm here with a friend. I … we were in an accident.

She's in examination room 3. I'll wait there." I remembered that I was also supposed to find a doctor and see what was taking so long for him to treat Maggie.

The nurse gave a curt nod. "Kevin Davis. Exam 3. Okay. I'm busy, but when I can, I'll pull the chart and see what happened." She turned and walked away, hollering over her shoulder, "I can't promise anything."

I made my way back to the nurses' station, on the hunt for a doctor.

An hour later the doctor was putting a bandage on Maggie's freshly stitched leg. Maggie kept smiling at the doctor and telling him what a wonderful job he was doing. It was a good strategy. The doctor seemed to take extra time and care with stitches. He was going over a list of dos and don'ts with Maggie when the nurse walked into the room. She held a file folder in her hand. She looked at me, then back at the file folder. "You're Mrs. Davis?"

"Yes, Kate Davis."

She shrugged. It didn't matter. She'd gone to the trouble of digging up the chart and she was going to tell me what was in it regardless if I were Mrs. Davis or King Tut. "According to this," she pushed her finger toward the folder, "there was no watch. Not only that, there weren't any clothes, either."

"I don't understand."

She glanced at the chart. "Kevin Davis arrived at this hospital naked."

14

I turn the lock, closing the Wee Book Inn for the night. I'd pulled a double shift, covering for Percy. I hop in my car and turn up the radio loud. I drive with the windows down to stay awake and alert. When I pull into the driveway, my legs protest. I'm happy to be home, but too exhausted to want to get out of the car. I haul myself out, check the mailbox—bills, should have left them where they were—and open the front door. "I'm home," I call.

Kevin runs to the door; he's bare-chested, holding a dark blue dress shirt. "Did you wash this in hot water?"

I kick my shoes off. "No. I don't wash much of anything in hot water. And hello to you, too."

He holds it out. "It's shrunk."

I take the shirt and examine the tag. "It says dry clean only." I toss it back to him. "Did you dry clean only?"

Kevin follows me into the kitchen. "Not funny, Kate. This shirt cost more than a hundred dollars."

My mouth is full of croissant. It's nine-thirty and I'd missed dinner. "What? Why on earth did you buy a shirt that costs that much and then toss it in the laundry?" I shake my head, staring

*at the shirt. "Scratch that. Why did you buy a shirt that costs
that much, period?"*

*Kevin speaks through clenched teeth. "I thought you read
the tags before you threw them in the washer."*

*I run a causal hand down his torso, from his shoulder to
his navel. "I thought you talked to me before spending that
much money for one shirt." I climb the stairs, still munching the
croissant.*

He follows me, ranting about the shirt.

*In the bedroom I change into my pajamas, half listening.
He thrusts the fabric toward me, not quite in my face, but just
under my chin. He pulls his hand away quickly, as if realizing
he may have gone too far. "It's silk, you know."*

I didn't know. I couldn't even recall seeing it before now.

*I turn the tap on and wet my toothbrush, raising my voice
over the noise of running water. "We'll never get our five-bedroom house if you keep buying hundred-dollar shirts," I say it in
a singsong, slightly teasing voice, hoping to relax him.*

He hollers back, "You're missing the point completely."

*I walk back to the bedroom, toothbrush in mouth, and
stick my head in the room. "I'm sorry the shirt is ruined. Really
I am. But it's just a shirt, Kevin." I return to the bathroom. If he
made any reply it was lost in a stream of flowing cool water.*

My hands shook as I dialed the hospital courtesy phone. I turned
and looked at Maggie sitting in a wheelchair in the hospital

corridor. She raised her eyebrows at me in question and I held up my hand, palm forward, in response. It took two attempts before I was able to punch in the correct series of numbers. I finally succeeded, then accidentally dropped the receiver and stood, dumbly, watching as it swung like a pendulum from the cord. I picked it up and squashed it to my ear. I heard the ringing of the phone and the wail of a distant siren at the same time. After two more rings Heather answered.

"Can you come and get me at the hospital?" I said into the phone.

"Kate, what happened? Are you okay?"

I squeezed the receiver. "We're fine. Can you come and get us?"

"We?"

"Maggie Cunynghame and me. I'll explain when you get here." She agreed, and I hung up. I stared at the numbers on the phone.

I felt my heart banging, two-fisted, against my ribs. My sister had lied to me. And I was going to find out why.

My stomach clenched with impatience. It had been a long process of waiting, loading and unloading Maggie from Heather's compact car, installing her in her home, ensuring her comfort and safety, and promising to call every hour to check on her. On our way out I looked back to see Maggie sitting in a recliner, swaddled in blankets and piled high with her cordless phone, remote control, box of tissues, and two cats. A cup of steaming tea sat on a small table beside her. Her new crutches were within easy reach. She gazed lovingly at the television and didn't even look up when we stepped out the door.

I walked to the car, suppressing a gag of nervousness. I needed to ask Heather about Kevin's clothes. She couldn't have gotten them from the hospital if Kevin wasn't wearing anything when he arrived. Where did she find them? Why didn't she tell me?

I eased myself down into the passenger seat and felt the dull throb in my neck return. The painkillers they had given me were wearing off. I fished in my purse for the prescription the doctor at the hospital had written for me, and showed it to Heather. She glanced at it and nodded, yes, we'd head to the drugstore next.

She backed out of Maggie's driveway. We rolled slowly past the debris of the accident still lying on the road. Glass from my broken headlights, bits of yellow from the side of Maggie's car. *I did that,* I thought. I looked at the pieces of car scattered on the ground and felt an odd sense of disconnection from them. It had happened, but it felt unreal. I carried the impact of the moment in my aching muscles, yet my mind couldn't connect with the events. As if my psyche was already too full of events to process and trauma to make sense of, so it rejected this newest piece of information. Yes, it said, we've been in a crash, but I can't deal with that right now. As we drove past, a silver fragment of my bumper gleamed up at me like a wink.

15

I stood at the tall pharmacy counter and slid my debit card through the slot on the machine. I idly punched in my numbers and turned to look at Heather. She was studying a bottle of some kind of herbal medicine. She looked beautiful in her baby blue T-shirt and creamy cotton shorts. She pushed her hair to one side. She read the ingredients label off the bottle. Her lips moved as she read. She was my brilliant, ordinary sister. And a liar.

"Rejected," said a voice from behind me.

I turned and faced the pharmacist. "Excuse me?"

"The transaction," the pharmacist said, sliding the card toward me.

I stared down at it. How can a debit card be rejected?

"It says nonsufficient funds," came the reply to my unspoken question.

"Non—" I began. Frozen. Donna had told me that the bank account was frozen but that she would take care of it. That was over a week ago. *She must have forgotten*, I thought. "Heather," I called, not bothering to turn around.

My sister came and stood beside me. I held up my useless bank card. She looked at it, then at the pharmacist, then back at me. She reached into her purse and pulled out her wallet.

~◉~

The two painkillers went down with water. Heather took the glass from me and put it in my sink.

She gave me a gentle push toward the living room. "You'll feel better in a few minutes."

I sank into the sofa and felt an immediate sense of relief and weariness. I closed my eyes.

She stood, looking at me. "You need me to stay?"

I shook my head. "Heather, I need the truth."

"Truth? About what?"

"Kevin's clothes," I said as I opened my eyes in order to see her reaction.

Heather's face turned to wood, an expression I couldn't interpret. Her eyes darted back and forth like two trapped birds. She sat down hard on the sofa. I leaned toward her.

"I asked about Kevin's missing watch at the hospital. The nurse said there was no watch. More than that, Kevin had been naked when he arrived at the hospital."

"Watch," Heather said in a dull whisper. She looked down at her hands.

It confirmed what I suspected. I'd never mentioned Kevin's missing watch to Heather, but she already knew it had not been among the articles of clothing she'd brought back to me. Could I get her to tell me the truth? "The day of the funeral, I asked you to come with me to the hospital, to get his things. You said you'd go alone instead."

"I did," Heather said. "Then I brought them here. You were sleeping, so I put them at the bottom of the bed and left."

I had had a dream that night, of Kevin standing over me. When I awoke, his clothes were lying at the bottom of the bed. It must have been Heather I sensed in the room.

I shook my head. "How did you manage to get his clothes from the hospital if he had been naked when he arrived there? They never had his clothes in the first place."

Heather spread her hands out in front of her. "Obviously the nurse today got it wrong." She placed her hands on her knees and gave me a sad smile. "Kate, you've had a long, rotten day. The last thing you need is to get worked up about a simple misunderstanding."

I furrowed my brow. "She read it right off the chart."

"So what? So someone wrote wrong information on a chart." Heather threw her hands around. "I'll bet it happens all the time. The clothes at the bottom of your bed were the ones Kevin was wearing that day, right?"

"Yeah …" I said in slow motion. Or, at least they could have been. I still could hardly remember anything about the morning of the day he died, including what he'd been wearing. But they were Kevin's things. I didn't see any point in mentioning my memory loss to Heather. I also didn't tell her how my head was beginning to feel loose and disconnected from my body.

"Well there you go," she said like she had just closed the case. "Whoever wrote that in the chart must have not seen Kevin until after the doctors had removed his clothes."

I felt a rush of warmth through my limbs as all the muscles in my
body seemed to relax at once. The pills were taking effect in a hurry.
"Removed them?"

Heather leaned forward. "They would have needed his clothes
out of the way in order to work on him. To try to save him."

I leaned back and closed my eyes again. I tried to picture it;
white coats, bright lights, hands pushing and pulling clothing out of
the way, sharp voices calling urgent orders. It made sense.

A warm exhaustion filled my bones and turned my muscles to
liquid. "Painkillers," I mumbled and eased into sleep.

"You'll sleep your life away," Kevin said.

My eyelids drifted open, then slammed shut. My limbs were
loose and indistinct. Where was I? "Where are you?" I said, my voice
thick and veiled. Silence. I should have known better. Questions
were a no-no. I moved my hand, but it wouldn't move. I tried my
finger, but I couldn't feel it. "Drugs. I took drugs."

"You're Briar Rose, sleeping your life away." His voice was soft,
slightly mocking.

"I can't feel anything."

"Once, you had the flu and slept for twenty-six hours." He
sounded close, as if whispering in my ear.

I lifted my arm to touch him, but it just lay there on the couch.
"I'm awake now."

A soft laugh, like a rolling mumble. "You're sleeping."

"I wish I could touch you."

"And once, you stayed up for thirty-six hours straight. I don't know why."

I counted my breaths, like sheep, four, five. "That was when Dad died. I couldn't sleep." Ten, eleven. "Is it good to be dead?"

Silence.

Eighteen, nineteen.

16

I had a lot to do. It was 2:30 in the afternoon and I'd accomplished exactly nothing. Rendered useless by a backlog of guilt, indecision, and painkillers, I sat at my kitchen table drinking my fifth cup of coffee and stared at the blank sheet of paper in front of me.

I tapped my pencil in time with the ticking clock. I sipped my coffee. I needed to make another list. Maybe it would organize my thoughts, spur me to action. My hand drifted to the paper and the pencil wrote: *Call Maggie.* Guilt slithered down my throat into my gut. How could I have hit her with my car? What was I thinking, pulling a U-turn like that? I owed her so much. She had visited me after Kevin's funeral, when I needed someone to talk to; offered encouragement and a list of counselors' names. And how did I repay her? I slammed into her car and sent her to the hospital with a gouged leg. Not cut, gouged. Thirty-two stitches. That was two days ago. I picked up the phone and dialed.

Maggie's voice boomed out of the receiver, "How's the neck, pet?"

I reached back and touched my spine with the cool coffee spoon. "Better. What about your leg?"

She let out a short chuckle. "I'll live."

"I'm sorry I haven't come to see you."

"You're in abominable pain. I know, your sister told me."

"Heather told you? When?"

"She was here this morning. She's been checking on me a couple of times a day. What a gem, that girl."

"Yeah," I said in a slow, dull voice. "She's matchless." I gave my head a feeble shake, hoping the details of my recent conversation with Heather would fall loose. All I could recall was Heather's voice, fast and high pitched.

"About your car," I said to Maggie. "We never exchanged insurance information."

"Let's take another day or two just to be injured. Paperwork can wait. You won't be charged. I told the police they can't charge you with anything. They said they wouldn't. Nice chaps."

"Charged?" I hadn't thought of that. A laser of pain shot me between the eyes. How many things are there in the world that I hadn't thought of? Frozen bank accounts, life insurance, mortgage papers, police charges. Watches.

I gulped my coffee and briefly wondered about mixing caffeine with codeine. My right leg twitched.

Maggie's voice pulled me back to the present. "Just a ticket, that's all. And as for the car, well, I was thinking of getting a new one anyway. The smashup just helped me make up my mind about it. As soon as I'm up to it, I'm going to the dealership and pick up that PT Cruiser. Have you seen it? It's purple. Gorgeous, just gorgeous."

I couldn't believe how happy she sounded. "I'll bring you some food later on," I said, thinking of my well-stocked freezer. "Compliments, again, of Heather."

"No need, dear. Several ladies from the church have been comin' round bringing me meals. I'm a well-fed cripple, I assure you."

Maggie was apparently inundated with visitors as she recuperated. I cast a glance around my blank kitchen. Heather hadn't been back since the day of the accident. I had run her off. Bullied her with my suspicions and questions.

I hung up and went to work on my to-do list. I put a line through *Call Maggie*. Under it I wrote *Call Donna*. I needed to figure out my finances. I ran a soft finger over the numbers on the phone. I dialed a different number instead.

The phone rings and I jump up from my seat on the floor to answer it. I hop over two sets of legs and swerve around a couple lost in conversation by the stairs. Our small house is bursting with friends. I reach the phone on the fifth ring. It's Blair. I push the receiver tight against my ear and plug the other ear with a finger. "Where are you? Everyone is here already."

"Listen, I don't think I'll come." Blair's voice is muffled. I barely hear him above the racket of music and talking.

"How come? Are you sick?"

He sighs, "Just not up to a party tonight."

I wave dismissively, even though he can't see me. "Oh, come on, just get over here. You'll have fun. The place is hopping with cute chicks."

"That's the last thing I'm interested in, Kate." It's not like him to be testy. "I can't take it anymore."

A roar of male voices drowns out all other sounds. A group of guys pushing each other's shoulders in good-natured challenge. Something's up, I think, smiling. "I think the guys are planning something—maybe a game of football out front," I tell Blair.

"Kate, you and I need to talk," he says. I look at the friends milling around our house. Then I spot her. A pretty blonde standing by herself in a corner, looking around as if searching for someone. Ah-ha. I can't recall her name, there are so many to keep straight, but I recognize her as one of Blair's girlfriends. She looks cute and pouty and I think to myself that Blair must be avoiding running into her.

I'm about to say something when a hand reaches out and pulls me into the kitchen. Kevin, smiling and flushed in the overheated house, says, "Who's that?"

"Blair. He doesn't want to come."

Kevin takes the phone from my hand. "Be here in five minutes, dude. We're going to scrimmage in the front yard and I need your passing arm." Kevin hangs the phone up. "He'll come." He's still holding onto my arm.

I look at the phone. "He sounded upset."

He lifts one brow. "He's fine. And besides, I'm the only man you need to worry about." He smiles in a lusty way and we laugh. "Having fun?" he says.

"A wonderful time," I say, trying to free my arm from his grip and rejoin the party, but he holds firm. Something in his eye makes me stop short, catch my breath.

He takes a half step toward me. "You look amazing tonight, Mrs. Davis." He speaks from the back of his throat, making his

*words sound low and growling. The party can wait. He leans
down, our foreheads touch. He says, "You are so beautiful, you
know that?" Then he kisses me. He takes his time as if our house
wasn't full of people. He lingers over my mouth until I no longer
hear the din of people talking, music blaring. When he lets me
go he says, "I'm having a good time too." He saunters off and
joins a group of guys talking hockey. I watch him for a moment,
everyone so at ease with each other, and I am overcome by a
feeling of belonging. Loved by our friends, yet having a secret
place in the midst of them where he and I are alone, even in a
crowd.*

I picked up the phone and dialed.

A deep voice. "Hello?"

"You said if I ever needed you—"

"I'll be right there."

Blair rapped on the kitchen door. I opened it and said, "Hi. Let's
walk."

We headed uptown, toward the elementary school. I walked fast,
like something creeping and relentless was following us. Blair easily
kept pace, his long legs taking one stride to every two of mine. It
looked like he was growing his hair out. He was wearing a faded
T-shirt the color of pea soup that read, "Don't should on me." He

looked young and moppish. A perk of operating a skateboard shop, I supposed.

We entered the deserted school yard, and I headed toward the playground equipment. The school had recently installed an immense tire swing that looked as though it could hold six or seven children at one time, maybe more. It could swing back and forth and spin around at the same time, like an amusement park ride.

I walked over to the tire, swung one leg up and over, and sat down, straddling it like a horse. Blair did the same, across from me, and then leaned back onto one of the three chains suspending the swing. He closed his eyes and raised his arms up, folding his hands behind his head. His body looked strong, like flesh stretched over granite. I swallowed hard and looked away. We swayed on the swing for a long moment.

Blair opened one eye and peered over at me. "I'm glad you pulled me away from work to enjoy the sunshine with you. But, on the phone, you gave me the impression that you needed me for ... something."

A shard of guilt stabbed at me. What *did* I need from Blair? Other than to ease my loneliness? I hadn't seen another human being since Heather had left me sleeping on the sofa. I didn't know what I needed. Maybe just some company. Human company. The kind that had a body to go with the voice. Unlike Kevin. What strange comfort it was to hear Kevin's voice. When he spoke, he was all that mattered, all that existed. He filled my mind, my life. But his voice was a cold shock each time he spoke. I never knew, could never predict, when he might speak. And when he fell silent, I was left wrung out, alone, pulsing with fresh loss.

"I'm not sure what I need, Blair. I'm sorry ..."

"Hey, don't cry." Blair's voice was soft and deep.

Blair pulled his leg over the swing and stood in the center of the tire. He reached down and touched my cheek, pushing the tears away. More fell to take their place. "I shouldn't have called you. There's no emergency—nothing. I guess I'm feeling ... lonely." I reached for his hand. He squeezed mine.

I stood and, without thinking, pulled him close. I wrapped my arms around his neck and buried my face there. I just needed to be close. To somebody. He smelled like soap. I felt his hands on the small of my back, then his arms wrapping around me.

I looked up into his gray eyes. "I've developed a tendency to soak your shirt with tears whenever I see you."

His laugh was a soft rumble deep in his chest. His finger touched my damp cheek. "I don't know how to help you. It kills me to see you like this." He gathered me to his chest and spoke into my hair. "I want to reach into the center of you and pull out all the pain." He leaned back a little and cupped my face with his hands. "How do I do that? How do I fix you?"

My lower lip quivered as I gave a weak smile. "I don't know."

Blair gazed into my eyes. He leaned in and kissed my lips so softly I wasn't sure it was happening. He made a sound, a tiny groan, and pressed his mouth down harder.

I kissed him back. Eyes closed, wrapped in the sensations of intimacy, I reveled in his touch. We stood in the middle of the tire, in the middle of the school yard, our mouths sliding gently together. *Kevin.* I felt his hands running up and down my back. His touch brought my pent-up longing to the surface. Oh, how I'd missed this. How I'd missed *him*. My heart knocked in irregular thumps. Blood rushed through my body, filling my ears with an urgent roar, like rushing water. The water became a shout. The shout became a voice. *Kevin.*

I gasped and pushed Blair hard with both hands. He stepped back, his arms flailing, as he flipped over the swing, landing on his back with a dull thud.

"What the—?" he said.

"Did you hear?" My voice was high and thin.

"Hear what?" Blair pushed himself up and stood looking at me, his face pinched with confusion, and probably lower-back pain.

"*Kevin*. Did you hear him?"

Blair shook his head, quick jerks, "What are you talking about?"

I looked around the playground, uncertain of what I was looking for. Maybe Kevin? *No, that's crazy.*

My chest tightened with fear. I lifted my hands to my mouth in a speak-no-evil gesture. I stared at Blair, shaking my head back and forth like a mantra.

Blair's eyes flashed with fear. "Are you all right?"

"I'm going crazy. Help me." My voice climbed higher and louder with each word.

Blair tried to take my hands in his. I jerked away from his touch. "Kevin—he was yelling. Telling me to stop kissing you."

Blair blew out a long breath. He seemed relieved, like the mysteries of the universe had opened to him and he saw they were no big deal after all. "Kate, I'm so sorry." I opened my mouth but he held up his hand. "I shouldn't have kissed you. I shouldn't have done that to you."

"I heard—"

"Kate, I understand. There was a voice in my head telling me to stop too. I ignored it, and I shouldn't have."

I shook my head at him. "You don't understand—"

He nodded at me. "It's my fault. I know what you've been going through, how hard it's been for you. I feel like a cretin for taking advantage of you. Please, tell me you forgive me."

I stared at the dirt on my shoes, trying to find the words to tell Blair about the other times I'd heard Kevin speak. *He'll think I'm crazy.*

Blair must have misunderstood my silence because, after a moment, he said, "Kate, please say you don't hate me."

"I don't hate you," I said, surprised he thought I might.

He gave me a feeble smile and said, "Come on, I'll walk you home."

We walked back to my house in silence. I clung to the edge of the sidewalk, careful not to touch him.

17

After Blair dropped me off at home, I stepped into the kitchen and shivered in spite of the summer sun. I poured a glass of water and downed it all at once.

"Well, look who's here," Kevin said, hissing. "Sad Kate. Poor Kate. So alone she had to turn to her husband's best friend for comfort."

"No," I whispered.

"You liked it, didn't you, Kate? Tell me. Tell me how much you liked it."

"Stop—"

"It's you who needs to stop. Stop acting like a prostitute. Stop throwing yourself at men." His words exploded in my head. The room expanded, then retracted. I pitched to one side, catching myself against the wall.

I sank to my knees. My head throbbed. "Please, I didn't. I don't know why you're saying these things."

"Whore." The single word pounded like a bass drum inside my head. It was followed by a stream of other words, vile, obscene words I'd never heard Kevin say before. Shocking words that, when strung together, were like snarling dogs. I pressed my hands to my temples.

"No. I love you, Kevin. Stop. You're killing me."

Kevin's voice pierced me behind my eyes. "Listen to you beg. Is that what you did? Did you beg him, Kate?"

"No, please … I didn't do anything. I love you. Please, Kevin—"

"Yeah, beg me, Kate. Beg me like you begged him."

I couldn't breathe. Spots of color burst before my eyes—scorched green, molten white, festering red, until there were no colors at all.

I'm dreaming, or awake. Kevin holds my hand. I can't see him, but I know it's him. I sense nothing but white—a sheet of white nothingness all around me, and the pressure of Kevin's hand holding mine. I try to turn my head, but nothing works—not neck, not arms, not legs.

Am I lying down? Yes, I must be, even though I feel nothing beneath me. I don't know where I am, but I'm not afraid. Kevin's hand squeezes mine and I wonder if this is what it feels like to die, to be dead. I'd like to open my eyes, but they don't open. Or they do, but there is nothing to see.

Kevin squeezes harder and I want to tell him to stop but I can't speak. The whiteness around me begins to throb; it moves in, retreats, then pushes toward me again. My hand hurts now, Kevin squeezes so hard I fear he might crack a bone. Why won't he stop? Doesn't he know he's hurting me? The whiteness pulses and grows brighter, in and out, back and forth until it is a pinpoint of light. I try to cry out as Kevin's grip increases, snapping bones. I want to scream.

I awoke on the kitchen floor. Even before I tried to move, I knew I was in pain. I was on my side, my arm pinned beneath me, my hand tingling from resting at an odd angle. My head throbbed. My neck was held in place with pins of agony. I straightened my left leg and felt my joints push back. My hand looked red and swollen. I rotated my wrist, relieved nothing was broken.

In slow, clumsy movements, like a turtle trying to stand erect, I pushed myself up onto my knees, then I grabbed the edge of the countertop and hauled my body up. For a moment the spots returned behind my eyes. Popping, obscene colors of anger and lies. Panic rushed into my lungs as I clutched the counter. Fresh tears bubbled from my eyes and spilled, headlong, onto the floor. I felt as if I'd been beaten with fists rather than words. I touched my lips, half expecting to see blood on my fingertips.

I shuffled to the living room and lay down, sinking deep into the sofa cushions. I picked up a pillow and held it.

What if it started again? What if Kevin's voice came back, angry and punishing? The thought terrified me, but I listened anyway. Maybe I could talk to him and make him understand.

Why? Why did he say those things? I opened my mouth to call his name, but stopped. What if he answered? What if he didn't? I wasn't sure which would be worse.

There was no trying to tell myself it was all my imagination, a dream, a hoax created by my unconscious or painkillers. Kevin's voice was powerfully real. A force inextricably joined to me. Unbreakable. Isn't that what Eliza had told me? We're all connected, she had said.

To each other, and to the spiritual realm. Kevin was proving there was no uncoupling, not even in death. We were bound by unseen ropes as real as iron.

When Eliza Campbell had first told me of this idea of being eternally connected to Kevin, it had helped ease some of the grief. Now I was terrified. I didn't want to be tied to this Kevin who screamed at me, pummeled me with vile words of hate.

What had Maggie said to me on her first visit? Things can get much worse. I hadn't understood what she meant then, but I did now. She was right. I was smack in the center of worse.

I sat up, feet on the floor. My body cried out in protest. I needed to take something for the pain.

In the kitchen I reached for the bottle of codeine and selected a pill.

"Whore." Kevin's bark echoed through the room, bounced off the walls and knocked me off balance.

The bottle dropped from my hand and the pills scattered everywhere. My mind chanted a mantra, "No, no, please God, no."

I had to get to the phone. I took a step and heard a sharp popping sound. I jerked my foot up, as quickly as if I'd been shot. On the floor, a crushed codeine pill. My heart pounded. I picked my way through the maze of painkillers as if it was a minefield. "Liar," Kevin bellowed, his voice reverberating through my skull.

I screamed.

18

I stood in my kitchen and pushed number two on my speed dial. I leaned my shoulder against the cool wall and sobbed, praying Heather was home.

Heather picked up and I whispered into the phone, my voice jagged, "Heather. This is going to kill me. I can't—"

"I'm coming over," she said.

She must have broken a few speed laws to get to me as fast as she did. When she walked in, she stared with a wide-eyed look of shock on her face. "What's happened?" She took a step toward me. I heard a pop as her heel crushed one of the pills still strewn on the floor. "What is going on?" She picked her way around the pills toward me. I stood in silence, staring back at her, lips trembling. She lifted her hand up to my cheek. I flinched.

Heather dropped her hand. "You're scaring me. What happened?"

"It's Kevin," I whispered.

Her head jerked back. "I don't understand."

"He's angry, Heather. He's yelling at me."

"Yelling?" she placed her hand on my forehead, as if checking for fever.

I nodded like an obedient child. "He's saying horrible things. Calling me names."

"Kevin is? Kevin is yelling and calling you names?"

Was I stuttering?

Maybe it was out of relief that Heather was there and that I wasn't alone anymore, or maybe it was insanity's full embrace, but I felt a sudden urge to giggle.

A laugh, a floating burp of hilarity, burst from my lips. "You think I'm crazy, huh?"

Heather gave her head a fast shake and opened her mouth.

I cut her off with a loud hoot of laughter. "I do. I think I'm crazy, Heather." Tears flowed down my cheeks as I shook with laughter. "I feel exactly like I'm crazy."

Heather took my hand. "I'm taking you to the hospital."

"Have you been talking to God?"

"No, I've been talking to Kevin."

The on-call doctor in the hospital psych ward glanced up from the chart he was reading. I thought I saw a look of weariness in his eyes, but he just adjusted the glasses on his nose and looked back at the file. I sat across from him, hands on the small table in front of me, and studied his bald spot.

The doctor poised his pen over the file and looked at me. "Does this 'Kevin' have supernatural powers? Can he perform great things?"

It was an odd question, but this was an odd place. I figured there was a good reason he asked. I thought of a story Kevin had told me before we were married. When he was ten, he had ordered X-ray glasses from the back of a comic book. They didn't work, but instead of wasting money by throwing the glasses away, he used them as part of a mad scientist Halloween costume. I had been impressed that a ten-year-old boy would be so responsible with his money.

I looked at the doctor. "Well, I don't know about great. But he's very thrifty."

Without missing a beat, the doctor said, "Kate, do you know where you are?"

"Yes. I'm in the hospital." I glanced around. "In an exam room."

"What day is it?"

"Trick question," I said, louder than I intended. "It's night."

He took off his glasses and looked at me.

"Sorry," I said. "It's Thursday."

"What year?"

I told him.

He made a brief note in the file. "You seem coherent."

"Thank you." The giddiness from earlier threatened to return. I squelched it by looking around the room. Signs of previous violence were everywhere. The walls were pockmarked with shoe prints and holes, as if someone tried to kick and claw their way out of the room. The bed to my left was a small exam table like you'd find in a doctor's office, rather than a regular hospital bed. Black straps resembling seatbelts hung down—restraints.

"Who brought you here?" The doctor said.

"My dead husband."

His head jerked up as if I had drawn a pistol. His eyes darted over my face, hands, and clothes. Maybe searching for clues of a recent murder. *It must be difficult to work here,* I thought.

"He's been dead for over a month. I mean, he died over a month ago. I didn't kill him. He did that himself. No, I don't mean he killed himself. He died. By himself. I mean, I didn't help him." My voice became a tiny squeak. "He died."

The doctor rubbed his eye with a finger. "I meant did someone come with you to the hospital tonight? Did you get a ride, drive yourself, take a bus, walk?"

Stupid. "My sister, Heather, brought me."

He made a few marks in the file. "Okay, now. I hear you say your husband died. What has happened since then that has brought you here tonight?"

"Well, he talks to me."

"Your husband?"

Who else? Didn't I just say that? Okay, calm down. Answer the question. "Yes, my husband," I said and smiled brightly to show how cooperative I was.

He didn't smile back. "What does he say?"

"Nothing. Nothing important, anyway. Just daily stuff. The kettle is boiling. Go wash the cereal bowls. He's cold. That sort of thing."

The doctor made a muffled "uh-huh" sound, but offered nothing more.

I took a deep breath. "Except the last time." I began to shiver in the stale room.

"When was the last time he spoke to you?" he asked.

I couldn't stop shivering. I ran my hands up and down my arms, trying to infuse them with warmth. "Today. I—I kissed someone." I felt embarrassed to say it out loud, like a teenager caught in the backseat of her father's car. "I don't even know why I did it. We were just talking and then he kissed me and ..." My voice dropped to a whisper. "Kevin saw."

The doctor opened his mouth, and then closed it again.

"You know that old saying, 'Sticks and stones can break my bones'?" I said.

"Yes."

"Kevin's words hurt me."

"I'm going to recommend we admit you for tonight. "

"A danger?" Heather hollered as she thumped down the hospital corridor. She was taking me home after my overnight there. "You, Kate, are not a danger to anyone."

In my mind's eye I saw the hood of Kevin's Mazda rive the side of Maggie's Mustang. *Was I?*

But I said, "No, I wouldn't hurt anyone."

Heather flung her arms above her head. "That's my point. How dare they say you would?" I'd never seen her so agitated. Every step was a declaration, every gesture so sweeping, I felt the desire to duck out of the way.

"They didn't really say that." We moved through the automatic doors together and walked toward Heather's car. "They said they wanted to assess if I was a danger to myself or other people."

Heather shot me an annoyed look. "Same difference. They're the crazy ones." She yanked at her purse until she produced a set of keys. I stood beside the passenger door, waiting for her to unlock the car. Over the roof of the car, I watched her fumble with the keys. I heard them hit the pavement, and then heard Heather swear under her breath.

It was only eight in the morning, but the sun blazed with ardor, promising a hot day. I felt like a warmed-over piece of toast. I hadn't slept at all. "You okay over there?"

Heather glared at me over the roof of the car. "Okay? No. I'm definitely not okay, Kate. I'm the total opposite of okay." She pointed the remote-control door opener at the car and jammed a finger down on a button. The trunk popped open.

Heather and I watched the trunk lid bob for a moment. She pushed another button and I heard the door locks click open. I slid into the passenger seat while Heather closed the trunk with a slam. I reached for the seat belt.

Heather got in and stared at the dashboard. I watched her out of the corner of my eye. She put her head down on the top of the steering wheel. I contemplated offering her a *there-there* pat on the shoulder, but I kept my hands in my lap. I hadn't expected Heather to react this way. In truth I hadn't thought much about how my situation had been affecting her. My panicked phone calls, my accusing questions. Throwing her out of my house. It must have been difficult.

She cast me a sideways glance. "What happens now? Do you have to go back?" She jerked a thumb toward the hospital. "Or what?"

"I'm really sorry about all of this—"

"No. Don't be sorry. Let's just move ahead. What happens next?"

I shifted in my seat. "Heather, I can see this is hard on you. I feel terrible—"

"I know you feel terrible," she bellowed, hands flying in the air like demented butterflies. "I feel terrible. Mom feels terrible. Everyone feels terrible." She looked at me, eyes brimming with unshed tears. "All I want is to get us from terrible to … to … not terrible. Better. Good, even."

I pressed my lips together, not knowing what to say.

Heather looked straight ahead, out the windshield. "We used to be good. You. Mom. Me. We had happy lives and happy times together …" Her voice drifted off. She pulled in a long breath. "So what's the next step for you?"

I swallowed a lump of misery. She was right. Somehow I had to get through this train wreck of fear and pain. "They set up an appointment for me with a doctor in the city next week. A psychiatrist." I shrugged. "Maybe that will … make things better."

Heather gave a slow nod.

"The doctor here at the hospital said I need to begin treatment with a Dr. Alexander, because he specializes in this sort of, um, problem."

"Which problem?"

I examined my hands on my lap. "Hearing voices sort of problem."

Heather started the car and backed out of the stall.

When we arrived at my house, I told Heather she should leave, go home, that I'd be fine alone, but she ignored me and started picking up the codeine pills on the kitchen floor. Part of me resented the help. I wasn't a child who required watching, and I could clean up my own messes. On the other hand I was relieved she was staying. Maybe Kevin would leave me alone with Heather here. And it gave Heather something to do, a place to direct her energy.

So I left her tidying up the kitchen, and wandered into the den. I was looking for a package of blank recipe cards and a pen. Kevin used the cards to write out speeches he occasionally gave at bank functions.

I took the top card and began to write. There was much to tell the psychiatrist, and I wanted to get it right.

19

Two days later I arrived at Dr. Alexander's thirty-first-floor office with fifteen recipe cards tucked into the side pocket of my purse. I had written every important event that had happened to me since Kevin died. I didn't think I would end up using the cards, but I felt better knowing I had them with me. Their presence calmed me. This was a different experience from the counselor's appointments I had before. This was serious. This was mental illness.

I had gone to counseling by my own choice. A woman looking for answers, poking around her own mind. But now I was being shoved toward a medical doctor. A part of me felt like a schoolgirl being called to the principal's office. I could protest, but I was told in calm, certain terms that it was in my best interest to comply.

Dr. Alexander's waiting room was painted tranquilizer taupe. Classical music played softly from the ceiling. A secretary asked for my insurance details and medical history in calm tones. No other patients were waiting. I sat in a low chair and hugged my purse, waiting to be called.

After what seemed only seconds, the secretary stood and called me. She walked me to an enormous oak door, our footsteps swallowed by the thick carpeting. She pushed opened the door and led me into a large, wood-paneled room. My first impression was something like "zowie."

It was an expansive space, more like a living room than an office—that is, if the living room was six hundred square feet of opulent luxury on the thirty-first floor of a downtown high-rise. Straight across from me a bank of windows covering the entire wall looked out on an impressive view of the cityscape, including a part of the river. In front of the windows, a massive wooden desk, larger than some people's apartments, glistened in the sunshine.

To my right I noticed a couch and chair placed in a formation that suggested their therapeutic purpose—sofa against the wall, chair positioned just above the arm of the sofa. Tastefully framed art covered the walls. Plush, neutral carpet hugged my feet. The entire room seemed to say, "Shhh. There, there."

The secretary offered me a choice of bottled water, herbal tea, or decaffeinated coffee. A gentle variety of drinks to soothe bruised psyches. I asked for water. She left the room only to reappear almost instantaneously holding a chilly, clear bottle. *Magic,* I thought as I accepted it.

She smiled and silently closed the door behind her. I blinked at the opulence of the office and sat down on the couch. It seemed to embrace me and I sank into its folds. I put my water down on an ornate wooden side table and stretched out on the sofa. This place seemed specially designed for people to spill the contents of soul and psyche onto the soft pile carpet. I let my thoughts drift and bump gently up against the caramel-colored walls.

I heard a door open.

Dr. Alexander contrasted with the comfort of the room, exuding a lofty confidence. I could picture him striding the halls of hospitals insisting everyone get better. He was tall, but from my position, seated on the couch, he seemed gigantic. He walked over to where I was and towered over me.

He offered a huge, meaty hand. "I'm Dr. Alexander," he said and sat down on the leather chair. I sat ramrod straight on the edge of the couch. His presence unsettled me and I felt unable to look directly at him. I silently wished for a few more minutes alone in the room.

I threw him a quick glance. "Hello." I looked down at my shoes.

I glanced at him again. Something was definitely strange. Something about his head.

I raised my eyes and met his gaze. I thought he was cocking his head slightly to the right. I peered harder. No, his chin and forehead were a line running straight up and down. It wasn't his head that was tilted.

It was his hair.

He was wearing a rug. It was sitting atop his head, slightly off center, causing the illusion.

Dr. Alexander said, "We are going to spend the next forty-five minutes together." He reached up and scratched his temple briefly. As he did, the toupee wiggled, and then settled back to its original, offside position.

I was transfixed. "Okay," I said to the toupee. I reached into my purse and pulled out my recipe cards.

"What does the voice tell you?" Dr. Alexander asked.

The voice? I told him it was Kevin's voice. Not an anonymous voice. Kevin's. Dr. Alexander and I had been talking for twenty minutes. I had self-consciously read the contents of the first two recipe cards aloud. He had made no comment as I moved from card one to card two. It wasn't until the end of card two, the part about hearing the voice of my dead husband, that Dr. Alexander seemed to get interested in what I was saying.

I sat slumped on the couch, too self-conscious to lie down. "He doesn't really tell me anything. I mean, we are not having conversations about the hereafter. He doesn't tell me what heaven looks like, or how my Great-Aunt Clara is doing." I picked at the corner of the recipe card. "I mean, he doesn't tell me stuff. He just talks, comments … on … things."

"What sorts of things?"

I threw a look at Dr. Alexander. He sat motionless, eyes glued to the notebook in his hands. I glanced at the top of his head. It was still there, still perched askew.

"Uh, day-to-day things," I answered. "I burn the toast, that kind of thing." I felt like a broken record. How many doctors would I tell about this? Maybe he didn't have my records from the hospital yet.

"Why toast?" he asked, his pen poised above his pad of paper. *Probably about to write "whacko" in medium blue ink.*

I stared at the carpet. "What do you mean?"

Dr. Alexander made an *ahem* sound. "Why would he say something about toast, in particular?"

"Because it's toast, in particular, that I burn," I said. I couldn't think of a better explanation. If I knew why Kevin said the things he said, I probably wouldn't be here.

Dr. Alexander lowered his notepad to his knee and reached up to scratch his forehead with his pen. I couldn't bear to watch. "I see," he murmured, then fell silent.

I pushed the toe of my shoe into the carpet and clutched the edge of the couch.

Dr. Alexander flipped back a page of his notebook and seemed to be enthralled by what was written there. "And this last time he spoke to you, just before you were admitted for observation, what was he talking about then?"

I swallowed hard.

"Can you talk about it?" he said to the notepad.

I pulled an invisible thread from the couch. Could I? Up until that moment, it hadn't occurred to me that I could choose to talk or not to talk to this man. I suppose I felt that I had to tell him everything. That was the reason I was sent here, wasn't it? I rolled the choice around in my mind. I looked at the brown toupee, still perched crookedly on the top of his head. "I'd rather not."

Dr. Alexander gave me a long, steady look. "I'm going to pre-scribe something."

"Prescribe? Like a drug?" I said stupidly.

He pulled a prescription pad from his jacket pocket. "An antihallucinogen."

A shock pulsed through my body. "Hallucinating? Doesn't that mean seeing things?"

He handed me the prescription. "Not necessarily. These will help with the delusions."

I stared at Dr. Alexander's toupee. I may be hearing the voice of my dead husband, but it was clear to me which one of us was delusional.

20

It had been a couple of weeks since the night Kevin screamed at me and Heather had taken me to the hospital. Silent weeks. I had moments when I believed it was over, the voice was gone, and other times I felt sure it would return.

I had arrived at Dr. Alexander's office for my third visit sporting new state-of-the-art UV-protection sunglasses that I had bought the other day. They guaranteed to keep my eyeballs as safe as if I had them wrapped in tissue and stowed in my coat pocket. For what they cost, they should also do my laundry.

I wasn't looking to become a material girl, but I had done a lot of shopping lately. Donna had finally come through, unfreezing my account. The first statement since Kevin's death had come a few days before, bearing only my name. The balance made my eyes hurt. So much money. And shopping provided me with something to do besides skulk around my house and not answer the phone. And the phone kept ringing, the answering machine collecting each message for me, storing them inside the flashing red light on my phone. My sister's endless questions; Blair's teary, long-winded messages about how sorry he was to have "crossed the line of our friendship"; my mother's brief but steady "just checking in" calls. And Maggie.

Heaven help us all from Maggie and her machine-gun approach to friendship. She called nearly daily, leaving meandering messages peppered with questions ranging from where under God's blue skies could I be at this hour (I had stopped answering the phone or returning calls, but Maggie apparently concluded that I was cavorting all over town at all hours of the day and night), to asking for details about my therapy sessions. "Does he have a couch? Does he wear a beard? Freud had a beard." Twice I hid behind the living room curtains and watched Maggie limp up to my front door. She rang the bell, knocked, sometimes both at once before giving up and shambling back to her car.

I wasn't answering the phone or the door because I didn't have a sane answer for the question, "How are you?" The answer changed at any given moment. And while I was home, the answer could best be described as "uptight." I mostly just clung to corners and tried to make myself very small, like a ball, on the floor.

But Dr. Alexander's office in the city was like another world, safe from the mundane yet traumatic life back in Greenfield. I felt more like a happy tourist in his office, far away from the life that troubled me. I found myself arriving in the city earlier than necessary for my appointments and strolling downtown sidewalks, peering into store windows, and buying things I didn't need at a probably alarming rate.

On my feet was a pair of creamy leather sandals that rubbed a bit on the right heel, and a matching handbag so teeny I could only cram in a credit card, driver's license, and coral-sunrise lipstick (also new). These were the spoils of sudden wealth and a newly developed desire to avoid being home alone.

Now that the insurance issues were dealt with, my bank account out of the freezer, and my bills were being paid, I had money to do whatever pleased me. Problem was, I was fast running out of things that pleased me. This, according to Dr. Alexander, was a good thing. He called it shop-therapy and warned it had very short-term benefits and long-term complications.

Dr. Alexander peered at me over his desk, reading glasses perched on the end of his nose. "What do you think about joining group therapy, Kate? I think you'd get a lot out of it. There is a grief group starting soon." He rifled through some papers. "I don't know when." He pushed a button on his phone. "Sally?" Sally didn't respond. He pushed another button. "Sally!" he hollered.

I heard a soft sigh from the phone. "Yes, Doctor?"

"What're the dates for Laura-Lea Autumn's group?"

"Wednesdays at 6:30 starting next week," Sally answered immediately.

"You catch that?" Dr. Alexander said to me. I nodded.

"Laura-Lea is very good. Young, so you'll be able to relate to her. Lovely girl. Smart, too. Runs a good group."

"Uh, okay," I said blankly. At least it was another excuse to get out of the house.

"I'm glad that's settled," he said. "I'll let her know you'll be taking a spot in the Wednesday evening group.

The following Wednesday, I arrived at the run-down Glen Hills Community Center for my first group-therapy session. It was in the heart of a poor and crime-ridden neighborhood in the city. The center was a floppy-roofed building shaped like a giant Quonset.

I parked in front and got out of the car. I looked at the neglected surroundings, then took a careful moment to lock the car doors and gave the hubcaps a glance. I hoped they'd be there when I returned.

I noticed the double doors of the hall were painted a too-bright blue, a strong contrast to the dirty beige walls. The wind picked up some garbage and swirled it around in the small alcove beside the doors. I took a deep breath. Keep an open mind, I told myself.

Inside, I saw a handwritten sign that read Group Therapy, with an arrow pointing to a narrow hallway. Straight ahead was another set of double doors. I peeked inside, then went down the narrow hall. The room was identified by another handwritten sign posted on the door.

I was the first to arrive. The room was so drab and utilitarian I wondered how anyone was supposed to feel better while sitting in it. It had the ambience of an abandoned classroom.

Two walls were taken up by peeling chalkboards (no chalk in sight). A third wall was covered by an orange pushpin board that was covered with an assortment of government-issue public health posters. One listed the symptoms of depression. I read the first three—depressed mood, inability to enjoy activities, problems concentrating—but it was too discouraging to finish. Another warned of HIV/AIDS and the high-risk behaviors that can lead to contracting the virus. I merely glanced at it. I knew I wasn't in the high-risk category. I'd never done drugs of any kind. Also, I had never engaged in what the poster described as "casual sex." Kevin and I were high school sweethearts. We were each other's first—and only—lovers.

Other posters on various topics hung haphazardly from single pushpins, offering phone numbers to hotlines, mental health tips, and safety advice. On the corner of the poster listing the dangers of hepatitis C, someone had scrawled "this sux."

Folding chairs were arranged in a circle in the center of the room. I was about to walk over and sit when a woman entered and without a glance in my direction grabbed a chair and carried it to the far wall. I stood, uncertain if I should do the same. Soon others arrived, two more women and three men. Each of them picked up a chair and found a spot along a wall. Everyone seemed intent on having the maximum space between them.

I selected one of the two remaining chairs and started to pull it toward the orange bulletin board, but about halfway to the poster the chair started making a horrible farty noise. Every head turned in the direction of the squealing rat-a-blat-vvvtt being emitted from my chair.

I stopped and cast a longing glance at the exit. I could just flee. Run away and never return. But everyone was looking at me.

Paralyzed by indecision, I finally slumped into my chair and stared at the floor. How was I going to get through this evening? Clearly I was the only crazy person here. I stole a glance around the room. I saw seven completely normal-looking people.

The woman who I assumed was Laura-Lea Autumn, the group facilitator, entered the room at precisely seven. Or at least her breasts did. The rest of her body followed seconds later.

The men in the room visibly brightened. The women, me

included, did a quick breast check. I glanced covertly down at my chest and mentally conceded, "Yep, I'm out of the game."

The short blond man in the gray wool pants (in the summer?) and checkered blue tie stared at Laura-Lea like he could hear "Make the World Go Away" in full orchestra. I crossed my arms over my chest and slid farther down in my chair.

Laura-Lea marched to the center of the room, and, hands on her oh-so-slim hips, she planted her feet far apart on the floor. I wouldn't have been surprised if she'd produced pom-poms and broken out into a catchy cheer. She turned a slow circle, looking everyone in the eye. She was smiling in a way that was both perky and intimidating. As she turned, she pointed with a long manicured finger to the spot where the chairs had been. Clearly she wanted us to return our chairs to the middle of the room. We obeyed the silent command, fashioning a reasonable facsimile of the original circle.

Laura-Lea sat in her chair, smoothed her white cotton pants, and placed both hands on her knees. "We are here tonight to begin to heal." She leaned forward, looking around the room. Heads bobbed in agreement—yes, yes, we're here to heal. She smiled, seemingly satisfied with this response. "The whole point of group therapy is to heal ourselves, and" —her voice dropped to a soft, but oddly adorable whisper— "to heal each other." More nodding, a few murmurs of agreement. Wool Pants Guy closed his eyes for a moment, as if savoring some sweet aroma.

Laura-Lea took a long, meaningful breath. "We're here to share our innermost beings with each other. Our thoughts. Our hopes. Our dreams. Our very souls. Each one of us will stop at nothing until we have laid bare our greatest pain." She let out a soft sigh. "But first, I need to have you sign these confidentiality forms."

After group therapy, I walked through the foyer, surprised to hear a cacophony of voices, whistles, and the sound of balls bouncing off various surfaces.

Basketball, I thought as I walked across the foyer toward the gym. Kevin had loved basketball. He played it all through high school, always wearing jersey number three.

I pulled the door open a crack and looked in. From my Peeping-Tom vantage point I could only see half the gym. Several teenagers were gathered in the key, watching the ball circle the hoop as it decided which way to fall. When it spun into the basket, there was simultaneous cheering and booing. Two boys exchanged a fast and complicated-looking handshake and ran down the court, out of my view. I listened for a moment, and then pulled the door open enough for me to squeeze through, into the gym.

No one noticed me; they just kept playing. The teams appeared to be red bandannas versus blue. A tall, skinny boy with a red bandanna tied around his wrist was dribbling fast down the court. A girl, shorter, but still no slouch in the height department, sped ahead of him and planted herself directly in his path. I was sure they would collide, causing a foul on the red team and, undoubtedly, causing the girl physical harm. In the moment it took to suck my breath in, the boy stopped, pivoted away from the girl, and landed a bounce pass to a teammate who took it up court and scored.

The red team screamed out a victory sound; high fives all around. For a moment the boy and the girl from the blue team stood facing each other in the middle of the court. Her back was to me. He looked down at her with a grim expression, like he was about to call Louie the Fixer to come take care of her. Then his face cracked into an enormous grin. The girl shoved him hard with both hands. She turned so I could see her face. She was smiling. "Jerk," she said in a casual voice. They walked to their respective benches.

When the game resumed, I decided to leave. It had already been an eventful evening for me and I was tired. I had my hand on the door when I heard a male voice call, "Who dat?" I pushed the door open.

Another voice: "Hey, wait. Where you goin'?"

I turned. The two teams were standing in the middle of the court staring at me. The tall girl raised her hand to her waist and gave me a quick wave. I bent my elbow, hand at my belt, and jerked it at her in response.

A man with a whistle around his neck was walking toward me holding a clipboard in his left hand and extending his right hand, a long-distance handshake. He stopped in front of me, still offering his hand. "I'm Jack."

I gave his hand a quick shake. "Kate. Sorry to interrupt. I was just leaving."

He gestured toward the court. "You wanna play? You're welcome to join in." He looked down at my strappy black sandals. "Or watch." He grinned at me.

"Hey, coach, think fast," someone called.

Jack turned and ducked just in time for me to see a basketball coming full speed toward me. I was about to throw my hands up in front of my face when the ball made contact with my nose. I made a sound like *gah* and grabbed my nose.

I felt a hand push my forehead back, forcing me to look at the ceiling. I heard Jack's voice, "Are you okay?" He gave me no time to answer. "Head up. Keeps the blood from going everywhere. I'm going to take you into my office; I have a first-aid kit. Keep your head back." He took hold of my elbow and started walking. "Look out, guys." I watched the light fixtures go by as I walked beside him.

I heard a door open. We must have reached his office. "You guys keep playing. I'll be back." Jack led me into his office and eased me into a chair. I stared at a brown water stain on the ceiling.

I heard rummaging, and then Jack was beside me, pressing white gauze to my nose. I tried to straighten my neck, but Jack pressed down on my forehead again. "Just keep your neck bent like that. It'll help stop the bleeding."

I reached up and touched the side of my nose. "Ouch." My voice sounded nasal. I offered a pathetic smile.

Jack lifted the gauze from my face. "I think it's okay. The bleeding, I mean."

I straightened my neck, waiting for blood to rush down my nasal passages. It didn't. I looked around.

The cinder-block walls of the office were painted institutional gray. The furniture consisted of a metal frame desk with a chipped tabletop. Behind the desk was an old office chair you'd expect to see in the steno pool, and a white mini fridge. I was sitting on one of two orange plastic molded chairs. A metal four-drawer filing cabinet sat in the corner. Posters of basketball players in various poses of action or victory were taped to the walls. The room was surprisingly quiet considering its proximity to the gym.

"Thirsty?" he asked, pulling two bottles of water out of the fridge. He thrust the bottle at me.

I caught it. "Thanks." I held the cool bottle to the side of my nose. "Ah, that's better."

Jack sat on the steno chair, propped his feet up on the desk, and leaned back until he was nearly horizontal. He smiled and then tipped the water bottle back and drained its contents in several loud gulps.

I uncapped my water and took a self-conscious sip. "I'm feeling better. Thanks for your help." I felt embarrassed for bleeding in front of a stranger. "I should get going." I reached down for my purse. It wasn't there. I must have dropped it when I was hit with the ball.

Jack swung his feet off the desk and sat up. "I'm sorry about what happened. Big Tim and me, we have this thing. Every once in a while, he yells 'think fast' and throws a ball at me. Each time I duck, and the ball goes sailing over my head. He thinks it's hilarious."

I recapped my water and raised an ironic eyebrow. "Hilarious."

Jack spread his hands out in front of him in a helpless gesture. "Tim has developmental delays. He isn't always the best judge of when it's appropriate to chuck a ball at me and when it's not. He didn't mean to hurt you. Anyway, I'm sorry."

I chewed the inside of my cheek. My nose throbbed. "It's okay. Just one of those things, I guess." I thought about it for a second, then mumbled, "Kinda par for the course, lately."

Jack propped his chin up with his right hand. "Huh?"

I shrugged. "Oh nothing."

"Anything you want to talk about?"

I flashed a halfhearted smile. "No."

"Ah, a woman of mystery."

A laugh pushed its way out of my mouth. "Nothing as interesting as that." I stood up and grabbed the doorknob. "Thanks for helping me with the ..." I looked down and saw splatters of red on my blouse. "Blood."

I opened the door and walked straight into Big Tim's chest. "Oof," I said. It seemed he had been listening at the door. A quick peek behind him showed me that he hadn't been alone. I blinked at the group of kids as they all suddenly thought of something else to do and wandered off to do it. All except Big Tim.

I stepped back into the office and looked up at him. He held my purse up. "Sorry I creamed you with a ball. You dropped your purse."

I took my purse from him and smiled. "Thanks, Big Tim." I glanced back at Jack. "Nice meeting you." I touched my nose. "Well, mostly nice meeting you."

Jack grinned and gave a shrug. "Anytime you get beaned with a ball ..."

I shook my head. "How embarrassing." I walked out of the office and across the gym, still shaking my head.

"Hey!"

I turned to see Big Tim holding a basketball out to me. "Do you play? Wanna shoot some hoops?"

I held my foot up for him to see. "Wrong footwear, sorry. Maybe some other time."

Big Tim's face broke open in a toothy grin. "Great. When? Tomorrow?"

Jack stood in the doorway of his office, leaning against the door-jamb, his face an open question. I turned my gaze back to Big Tim. "I can't tomorrow, sorry."

"Okay. How about the next day?"

Jack sauntered over and patted Big Tim's arm. "Hey, buddy, Kate was just popping in for today only. A one-day deal. Okay?" Jack lifted his head and hollered to the group, "We have time for a quick one. Team up, everyone." He looked at me. "But you are welcome to come back anytime."

I gave a you-never-know shrug. "Sorry I interrupted the game." I pushed the gym door open.

"Hey, lady, Jack's friend," said Big Tim. I turned and looked at him. "Next time bring your basketball shoes."

I raised my hand in a quick salute. "Right."

21

I stood at the top of the steps leading to my bedroom and fingered the journal I'd bought. Over the past two weeks I'd met with Dr. Alexander another four times. He had assigned this "homework," as he called it—journaling—at the first of those four meetings. Dr. Alexander was big on gradual sensory flooding—something I'd never heard of before. It was, essentially, baby steps toward "robust mental health."

Baby step number one was for me to purchase a journal. "Nothing fancy, just bound paper with lines." The book I held wasn't just any journal, though. I wouldn't be jotting down my girlish daydreams beginning with *Dear Diary* in swirly script. I wouldn't be dotting my *i*'s with little hearts and finishing my sentences with tiny daisies instead of periods. I browsed the racks of journals at the bookstore, wondering what sort of cover would be appropriate for a journal that was to detail the ebb and flow of my fear. Especially my fear to reenter my bedroom. It had been over two months since Kevin died, and I was still sleeping in the living room.

Dr. Alexander instructed me to stand at the top of the stairs, journal in hand, and look at my bedroom door. I was to write the date and time of this exercise in my journal, and document how many steps I was able to climb. Beside that number I was instructed to rate my fear on a scale of zero to ten. Zero meaning I was bounding into the room, whistling "Mack the Knife," not a care in the world, and ten meaning I was crawling away on all fours, weeping and hyperventilating into a paper bag. I was to bring my journal to our sessions so we could discuss my progress.

So far I'd gotten as far as buying the journal. That was my progress.

I had decided on a compact notebook with a two-tone hardcover in brown and black. The pages were unlined and completely void of my thoughts, experiences, or processes. It wasn't that I didn't understand Dr. Alexander's intentions. It *would* be an important step to sleep in my own bed again. But something inside of me, some niggling ghost, vaporous and intangible, told me that where I was sleeping wasn't the biggest deal in my world. Important, sure, but not my top priority.

Dr. Alexander said I wasn't sleeping in my own bed (I wasn't even setting foot on the second level of my home, except for the occasional and desperate shower) because of some "innate fear." He wanted me to pinpoint the cause of my fear and then overcome it, in order to begin to reclaim a normal life. What I couldn't explain to him was that it wasn't fear that kept me from climbing the stairs. I didn't have heart-pounding panic attacks each time I walked by the stairs or used the shower. I just *couldn't* go into my bedroom. My feet wouldn't take me there. I just stood as if someone had nailed my feet to the floor.

I fingered the journal's sturdy cover, looking at the partially opened bedroom door. I opened it to the first page.

"You're a reader, not a writer," Kevin said.

My body went rigid. My joints straightened, and my head began to ache.

"This isn't real." But my voice was a murmur, an undertone below the roaring in my ears.

I was afraid now. Okay, give the fear a number, just as Dr. Alexander had explained. Ten? One hundred?

His voice undulated, swirling in through my ears and rising like fog in my mind. "Go upstairs. You know you're mine."

I closed my eyes in a hysteria of fear and need. I could almost feel him; his presence pulsed just beyond the walls of my home, just beyond my fingertips.

"Stop. Please, stop." I chanted reality in my head, praying it would push the voice aside. This isn't happening. You're not real.

His voice, like a caress, blew across my face. "Kate. My wife."

Warm tears flowed. He was as real as he'd ever been in life. Real enough to send me to the psych ward, to make Dr. Alexander's mouth pucker with concern, to make my body ache. I gazed into the bedroom. "There's nothing for me in there anymore."

"Mine." He said the word tenderly, my lover returned from a long sojourn. Instantly my mind filled with memories of Kevin and me together. His warmth, his touch, the abandon he brought me.

I clutched the wall, fearful I'd fall backward down the stairs. I sank to the floor. A sob wrenched free, pulling my breath out with it as fresh grief rushed in to fill the void. Fear and grief tossed me between them. Fear for my sanity, yes, but mostly fear that his voice would turn menacing again. But grief, too, longing for my husband. For his solid touch, his fresh scent, his dependable presence. I pressed my palms against my temples. "I don't want to remember anymore."

I could hear his disapproval, like the shaking of a head. "You've already forgotten too much."

Kevin's voice is a stern whisper. He's calling from work and I can tell he doesn't want to be overheard. "You forgot?" he says, for the fourth time.

I open the fridge, close it, open a cupboard door, peer in, close it. "I'm sorry. I had to go in to work today. Percy was sick. He ate bad fish. It just slipped my mind."

"My boss is coming to dinner for the first time and it slips your mind. What am I supposed to do, Kate? She just came in here and said she'll be ready to go in half an hour."

"Can't we just go out?" Back in the fridge I find a bowl of fuzzy scalloped potatoes. I try to recall the last time we had scalloped potatoes. I don't think I even know how to make scalloped potatoes. Kevin's loud breathing interrupts my thoughts. "Donna wants to see our house and I told her you were a wonderful cook. She's expecting a home-cooked meal."

"Kevin," I say in a reasonable tone, as I throw an empty box of stone-wheat crackers into the recycle bin by the back door. "This isn't The Dick VanDyke Show. You won't lose your job because your wife forgot to make a pot roast."

For a moment he is silent, then: "You think this is funny?"

I shake my head at the phone. I did think it was funny. But there was no sense trying to get him to see the humor. Clearly this was important to him. "No. Sorry. It's just that there's nothing I can do about it now."

"We're eating at home tonight. Call the caterer." He slams the phone in my ear.

I stare at the phone. He hung up? Call the caterer? Like I'd ever used a caterer before? Like we had one on speed dial? Okay, Kate, think. Your husband is about to have a stroke unless you can whip up an eight-course meal in the next thirty minutes.

There was a caterer we had used at work. It was supposed to be oh-so-chichi, but Mandy, the manager of the Wee Book Inn, had ordered the cheapest lunch tray, consisting of champagne crackers, cheese cubes, a spinach-and-avocado dip, and an antipasto only Percy would eat. "It's a pity Mandy didn't go for the good stuff," Percy said. "They make a pimento and goat cheese stuffed-olive platter that is" —*he held his hands up by his ears, praising the food gods*— *"to die for."*

What was the name of that place? I look at the clock. The second hand ticks like a time bomb. I reach for the yellow pages and start flipping through. "Any port in a storm," I mumble.

We eat and eat. The food is good. Too good. Every third bite Donna winks and says, "You must give me the recipe." She waves her bone-thin hand and asks for my e-mail address. She calls me a culinary genius. I turn red, and I hope she thinks I'm blushing.

I cough into my napkin and remind her to save room for the crème brûlée. Donna makes a tiny O with her lips and says, "How Continental! Do you bake yours in a water bath?" and for a flash I want to throw up my hands and walk away from this sham.

I stand with my mouth open, waiting, hoping something intelligent will pop out. But she turns back to Kevin and they start talking about how federal foreign policy may affect interest rates.

I flee to the kitchen. I take my time arranging the crème brûlées, each snug in its own individual serving cup (white china; I had to pay a ten-dollar deposit on each one before the caterer would think about entrusting me with them) on a tray. I pour coffee into a white decanter and manage to find three matching white mugs with a crisp black strip around the rim. Pretty. Or, as Donna would say, Continental.

I place the tray on the table and Kevin snatches up one of the crème brûlées and places it in front of Donna, as if he's afraid I'll forget my mother's mantra, "Guests first." I pour coffee and Donna offers me a dazzling smile. Her teeth are perfect. Straight, bright white. I'm sure each time she visits the dentist he cries with pride. She points her fork at me. "The important thing to remember is to stay focused."

I pour another cup of coffee and nod, pretending to know what she's talking about.

She cracks the burnt-sugar shell of her crème brûlée, but doesn't lift the spoon to her mouth. She's Angelina Jolie thin, and I wonder when the last time her taste buds witnessed eggs,

sugar, and cream in any combination. She puts the spoon down,
opting instead for a sip of black coffee. "You understand, Kate,
how important the next couple of years will be for Kevin." It
isn't a question. "He's jumped a number of hoops already and
corporate has their eyes on him." She gives a conspiratorial
wink. "I've made sure of it." She holds up her coffee cup as if it
were cabernet in Waterford glass. "Here's to the fast track!"

Kevin gives his aw-shucks grin and looks down. It's the look
that makes my heart skip a beat every time. He raises his cup,
clinks it against Donna's, and then touches the lip of my cup and
holds it there, looking into my eyes. "Exciting times, babe."

I smile back, then turn to Donna. "What does 'fast track'
mean for us? Will Kevin be running the branch someday?"

She plunks her coffee cup down hard and some slops over
the edge and dribbles onto the tablecloth. Her eyes narrow at
Kevin. "You've discussed this, right?"

Discussed what?

Kevin nods and talks fast. "Kate is my rock. She supports
me all the way." He puts his hand over mine. "Don't you?"

I nod vigorously. "Always." This is my Kevin, the warm,
affectionate man who shares my hopes and dreams. Even if it
means calling the occasional caterer and passing a ridiculously
elaborate meal off as home cooking.

Donna beams at the two of us. "Here, here," she says,
thumping the table with her hand. "It may be old-fashioned,
but 'Stand by Your Man,' I say." She sits back in her chair and
sips her coffee, seemingly satisfied with all she surveys. "With
your wife's support, there's no limit to what you can achieve."

Kevin smiles at me, then looks at my empty crème brûlée dish and quickly frowns. "You're finished already? Honestly, Kate, if you slow down, you might actually taste your food."

2 2

The next night was our second session of group therapy. After spending the first half of the session going over and discussing the group rules, Laura-Lea pulled her T-shirt down, stretching it tight over her curves, and asked, "Who will volunteer to begin with their story?"

I got busy avoiding eye contact by straightening my purse and another bag I brought that held my tennis shoes. If there was a basketball game going on after our session was done, maybe I'd join in. Big Tim had invited me, after all.

Laura-Lea cleared her throat, still waiting for a volunteer. I stared at my shoes. She explained that she expected each one of us to take a turn opening a session, and that "this would be a good chance to get it over with if we were feeling nervous."

I stared at my feet. I sat beside Grace, a tiny, birdlike woman with dark hair and tired eyes who never sat still. She twisted in her seat. She was wearing sandals and her toes turned in when she spoke. "It's difficult for me to talk in public."

Laura-Lea said, "I understand. It can be hard to find the right words."

Grace shook her head. "No, it's not that." She slumped in her chair as if her bones had slid out of her body. "It's ... well ... I was eighteen when I married Jim. He was an outgoing guy, loved to talk. Talk, talk, talk. That's all he did for over forty years. He constantly interrupted me. I doubt I finished a sentence in all those years. Yak, yak, yak. Now he's gone." She held up two limp hands in an empty gesture. "The funny thing is I still can't finish a sentence. He still jumps in, interrupts me. In my head, you know? It's like he's still right here beside me."

My heart thumped out a Morse code message. Maybe Grace would understand. I swallowed hard. "He interrupts you," I said quietly, looking at her.

Grace's body recovered its bones and she sat ramrod straight. "Well, not exactly. I imagine it. It's just in my head. It's not as if I actually hear him interrupt me." She winked at me. "I'm not crazy."

It was my turn to slump in my chair. I went back to studying my shoes.

Laura-Lea said, "Grace, would you like to continue with your story?"

"No, dear. Not tonight."

Another woman spoke up. "I'll go." I squeezed my eyes shut in relief.

Janice Grear was fifty-eight years old and had been a widow for just over four weeks. "I wish I missed my husband more."

I looked at Janice in confusion. She must have meant to say that she missed him more and more, or something like that. I glanced over at Laura-Lea, waiting for her to correct Janice. But Laura-Lea was leaning forward, nodding her head in what appeared to be compulsive agreement. "Yes." Nod, nod. "Okay, Janice." Nod. "Tell us."

Janice took a deep breath. "We'd just begun our annual vacation to Pigeon Lake. We'd been renting the same cottage for the same two weeks every year for almost thirty years. This year I told Norman that I wanted to rent a different cabin. One of the newly remodeled ones with a dishwasher, but Norman said forget it.

"Anyway, we were at the gas station. I had popped into the convenience store to pick up some gum and a paperback for the beach. A good one, not one of those trashy books with people kissing on the front cover." She turned to me. "You know the ones I mean."

I knew.

I'm standing at the checkout counter of Food-Friendly Grocers. There's a rack of recent best sellers nearby, which is handy because the line I'm in is as long as the Great Wall of China and the cashier is wearing a huge yellow button I can read even from this distance that says, "I'm in training!"

I scan the book rack. There's a romance novel, proudly commanding the #6 best-seller slot and I can't take my eyes off it. I'm not looking at the title or author, I'm staring at the shirtless hunk on the cover. He's holding a woman who's bending backward as if she's about to faint, but she's wearing a leotard so perhaps she's trying out a particularly tricky yoga move and needs a spotter. I mentally superimpose Kevin's face over the man on the cover. Kevin: shirtless, his shoulder-length hair flying—okay, not flying, more like lifting gently but mannishly in the breeze. Problem is Kevin doesn't have long hair. He has clipped banker hair. And he is nearly always wearing a shirt. He's more a poster child for the Young Republicans than a romance hero.

Someone behind me clears her throat in that loud way that says "You're doing something wrong, and would you be so kind as to stop doing it?" I turn and the woman jerks her head at me in a move-along gesture. The line has moved up, and I didn't move up with it. I push my cart ahead, craning my neck at the book cover. When was the last time Kevin and I had spontaneous fainting yoga?

"Get a grip," I tell myself.

The woman behind me says, "Excuse me?" One hand on her hips, the other squeezing a lemon like she was about to throw it to center field.

"Sorry," I say and turn back to my cart. I don't know if I'm embarrassed or sad or what. I glance back at the woman but she's not looking at me anymore, she's eyeing the romance cover too.

She shakes her head, pointing at the book. "Tell me, when was the last time you saw a man looking like that?" She starts laughing, shaking her head. "Mine looks more like the Pillsbury Doughboy than Fabio." She chuckles to herself. "No six-pack on my man. He's wearing the whole keg." She laughs in earnest.

I could tell her Kevin looks like that. Not his hair, but he was tall, and handsome. With his hair clipped and in his tailored suit, he could easily be mistaken for a recent Navy recruit. And under that suit his six-pack is still there, made slightly softer from hours of sitting behind a desk, but definable all the same.

My bread is squashed. I grab the coffee can and carton of eggs with equally firm fists and pound them onto the conveyor belt. Grapes dribble juice onto the belt. I'm taking my sexual frustration out on my produce.

Okay, my frustration isn't just sexual. Sure, I'm in the grocery store ogling the hunk on the cover of a romance novel, a strong clue something is amiss, but it's more than that. I miss Kevin. Even when he's home, I miss him. He's preoccupied.

The woman behind me is flipping through the pages of the romance novel, shaking her head and smiling at the same time. She glances up and catches me staring. She holds the book out. "You want to buy it?"

Her smile slides from amused to knowing and I turn away, mumbling, "Nah." But it's not because I don't like romances. My taste in books runs from the Romance period to the modern era. Wuthering Heights *to* Emma, Gone with the Wind *to* Jane Eyre. *Didn't I just recommend* A Farewell to Arms *to two different customers at the bookstore?*

I don't want the book because it's not a paper romance I'm after. I have the real thing at home … or I had it. Somewhere along the line, we've gotten off track.

It's easy to blame Kevin, I consider as my groceries move along the conveyor belt. It'd be easy to say it's his fault for work-ing so hard and such long hours, and only cuddling up to The Economist, *but that's not accurate either. It takes two to tango, and I haven't put on my dancing shoes for a long while.*

I pay the cashier; the only bright thing about her is her yellow button.

A boy stacks my food in the cart and grunts, "Yep," when I say thank you.

I push the cart toward the exit and I'm thinking about dancing; I'm thinking about romance novels and Kevin's bare chest.

Janice was in the middle of a long tangent about the filth for sale on gas station book racks when Laura-Lea prodded her to get to the point by clearing her throat in a pointed way.

Janice sat straight in her chair. "Well, anyway, I was buying a book and Norman was outside at the air pump, filling the giant inner tube we keep for the grandchildren. They love to take it out on the water and bob around. Why I'll never know, but they do. When I came out of the store, I told Norman he was overfilling the tube, but he paid me no mind, as usual. I was walking to the car when I heard a bang. I turned to see Norman flying through the air at a terrible speed. He landed some fifty feet away from the air pump. I knew he was dead before he hit the ground. It was exactly something he would do."

Janice looked around the room. "Don't get me wrong, I've shed a tear or two, believe me. I cried at the funeral when my dear friend Betty March got up and played 'Onward, Christian Soldiers' on the organ. She muddled up the middle, but it's the thought that counts, don't you think?" she said, eyeing Laura-Lea, who was still nodding.

No one spoke. Bobby, the short one wearing wool pants, cleared his throat and cast another longing look at Laura-Lea. Richard, tall and distinguished-looking, threw a look of distaste at Mimi, who sat holding her chin with her hand, staring at a spot on the floor.

Janice sat up straighter in her chair and cleared her throat. "The hardest thing I've had to deal with since Norman's death is guilt. Guilt over the fact that I don't miss him very much. I tried to, but he's a difficult man to miss. I came here because I've no one to talk to about this. My family is heartbroken, you know? So I can't very well tell them that I'm fine with the way things are."

Laura-Lea reached over and patted Janice on the hand. She whispered what looked like "Good job" and then sat up in her chair to address the group. "I would like someone to share their reaction to Janice's story. Tell us how you felt while you were listening to her talk."

Grace looked at Laura-Lea and said, "It was very sudden. That's what I thought."

Laura-Lea gestured toward Janice. "Tell her, Grace, not me."

Grace shifted in her chair so she could face Janice. "When you were talking about what happened to your husband, I thought, that it was very sudden. It must have been a shock."

Janice nodded to the crumpled tissue in her hands.

I folded my arms over my chest, feeling a sudden compassion for these women. "My dad died suddenly," I said.

Laura-Lea leaned toward me. "Are you here grieving the death of your father—" she looked down at a piece of paper in her hand "—Kate?"

"No."

"Oh. Would you like to share with the group your reason for being here?"

"No."

Laura-Lea's head jerked sideways and her mouth snapped open and shut, like someone was reeling her in.

"I mean, not today," I said.

She pressed her lips together in a facsimile of a smile and turned in her chair. "Janice, next group I want to start with your story, right where you left off. Okay?" She checked her watch. "We took up a lot of time going over the group rules, so our time is up. Chairs back against the far wall, please. See you next week."

We filed out in silence. I was sure I would dream of Norman flying.

In the foyer I listened to the sounds of basketball for a moment, then changed my shoes. In the gym four groups of kids were playing, two on each side of the gym. Big Tim missed an easy shot inside the key, and then looked around to see who might have noticed. He spotted me, his eyes opening wide, his face breaking into a smile. He waved with both hands and jogged across the court toward me, leaving his teammates shaking their heads after him.

"Hi, Jack's friend," Big Tim huffed in my face.

I took a half step backward, but returned his smile. "Hi, Big Tim." I pointed at my feet and wiggled my toes in their canvas tennies. "I came dressed properly this time."

Big Tim clapped his hands once and hollered, "Awesome."

I held up a cautionary hand. "No 'think fast' throwing today, okay?"

Big Tim wrote an X on his chest with his finger and then held up his hand Boy Scout–style. "Promise. You're on my team."

He took off running and I jogged behind him, meeting the rest of our team at the top of the key. The tall girl I recognized from my last visit stared at me with an expression of blankness. I held up a hand in greeting. She turned away.

Big Tim handed me a blue bandanna. "Us against red."

I noticed the girl had her blue bandanna tied around her wrist. I followed suit, which drew a look of boredom from my fashion mentor.

Big Tim stood on the out-of-bounds line, dribbling the ball, and called, "Blue's ball." He was looking to his right, away from me, but without even glancing my way, he threw the ball at me. Surprised, I missed and the ball sailed by me.

The girl threw her hands up and yelled a single word.

"Sekeena." Jack's voice came from behind me. Sekeena's face flushed, but by her expression, I didn't think the flush was from embarrassment. Her eyes sparkled even as she dropped her head and mumbled "sorry" to her high-tops.

Jack stood by his office door, calm and casual. He held a clipboard in one hand, his arms crossed over his chest. He wore black sweatpants, a white cotton T-shirt, a stopwatch, and a smile. He crooked a finger at Sekeena. "Come 'ere."

I watched the girl saunter slowly toward Jack, as if she knew he would wait for her no matter how long it took her to arrive. Jack stood by his office door, the pleasant expression on his face never changing. The game continued around me, but I stood, transfixed, watching Jack and Sekeena.

When the girl finally reached him, Jack placed a hand on her shoulder, forcing her to stand an arm's length away. He bent his head and spoke to her. The sounds of the basketball game drowned out their words. Every few seconds Sekeena's head bobbed in a quick nod. When Jack was done speaking to her, he turned her toward the game and gave her a gentle push. Sekeena walked toward me. She stood in front of me for a moment and offered her hand. I shook it. She glanced at the floor. "Sorry for my language."

"No worries."

She pursed her lips in a half grimace. "We cool?"

"Yes."

She stared at the floor. "Cool."

I glanced up at Jack, who was now reading from his clipboard. I was struck by the stillness that radiated from him into the space around him, a palpable peace.

He glanced up and caught me staring at him. He lifted a hand in greeting and I returned the gesture. He didn't seem surprised to see me. I looked back at the game, which was proceeding well in my absence, and then walked over to Jack. He smiled into my eyes in a way that felt like a steadying hand at my elbow. Solid, calm, protective, kind. What a strange man, I thought.

Jack looked down and made a mark on the clipboard he was holding. "Nice to see you, Kate."

I shifted one foot to another. "I thought it might be fun to take Big Tim up on his offer."

He studied the clipboard. "Glad you did."

I tapped the sheet he was examining. "Game plan?"

He looked at me. His eyes were blue. "Sort of. It's for Sunday. We have a service here Sunday mornings."

It took a second to register. "Service? Like church service?"

Jack nodded.

"Are you a pastor or something?" I asked.

He looked at me for a long moment. "Follow me," he said, then turned and walked into the office.

An odd response, I thought as I followed him. Maybe he was an incognito Buddhist monk but couldn't say so because everyone is supposed to find their own path to enlightenment.

Jack pushed the door closed. "It's noisy out there." He smiled a lopsided grin and said, "The short answer is yes."

"Pardon?"

"The answer to your question. I'm a pastor—or something."

I cocked an eyebrow at him. "What's the something?"

"Well, I'm a pastor of sorts."

I sat in the plastic chair across from him. "I didn't know pastors came in sorts. Then again I don't know much about pastors."

Jack propped his feet on his desk. "Well, I'm not what you would call a regular pastor. I don't actually have a church." He seemed to think about it for a moment. "Well, I have a church; I just don't have a building."

I pulled a face. "Well, that clears it up. Thanks."

Jack laughed. "Glen Hills Community Center serves as our makeshift church building each Sunday morning." He explained that a small, but loyal, group of people from the neighborhood filed into the gym each week dragging with them the equipment required for the service. "We always start late. Many come still hung over, the music is terrible, but we do it anyway," he smiled. "I play the drums."

He said that each Sunday the group would transform the gym into a church. Jack brought his worn set of drums, a girl named Jeannie brought her slightly out-of-tune keyboard, offering it for use with such pride and happiness that Jack said it broke his heart. Two others brought an electric and a bass guitar to round out the sound. "And hopefully drown out the keyboard," Jack said.

The community hall provided a portable speaker, he said, that could transmit the music or Jack's preaching, but not both at the same time. The group would set up the few chairs available to them, but many ended up standing for the entire time. Some would walk around while Jack was speaking. Some slept, Jack said. In winter the chairs would fill up with people who were just happy to get out of the cold for a few minutes. It sounded informal by any standard, but Jack said he believed it was the most important thing he did each week.

I pointed to the door of his office. "So the basketball is just a sideline?"

Jack raked a hand through his dark hair. He could use a haircut, I thought.

"It's part of a youth program I run," he said. "The kids can come anytime during the day. There's a bunch of stuff they do, but Wednesday nights we play basketball."

I nodded, just wanting him to keep talking. I was amazed how calm I felt listening to Jack. Almost tranquil. Not unlike the feeling I got from Dr. Alexander's sofa. Something about his voice. I gave him a smooth smile, grateful for this quiet feeling.

Jack cocked an eyebrow at me. "Your turn. Tell me about Kate."

I didn't want to talk about me. "Nothing to tell, really. I don't run a youth program, or anything else for that matter. I don't do anything." I paused. "Actually I don't even have a job."

Jack pushed his lips out, a weird fish impersonation, but I could see he was thinking. "I see."

I got up and walked to the door. If I stayed any longer, he'd try to get my whole story. I wasn't interested in telling it at that moment. "I actually came to play, if that's all right. I mean, Big Tim did invite me."

Jack was on his feet. "I'll grab my whistle and meet you out there."

An hour later I was covered with sweat and had acquired four bruises, two on my legs, one on my forearm, and one on my butt at the final whistle. I smiled at Jack, feeling the endorphins course through my body. I hadn't broken a sweat in months. It felt good. High fives flew and Big Tim bounded toward me with a massive grin. He picked me up and whooped.

I gasped, winded from the bear hug and the running. "Did we win?" I had no idea what the score was.

Big Tim shook his head, still smiling. "Nope." He put me down.

Sekeena sauntered by me. "Not bad. For your age."

"Thanks." I gathered up my belongings and turned to wave at Jack. "Bye."

Jack jogged toward me. "Hey, wait a second." He took my elbow, steering me toward the door, away from the others. "I've been thinking. If you … need a job … there could be a part-time position here for you. I wouldn't be able to pay much, but—"

I smiled, interrupting him. "Oh, Jack, no. I mean, thank you. That's very kind. But when I said I don't have a job, I didn't mean I was looking for a job. I just … came here to play. Just for fun."

"Right. Sure. Good," Jack stammered. Was he embarrassed?

I turned to go. "Bye. Thanks again. I'll come by another day, maybe."

Jack waved and mumbled something I couldn't hear.

23

Friday evening I fumbled for my keys, juggling two bags of groceries and my purse, trying to get my front door open. I dropped the keys and howled out a long "Arrggh."

As I reached down to grab the keys, the front door swung open. Blair stood in the doorway, arms reaching out for one of the grocery bags. "Let me help you."

"Arrggh!" I said again, this time directed at Blair. He backed into the house and turned sideways in a please-come-in gesture. "I used my key. Sorry I freaked you out, but I need to talk to you. And you haven't returned my calls for weeks."

I walked past him into the kitchen and put the grocery bag on the counter, still panting from the scare. What was with men wanting to scare women?

Blair followed. "I've tried coming by, but you're never home when I do. Finally I decided I would just let myself in."

I looked him up and down. "Lie in wait, is more like it."

He straightened his spine. "That's what I've been reduced to, yes. Do you have any idea what this has done to me? How torn up inside I am?"

I frowned. *He* was torn up? The poor boy. I wondered how he'd like to spend five minutes inside my head.

"Did you know I was in the hospital?" I starting pulling groceries out of the bags and putting them away.

Blair opened the fridge so I could put the milk in. "Didn't you listen to my messages?"

I glanced at the phone, realizing I hadn't checked the machine in a while. I walked over and hit a few buttons. A mechanical voice informed me I had thirty-six new messages. Ouch. Okay, maybe I'd been a bit too distant. Blair didn't know what was going on with me. All he knew was he kissed me once and I landed in the nuthouse. He probably blamed himself. "Blair, I'm sorry," I said.

I heard rustling and the fridge door close. He was putting my groceries away for me. I turned and saw Blair's eyes filled with tears.

He held a hand out to me, and then let it drop to his side. "I never—not in a million years—I didn't mean to hurt you."

"You didn't hurt me."

"I—"

"Sit down." I pulled a chair out from the table. "I'm going to tell you what happened. It's going to make you run screaming from this madhouse, but I'm going to tell you anyway."

And I did.

Blair sat at my kitchen table staring at me, his head moving back and forth like he was watching a slow tennis match. "What does all this mean? Are you—?"

"Crazy?"

He looked down at the table.

I shrugged. "No. Maybe."

"Do you still—?" He pointed to the ceiling and made a swirling motion with his finger.

I looked away.

He got up from the table and started pacing. He stopped behind me, hands on the back of my chair. "Did I—?"

I turned my head, trying to see him in my peripheral. "You aren't responsible for the voice in my head."

I felt his hand on the back of my head as he fiddled with a strand of my hair. Goose pimples rose on my neck and ran down my arms. "I didn't help." He spoke quickly, as if anticipating the question. "You've been under so much stress. Kissing you just added more."

"Stress?" I turned toward him.

He nodded. "You were under a lot of stress even before Kevin died. No one can blame you for reacting to it."

"I was?" Why was I under stress before he died?

Blair blinked rapidly for a moment. "Yeah, you were pretty sick for a while there. You don't remember?"

I turned back to the table. Kevin had been right. I'd forgotten too much.

Laura-Lea called it inappropriate self-disclosure.

Malcolm Peters had volunteered to open my third group session with his story of loss. He had launched into a bizarre monologue that began with his mother's failure to breast-feed him and meandered to stories about the holes in his underwear, his childhood bed-wetting problem, and pet names he had invented for his various body parts.

He talked nonstop for twenty minutes. It was like he was holding the group hostage with words. Like his voice barred the doors and bound us to our chairs. He spoke to the floor, never looking up, in flowing tones that never allowed for interruption. "I was fifteen and my older cousin locked me in a room with two girls. He said he wouldn't let me out until I had slept with both of the girls. If that isn't rape," he drew in a breath and shook his head slowly, "I don't know what is."

I choked out a cough. Janice and Grace both sucked their breath in. Richard Lieberman shook his head. "For the love of Pete." He looked at Laura-Lea. "Are you going to put a stop to this?"

Laura-Lea blinked at Richard. "Do you want to share your reaction with Malcolm?"

Richard balled up a fist. "Are you serious?" He turned sharply in his chair to face Malcolm, who was still staring at the floor. "My reaction is *shut up*."

I choked on a ball of discomfort. Beside me Grace slammed her spine against the back of her chair. Laura-Lea pouted. "Richard, you are not respecting group rules when you use that language."

Richard's face turned a pulsing red, like he was trying to push something out. Or hold something in. "He's the one who's not respecting group rules." Richard flung a hand in Malcolm's direction. "Nothing he's said tonight is even remotely connected to why we are here. He's just prattling on about outrageous … garble." Richard had a point, but his anger made me uncomfortable.

Mimi Jones was sitting beside Richard, nodding her head at his

every word. Apparently she wasn't feeling as ill at ease as I was. She
hadn't spoken in the first two sessions, but now she raised her hand
and wiggled her fingers at Laura-Lea. "May I speak?"

Laura-Lea leaned forward, revealing her impossible cleavage, and
gave Mimi a long blink. "You don't need to ask permission."

Mimi cleared her throat. "I just wanted to say that I agree
with Richard." She picked up a long, manicured hand and placed it
on Richard's knee. "I see beyond his harsh words, into his meaning …
his intent." She left her hand where it was, and turned her gaze on
Malcolm, who was still studying the floor. "Richard's point is that this
group has a singular purpose. Isn't that right, Richard? And you" —she
flicked her other hand toward Malcolm— "are off track."

Richard turned in his chair, shifting his knees out of Mimi's
reach. "He's not just off track. He's a train wreck."

Laura-Lea stood up, both hands in the air, like she was counting down the starting beat for the string section. "I hear what all of
you are saying. Richard, I hear your frustration. Mimi, I hear and
appreciate your empathy. Malcolm, I would like your reaction to
Richard's comments."

Malcolm's head bobbed on his chest, from laughing or crying, I
couldn't tell. "I don't understand what you said."

I left the session expecting to hear the sounds of basketball, but all
was quiet. Inside, the gym was dark, except for a line of light that
shone from under Jack's office door. I crossed the gym and rapped
softly on the door.

"Yeah?" Jack's voice called, then the door opened. He wore a rumpled suit jacket, his tie hung in two straight lines from his neck, the collar open. He finished the look with a pair of faded jeans.

"Hi, Jack."

For a moment he just looked at me, as he would a stranger, then he said, "Kate. Hello."

"No b-ball tonight?"

He pointed to a plastic orange chair and I sat, a creeping feeling in my stomach. Something was wrong. He sat down in the other orange chair, our knees nearly touching. His blue eyes were red rimmed. He cleared his throat.

"Big Tim was shot and killed last Friday. Today was the funeral."

"Shot? H-how?" I said.

Jack ran a hand over his face. "He was walking to the store to get some milk for his mother and got caught in gang crossfire." He looked away, his jaw working like he was trying to swallow something.

I touched his knee, a fast tap of sympathy. "Just like that? He just went to the store and …"

"Yeah, just like that." He snapped his fingers.

"Did they catch the guys who did it?"

Jack snorted a sound of disgust. "Police are looking into it, but it's a nearly impossible task. No one talks to police, they're all too afraid. They can collect evidence, but without witnesses to identify the people involved …" He shrugged.

We sat in silence with the truth we both understood. A life can be wiped out without anyone being held responsible. Without anyone saying they were sorry. I looked at his wrinkled suit jacket. "Did you perform the funeral?"

Jack leaned forward and rested his chin in his hands. "Yeah, at the Baptist church down the street. Most of the kids from basketball were there. Tim's mom and aunt, and his brothers and sisters." Tears ran down Jack's face. He made no attempt to brush them away.

I clasped my hands in my lap. "I wish I'd known. I would have come."

He sat back. "I have no way of getting ahold of you. Although, to be honest, it never occurred to me to try. You live around here?"

"No."

He waited.

I gave a half smile and said, "I'm from Greenfield."

He stood. "Nice to see you again, Kate from Greenfield. Can I walk you out?" He had dark circles under his eyes, and his skin was pale under his five o'clock shadow.

"Yes, thanks."

He walked me to my car in silence, then, "Good night, Kate."

I opened the driver door and stood, looking at him over the roof. "Where's your car?"

He pointed to the side of the building. A bicycle was propped against the wall. "My wheels. I don't own a car."

I looked down the dark street. Most of the streetlights were burnt out, giving the road a Sleepy Hollow feel. "Can I offer you a ride home?"

He shook his head. "Biking will help clear my head. But thanks anyway." He pointed at me with both hands. "Maybe another time?"

"Sure."

He walked backward toward the bike. "I'm glad you stopped by tonight, Kate."

Mandy looks at me as if I've suddenly grown a third eye, but I can't stop smiling. She glances down at the paper on her desk, then at me. "Can you tell me why? Did you get another job?"

"No. And I won't, not for a while."

She gestures to my resignation letter. "Aren't you happy here?"

"Yes, very much. I've enjoyed this job, but things have changed for me at home and I need to step away."

"What if I move you to part time?"

I shake my head. "Thanks, but no. It wouldn't work." I have to squelch a burst of laughter that's threatening to burst out of my mouth. I don't want to offend Mandy, but I don't want to give her all the details of why I'm quitting. I want Kevin to be the first to hear.

She reaches across the desk, trying to hand my letter back to me. "Can you stay for a couple more months? Just until the Christmas rush is over?"

This pulls on my heartstrings. I love working here at Christmastime, sharing favorite books with frenzied shoppers who fill the store with energy and purpose. But I need to be firm. For once, I have to stick to the plan I've made, no more waffling. No more excuses. I pull myself up to my full height, all five feet, four and a half inches.

"Sorry, Mandy. I wish I could, but ..." She gives me her pleading face, an exaggerated frown and big eyes. It's comedic, and I know she's resigned herself to the fact that I'm leaving. I stick my hand out and she looks at it for a long moment before shaking it.

"Come back anytime, Kate."

I grab my purse and head out the door. "Thanks!" I holler, glad to have finished the task. I step out onto the sidewalk, head up, ready to start a new phase of my life. I check my watch. Five thirty. Kevin will be home soon. I walk home humming.

24

The morning after group therapy, in my kitchen, I hung up the phone with the insurance agent and looked at the figure I'd written on a pad of paper. I was finally dealing with the financial implications of my car wreck. The number on the paper was huge. I sighed. I'd just received an education in the finer points of car insurance. It seemed Kevin didn't have the proper kind of insurance on his leased Mazdaspeed3, and fixing it would be costly.

I dropped the pencil onto my kitchen table and sulked. Why didn't he know to put gap insurance on the car? Sure, I'd never heard of it until moments ago when the insurance agent told me about it, but it was Kevin's job to know these things. He had been fastidious about details such as insurance, investment, and squeezing every last dollar out of a contract. For some reason he'd messed up on the Mazda.

I got up to put on the teakettle. I noticed a slight tremor in my right hand. The kettle trembled in my grip, and I couldn't steady it no matter how hard I tried. I set the kettle down with a plunk and pulled a long breath in through my nose just like Laura-Lea taught us. Dr. Alexander—who I still saw once a week—had told me to take note of physical signs of stress because they can be gateways to what he called "cathartic breakthroughs." I didn't know if a cathartic breakthrough was something I particularly wanted, but he said they were important.

A sudden tremor I couldn't control could be a sign that my body was attempting to relieve stress—in other words, it was trying to tell me something. I let my breath out in a slow, thin line between my lips. I took another slow breath in and closed my eyes. Dr. Alexander had said I could mentally journey through my body in order to locate what he called the "seat of emotion."

"We feel different emotions in different parts of our bodies," he had told me.

Eyes closed, I imagined traveling through my body, looking for the part that was feeling stress.

First I checked out my heart and lungs, and then moved on to my stomach. Everything seemed normal. I moved down to my legs and feet, then back up to my arms and hands. Nothing. The kettle boiled. I opened my eyes and reached for a cup. My hand trembled as I placed the cup on the counter.

"I don't know," I said to the kettle. "Maybe this is just malarkey." I closed my eyes and repeated the exercise. This time it occurred to me that I should examine my back, spine, and neck. My eyes opened wide as I reached around and touched the base of my neck. Something was rolling around in there, like a tiny ball, in my spine. Now what? I thought back to Dr. Alexander's instructions.

I could hear his instruction, "Picture the stress, Kate. Give it a form, give it substance."

I pictured the ball as a marble lodged between my vertebrae. I mentally reached out and touched it with a soft, exploring finger. It was hard, but instead of feeling cold as I for some reason expected, the marble was hot, like fire. The moment my finger made contact, it howled and then let out a growling yell and began to spin faster and faster. Startled, I pulled my eyes open, gasping for air. "That's enough," I said. I sucked on my fingertip as if cooling a burn.

An hour later I took a sip of cold Earl Grey and spat it back into the cup. I had been thinking about the marble of anger, but I was still staring at the enormous sum the insurance company quoted to fix Kevin's car.

I dragged my hands over my face and stared at the number again. My Ford was getting old, but was fixing the Mazda the best solution? I reached back and rubbed my shoulder. With one finger I touched the spot on the back of my neck where I had "seen" and touched that spinning, burning hot marble of anger.

I was angry. I had told Blair as much, but after the marble experience, I realized that I had probably been angry for a long time, even before Kevin's death. But my Swiss-cheese memory hadn't told me the whole story. Bits and pieces continued to come, but never enough for me to see the whole picture. I supposed that hearing Kevin's voice wasn't my only mental health issue.

I sat and contemplated my mental health. No doubt I was doing better than the Kate who sat unbathed and rumpled on the living room floor day after day after Kevin died. In fact I was the opposite of her. I was barely ever home. Sure, I was still sleeping in my living

room, but I'd made remarkable progress. Hadn't I? I was improved
from the Kate who snapped harsh words at her sister without warning or warrant, ordering her out of my house. My conversations with
Heather were quieter now, calm, sparse dialogues centered on our
mutual desire to lead normal lives, to be normal people. For me to
be cured.

But cured of what, exactly? Dr. Alexander had no hesitation in
labeling my condition as mental illness. He had handed me a prescription (still sitting, unfilled, on my counter) with the assurance of
a man who knew crazy when he saw it. But I flinched at the label.
I didn't feel mentally ill. Fractured maybe—a temporary fissure that
would, in time, heal. But ill? Mental diabetes? Cancer of the thinking? No, I couldn't accept that. Besides, I was improving every day.

A picture of a burning, spinning marble formed in my mind.

I pushed the teacup away, frustrated. "Am I fixed or not?" I
muttered.

"It's not worth fixing," Kevin said.

I shot out of my chair, slopping Earl Grey onto the table. My
heart expanded and fell in huge, pulsing thuds. "No. Stop. Don't do
this. I don't want to do this."

Kevin's voice came calm and easy. "I don't think you should."

I shook my head, trying to clear it. Fear roared in my ears,
drowning out his words. "Should what? This makes no sense."

"I agree."

Even as my skin rose up in goose pimples and my heart began to
pound, some part of my mind yelled out. *Don't listen. Make it stop.* I
crushed my fists into my eye sockets. "I'm not going to do this."

Kevin's voice was conversational. "Don't do it."

Tears flowed down my cheeks. "What do you mean, 'don't'? You're doing it, not me." I thought about running out the back door. Would his voice follow me? I remembered the afternoon in the playground with Blair. Kevin's voice had followed me there. There was no reason to think it wouldn't now. Desperation flooded my body. "I can't do this anymore."

Kevin said, "It's not worth it."

Worth? He thinks I'm not worth fixing? That I can't get better? I raised my face toward the ceiling and roared, "I'm worth it. My sanity is worth it."

"The car isn't worth fixing," came the unfazed response.

Slow realization, like a sunrise on a rainy day, dawned and pulled the tension out of my body. I felt like a deflated balloon. "You're talking about the car."

"It sounds like waves in the ocean."

Ocean? We were miles from any ocean. "I don't understand."

The kitchen clock ticked in the silence.

"Why is this happening?" I said to the air.

I could hear my own breathing, the rapid little breaths that were flooding my brain with too much oxygen, making me feel dizzy. "This has to stop, Kevin. I need you to stop doing this. Do you hear me?"

Nothing.

Inspiration struck; a benevolent poke in the eye. I knew what to do.

I grabbed the phone and dialed. "No more arguing with a dead guy," I mumbled.

Dr. Alexander's receptionist, efficient as ever, answered in one ring.

"Hi, Sally," I said, "Listen, Dr. Alexander told me to call him if I heard Kevin's voice again."

Sally's smooth tones slid over the phone lines. "Hold the line, Kate." The sound of rushing water filled my ear. Dr. Alexander didn't believe in playing music when a patient was put on hold. Instead I was treated to the sounds of nature, in this case, water. It irritated me. I had to pee. The soundtrack was approaching what sounded like Niagara Falls and I was crossing my legs hard, when Dr. Alexander's voice came on the line.

"Yes, Kate, I'm here." That was his line. No *What's the problem?* or even *What is the nature of this call?* Just, *I'm here.*

I clutched the phone hard. "Kevin. He spoke."

"When?"

"Just now. Minutes ago. I called you right away."

He mumbled something that sounded like *excellent.* "What did he say?"

My bladder poked at me. I bit my lower lip. "He said I shouldn't bother to get the car fixed."

There was a long pause. "Anything else?"

"He hears the ocean."

Another pause. "I see."

I gave my head a quick shake. "But, listen, the reason I'm calling is because I've figured out how to make him stop talking."

I heard rustling paper. "You're taking the medication as I prescribed?"

I rolled my eyes. "That's not the point, Dr. Alexander. Listen to me. I know how to make Kevin's voice stop. There are rules he follows. I've been trying to figure them out for weeks. But I was always trying to figure out how to get Kevin to talk more. You see? I wasn't trying to get him to stop. I was trying to get him to talk. I've always known how to get him to stop talking. It's simple. Whenever he speaks, I mention something personal—like how much I miss him. Or I ask him a question. He can't seem to answer direct questions. That's one of the rules. You see? I can control it. So I don't need to be afraid anymore. "

"I'd like you to come in this afternoon."

I shook my head. "Don't you see? I have the control. All this time I thought I had no control. But I do. I have all the control. I can make his voice stop."

Dr. Alexander cleared his throat. "Can you be here by 2:30?"

25

"Why can't you cooperate with me?" Kevin says, running a hand through his hair. I notice it's thinning at the top. I can see veins of scalp snaking through his short-cropped hair. When did that happen? Is he going bald? "I'm building a whole new life here."

We're in the kitchen, at breakfast. I hold the coffeepot in my right hand, poised above Kevin's favorite mug, but I don't pour. "We don't want a whole new life, Kevin. We want our life, the one we planned since high school."

Kevin's arms fly in a gesture of frustration. "Plans change. People change." He lowers his voice to a near whisper. "I've changed. I want more from life than just getting by."

I gape at him. "We're not 'just getting by.' We have a house, two cars, our bills are paid, there's money in the bank. We're doing well. Great, even." I pour the coffee and set it down on the kitchen table.

He stands, arms crossed, looking at it as if it might be poisoned. He presses his fists onto the table, supporting his weight. "Exactly. And why is that? I'll tell you why, it's because I've worked hard to

make it that way. But you decide to quit your job without even
telling me. It seems the only thing you want is to drag me down,
hold me back." He sits down hard on one of the kitchen chairs and
the table shakes. The coffee flops around inside the cup, but doesn't
spill. "Don't you see? I've been offered the world. Donna has told
me time and again that the sky is the limit for someone like me.
She's shown me the brass ring, and I want to reach for it."

I skid a chair over beside him and sit. I touch his arm.
"Kevin, I'm not—"

He holds a hand up in front of my face. "I want the whole
show, Kate. I don't want to sit here in this go-nowhere town for
the rest of my life. I have a real future and I've no intention of
blowing it."

"Go-nowhere? You love this town. We grew up here."

His face turns red and he shouts, "See? You're doing it right
now. I'm talking about the brass ring, a future filled with pos-
sibilities, and all you can do is sit there talking about the past,
and how you love this nothing of a town."

I blink twice, then again. His temper, his yelling—coming
from nowhere—startle me. We've disagreed before. I know there
have been times I've stretched his patience thin, but he's never
yelled before. I've never seen his face bloat with anger, swell-
ing his eyes and stretching his skin with violence. Some small
instinct tells me to be still, be quiet, don't move. But I push
against it, shoving aside the warning that the man I'm speaking
to now is not like the man I once knew. "Nothing? How can
you call Greenfield nothing? You love this town. You've always
talked about staying here and raising our children in a safe—"

Kevin shoots out of his chair, roaring like a grizzly. "You talk as if everything were already decided. Like there's nothing left to discuss." He rakes his hands over his face. "You don't hear a word I say. You won't listen."

I stand and put a hand on his shoulder. He turns fast, raising his hand. In a flash I see his palm, then feel a sharp sting, the force of which throws me off balance. I grab the back of a kitchen chair to steady myself. I'm not even sure what happened, not sure where the pain came from. I look at Kevin, his mouth is open, his hands limp at his sides, the red fury gone from his face. In fact his skin is pale and slightly green, as if he's suddenly caught a stomach flu. I shake my head, once, twice, imitating him as he shakes his head, no, no.

I raise my hand to my face and feel the burning spot on my cheek. Kevin's eyes fill with tears, he keeps shaking his head, whispering, "No, no." His hand reaches toward me, to steady me, catch me. I grab hold of it, like a lifeline, a buoy in dark waters.

"I'm sorry," I sob. "Kevin, I'm so sorry. I didn't mean to—"

He shushes me. "It's okay. Everything is okay."

I look into his eyes, nodding, searching. "It's okay," I say.

He leads me to a kitchen chair, our movements stiff and shuffling like we were suddenly very old. We sit, slow and jerky, side by side, his arm around me like a cloak, his other hand rubbing my hand and arm. I cling to him, hide my face in the crook of his neck. I'm shaking, bereft as a refugee. I close my eyes.

Kevin holds me close, tucking me under his arm like a

child. "It's over. It was nothing. I didn't mean it. Okay? I love you; I'd never hurt you."

I nod. I cling to his neck. I say, "It was nothing." I want it to be okay now. To be over. To have never happened at all.

At 2:28 I pulled up in front of Glen Hills Community Center, miles from Dr. Alexander's office. He hadn't believed me when I had called him, hadn't even listened to what I had to say. I felt no compulsion to keep the impromptu appointment. I sat in my car, looking up at the bright blue doors. The community center had begun to have an effect on me. A kind of attraction I couldn't define. When I wasn't there, I thought about being there.

I closed my eyes and was immediately able to conjure up the sensations of being in the group-therapy room. I could smell it (damp gym odor mixed with coffee). I could see the faces: Janice jabbing a tissue at the tears that wouldn't come. Grace who flittered on her chair like a nervous hummingbird. Mimi, who was constantly touching people and displaying her cleavage despite the fact hers could never compare to Laura-Lea's extraordinary buoyancy. Bobby, who obviously pined for Laura-Lea.

I wondered what Bobby's story was. What loss had brought him there? He hadn't shared his story yet. Then again, neither had I. I usually sat staring at my shoes, feigning indifference while I absorbed every detail of the conversations.

I was beginning to feel connected to these people somehow. Even Malcolm held a fascination for me. What possessed a man to rattle off the most bizarre personal events imaginable to a group of people he didn't even know? I could barely recall my memories, and even though they were coming back over time, it was a slow, unsteady process. But being there, with people who were at least as muddled up as I was, felt like balm. Perhaps in time they would help me piece together the remaining missing pieces of my memory. Maybe then I would feel brave enough to share them. And tell them about the voice that haunted me.

Plus I knew I wouldn't be allowed to sit and soak up the atmosphere for much longer. Soon Laura-Lea would insist I share my story with the group. It was expected. At the last session I saw her eye me at the beginning and look like she was about to say something to me. I ducked my head down, letting her know I wasn't in the mood to talk. I didn't relish the prospect of talking about Kevin's death.

I sat in the car until the clock read 2:30, in an act of stubborn determination. Then I got out and did a quick sprint to the hall. Once inside I noticed an odd fluttering sensation in my stomach. Nerves? Guilt? I wasn't supposed to be here. I was supposed to be downtown getting lectured to by a psychiatrist. And who would be here on a Thursday afternoon? Not Laura-Lea, not the group-therapy gang, not the basketball players.

Jack. That's who would be here.

When we had talked the night before, I had felt a sense of … what? A kind of relief, I supposed. The news of Big Tim's death had been a shock, but it had felt good to be on the other side of grief for a while. To be the one offering comfort rather than receiving it.

I pushed open the gym doors and was surprised to see a group of teens milling around under a basketball net on one end of the gym. A boy held the ball under his arm and spoke to the small group gathered there. I couldn't hear what was being said, but the feeling in the gym was hushed, subdued. These must have been friends of Big Tim, apparently skipping classes in order to gather together here.

I stopped short, holding the door open, not wanting to disturb the conversation. Jack came out of his office and walked over to the group. No one noticed me. The moment Jack stepped into the circle, Sekeena began to sob. Jack tucked her under one arm and gave her a hug. She clung there, crying into his shoulder. The boy with the ball put a hand on Jack's shoulder and Jack returned the gesture, reaching out with his other hand and grasping the boy's arm. The rest of the group stepped closer, a circle of shared grief.

I stepped back into the foyer and closed the door silently. I would have been an intrusion on the group of longtime friends. I'd only known Tim for a short time. In my car again I pulled away from the curb, the image of the group, clinging to each other, sharing their tears and hurt, swimming before my eyes. A pain, like a toothache, filled my heart. Losing Tim was tragic, but to see them huddled together, shouldering each other's grief made me ... jealous.

26

The following week, I walked down the hall toward the group-therapy room and saw Laura-Lea standing at the door.

"I want to chat with you after session." She touched my arm. "Can you stay?"

I swallowed hard, my stomach doing a tiny flip. "Sure." I had a pretty good idea what Laura-Lea wanted to talk to me about. Not only had I blown off the emergency appointment with Dr. Alexander, but I had skipped our regular appointment. I knew I needed his help, but I couldn't face his quiet look, his pen and paper, his inquiries about the medication. I needed a break from the scrutiny.

When everyone was seated, Laura-Lea looked me in the eye. "Kate, it's your turn to begin session."

Apparently, not only was I to talk with her about my disappearing act of the past week, but I was also to share my story.

But I was cornered, so I nodded.

Laura-Lea nodded back.

I took a deep breath and let it out slowly, just like Laura-Lea had taught us.

I glanced around.

Grace shifted in her chair.

Richard coughed in a fake way.

Mimi adjusted the front of her V-neck top to maximum effect.

Bobby openly stared at Laura-Lea.

I froze, feeling the weight of their stares. I glared down at my shoes. "I'll start next week's session instead, okay?" I said finally.

Laura-Lea puckered her lips in a doubtful expression. "You said that last week."

"Oh, yeah. I forgot."

She flicked her hands at me, like shooing a puppy out the door. "It really is your turn to begin the session, Kate." As an afterthought she added, "Remember, this is a safe place. You can say anything here." She said it smoothly as if explaining the return policy at Walmart. But I knew differently.

I glanced at Malcolm, remembering the way the group had swiftly judged and convicted him after his bizarre monologue. He still came to each group therapy session, but now he said little. His opinion was never sought by anyone in the group, not even Laura-Lea. He had been, by silent majority, relegated to the fringe of the group. Safe was a crock.

But short of bolting from the room, there was no way of out this. I cleared my throat. The image of the teenagers and Jack clinging together in their grief came to mind. Would it be so awful to share my grief? I didn't have to tell them everything, did I? I didn't have to tell them about hearing Kevin's voice. I didn't have to tell them anything I didn't want to. They wouldn't know the difference. "Uh, three months ago my husband died unexpectedly. I mean, he wasn't sick or anything beforehand. And I guess I've had a hard time, uh, coping since then."

Richard rolled his eyes. "And?"

I looked at Laura-Lea for support. True to form she nodded vigorously. I nodded back. "And, uh, it's been hard."

Grace turned to me. "Hard in what way, dear?"

I sucked on my upper lip. "Really, really hard."

Richard crossed his arms. "Oh for—. Talking to you is like pulling teeth."

Here we go ... I gave him a pleading look, but he just continued.

Richard smirked at me. "You come to group, sit slumped in your chair—your body language is very closed off, did you know that? You say almost nothing. And when you do talk, you give these one- or two-word answers." He turned to Laura-Lea. "I find it difficult with her in the group. I wonder if she really wants to be here."

I sat feeling like a stick of wood.

Laura-Lea opened her mouth, closed it, pointed to me, and then pointed at Richard, like she was playing a game of eeny-meeny-miny-moe.

Mimi cleared her throat. "Richard, I think you're being unfair to Kate. In my opinion—"

"Your opinion is of no interest to me," Richard roared. "I don't know why you're here either. You get all dolled up with makeup and low-cut blouses. It's more like you're on a man hunt than grieving."

Mimi clutched the neck of her blouse. "That's unnecessarily harsh. Why are you always so harsh with people?"

Richard leaned toward her. "It's called tough love."

She crossed her arms. "You don't love me."

He stared at her. "I do. In an existential way."

She gave a snort and turned away. At the same time, she tossed a get-a-load-of-him look at Janice. Janice glared back at Mimi.

Grace lowered her eyes and folded her hands on her lap like she was about to break into prayer.

"We're here to help each other," Laura-Lea mumbled to no one in particular.

I nodded vigorously, overcome by a sudden desire to comfort Mimi. "Th—that's true. And we are helping each other." There was a hint of desperation in my voice. I wanted this group to get along. I wasn't sure any of this was helping anyone, but I had a tremendous need to be here. With them. Week after week. Like a TV show, a vitamin pill, a full-time job, I wanted us to always be here. To stay the same. I needed the steady knowledge of Wednesday night.

I turned to Richard. "I want to be here." I closed my eyes and tried to think what Laura-Lea would say. "I hear what you've said, and I promise to be sensitive to your ideas."

Richard gave me a curt nod. "Good."

Mimi pounced. "Yes, it's good that she listens to you, isn't it, Richard? That's what you want from women. For them to listen and obey."

Richard turned an alarming shade of purple. He crushed out his words between his teeth. "Mimi, stop. I'm not having this discussion with you."

She threw an arm over the back of her chair, ready for anything. She resembled Joan Crawford in *Mildred Pierce*. "Oh, yes you are. You just accused me of being on a man hunt. Well, who asked who out to dinner? You. Remember? You asked me. I didn't chase you. You did the chasing, mister."

My eyes bulged from their sockets. They were dating?

Grace slapped a hand over her mouth.

Malcolm tittered.

Janice rolled her eyes.

Richard was on his feet. "Shut up, Mimi."

Mimi, undaunted, leaped off her chair. "You can't bully me. That's what you are—a bully. Why don't you tell the group about your dear wife, Richard? Tell them how you miss having her clean your house, cook your food, and wash your clothes. Tell them how you needed to slap her around sometimes."

The rest of us sat, risking tennis neck looking from Mimi to Richard, to Janice.

Laura-Lea shot to her feet and stood in the center of the circle. "I'm going to lead the group in a cleansing exercise. Everyone sit down and close your eyes. You, too, Richard. Breathe deeply through your nose."

I closed my eyes and filled my lungs to bursting.

At the end of the session, Mimi, who was supposed to have been calmed by twenty minutes of deep breathing, slammed out of the room. Richard sighed and then slowly made his way out, carefully holding the door for Janice, who was refusing to look at him.

I added my chair to the stack by the far wall and Laura-Lea tossed me a weary look. "Got a second?"

I nodded.

She leaned against a stack of chairs. I wondered if they were the same ones Jack used on Sundays. "Dr. Alexander asked me to speak to you if you came to group tonight."

I sucked my lower lip in. "If?"

"Seems you were a no-show for an appointment with him last week and then again for your regular appointment on Monday. Can you tell me what happened?"

My head jerked. "It wasn't really an appointment. He had asked me to call him if … if I wanted to. I had called him and he asked me to come see him if I could. But I was feeling better, so I decided not to bother him further." I shrugged to prove how trivial it all was, but my eyes filled with tears.

Laura-Lea put her hand on my arm, the casual touch of a caregiver. "What about Monday?"

I frowned at the floor.

"There's more that you aren't telling me."

"I'm not crazy," I said, inching away from her.

Laura-Lea's eyebrows snapped together in a look of confusion. "No one is saying you are."

I took a few more steps backward, creeping toward the door. "I'm not. No matter what Dr. Alexander told you. I have this under control."

"Dr. Alexander is concerned. He cares what happens to you."

"That's good to know. Thanks for telling me." I shook my head, still edging toward the door. She made no effort to stop me.

She sighed. "He asked me to tell you that he would like to see you tomorrow morning."

I stopped in the middle of the open doorway. "I can't tomorrow. I have an appointment at the bank." Another lie.

"Fine. I'll tell Dr. Alexander you'll be at his office late morning, after you're finished at the bank." She turned her back and began collecting her things.

I watched her for a moment, and then headed for the door.

The sounds of basketball filled the foyer. The crew was back, meeting again. I listened to the sound of the bouncing ball, the squeak of sneakers against the peeling wax on the floor. The image of these teenagers, just last week, huddled, hugging, grieving, filled my mind. I pushed the door open. The group was smaller than usual, but playing hard. Jack blew the whistle on a foul and pointed to the top of the key for the teams to assemble for the two-shot. He spotted me and jogged over. "Good to see you, Kate."

"You too, but I'm not going to stay tonight," I said. "I just wanted to say hi. But I'll stay next time, okay?"

He squinted. "Everything all right?"

I squared my shoulders. "Yes. I've figured some things out, I think." *Even if my own doctor doesn't believe me.*

He patted my arm. "Sounds like good news."

"You know what? It just might be." I smiled. "I think things will work out."

27

Early the next morning I walked into the bank and was slapped by a blast of cold air. It bounced off the bare walls and the polished tile floor, searching out a soft, receptive surface to absorb its chill. I had told Laura-Lea I had an appointment at the bank, and while that wasn't strictly true, it was a good idea. If I was going to take control over my life, I needed to begin immediately. Kevin's safe-deposit box was a good place to start.

I took a few steps and then hesitated, uncertain where to go. I eyed the line of silent customers waiting for the next available teller, and then the massive desk behind which a woman sporting a tight bun looked firmly down at whatever task was before her. The sign hanging directly above her head like the sword of Damocles, read *Reception*. Beyond her desk were rows of other desks, occupied by slow-moving, silent bankers. There was no sign reading *Safe-Deposit Boxes*.

A woman breezed past me and joined the long line for a teller. I decided on the receptionist.

I walked over and peered down at her scalp, visible due to her severe part. The bun-headed woman didn't look up. I cleared my throat, surprised at how loud it was as it ricocheted off the bare walls. Bunhead, still looking down, held up a finger, indicating she would be with me in "one." One what, I couldn't say. Finally she looked up. I expected her to speak. To say hello or "Can I help you?" She only raised her eyebrows, making a *What is it?* face.

I leaned toward her. "Good morning. I'm here for a safe-deposit box."

Bunhead looked at me with eyes half closed. "What size?" She pulled out a form and placed it in front of me.

"Sorry, I don't know. I've never seen it before."

She glared up at me for a moment, and then sighed. "Are you here to acquire a box, or to visit your box?"

I nodded like an eager child. "To visit. I'm Kate Davis. Kevin Davis's wife."

Bunhead stood at attention. She held her palms up in a don't-go-anywhere gesture as she began to walk. "I'll be right back."

Moments later I saw her walking toward me, Donna Walsh right behind her.

Donna's face was a sea of glass, calm and unreadable, but she walked at a quick pace, brushing past Bunhead. I was surprised she wasn't winded by the time she reached me. She did look tired, though. Dark circles framed her gray-green eyes (contacts?). She appeared to be wearing too much makeup. Her skin looked sallow under the sheen of her blusher. She looked both regal and haggard, a queen with insomnia. She stopped directly in front of me and bent her head until we were nearly touching foreheads, like she was going to suggest a handoff and call "Hut!" She put a light hand on my shoulder. "Linda tells me you're here about Kevin's safe-deposit box." She jerked a thumb toward Bunhead.

Donna's perfume was oddly familiar. I wondered if it was the one my mom had recently switched to. I held up Kevin's gold-colored key.

"Come this way," she said. She turned sharply on her heel and walked back the way she had come. Bunhead resumed her position at her desk, reunited with her absorbing task, and I scurried after Donna.

We walked past the rows of desks and then turned left into a corridor. Donna opened the second door to the right, switching on the lights as she entered.

She turned to face me. "There are a few things to sign. I wish we could skip it, but the bank has to have all its i's dotted and its t's crossed." She rolled her eyes at me in a conspiratorial way. I found myself nodding and rolling my eyes too. "No problem," I said. We were like sorority sisters sharing a mutual dislike for the college dean.

"I'll bring the forms in to you. You need to read and sign them before we can open the box."

"Sounds good. Thank you," I said. She turned to leave.

She took a step out of the room and then spun around to face me. "By the way, do you have the forms we require?" I pulled out Kevin's death certificate and a copy of his will from my purse and handed them to her. She took them without looking at them and then left me alone in the room.

The room was stark white. Fluorescent lighting glared down from above. Two large, framed watercolors, painted in forgettable pastels, hung on two of the walls. A desk and chair sat against the far wall. A small photocopier stood in the corner, a wastebasket beside it.

I sat in a chair and waited.

I heard a soft knock, and Donna entered holding a file folder. "Take your time going through these, and sign at the bottom of page four." She handed me the folder. "Normally we require all kinds of additional ID, but we'll just make a copy of your driver's license. I'll vouch for the rest. When you're done looking over the papers and have signed, dial 232 on the phone. That's my extension."

Four pages of legalese. Who would read through four pages just to open a safe-deposit box? "Wait," I said. I took the file and turned to page four. I signed my name and handed the file back to Donna. "Done."

Donna took the file, frowning at it like she was no longer sure what it contained. "All right. Follow me."

She led the way into a vault containing row upon row of tiny numbered doors that covered three full walls from floor to ceiling. It appeared the boxes came in at least three sizes. The smallest doors were rectangles, three or four inches high and eight or so inches long. Others were large squares, the size of an award plaque. The largest ones were the size of a desk drawer.

Donna pointed at number 123. It was one of the midsized ones, which surprised me. I was expecting a small box where he would have kept a copy of the mortgage, insurance, a few investment papers, and not much more.

Donna pointed to the keyhole. "It's a two-key system. I insert and turn my master key first. Then you use your key to open the door. I'll remove the box for you and take you back to the room we were in before. Your key will also open the box." She inserted her key, turned, and then withdrew it. Then I stepped up, inserted my key and turned, and opened the door. The box itself was set into the wall like a drawer. Donna grabbed the handle and pulled it out of the wall. "Follow me," she said again as she marched out of the vault.

Back in the room Donna set the safe-deposit box down on the desk. "Take as long as you like." She indicated the phone. "And remember, when you are done, call extension 232."

I waited several beats after Donna left before I lifted my key to the lock. The hinge was on top of the box, so it opened like a chest. I flipped the lid open and peered inside. The box wasn't even half full. Various papers, envelopes, and official-looking documents were spread around at the bottom of the box in no apparent order. Why did Kevin have such a big box? I reached in and lifted out an envelope with the name of the bank on it. Inside were the mortgage papers with details of the insurance. I put the documents in my purse. The mortgage was paid in full now, through Kevin's insurance policy, but it brought me no joy to know this.

I sat on the chair and reached into the box again, grabbing the next document on the pile. I moved slowly, methodically. I examined each item in its turn. I didn't bother looking into the box as I reached in for the next paper, then the next. Which is why I didn't see it until I had gone through over half of the contents.

Something sparkled from the far corner of the box. Something metal, stainless steel maybe. I reached in and pulled out a skinny digital camera.

I wouldn't have been more surprised if I had pulled out a hissing cobra. The front of the camera told me it was 8.1 megapixels and came equipped with optical zoom. I turned it over. Most of the back was made up of a viewing screen. There were two small buttons above the screen, one with a green arrow, the other a red picture the shape of a camera. There were other dials and buttons on the camera, with markings that meant nothing to me. I found the *On/Off* button on the top of the camera and pushed it. I was treated to a view of my feet on the viewer screen. I pushed another button and took a picture of my feet. I turned one of the dials. Nothing special happened. I pushed on the button with the green arrow and a picture appeared on the screen. This one didn't look like the one I had taken of my feet. It was framed by what looked like a reel of film, giving it the appearance of a scene from a movie. Maybe it was a movie. The picture inside the film reel was of a room I didn't recognize. A chair, in front of beige curtains. I pushed another button and the screen went blank.

I pushed several more buttons, none of which brought the video back. Then I hit the green arrow button and not only did the picture come back, but it came to life.

When Kevin's voice leapt from the camera, I nearly dropped it. "Room 1842. Check it out. Ugliest hotel room I've ever seen." The image panned around the room, zooming in on the mini fridge, the coffeemaker, the closet. The bed came into view, rumpled covers, pillows tossed here and there. I heard Kevin's voice. "Ah, now the bed. Here, in glorious contrast to this ugly room, we find the most beautiful woman I've ever seen." A long, bare leg came into view. I heard giggles. The camera followed the bare leg up until it disappeared under the covers. The camera continued its slow ascent, up toward the head. A hand with long, painted fingernails; an arm; a bare shoulder. A voice, "Hey, lover." A face.

My vision blurred with tears so that I could barely make out Donna's face as she smiled into the camera.

28

"I don't understand, Kevin." I'm standing in the foyer of our house, in front of the door. I'm a human barrier, a blockade of flesh and bones.

Kevin crosses his arms across his chest, placing his expensive new suit in danger of developing elbow creases. It's dark blue, nearly black. His tie matches precisely. He looks like a G-man in a B movie. More a costume than a suit. But I don't say this. I also don't tell him how I barely recognize him, how the long hours he keeps is turning him into a stranger. How the way he shakes his head at me makes me want to cry. He pulls a face. "You're being ridiculous."

"Explain it to me again."

His eyes roll up and to the left. "I don't have time for this. I have a dinner meeting."

I throw my hands up. "Your client can wait for a few minutes."

His eyes narrow. "You have no idea what my client can or cannot do. You haven't the first clue about it, Kate."

I swallow hard, my nerves fraying. He's angry, and so am I, but I see the clouds gathering around his head, I see his eyes turn to granite, and I back off a bit. "You're right, I don't know. I need you to explain it to me; I need your help to understand." I hold my hands out, palms facing him, to soften my words, to cool his anger. "Five thousand dollars is a lot of money."

He snorts. "That's your problem, Kate. You honestly think five thousand dollars is a lot of money. It's not. It's chump change in the circles I'm breaking into." He snaps his fingers. "It's a night out to these guys."

I close my eyes and pull in a long breath, steadying my voice. "But you aren't one of those guys, Kevin. You're you. This is us, remember? You and me. We don't spend five thousand dollars on a suit." Despite myself I feel my bottom lip tremble. "You didn't even talk to me first."

He puts a finger under my nose. "Oh great, here come the crocodile tears. Do you honestly expect me to stand here with a client waiting while you have your little boo-hoo? This is crap, Kate." He grabs me by the shoulders and shoves me away from the door. His fingers sink into my flesh.

I grab the lapels of his five-thousand-dollar suit.

He takes hold of each of my wrists and twists opposite ways. I cry out in pain and release his jacket. The material is crushed and wrinkled. He doesn't let go of my wrists.

"You will stop this now. Do you understand me, Kate?" His low voice is like gravel in my ears. He gives me a fast shake. "End this now, or I'll end it for you."

I stare up at him. "What do you mean, end it for me?"

He lets go suddenly and I nearly fall backward. He steps

toward the door, one hand on the knob. "I don't want to do this right now."

Some unknown horror floods my body. "Do what?" It's a whisper.

He shakes his head. "This is the wrong time to talk about this."

I reach out for him, and he takes a step back. I look down at my wrists, red and bruised from his hands, and pull my arms back. "Kevin, no."

His body goes loose, relaxed, and I see it in his face, the decision he's made. I push past him and open the front door. "Just go to your meeting." I flap my hand, shooing him out the door, but he doesn't move. He opens his mouth. I push the door wide open and pull on his arm. "Go, just go."

"Kate, I've been trying to find a way to tell you—"

I clamp my hands over my ears. "You're late. Go."

He gives me a long, searching look, then walks out the door into the darkening evening.

My hands shook as I held the camera. A part of me wanted to throw it down, crush it beneath my heel. But I held on to it with strong, almost protective hands, staring at the images as I hit *Play* over and over again.

Every time I heard Kevin's voice it was a fresh beating, a new assault. But I couldn't stop. Each time the image moved to the bed I held my breath; maybe this time she wouldn't be there. Maybe it would be me instead. Maybe it would be empty. But each time it was her saying, "Hey, lover." It was her smiling up at the camera. Her reaching out for Kevin, imploring him to put the camera down and join her in the bed.

When the clip ended, my finger would hit *Play* again. Some suicidal part of me was searching out every morsel of misery, bathing me in pain.

I watched the scene until I could see each detail in my mind. I closed my eyes and replayed the scene. Each shade of beige. Each surface. Each sound. Each word. I felt sick.

I opened my eyes and felt a fresh jolt of surprise. While absorbed in the video, I'd forgotten where I was. I was in the bank, and Donna was on the other side of the door. My heart skipped a beat, and then started pounding hard, as if I were running a marathon. I stared at the door as if Donna might fling it open at any moment. Nausea swelled in my stomach. My body broke out in sweat. I grabbed the wastebasket and vomited into it.

I wiped my mouth with my sleeve. "I've got to get out of here." I looked at the phone. What was the number I was supposed to dial? No. If I dialed the number—whatever it was—Donna would answer. She would come into the room. She would look at me, speak to me. I glanced at the wastebasket. The air was becoming increasingly unbreathable.

I sat on the chair and set the camera down on the desk. I closed my eyes. Immediately images from the camera sprang up before me. Her leg. Her arm. Her face. I bent over in my chair until my face rested on my legs and sobbed.

After a long while I sat up. A thought came: *Just leave.*

I grabbed the camera and my purse and headed for the door. I glanced back at the room. The safe-deposit box lay open, exposed to the world. Several pieces of paper were scattered on the desk beside it. A terrible odor rose from the wastebasket. I pressed my ear against the door and listened as I turned the knob in slow motion. I heard nothing. I pulled the door open a crack and with one eye peered into the corridor. Empty. Good.

I inched the door open a bit farther and stuck my head out. No one. Good. I slid out of the room and stood in the hall for a moment, getting my bearings. I started at the end of the hallway. Do I turn left or right? I couldn't remember.

The hammering of my heart moved my feet down the hall. I turned right and kept my head down, walking fast toward the main lobby. I glanced up and saw Bunhead's desk ahead of me. I put my head down and sped past her. True to form she never looked up.

I approached the bank's main door and pushed. Nothing happened. The door wouldn't open. Panic filled my lungs, choking me. They had locked me in! I stared at the door in disbelief. Outside a man approached the bank. He arrived at the door and pushed. It swung open silently, admitting him with ease. The door closed behind him while I stood dumbly staring at the sign affixed to the glass. *Pull.* I pulled the door open, stepped out onto the sidewalk, and ran toward my car.

I lurched at the car, throwing my purse and the digital camera into the front seat. I jumped in and went to turn the key. Where was the key? I wasn't holding the key. I grabbed my purse and dumped its contents onto the passenger seat. No keys.

I could barely see through my tears. I groped the contents of my purse. Not there. I hollered out a scream of frustration. I just wanted to get as far away from the bank as possible as fast as I could.

Where were the keys? Did I leave them in the bank beside the safe-deposit box? The thought of having to go back into the bank made my stomach lurch. I thought I might vomit again. I'd walk home if I had to. I wasn't going back in there. *Think, Kate, think. Where are your stupid keys?*

I gripped the useless steering wheel. *Wait.* A distant thought was dawning. "How'd I open the car if I left the keys in the bank?"

I pushed open the door and stepped out, banging my head on the door's frame. With a hand on my quickly swelling forehead, I looked inside the car. The keys were lying on the driver's seat. I'd been sitting on them.

"Idiot," I told myself. And here I'd thought I'd been getting better.

29

I stood on the brakes, screeching to a stop in front of my house. I grabbed the camera and went to the front door, opened it.

"Kevin!" My voice bounced back in the hollowness of the house. It mocked me. I turned my face to the ceiling and screamed. "Come out, Kevin! No hiding now. Now it's my turn to shout." I ran into the kitchen and tossed the camera onto the table. "It's my turn to attack you. Come out, *liar.*"

My body shook with rage as the images on the camera flashed in my mind. The images I had carefully committed to memory.

"What have you got to say to me now, Kevin?" I swore into the silence.

Every step since Kevin's death had to be retraced. I had grieved the wrong things, weighted the wrong losses, held the wrong regrets. Nursed the wrong memories.

I spun on my heels and made a fast dash for the stairs. Taking the steps two at a time, I called out, "I'm coming for you, Kevin."

At the top of the stairs I flung myself against the bedroom door. The frame cracked as the hinges pulled away from the wood. The door flew open so hard the doorknob punctured a hole in the wall.

I advanced to the closet and wrenched the doors open, exposing the soft cotton clothes inside. Kevin had claimed the largest portion of the closet, his silk shirts and ties, his expensive suit jackets needed "room to breathe" so they wouldn't wrinkle. I grabbed at one of Kevin's suits. The jacket pulled off easily, but the pants hung from the wooden rod. I snatched them up and threw them onto the floor behind me. I seized four silk shirts and the silk fabric ripped. I threw them on top of the jacket on the floor, grinned at the shirtless sleeve I held in my hand. I tossed it aside.

Once again I reached into the closet and grabbed a chunk of dress shirts and pulled. Bits of broken hangers flew out at my face, but I brushed them aside and threw the clothes over my head and onto the floor behind me.

I yanked on his tie rack and the nail of my index finger bent backward. I screamed in pain, but attacked the closet yet again. Tears streamed down my face, blurring my vision as I reached in, feeling for anything that was his. I used the palms of my hands to push them off my face. "No more tears," I said, then louder, "No more crying over you, Kevin! I won't get it wrong this time." I pulled down hard on the tie rack and the hanging end snapped off. I turned and hurled the rack across the room. It landed on the dresser, smashing into a framed photo of Kevin taken on our honeymoon, before sliding to the floor.

Panting, I turned and attacked the closet again. I reached deep inside; I took hold of another handful of clothes and pulled them down. A piece of plastic hanger broke loose and caught me on the cheek. I shrieked in outrage and pain. I gazed at the blood on my hand and howled like a mad dog.

I moved to the window and pushed it open. I used the heel of my hand to try to shove the screen out of its frame. It wouldn't budge. I stepped back and in one swift motion flung my leg up and kicked the screen out of its frame. It flapped to the ground below, landing with a soft metal sound.

I stalked over to the middle of the room and grabbed up an armful of clothes. Back at the window I leaned out and shouted, "Talk to me now, Kevin!"

I threw the clothes out the window until they littered the front yard with fabric and broken hangers. Sweating, I snatched up another pile, then another, until nothing remained on the floor.

I swung around, scanning the room, and spied the broken picture frame and neckties near Kevin's chest of drawers. Something under the bed caught my toe. I dropped to my knees and pulled out the leather-bound book on aviation I had given Kevin for our third wedding anniversary. It was thick with dust. Inside I had inscribed *Just you and me, babe, forever.* I pitched it out the window like a Frisbee.

Back at the bed I gathered up bedspread, sheets, and pillows. The faint scent of Kevin stuck to his pillow. I hurled it out the window and sent the rest of the bedding out behind it. I went back for the broken picture frame and scooped it up, cutting my hand on the broken glass. I flung it out the window, listening to the tinkle of glass far below.

I moved to his dresser and pulled open a drawer. His neatly folded clothes mocked me. I wrenched the drawer out from the dresser and dumped his tidy socks out the window. Then I heaved the drawer out the window after them. It hit the driveway with a satisfying crash.

I grabbed the next drawer and heaved it out the window too. Two more drawers followed, each crashing on top of the one before it.

I stood, panting hard, and looking at the hollowed-out dresser. I dragged it to the window as if it weighed nothing. I tipped it, then lifted the bottom, then hurled it out the window. The crack it made when it hit the ground made me smile.

I stood at the open window and listened for his voice. Nothing.

I crawled to the closet and loaded my arms with Kevin's shoes. They too were pitched onto the front lawn. At the back of the closet, lying like a puddle, was Kevin's high school basketball jersey. Number three. He'd worn this jersey through four years and three championship games. He had called it his lucky shirt. I held it to my face, breathing in Kevin's faint scent.

The worn material was soft and cool against my cheek. The deep forest green had long faded to a soft jade. He was wearing this jersey the first time I saw him. He had been shooting baskets in the gym when a friend and I peeked in to watch. We giggled and nudged each other every time he went for a jump shot. He was glorious. It was more than a jersey, more than a high school team uniform. He cherished this faded green tank. For him it represented all he was in his youth, and all he hoped to accomplish as an adult.

I carried it downstairs and into the kitchen. Holding the jersey tightly, I rummaged in a drawer until I found what I was looking for. I went back upstairs and sat in the middle of the bed I hadn't touched in months. A sweet breeze blew into the room. I could hear birds—robins, I thought—singing. A great calm filled my mind. The fury had seeped from my body. I calmly held up Kevin's prized jersey and used the kitchen scissors to cut it into dozens of small pieces.

When I was done, I scattered them around the stripped mattress and floor, cotton petals strewn over the funeral pyre of our bed. I stretched out on the bed. I listened to the silence for a few moments, and fell into a deep sleep.

I awoke to the sound of pounding. I blinked at the ceiling, waiting for it to stop. It did. I heard, instead, the sound of the front door opening. "Kate?" Blair's voice. "Are you here? Are you all right?"

I sat up and raked my hand through my hair. Bits of green cloth fluttered down. Why wouldn't I be all right? "I'm up here."

Blair's footsteps echoed up the stairs and then he appeared at the bedroom door. His face went from concern to horror as he looked around the room. Finally his wide-eyed gaze rested on me. "What happened? Are you hurt?" He walked to the bed and bent down to look at me. His hand brushed my cheek and I flinched as it made contact with a cut on my face. "Who did this to you?"

I gave a short snort. "Kevin."

Blair gripped my shoulders. "Seriously, Kate. Tell me what happened."

I pushed his hands away and got off the bed. Bits of green fabric littered the mattress and carpet. The scissors were lying on the floor. I looked at Blair. "I'm not joking. And why are you here?" Without waiting for his response, I walked out of the room and headed downstairs.

Blair followed. "I was driving by and saw your front yard. What happened out there?"

I opened the front door and walked out across the lawn, wading through ripped clothing and broken hangers. A large shard of wood had been ripped away from one of the dresser drawers and was plunged into the ground like a toy Excalibur.

I moved to the sidewalk. Debris covered the lawn as if the house had sneezed it out.

Blair stood beside me, gazing at the aftermath of my rage. "Please talk to me, Kate."

I turned and took his face in my hands, bringing it close to mine. His eyes questioned me, but I pressed my lips against his in a long, slow kiss. I took my time, feeling the warmth of his lips on mine. I slid my arms around his neck and he curved his arms around my waist. For a moment nothing else existed. Then I felt his hands firm on my arms as he pushed me away.

"Stop. This is crazy. Tell me what's going on."

I stood very still, listening. Nothing. No yelling, no voice, no Kevin. I shrugged. "I got some bad news today. Let's go back inside."

I could feel his frustration as he followed me into the kitchen. "Thirsty?" I said.

Blair's face flushed crimson. He swore under his breath. "No. What's going on?"

I opened the fridge door and peered in. "So you just happened to be in the neighborhood?"

He pawed at his face with both hands. "I drive by your house every day. I have been for weeks. To check on you, I guess."

I took a long gulp from an orange juice carton, then studied Blair. He was breathing hard, like he'd just finished jogging around the block. His eyes were wide with concern or annoyance. I swallowed the juice and it burned down my throat. "I didn't know you did that."

Blair exploded. "Tell me why your front lawn is covered with broken furniture."

I shrugged. "I did that."

"You? Why?"

I was tired, despite my nap. Maybe even delirious. "I went to the bank this morning to empty Kevin's safe-deposit box. I found that." I pointed to the camera sitting on the table.

His gaze followed my finger. I expected him to shrug or say "So what?" Instead he stared at the camera with a look of utter collapse. He closed his eyes, inhaling sharply, like he'd just been stabbed.

"Oh, no," he whispered.

I stared at him in disbelief, nearly dropping the carton. Did he know about the camera? How could he? He stood pale-faced, staring at it. He knew. He'd always known.

With tear-filled eyes he said, "I'm so sorry."

I put the orange juice back in the fridge, then picked up the camera and clicked it on. Blair made no move to stop me. I ignored the video, clicking past it to the next shot. One after another I viewed the shots, mostly of Donna in various poses, smiling, and thankfully, fully clothed.

The date appeared in the bottom right-hand corner of each picture, and the order of the pictures took me back in time. I scrolled and scrolled, mentally blocking the many pictures of Kevin and Donna together, until I came to the picture I was afraid I'd find. In it Blair's arm was stretched out in front, obviously holding the camera.

He was sitting on a couch, Donna on one side of him, Kevin on the other. They were squeezed tight, cheeks pressed together. It was a photo booth sort of picture, one you'd expect to see drop from the slot along with three other equally goofy shots. No one was serious. They were just having fun.

I didn't look up from the camera. "Where was it taken?"

Blair sighed. "My apartment."

"I hate you." I opened the back door. "Get out."

He stood still for a moment, then walked out the door. I watched him cross the yard and pull the back gate closed with a soft click. When he was gone, I stepped outside and walked toward the garage. I noticed the lawn had recently been mowed and the flower beds watered. The bleeding hearts were in full bloom, the hollyhock nearly as high at the roof. Someone had been taking care of my yard.

I stopped about ten feet from the garage, then hefted the camera like a baseball. I pulled my arm back and then hurled it at the garage. Pieces flew in all directions. I went back inside, and closed the door firmly behind me.

30

The elevators opened with a sharp *bing* sound. I hurried down the hall, my sandals making a *thwick-thwack* sound as I walked. I pushed open the door of Suite 3106 and rushed to Sally's desk. It was nearly five o'clock, but she smiled as if she'd been expecting me.

I glanced at the massive door that led to Dr. Alexander's inner office. "Is there a chance—?"

Sally gestured to the chairs that lined the wall. "Take a seat."

I sat, tapping my right foot like a jackhammer. I watched Sally's back as she talked on the phone. I couldn't hear a word.

She hung up the phone and turned to face me. "Dr. Alexander can see you now."

My head snapped back in surprise. "Right now?"

Sally got up and stood beside Dr. Alexander's office door. "Right now." I followed her into the office. She dropped a file on the doctor's desk and then left me alone in the room. I moved to the couch, my usual place, then got up and paced the room. I walked over to Dr. Alexander's desk and sat in one of the two chairs in front of it. Another door opened, and Dr. Alexander appeared, straightening his tie and jacket. He sat across from me and opened the folder on his desk. "Nice to see you again, Kate." He said this while reading from the folder.

I said nothing.

He looked at me. "I was wondering if you were going to show up today. I'm glad you did."

Show up? What was he talking about?

He glanced at his wristwatch. "Late, but here nonetheless."

Late? I tried to remember. Laura-Lea. She had told me last night Dr. Alexander wanted to meet with me. Was it only last night? I opened my eyes and saw Dr. Alexander watching me closely. "Your right leg has a rather violent tremor."

I looked down; my leg jerked like Thumper. I pushed it down with my hand, to still it. "I guess I'm wound up. This morning I found out Kevin had been cheating on me."

He raised an eyebrow. "That is terrible news. I can see how that would upset you." He watched me for a long moment, then opened a drawer and pulled out a prescription pad. He scribbled on the pad, ripped the page off, and slid it across the desk. "It's mild, but I think it's all you need right now. You drove in yourself?"

I stared at the prescription on the desk. "Yes. Mild what?"

Dr. Alexander leaned back in his chair. "Sedative. It'll help you relax."

I shook my head. "I don't want to relax."

"You need to."

I held my palm up in a stop-right-there gesture. "Have you ever gone hiking? Kevin and I went hiking on a trip to the Rockies not long after we were married. He took me on this long path way up high on the mountain. He said I'd love it, but I didn't. We got off the marked trail and Kevin couldn't find it again. He lost the bear bells—the ones you're supposed to shake while you walk so you don't sneak up on a bear and get eaten. The day turned cold and we weren't dressed for cooler temperatures. I twisted my ankle and it swelled up bigger than my head." Dr. Alexander opened his mouth to interrupt me, so I raised my voice. "The point is, as miserable as the hike was, as painful as it was to walk on my sprained ankle, I needed to do it. I had to get back to our campsite—to safety.

"That's what I need to do now, Dr. Alexander. I need to keep walking; press on so I can get through this."

His chair squeaked. "Kate, I want to help you, but it seems you won't let me. You miss appointments, you won't follow the medicine regime I set out, and now you're refusing a second prescription. You say you want my help, but you ignore my advice. It makes me wonder if you really want to get better."

My face flushed hot. "Of course I do. But did you hear what I said? What I just found out? You can't expect me to be relaxed."

He pressed his palms flat on the desk. "I understand, Kate. And I'm sorry about your news. But still, you're hearing voices, Kate. No amount of talk therapy is going to cure that symptom."

"One voice," I screamed. "Not voices. Just one. Just Kevin's rotten, lying, cheating voice." I balled my fists by my side. Why couldn't anyone get it right?

Dr. Alexander sat in silence as I bawled on his desk. After a moment he pushed a box of tissues at me. I took one and blew my nose. "I'm sorry. I shouldn't have yelled."

He nodded once. "S'okay."

I looked up at him through wet lashes. "I want you to listen to me, to believe me."

"I do believe you, Kate."

I blinked at him, deflated. "And if I don't take the medication …?"

Dr. Alexander folded his hands in front of him. "Then it would be best for you to seek a new doctor."

A shock ran up my spine. "New doctor?"

His expression was blank, unreadable. "If you refuse to follow my treatment regime, I don't see how I can help you."

The sunlight assaulted my eyes as I stepped out of Dr. Alexander's high-rise building. I squeezed my eyes shut and felt my thoughts, like ticking bombs, circling me.

Mobs of people rushed around, moving as if with a single heartbeat, in and out of buildings, on and off buses. Downtown pulsed and throbbed. A woman yelled into a cell phone, a man with a briefcase bumped shoulders hard with another man and hurried on. A hot-dog stand manned by a grubby-looking guy who may or may not have been homeless. But I was alone in the throng. Alone with my contemplations, my musings, my stupidity.

After Dr. Alexander's ultimatum I was disorientated, unable to adjust to the reality that I wasn't the only person left on earth. That I wasn't the only thing that mattered.

Dr. Alexander's warning—threat?—hung on me like a damp towel. There were requirements, expectations I had to fulfill if I ever wanted to be considered well. It seemed what constituted "well" was a process best left to the professionals. So many rules I hadn't learned.

What had Kevin's requirements been? What had he expected of me in order to keep him from having an affair?

I stood on the bustling street corner and gulped in a lungful of air. Across the courtyard the hot-dog vendor dropped a wiener on the sidewalk and, as he bent to retrieve it, his customer walked away, shaking her head. He straightened up and looked around, bun in one hand, frankfurter wobbling on the end of his tongs in the other. His expression said, "Where'd she go?" He looked across the courtyard and we accidentally locked eyes. He shrugged. I shrugged back. Sometimes it's a small thing that causes someone to walk away from you.

That evening I drove out of the city, turned down exit twenty, and noticed a billboard. A man's face, fat and smiling, filled more than half the board. He pointed Uncle Sam–style at the traffic below. Beside the gigantic head was his name, Reverend J. D. Slater, and a slogan, *Miracle Working Power—Today!* Under that, a phone number. I chanted the number, memorizing it as I took the turnoff to Greenfield. I could use a miracle today.

Back at home I stood on the front sidewalk and surveyed my lawn. A riot of silk shirts waved in the breeze. The lawn covered in bits of bedroom debris that I would have to clean up. My only regret was I had lacked the strength to hurl them farther.

I pushed into the house, dragging my feet as if I suddenly weighed five hundred pounds. I'd have to clean up the mess sooner or later. I shut the door behind me, blocking the view to my front yard. *Later.* I sloughed to the kitchen, found the prescription for the antihallucinogen on the counter, and shoved it in my purse, a germ of an idea forming.

"Kevin?" I called his name in a loud voice, and then waited. Silence pulsed back at me. I walked to the living room. "Kevin? Are you really gone, or just hiding?"

I climbed the stairs to my bedroom. I crawled onto the bare mattress, rolled onto my side, and stared through the open window. I had expunged all obvious traces of Kevin from the room, had flung them from a great height. Now I stretched out on the bed and closed my eyes. As I fell asleep, two things were clear. My soul had been swept clean of Kevin. And I wasn't happy about it.

❧

The next morning I stuffed Kevin's ruined belongings into large green garbage bags. At one point a shard of plastic or wood bit into my hand and pierced my palm. I swore at it and kept going.

As I worked, I weighed the two theories of mental health. On the one hand Dr. Alexander believed a regimen of medication and talk therapy would, in time, cure me. Well, he'd never used the word *cure.* Improve? I kicked at a bit of smashed dresser drawer. Did Dr. Alexander believe I could be cured? That the pills would right the chemistry of my brain for good, solving all my … delusions, he called them delusions. And what had caused these delusions in the first place? Memory loss, Kevin's voice blistering with rage, then soothing with sexual advances.

On the second scale was the question Eliza Campbell had

introduced, that my issue was a spiritual one and had a spiritual cause. That the voice had more to do with a plugged connection to the eternal than it did with faulty wiring in my brain. But if that were the cause, what was the cure? What did spiritual people do when their pipes rusted out? Chant? Drink herbal tea?

On the one scale sat a regimen of pills and therapy that promised a cure, but offered no clue of the cause. On the other scale the cause was faulty connection, crossed spiritual wires, but I had no idea how to proceed toward a cure.

I shoved three shoes into the overflowing green garbage bag. It wasn't simply that Eliza Campbell's spiritual theory offered me a cause, it was the idea that I could fix my problem myself, without relying on medications. All I had to do was find someone who knew how to clean out people's spiritual causeways. I recalled Rev. J. D. Slater's phone number. *Miracle Working Power—Today!* I dragged a garbage bag into the back alley and tossed it on the pile. I went inside to call Rev. J. D. Slater and make an appointment for my miracle.

Two days later I turned into the parking lot of Rev. J. D. Slater's church. It was a massive building that from the street resembled a concert hall more than a church. I drove through a huge parking lot. A smattering of cars huddled near the front door. I parked beside a green Jaguar, wondering when I'd last seen a Jaguar. No one I knew could afford one. I got out of my Ford Focus and walked toward the main entrance. A large banner above the doors read *Welcome to Rhema Word Victory Church.*

I tried all three sets of double-glass doors, but they were all locked. I checked my watch. Was I early? No, I was right on time.

I stepped back and surveyed the doors. Maybe these were Sunday morning doors and there was some other entrance people used on weekdays.

I was about to walk around the building in search of another door when I spotted a doorbell set into the brick wall beside one of the doors. I punched it with my finger. Nothing. I pushed it again, holding it for several seconds. Still nothing. I cupped my hands around my eyes and peered through one of the glass doors.

It was like glimpsing paradise. Gleaming white marble pillars and floors blinked in the sunlight. The foyer was as large as the gym at Glen Hills Community Center. A tiny figure came into view—a woman with a pixie haircut gone terribly wrong. Her mouth formed what looked like a permanently etched frown. She unlocked the door and poked her head out. "Yes?"

I handed over the paper with Rev. Slater's name and phone number on it. "Hi there. I have an appointment with, uh, The Reverend?"

Pixie Woman pushed the door open and stepped back as I entered. She closed the door and locked it again. With military precision she spun on her heels and marched back into the church, waving an arm at me, indicating I should follow.

If she hadn't been walking at a breakneck pace, I would have taken time to ogle the surroundings. The lobby was expansive, with ceilings that soared, trying to reach God Himself. Light from the glass doors, as well as from a dozen or so skylights, poured in from every angle. I suppressed the urge to touch the leaves of one of the several massive trees that dotted the lobby. Each one was planted in its own dirt hole carved into the marble floor. The air was cool, almost chilly, despite the soaring temperature outside. Pixie Woman's low heels made a loud clacking sound as she strode toward our destination. The word *palatial* drifted through my mind.

Ms. Pixie ushered me into a waiting room and pointed to a chair. "I'll let The Reverend know you're here." She disappeared down a hallway.

I sat and scanned the magazines on the table in front of me. *Charisma, Spirit Led Woman, Pray!, Prophecy in the News.* I crossed my arms and sat back in the chair. After a long moment Pixie Woman clomped back into the room and took a seat behind a teeny desk. She turned to a computer screen and began typing.

I stared at her profile. "Excuse me—"

She spun in her chair. "The Reverend is praying and will see you when he's done." She indicated the phone by her elbow. Apparently he would call. She returned to her typing.

Huh. Praying. Maybe I should try praying too? This was a church, after all. God could be lurking around any corner. I shifted in my chair and lowered my head like I'd been taught as a child in Sunday school. I searched my memory for a prayer. There was one that started, *Now I lay me down to sleep.* Not helpful. I searched further: *God is good, God is great ...*

I squeezed my eyes shut, trying to dredge up the rest of the prayer. *Let us thank Him for this food.* I sighed and opened my eyes. How, exactly, does one pray? How do you know if it's a good time to talk to God? Maybe it's like a university lecture hall and you have to raise your hand and wait your turn until the professor points to you.

I lifted my eyes to the heavens—actually to the soaring ceilings of the church, they must have been twenty feet high, and pictured God pointing down at me, a gigantic finger in the sky, and a loud voice like an earthquake booming out, "Your turn, Kate Davis."

The idea made me moderately hysterical. *Calm down, Kate.* Of course it didn't work like that. Get a grip. Besides, who was I to think I could just prance up to God and start talking? Like, hey, God, I know we haven't talked much in the past twenty years, but I sure could use a favor.

I chewed my fingernail. Better to wait for The Reverend. He could introduce us, God and me. Like a mutual acquaintance at a party. He would chat us up until we were both comfortable, and then he'd leave God and me alone for a while.

Did I even believe in God? I squirmed on my chair. I didn't *not* believe in God. I'd never stomped my foot and said, "That's it! Proof of the nonexistence of God. Case closed." But miracles? When was the last time I'd seen a miracle? Or knew someone who had? No, no, I was fine. I wasn't asking to walk on water, I only wanted clarity, a path I could follow. Just an ordinary miracle. I just had no idea how to get one on my own. That's why I needed The Reverend.

Pixie Woman startled me out of my musings. "The Reverend will see you now."

I followed her to J. D. Slater's private office. She waved me in, and I came face-to-face with the man himself. He was a mountain, capped with greasy black hair instead of snow. He quivered toward me, a glacier on the move. His suit strained with the effort of containing his bulk.

He held out a massive paw, his voice deep and booming. "I *am* the Reverend Slater." He waved Pixie Woman away. "Sit, and tell me what troubles you today." He sounded as if he might burst into a sermon at any moment.

We sat on opposite sides of his desk. He eased himself into his chair, wheezing with the exertion. The chair creaked alarmingly, but held.

I chewed my lip. Where to start? I shifted in my seat, feeling more uncomfortable by the minute. Maybe this was a bad idea. No, I'd thought about this a great deal before I called. Just jump in, like a swimming pool. "Well, I've been hearing my dead husband speak to me."

The Reverend made a *humph* sound, not unlike the sound I'd heard a rottweiler make once. He moved his head, perhaps a nod, his head rolled up and down, folds of fat undulating under his chin. They momentarily hypnotized me. I blinked rapidly. "I was. But I'm not anymore." I spoke quickly. "I got rid of him, chucked him out the window, so now he won't talk." I frowned. Was I making sense?

He narrowed his eyes until they were almost invisible in the meat of his face. "The voices have stopped?"

"Voice. One voice." I held up a finger like a primary school teacher. "Yes, it's stopped. That's why I came to you. My psychiatrist thinks pills are the answer, but I've come to believe I'm experiencing a spiritual thing ... problem."

The Reverend made a deep rumbling sound. "I agree with you. This is spiritual. Doctors can't help you. Pills won't help."

I cocked my head. He was saying the same things I had said, but why did I get the feeling we weren't speaking the same language?

"Uh, certain things have happened in the past week that caused

Kevin to stop talking to me." I leaned forward, and he did too, spilling over onto his desk. I sought out his eyes, deep within the fleshy pockets of his face. "I need Kevin to speak to me again."

The Reverend fell back in his chair with a tremendous thud. "You've come here to ask for help in talking to the dead?"

His incredulous tone shook my already wavering confidence. "Well, just Kevin. I need to get some answers—set some things straight. He's the only one who can do that."

He seemed to think about this. He didn't move for a long moment, not even blinking. Then he folded his hands on his desk and peered at me. "I've spoken to God about this matter, and God has directed me."

When did he speak to God? Just now? I'd missed it. God directed him? How?

He held up a fat finger. "I'm going to ask you some questions. Your answers hold the key regarding how we'll proceed today."

I squirmed in my chair. He made it sound like a pop quiz I'd forgotten to study for.

He sat back. "Are you willing to attend services here for a minimum of six weeks?"

I started. "Six weeks? Here? Uh, I don't live in the city. It's a long drive to get here." He fixed me with a steady gaze. "I mean, I suppose I could."

"A church alive is worth the drive. Jesus isn't going to help you unless you are obedient to His Word."

"Word?"

"Do you believe the Bible is the literal and inerrant Word of the Living God?"

I tried to dredge up what I knew of the Bible. Fragments of stories and images flashed then faded in my mind. Stories of good guys and bad guys. A man named Noah, or Jonah, or maybe Moses, floating in an ark filled with animals; another man, being thrown from a boat (the ark?), and getting swallowed by a whale, a man in a den of lions. I had heard these stories in my childhood, when my parents would drop my sister and me off at church for Sunday school. I remembered believing these stories with the same kind of faith I had in Santa Claus. A wink-nudge-wouldn't-it-be-nice faith.

"I don't know. I've never thought about it before. I guess it could be." I thought of the book in Eliza Campbell's waiting room, the *Bhagavad Gita*. Wasn't that supposed to be scripture too? One look at Rev. Slater told me not to ask him.

He narrowed his eyes, but he was smiling, a Pillsbury Doughboy grin. "Have you exposed yourself to the demonic world by the practice of séances, witchcraft, or Ouija boards?"

My heart began a panicked tattoo. "What? No, of course not." I'd sat on sateen cushions in Eliza Campbell's elaborately painted counseling office, I'd sang and danced in my kitchen with my deceased husband, but that was a far cry from séances and Ouija boards.

He stood up. "Can you confess with your mouth, right here and now, that Jesus Christ is your Lord and Savior?"

I shrank in my chair. "I'm not sure I understand …"

He moved around his desk toward me. "Do you know you're a sinner who needs a savior?"

Sinner? He didn't even know me.

The Reverend stood in front of me as I sat in my chair. "It's

clear to me what's happened. I can see the path your feet are on."
He slapped his hands on the top of my head. Pressing down hard he
shouted, "Come out!"

My neck buckled until my chin pressed into my chest. What was
he doing? I clawed his wrists. "Stop!" I screamed, but the word stuck
in my throat. Only strangled, garbled noises escaped.

Rev. Slater sounded as if he were being choked as well. He hollered strange words, like a different language. He clamped a meaty
hand over my mouth and shouted, "Come out of her, foul devil!"

Devil? Terror swept through my body. I couldn't breathe.
Desperate, I tore at his hand, but he only pressed harder. "I command you to come out, you lying spirit!" He shifted his weight from
side to side, his hands like a vise around my head and face; we rocked
in frenzied rhythm. I pushed at his arms, screaming through the
meat of his palm.

I tried to slide off my chair and slip out from under his immense
weight, but he dug into my face and skull and held me in place. He
bellowed a mixture of English and gibberish. Desperate for a breath
I kicked his shin. He stomped his foot like a mad bull, but kept
rocking me from side to side, faster now until I could feel the metal
frame of the chair dig into my hip, first the right, then the left. I
kicked with both legs and managed to connect with his kneecap. He
roared with pain and tightened his grip on my head. "You can't win,
foul spirit. I claim this life!"

He's trying to kill me. I begged him, pleaded for my life, but his
hand over my mouth pushed the words back down my throat. I
needed air. Black spots exploded before my eyes. My hands dropped
to my side and I felt my body go limp. Surprisingly The Reverend

loosened his grip and then let me go. I slumped over and raked in gulps of air, a sob of relief escaped my throat.

He took two steps back from me. "Now I'm going to lead you in prayer."

I jumped up and ran for the door.

31

I put my pencil down and looked out the kitchen window. I felt like a wrung-out sponge. Exhaustion radiated from some deep pit inside me. The early September Sunday morning sun was bright through the window. I blinked at its impersonal brilliance.

I glanced down at my journal and the list I had spent the morning writing. It contained the names of everyone I had once believed I could trust. Kevin. Heather. Blair. The Reverend. I touched the bruise by my mouth with a gentle finger, still there after two days. It was a deep purple blotch from the corner of my mouth down to my chin and halfway across my jaw. I had gone seeking help, and ended up injured.

I included Dr. Alexander's name too. It irked me to think that I was only allowed access to the halls of mental health as long as I complied completely with his orders. Sure, I hadn't even tried the medications, but he hadn't tried things my way either. Mental health should be a partnership. I half blamed him for what had happened with The Reverend.

I liked my list. It helped me remember. It told the truth. I picked up the pencil and drew a dark cloud at the top of the page.

I hadn't put Donna's name on the list because she wasn't someone I had trusted in the first place. Still, her name sent shocks of fury
through my veins. Her smug, cool face as she waved to the camera.
Lover. The word had rolled off her tongue, effortless, as if she and
Kevin were two kindred souls, brought together by their mutual passion for conservative investment portfolios.

It shocked me how comfortable Donna seemed lying in that
bed. No nervous tittering, no guilty looks or pleading to turn the
camera off, *What if someone were to find out?* Instead she'd acted like
Cleopatra, ruler of all she surveyed. As if she had the right to be
there.

The woman had violated my life. Broken into it. But it wasn't as
if she'd picked the locks. She'd been invited through the back door
by the man I had trusted most.

I clenched my fists, snapping the pencil I held in two. Waves of
humiliation crashed down, one after another. I tossed the broken
pencil into the garbage and stared out the window.

Kevin's voice had said that I'd forgotten too much. But my
memories felt closer now. I could sense them circling from above,
like birds of prey.

I glanced at the list of names I'd written. Names of people who
told me they loved me. People I'd spent my life loving. Liars, every
one of them. Where would I go to find truth? I glanced up at the
clock. If I left now, I'd catch Jack before church was over. I grabbed
my car keys and headed out the door.

It was nearly noon when I inched my way into the gym and stood near the back. It had taken a long time in the car to apply enough makeup to hide the bruises left by The Reverend's giant hand two days ago.

Sunday at Glen Hills Community Center looked much like Jack had described it. A motley crew had assembled, some sitting in folding chairs, others milling near the back where I stood. Jack was wrapping up a talk about the highway to heaven.

An older man, wearing baggy coveralls and a yellowing smile, shook a paper cup at me and whispered, "Want some java?" He had the bulbous nose of a lifetime drinker; red and purple veins snaked across the center of his face. He didn't seem bothered that I had come in right near the end of the service. He could have been some-one's grandpa, if someone's grandpa had spent too many years at the bottom of a tequila bottle. Still, he looked sober now, clear-eyed. Shabby, but not dangerous. I shook my head and gave him a feeble smile as I slinked away. He smelled strange, like he'd recently bathed in lavender-scented mothballs.

At the front of the gym, standing on a makeshift stage con-structed of large wooden boxes, Jack, in jeans and a white T-shirt, was speaking into a microphone. His voice crackled through a single amplifier.

"The road to heaven isn't much of a road," he was saying. "It's more like a dusty trail, roughly cut out through the underbrush. Most people don't even notice it. It doesn't look like a path at all, so they walk right by. Others see it, but don't go down it because it's ugly. Dirty. Difficult. Overgrown. If they took the road to heaven, their progress would be slow, maybe immeasurable. They'd have to give up a lot because the path is narrow. So there's no room for bag-gage." Jack paced for a moment. "We've talked about all these things this morning. But maybe you're asking, 'Why would anyone decide to take an impossible road like this?'" Jack looked out into the gym and our eyes met over the heads of the people sitting in chairs. He smiled. "Because it leads to life."

"Baloney," a voice called from the audience.

Jack tore his eyes away from mine and gazed at a man in the second row. To my surprise he smiled. "How so?"

The man stood up. "I've heard that pie-in-the-sky crap my whole life. It's the same old story—*Do as I say and there'll be big reward in heaven.* Why should I give up my life here and now, just on the promise of some religious nut?"

Jack frowned. After a moment he said, "You shouldn't."

It was as if everyone in the room took a step backward. There was an audible gasp from the congregation. I wished I could see the man's face. "Exactly," he said.

Jack said, "But, tell me something, what is it exactly you'd be giving up in the 'here and now'?"

The man crossed his arms. "My freedom, for one thing. You reli-gious nuts like to keep people on a short leash." He swayed slightly and grabbed the back of the chair in front of him.

Jack nodded. "Ah, right. Freedom. Freedom to come and go as you please. Freedom to do anything you like without anything like guilt getting in the way."

The man held up a finger of his own. "I'm a good person. Sure, I've made mistakes, who hasn't? But I've got no regrets. I've lived my life on my own terms. Guilt is just something you religious guys made up."

Jack cocked his head. "Yeah, maybe it is. Or, maybe it's something God can use to get our attention. It seems to me the things people cling to in the name of freedom are the very things that have those people locked in chains."

The man sat down hard, waving a dismissive hand toward Jack, signaling the conversation was over.

The exchange amazed me. I'd never thought of a church service as a place you could speak your mind. Rev. J. D. Slater's fat face filled my mind. I doubted he would have tolerated someone questioning him. *Probably would have shot the guy.*

Jack smiled at the group. "It's lunchtime." He said a short prayer, then told everyone to go home. He jumped down from the platform and stopped in front of the argumentative man, offering his hand. The man shook it and they spoke for several minutes. When the man turned to leave, he was smiling.

Jack caught my eye and sauntered toward me. "Hey, don't run away. I need to help get this stuff packed away, but if you'll stick around, I'd love to chat."

"Maybe we could have lunch?" I said.

Thirty minutes later Jack and I sat across from each other at the Happy Eater Chinese restaurant. The food looked wonderful, but I wasn't a happy eater.

I pushed chow mein around my plate. "I literally don't have anyone else to talk to."

Jack shoveled an astonishing amount of moo goo gui pan into

his mouth and nodded. He swallowed hard. "I'm honored. You talk. I'll listen—that's all I can promise you. Beyond that, well, I'm not much help."

I raised an incredulous eyebrow. "Really? That's refreshing. I've spent the last few months talking with people who think they know everything, and it hasn't helped me much. But you're a pastor. How come you don't believe that you hold the truth of the ages in your back pocket?"

Jack stood up and reached his hands into his pockets, pulled them inside out so the material hung down in front, white and empty. He turned his open palms toward me, an imitation of a vaudevillian beggar. "I guess I missed out somewhere along the way." He sat down and scooped fried rice into his mouth.

I sipped my water. It was warm. "I don't think so. I saw how you talked to that man this morning. You didn't even get upset when he questioned everything you'd been talking about."

Jack lifted a shoulder. "They're all good questions. And anyway, he's come around a few times in the past few months. He's a drinker. Lonely, I think." He paused to shove more food into his mouth. Apparently he'd slept through the parental lecture to chew your food twenty times before swallowing. He waved his fork. "He's just trying to figure it all out. I wouldn't be helping him much if I yelled at him for disagreeing with me." He gave me a mock serious look. "But this is supposed to be about you, and here I am doing the talking."

"Is he a sinner?"

Jack paused, his water glass suspended halfway to his mouth. "I'm probably not qualified to say. I see he has problems, yes." He looked far off for a moment. "God is holy," he said quietly, almost to himself.

"Am I a sinner?"

He thumped his glass on the table. "Kate, where is this coming from?"

I gently touched my fork to the bruise near my mouth. "Two days ago I went to see this preacher—a self-proclaimed miracle man—for help. But when I explained why I was there, he called me a sinner." My eyes burned with unshed tears at the memory of the other things The Reverend had said and done to me.

Jack reached across the table, his hand falling just short of touching my hand. "What preacher?"

"Rev. J. D. Slater. He has a huge church over by—"

Jack interrupted. "I know where the church is. That's my father's church."

32

I made a strange sound, like a cat horking up a fur ball. "Your father?"

He tapped his chest. "I'm J. D. Slater Jr."

"I can't believe it," I said. There was something repulsive about the idea the man sitting across from me had been raised by The Reverend.

Jack leaned forward. "What happened?"

"He hurt me," I blurted. *In the name of God.*

Jack looked startled. "Hurt you?"

"He asked me a bunch of questions about the things I'd done, and before I knew what was happening, he was standing over me, one hand on my head, the other over my face." I ran two fingers down my chin, reliving the pressure of The Reverend's meaty hand pressing into my face, covering my nose and mouth. I inched my chair away from the table.

He pushed partway off his chair, hands on the table, leaned in, and squinted. "You're bruised."

I looked away, ashamed somehow of the marks on my face. As if I had been responsible for them. Yet I wanted him to see them, a witness to my encounter with his father's God. "I covered it with makeup as best I could." I stole a glance at him.

Jack sat down hard, as if he'd deflated. "Kate, I'm so sorry."

I nodded, but in my mind, I was back there, reliving the incident. "He shouted, called me filthy." My lip and chin trembled. "He said God had talked to him, shown him that I was a sinner. Is that what you believe, Jack? Would you say I'm a sinner?"

Jack's chin dropped to his chest; he squeezed his eyes shut. "I'll never call you names, Kate."

"Obviously your father's God hates sinners like me."

His hands clenched to fists on the table. A whisper. "No, Kate—"

I could almost feel his giant hands rocking me side to side, his deep voice rolling over me like an endless echo. "He kept yelling 'Come out!' as if he thought I was—" I couldn't bring myself to say the word. "My life has fallen to pieces and God's answer, it seems, is to blame me."

He kept his head down, jaw pulsing as he bit down over and over. "God loves you."

Love? What kind of love was it that made The Reverend bruise me? Would love spit words of hate and judgment in the face of someone who had come for help? Is that what love is to God? I shook my head. Was this the kind of love The Reverend had taught to Jack?

"Well, Jack, I don't want anything to do with a God who loves like that."

"It's like a devil gets inside my head sometimes," Kevin says as he runs his hand down my cheek, wiping the tears there.

We're in his car, parked on the side of a street we don't live on, somewhere on the west side of town.

"Let's go for a ride," Kevin had said, and I had jumped up, nearly ran to the car, anxious just to be near him for a while.

Ten minutes into the drive I had said something I shouldn't have. Actually I asked him a question. Sometime between "I do" and today, Kevin had started hating questions. At least the ones I asked. It hadn't even started out as a question.

I said, "You're doing so well at the bank, Kevin. I'm proud of you." And I should have left it there, let it lie, let it go. Should have known he was still upset I'd quit my job. "Don't you think it's time we start our family?"

His reaction was as sudden as a summer storm. He slammed his hand on the steering wheel. Then slammed it again. For a moment he rocked back and forth in his seat, then formed a fist and punched the dashboard. "Why do you do this to me?" he roared. "Push, push, push, that's all you know how to do."

I cowered in my seat, pressing myself against the door. "I just meant—"

He stood on the brakes, throwing me forward. The seat belt burned into my neck and shoulders. The car idled in the middle of the road. After a long moment he pulled the car over to the curb.

I started to cry.

He reached over to touch me and I shrank away without thinking. A flash of pain crossed his face. "Come here." He *touched my chin, my jawbone, my cheek. "It's like a devil gets inside my head sometimes."*

At his confusing words I say nothing. I feel afraid. Afraid of him and his anger. Afraid of losing him and everything we have.

He sits back and puts his hands on the wheel. A long, slow breath pushes out his mouth. "The last thing in the world I want is to hurt you. You know that, right?" He turns to look at me. "You know it, Kate, right?"

I nod. "I know it," I squeak.

He nods, assured. "And yet, here I am, hurting you."

"You didn't hurt me. You hit the dashboard, not—"

He interrupts. "Kate, I want a divorce."

3 3

I stared at the blinking red light on my kitchen phone until it was like a heartbeat in my mind. I had turned the ringer off after my lunch with Jack. That was two weeks ago. Two weeks of hiding out in my house, not knowing what to do. Two weeks ago I thought I could choose between medical therapy and spirituality. Now I had neither. I'd managed to rouse the ire of God by my sin, and Dr. Alexander by my missed appointments.

But instinct told me who had left messages. Mom, Heather, Dr. Alexander's receptionist. I didn't want to talk to any of them. And Maggie. I hadn't spoken to her since right after the car accident. A slice of guilt cut through my gut. She deserved better. They all did. I'd pushed them away for something they had nothing to do with—had no control over. In the case of The Reverend, they didn't even know what had happened.

I snatched the receiver and punched the code to access my messages: Mom, calling twice, just checking in, "Are you eating?"

Then Maggie's voice: "Kate darling, I'm just calling to see how things are going. Your mother tells me you're seeing a doctor in the city. Do call." Maggie again: "Kate? I hope all is well. I understand you're seeing a psychiatrist. I'd love to hear how it's going for you, dear. Do call."

Laura-Lea's voice came on. "You've missed two group sessions. Please call me when you get this message." As an afterthought she said, "I hope everything's okay." I jotted down her number, but what would I say? That I was avoiding group therapy because I didn't want to bump into the pastor that hung around the building?

In truth I longed for group therapy—missed them all, but if I went to Glen Hills, I would see Jack, and I couldn't face him. Couldn't face talking to him about the God he served. The God that didn't want anything to do with a sinner like me. He was an angry bully, not a loving God. Jack said God loved me, but he also said God was holy. The Reverend showed just what holy really meant: angry. God was a bully. And I was getting tired of bullies.

The bullies of the past few weeks stood up for roll call in my imagination: Kevin, my lover and tormentor, killing me with his kindness, and then with his violent words and accusations—and lies. Blair, and his lies of omission. Donna, the worst sort of adversary, hidden in dark corners, sabotaging from invisible places. And now Rev. J. D. Slater Sr., whose only saving grace was his inability to outrun me as I fled for my life.

Yes, it was time to start standing up for myself. To stop letting bullies push me around. I snatched up my keys and headed for my car.

I backed out of the driveway and sat for a moment, deciding if I should do what I was thinking of doing. My gaze followed the line from the front lawn up to my bedroom window, its screen missing. Maybe there really was a devil in me.

I drummed my fingers on the steering wheel. The Reverend seemed to believe there was.

I clutched the steering wheel, hands shaking. I tipped my head back against the headrest and tried to clear my mind. A question floated to the surface: *Why no phone message from Heather?* It wasn't like her not to call.

I swatted the question away and put the car in drive. I had more pressing matters to consider, like confronting the harlot who had slept with my husband. I steered the car toward downtown, toward First Bank and Donna Walsh.

34

I felt the familiar blast of cold air as I walked into the bank. I resisted the urge to bat it away with my hands. No need to draw undue attention to myself. Especially since my intention was to sneak into Donna Walsh's office without being noticed. I eyed the surveillance camera on the ceiling pointed straight at my face. I ducked my head.

Bunhead sat at her desk, looking down, the *Reception* sign still poised above her. I was glad for her aloof manner. It would make it easy for me to slip by her and find Donna's office.

I only got a few feet past a sign that read *Personnel only* when I heard her sharp "Hey!"

I sped up, made a fast left down a hallway lined on both sides with closed doors. I had no idea which one belonged to Donna. *Why don't they keep their doors open?* I had to read the names on the doors and outrun Bunhead at the same time. I glanced back. She was in hot pursuit, hollering "Hey!" every third step.

I reached the end of the hallway—a dead end—without locating Donna's office. I turned, made what I hoped was aggressive eye contact with Bunhead. I walked toward her. "I just want to see Donna. None of this concerns you."

Undaunted, Bunhead planted her feet, hands on hips. "You can't just barge in here."

I stopped in the middle of the hallway, a few feet in front of her. I needed to see Donna, but antagonizing Bunhead wasn't going to help me get what I wanted. I changed tactics. "We got off on the wrong foot here, and I'm sorry about that. I just really need to talk to Donna. I'm sure it's fine if I just—"

"It's not fine. Donna is in a meeting. She cannot be disturbed. And you have no right to be back here." She reached out as if to take my arm.

I took two steps back. "Disturbed? I have no right? That woman was sleeping with my husband, and you are telling me I have no right?"

She glanced at something behind me. "Keep your voice down."

I balled my hands into fists by my sides. "Don't tell me what to do!" I heard a click from behind me; the sound of a door opening.

I turned. Donna stood in the hall, closing her office door behind her. She eyed me with weary indifference, then looked past me. "I'll deal with this, Linda. Go back to your desk."

Linda made a face that said, "Are you sure?" and then took a few steps backward down the hallway as if inching away from a shootout.

I turned to Donna. "I want to talk to you."

Donna leaned against her door, the personification of impassive. "I figured that part out myself."

We stared at each other in silence, and then I jerked my head at her office. "Can we go in and sit down?"

"No."

I tossed my head back in surprise. "No? You want to stand in the hall and do this?"

Donna sighed. "There is no 'this,' Kate. There's nothing to talk about. You should just go home." I thought she'd go back into her office, but she didn't move. She held up a finger. "There is one thing; you left your driver's license the last time you were here." She arched an eyebrow. "You can pick it up at the reception desk."

I made a fast mental list of all the driving I had done since the day at the bank. *Oh man.*

Donna's eyes ticked through my features one by one. Her dull expression told me what she thought of what she saw. She smirked. "Good-bye, Kate."

I planted my feet. "I'm not going anywhere."

Her eyes narrowed slightly. "I understand you've been on medication since the funeral."

I wouldn't have been more surprised if she'd pulled a gun and demanded, *Your money or your life.* "That's not true."

She crossed her arms. "Really? I have it on good authority."

Authority? Who—?

"You've been hearing voices."

My heart pulsed like water bursting from a pipe. "You don't know anything—"

She pulled a face, like she had swallowed something distasteful. "I know a great deal. From a great many sources. Not the least of which was Kevin."

Where was this coming from? When had I lost control of the conversation? *From the moment you arrived.* "You're sickening."

She sighed. "I'm not. I'm realistic. I see the facts, and not some fantasy."

Fantasy? "I'm not—"

Donna held up a hand. "You act as if it's surprising Kevin would turn to me. His life had changed. I was his mentor, his confidant, and he told me many things. Such as his frustrations with his marriage." She said the last sentence with slow deliberation. "He couldn't believe how thick-skulled you were when it came to making changes. I'm starting to see what he meant."

I felt strange, off center. This wasn't how I intended this conversation to go. I'd come here to confront her; somehow she'd gotten the lead. "You're the one who pushed the changes on him."

She twirled a bony hand in the air. "No. I was the one who noticed Kevin's potential." She shook her head, as if words failed her. "He was something to watch, Kate. His energy. But you never knew that, did you?"

"You seduced him," I said. I was supposed to ask the questions, not her.

She laughed. "Oh please. He pursued me. And no wonder. He was tired of playing house with a woman whose biggest dream—" she tapped her chin with a long finger, "—*only* dream, really, was to be a mommy."

"He wanted a family too."

Donna tossed up a short laugh. "You're still living in a fantasy world. Did you know he put your house up for sale?"

I choked. "I don't believe you."

"That can't be helped." She touched one finger to another, as if she were about to list numerous points. "He'd already arranged for a real estate agent. He'd been planning to tell you; he needed your signature in order to sell. But he passed away before he had the chance."

All the muscles in my body contracted at once. Sell the house? Why would he sell the house? Unless he'd already bought another house somewhere else. And wasn't that always part of the plan? To buy a larger house and start a family? Just because I didn't remember him putting the house up for sale didn't mean he hadn't told me.

I cursed my spotted memory. No, it didn't mean anything. I righted my shoulders, pulling my spine up. "We'd always planned on selling our house. Kevin simply found another one for us and wanted to move quickly." I eyed her. Did she know I was lying? Not lying exactly. Just making it up, based on the bits and pieces I could remember.

Donna pushed away from the door and stood straight, assuming the casual stance of the unaffected. "I've been promoted," she said conversationally. "An excellent position at corporate headquarters in the city."

Why tell me? What did I care if she moved to the city or to a cupola in Tiananmen Square?

She shook her head ever so slightly. "I'd been given the green light to handpick my support staff. Kevin had been at the top of my list."

A jolt ran through my bones. "He was moving us to the city?" I sounded like a lost child. My mind raced, grasping at the darkness of my past for some memory I could use to orientate myself. Nothing.

Surprisingly I noticed a hint of uncertainty creep into Donna's gaze. "The details hadn't been finalized." She shrugged. "Kevin didn't want to hurt you. He had even talked to Blair for advice on how best to break the news to you."

Blair's name rolled off her tongue. Like a friend's name would. Further evidence of how fully she had infiltrated my life.

Donna picked a thread off the arm of her tailored suit. "He was concerned about your situation. He wanted to make sure you would be taken care of. It was touching, really, on some level. His last words were of you."

It was a sucker punch to the solar plexus. I hinged over. *His last words had fallen on her ears.* His dying hand had held hers, sought its warmth and comfort. It was Donna who served as the keeper of his secret thoughts, the priest of his last confession. My lips trembled. I closed my eyes and counted to ten, then twenty. I'd fly to hell in a paper plane before I'd allow myself to cry in front of her. As much as I hated her, hated that I had to ask her, I needed to know.

"What did he say?" I bit out the words.

Her eyes appeared unfocused, as if looking through me. "He said, 'Don't tell Kate.'" She gave a quick shake of her head. "Not very profound for someone's last words, I suppose. But he knew he was dying. He wanted to protect you from the truth, in order to secure your future."

"My future?"

Her head dipped, another nearly imperceptible movement. Her expression clouded. She whispered, "He didn't want there to be an investigation. Insurance companies have extremely stringent rules."

My eyes widened with realization. "The forms I filled out stated Kevin had died at work, at the bank." My stomach churned, debating what to be horrified about first. "He was with you. That's why they didn't give me his belongings. They never had them."

Donna's gaze fell to the floor, silent for a long moment. Then, "It's in your best interest to say nothing," she said quietly, returning to the role of the cool, efficient banker. "The payout on Kevin's insurance policy was so high precisely because they understand he died at his workplace." She lowered her voice. "If they get word of a problem, they'll start an investigation."

I didn't care about any of that. I didn't move. "You have his watch."

She sighed. "I have work."

"You're sick."

Her eyes narrowed to slits. "Stop throwing insults around. It's a difficult enough situation without—"

"I'll say what I please," I hollered.

She leaned forward. "Lower your voice."

I waffled. If I kept provoking her, she'd stop answering my questions. But I was reluctant to relinquish the bit of control I'd managed to gain over the conversation. "I'll pitch my voice where I choose," I said, my voice firm but low.

She looked away, head high. "Go home, Kate. You're like a child."

"You're a thief. And a liar!" I shouted.

Suddenly her office door opened. Someone inside had opened it, but I couldn't see who. Donna took a full step back and glared at whoever it was. "Close the door and sit down. I'll be right in." She gave me a cold look. "We're done here."

"We're done when I say," I said.

"Kate, go home," Heather said as she stepped into the hallway.

I stared at her like a village idiot. What was Heather doing in Donna's office?

Donna put a hand on Heather's shoulder. "It's okay. I'll handle things."

Heather ignored her, taking two steps toward me. "I know this is a surprise—"

My legs shook. "It's not a surprise, it's an ambush." I pointed to Donna, my voice shrill.

Heather held her arms out as if to pull me into an embrace, but

I maneuvered past her and shot toward Donna. I slapped her hard against the cheek.

For a moment she stood wide-eyed with shock, teetering. Then she rocked back and leaned against the wall. Her hand covered her cheek. She screeched, "You hit me!"

Heather pulled me away from Donna. We reeled backward together a few steps, my hand balled into a fist, ready to strike again. Donna howled in what I thought was an overly dramatic fashion. A bright red mark on her cheek swelled. I stared at it, confused. "I only slapped her," I said to Heather.

Heather shook her head. "You punched her."

I scrunched up my face. "No. I slapped her."

Our debate was cut short by the arrival of Bunhead, who marched toward us, pointing like a high school hall monitor. She stopped and moved to one side to make room for the two police officers behind her. The first officer was a man who looked too close to retirement age to be here. The second officer, a younger, nervous-looking man, stood a couple of paces behind. They stopped several feet away, eyes shining with adrenaline.

I didn't think, didn't spend a moment reasoning out the ramifications of my actions. I just reacted. I grabbed Heather and held her in front of me, a human shield.

Heather slapped at one of my hands. "What are you doing?" But I held her fast. She tried to twist out of my grip. "Stop it!"

The first officer, the older one, held a cautioning hand up, his other hand still hovering over his revolver. His fingers twitched.

Gun. The word filled my mind. He had a gun.

I rammed my finger into Heather's back. Maybe they'd think I had my own gun. "Stay back," I cautioned them. I lowered my voice, trying to sound authoritative. But the words poured out thick and growly. I sounded like an obscene phone caller.

Heather reeled up on her tiptoes. "Ow. Are you insane? You're hurting me."

No good. Neither officer moved. One officer's eyes flitted between me and his partner, like he was deciding between Tasering me or making a run for it. As if cued by some unseen Broadway director, they both undid the clip on their holsters and slid their guns out. The older cop spoke, "Take it easy, we just want to talk."

My eyes were riveted to his gun. "I talk better where there aren't weapons pointed at me."

Heather wriggled, trying to face me, "Kate, this is ridiculous. You don't even have a—"

I reached up and hooked my arm around her neck, and pulled her back against me. "Shut up," I hissed in her ear. She made a gagging noise and I eased off her neck a bit. I didn't want her vomiting all over the place.

I turned my attention to the police officers blocking my only way out. "All I want to do is leave." I rammed my finger deeper into Heather's kidney. "And I'm taking her with me."

Except they weren't looking at me. With guns still aimed somewhere near my eyebrows, they were both looking behind me. At Donna. For all my macho hostage-taking maneuvers, I'd forgotten the basic rule of kidnapping: Subdue everyone. I had Heather in a stranglehold, but Donna Walsh …

I turned my head until I could see her in my peripheral. She leaned against the wall, arms crossed, making broad facial expressions at the police officers. She looked the antithesis of panicked. The drama playing out in front of her was barely capable of holding her attention. Not only that, but she was able to move around, say and do anything she wanted. She was completely out of my control.

I turned toward the cops. The older one had inched toward me while I had been looking at Donna, his eyes flashing back and forth between Donna and me. He nodded, advanced a step, nodded, advanced. He held a hand out toward me like he was calling a kitten out of a dark corner.

I eyed the gun. Reality crashed down on me, a tidal wave in a tunnel. There was no way I was getting out of this. No way would they let me waltz out of her with my sister in a choke hold while they waved good-bye and shouted warnings for me to stay out of trouble. I let go of Heather all at once and leapt backward. Heather, unbalanced by her sudden release, teetered and then fell straight down like a pile of laundry. I threw my hands up above my head. "No gun," I shouted, but I was cut off as the full the weight of the older cop slammed into me and knocked me to the floor. My head connected with the carpet—a ridiculously thin weave—but before I could say, "Police brutality," he'd spun me onto my stomach and straddled me, sitting down hard on my back. His knee pressed against the middle of my spine.

He and his partner stood me up. Heather was crying in Donna's arms. Donna patted her on the back and stared at me with a blank expression.

The young officer put a hand on Heather's shoulder and asked, "Are you all right? Are you hurt?" But he was looking at Donna.

Donna moved toward the officers. "She struck me with her fist. I don't think the jaw is broken."

I rolled my eyes. "Oh, please. I barely touched you."

The young cop turned to Donna. "I'll need to speak to you privately about pressing assault charges."

Donna looked directly at the policemen. "There will be no need to press charges. This woman is a psychiatric patient. I have it on good authority"—she turned her gaze toward Heather—"that she is off her medication." She smoothed her already perfect blonde hair and gave the officers a demure, slightly pained smile. She may as well have batted her eyes and said, "Well, I do declare!" Both cops leaned in, hanging on her every word. "She's clearly demented," Donna said. "She needs a doctor."

35

Three days later Dr. Alexander sat tapping his pen on a pad of paper. Apparently he carried those two critical objects everywhere he went. Even to a psychiatric assessment center like the one I was consigned to. On his lap was a file folder with my name on it. My chart. Only in here, they don't call it a chart; they call it a behavior journal, and only mental health professionals could write in it. He fixed me with a pointed stare. "You're in a very dangerous place, Kate."

I slumped on the hard, scratchy couch of the interview room. "You're telling me. My roommate's suicidal and the guy who thinks he's invisible keeps following me around. When I tell him to get lost, he says I can't see him." I shook my head. "Yesterday he stole my green Jell-O. Right off my tray. Just yoink, and he walks away. I'm going to start locking my door."

"I was referring to your mental state. And your legal position."

I made a snorting noise. My legal position was what had brought him here. Because I had already been seeing him, the court appointed him to oversee the assessment of my mental health. *How convenient.*

Dr. Alexander wrote slowly with his medium blue ink pen. "You were nearly arrested for assault."

I raised a weary eyebrow. "Nearly arrested? Is that like being nearly pregnant? Either a person is arrested, or they're not."

"You've narrowly escaped a felony charge—"

I raised my hand high, like a bright student in the front row. "Three charges pending." I gave him a lopsided grin. "It ain't over 'til the fat lady sings."

"And now you're confined to this facility. How does that make you feel?"

How did I feel? I was locked up in a psych ward, with a suicidal depressant for a roommate. She kept going through my purse looking for something she could OD on. Then there was the anorexic who believed her food was being poisoned. To say nothing of the invisible man. And someone with a fair amount of clout had decided I belonged here among them. How did I feel? Unreasonably calm. For the first time in months, I didn't feel a thing. Didn't care. Couldn't make myself care.

One side of Dr. Alexander's mouth jerked upward in amusement, perhaps, or irritation at my silence. "How are you feeling now that you are taking the medication?"

Forced to take it would be more accurate. Twice a day for the last three days, my name had been called over the intercom. I was to go to the dispensary, stand in line, accept my paper cup of pills and glass of water. Then a guard wearing latex gloves would examine the inside of my mouth, shoving his fingers beside my gums, poking under my tongue. Once, a man at the front of the line spit his pills onto the floor. The guard and two orderlies sat him on a chair and poured them down his throat. When my turn came, I swallowed mine.

Dr. Alexander said, "I hope you are beginning to see that by not following my orders you made things worse for yourself."

I stared at my shoes.

"You held your sister at gunpoint."

I raised my finger, cocked my thumb back, and said, "Bang," pretending to shoot off my big toe. "I'm not hearing Kevin's voice anymore, did you know that?"

He sat back in his chair. "It may not have been a real gun—"

"It was my finger!" I said, louder than I intended. "It's not as if I walked into the bank carrying a real gun, or even a fake one for that matter. I didn't plan on any of it to happen the way it did."

Dr. Alexander gave me a steady stare. "In a bank, of all places."

I feigned indifference, picking at the nubby fabric of the sofa. It felt like burlap.

"Your attitude is nothing short of alarming, Kate."

I sat up and raised an eyebrow. "You think this is alarming? You should have been at the bank when those cops had their guns drawn. Talk about alarming."

"Kate," he said, using his deep, authoritative doctor voice. Apparently he was going to try a different tactic. I lowered my chin to my chest and pretended not to listen. He spoke in a low, nearly conspiratorial manner. "I'm disappointed in your recent choices. I was hoping you'd cooperate with this process."

He paused, maybe waiting for me to jump up and shout, "Three cheers for Dr. Alexander and his amazing patience!" I tipped my head back and studied a suspicious-looking crack in the ceiling.

"The only reason you're here, instead of in jail is because the woman you assaulted—" he paused, probably to check the name on his notepad, "—Donna Walsh, defended you. She was adamant they not lock you up. Whatever the issue between you two, I'd say you owe Ms. Walsh a debt of gratitude."

The crack in the ceiling started in the far corner and meandered nearly halfway across the room. I imagined it breaching, opening wide to allow the contents of whatever sat above—beds, desks, filing cabinets—to pour in on top of us. I closed my eyes, waiting for the deluge.

Dr. Alexander's voice rode above the waves. "I see you're not in a talkative mood. That's fine." He paused. I said nothing. "I want you to understand, Kate, I'm required to write up this conversation as part of the information that will be reviewed by the judge."

I opened my eyes and craned my neck around, checking to see if there was a corresponding crack in any of the walls, but I couldn't see any.

"And every other conversation we have until the assessment in complete. The more you cooperate with the process, the better your chances are of walking out of here without facing jail time."

I gave him a look that I hoped said, *You can leave now.*

He slapped the file folder closed and stood. "For as long as you're here, I'll be meeting with you twice weekly, a routine we will also continue after your release." He raised his eyebrows with significance.

I stared at the ceiling until I heard him leave.

36

Kevin and I sit in his Mazda, parked by the side of the road. His face is earnest, but tense. "The last thing in the world I want is to hurt you. You know that, right?" He turns to look at me. "You know it, Kate, right?"

I nod. "I know it," I squeak.

He nods, assured. "And yet, here I am, hurting you."

"You didn't hurt me. You hit the dashboard, not—"

He holds a hand up. "I want a divorce."

It's like a slap; I feel the sting on my face. I take a moment just to breathe. He doesn't mean it. He doesn't want a divorce, even if he doesn't know it yet. Christmas was only a month away; I'd already begun preparing. I had the perfect gift, already wrapped and waiting. I reached out and touched his cheek. "I love you."

He blows out his breath. "I know you do." He turns to me. "I love you, too. But everything is different now."

My heart soars. He loves me. Circumstances change all the time, but he said he loves me. It's all I need. I can live on that statement, use it to nourish myself in days of trouble, or times when his temper turns harsh. I can bathe in it, drink it, wrap it around my shoulders on cold days. I smile. "We've loved each other from the start, Kevin." I reach across the car and take his hand. It remains limp, but he doesn't resist. "And now," I say, pulling his hand over to me, "our love has created something wonderful." I lay his hand on my abdomen.

He stares at his hand for a long moment. Then realization dawns; I watch it ripple up his countenance until his whole face reflects the knowledge. He snatches his hand back, as if burned. "You're—"

I nod, my smile stretching wider.

Kevin doesn't move. I'm not sure he's breathing. For the longest moment he says nothing, does nothing.

Finally he raises his hand, pointing. "Get out." His voice is a low growl.

"What?"

"Get out," he yells, his face becoming purple.

"We're miles from home, I didn't bring my purse, I have no—"

He turns to me, eyes bulging. His hands push me toward the door. I fumble for the handle. I push the door open and tumble out of the car, nearly falling onto the sidewalk. Kevin doesn't wait for me to shut the door. The tires squeal as he hits the accelerator and peels off down the street.

The day after my meeting with Dr. Alexander, I went to the recreation room to meet Heather and Mom. Heather was sobbing quietly into a tissue as she sat on a nubby couch. My mother sat ramrod straight beside her, dry-eyed, and patted Heather's knee every few moments. I moved to an equally utilitarian straight-backed armchair across from them, speechless.

Except for Heather's occasional gasps and snorts, we were quiet.

What could I say to my family who had come to visit me in a locked psychiatric center? What conversation could I make? Sure, Mom, there are bars on the windows, but they make terrific cheese-cake for dessert every second Thursday of the month!

"It's not as bad as it seems," I finally said to both, or neither, of them.

Heather's head jerked up from her tissue. "Not bad? Are you crazy?"

"Apparently that's for the judge to decide."

My mother pursed her lips and looked from Heather to me and back again. It was "the face," the one she'd used when we were younger and I called Heather an idiot at the dinner table when she'd blabbed to our parents that I'd offered to show Lenny Hawkins my bra strap at recess if he paid me twenty-five cents (it was a dollar), and I yelled for her to shut her giant mouth and threw a bread roll at her. Mom's look always stopped us both cold. Even though we weren't kids anymore, and Lenny Hawkins was nowhere in sight, Mom's look sent us both to our corners.

I squeezed my eyes shut and rested my forehead in my palm. "I don't know why I grabbed Heather like that." I opened one eye a slit and looked at her. "I'm sorry."

It was my mother who answered. "I'm confident things will end up all right. It's a strange situation, yes, but, well, things have been hard for all of us lately." And with that my mother managed to swat the whole situation away. "You won't do it again, will you, Kate?"

My eyes flew open. Was she serious, talking to me like I was ten years old and caught stealing small change from her pocketbook? "No, of course not."

Heather wiped her nose with a tissue. "She can't. There's a restraining order in place. She can't come within one hundred fifty feet of Donna."

"What are you, a lawyer? Did you read the restraining order and commit it to memory?"

Heather looked down at her lap. "Donna showed it to me."

My eyes narrowed. "You're still talking to her?"

She fidgeted with the crease in her denim capri pants. "We're friends."

I jumped up from my chair. "Friends?" I roared.

A large security guard who had been standing, arms folded, by the exit hustled toward us. Heather held up her hands, surrender-style. "We're okay, nothing's going on."

"Nothing?" I loomed over Heather. "You befriend the whore who slept with my husband and you call it nothing?" I screamed so loud I could feel the veins in my neck strain with the effort.

The security guard reached me, one hand on my shoulder, one on his baton. "Easy now," he said as if I were a trained horse.

I jerked my shoulder away. "Buzz off." I turned back to Heather. "You come in here crying, spouting off like you have a clue about anything." The guard clamped his huge hand around my arm; I felt my bone under the pressure of his fingers, like a twig.

Heather placed a protective arm in front of Mom, like a driver coming to a sudden stop. The sight of it shielding, barring her from whatever harm I intended sent a howl of outrage though my body. I reached for Heather's arm.

Inches from Heather, I felt the guard forcing me back, using the pressure of his baton on my throat as leverage. I pushed the baton with both hands, furious at being treated like a wild animal. I gasped for breath. The room blurred.

Suddenly the baton was gone. I dragged in air, as if surfacing from a great depth. Heather and Mom huddled together on the couch, wide-eyed. I stepped toward them, to join them in their fear and wonder, but the guard held my upper arms from behind. "Settle down now," he commanded.

"I'm fine," I croaked. But was I? I wanted to call him names, scratch his eyes with my fingers. If he loosened his grip, I would. The indignity stung my eyes, my throat burned.

An orderly ran over to Mom and Heather and reached out with soothing arms. "Best you go now. She'll calm down. Maybe next time will be better."

They stood in unison, like compliant children. Mom stretched out a hand, but the orderly pushed it back to her side. "Time to go." He herded them to the door.

Heather looked back, mouth quivering. "We love you, Kate."

Love? There was no such thing as love. It was a word used to justify hurtful actions. Was it love for me that drove her to befriend the woman who tore my life apart? Love that had caused Kevin to betray me? Love that caused The Reverend to bruise me? What use was that kind of love? I tried to pull free from the guard's grip. "Shut up," I bellowed at her. I pried at the guards fingers. "Let me go."

He pulled me back against his chest and held firm. "You're going to spend some time in confinement."

"You're going to lock me up?" I shook my body, trying to loosen it from his grip. "For what? Having a cow for a sister?"

The door Mom and Heather had just gone through clicked shut. I twisted my lower body and tried to kick the guard.

"Let go," I said. "I didn't do anything wrong." In this place all you had to do was stand up when everyone else was sitting down— raise your voice when others say shush, show any emotion, and it was enough to get you hauled off.

The guard circled my waist with his arm and heaved me up. My feet flailed. I drew one foot back and connected with the guard's knee. He barely flinched.

Instead he called, "You, come here." Within seconds the orderly who had tenderly showed my family the door grasped my ankle with an iron grip. Together they half carried, half dragged me toward a second door that led to the patient rooms.

"Stop," I yelled. "Put me down." I kicked my free foot.

The orderly swore violently as my shoe connected with the side of his head. The other guard opened the door and the three of us lurched into the hall.

In the confinement room they tossed me on the bed and hurried from the room, slamming and locking the door behind them. I scampered to the door and pounded my palms against the heavy glass window.

"Call Dr. Alexander," I screamed through the door. "You can't do this to me. Call him!" But they were already out of sight.

37

I shivered on the narrow bed, although the room was warm. Humiliation streamed through my veins, and my body throbbed with pain. It hurt to swallow. I turned on my side and faced the wall. I'd been hauled away, thrown into a locked room like a naughty child. Dignity stripped.

I closed my eyes and listened to the sounds of the room, the hum of the warm air pushing through vents, the scurry of pipes behind the wall that sounded like footsteps. Feet pacing a wooden floor. Kevin's feet.

Kevin paces the living room while I watch the snow fall out the picture window. Everything looks clean, new, fresh. And cold.

"You've decided my fate with this pregnancy. That's what you think, isn't it?" He slaps his fist in his hand, punctuating the upbeats of his rant. "You know what this feels like to me? A trap. No matter how many times I've asked you to support me, your answer is this—" He gestures to my still-flat abdomen.

"I have choices. I can choose any path I want to take. I walk down whichever road I want to walk down." He says this like a mantra, a manifesto.

He suddenly stops his pacing and leans in close. "You think you can chain me here out of a sense of duty?" He teeters, and for a moment I think he's going fall on top of me. I cover my abdomen with my hand, but he catches himself in time.

He notices my protective gesture and raises an eyebrow at me. "Duty, eh, Kate? That's your choice? You think you can keep me here in this go-nowhere town, in this tract-housing neighborhood because of that?" He points at my belly again. "Is that how you want it?"

My voice comes from a deep well, distant, like an echo. "No." I avoid his eyes. I can't look into the face of this man I love, this man who has become someone I don't know, a stranger.

He looks at me with exaggerated patience. "No? Oh, really? Then kindly explain to me what it is you think this plan of yours is going to accomplish."

"I love you, Kevin. You're all I want."

He laughs and resumes his pacing. "I'm all you want, yet there you are, pregnant. At the worst possible time, you get pregnant. Do you know what you're doing to me? Do you know how insanely complicated my life is right now?"

"I know—"

"You don't know! If you did, you'd be supporting me instead of doing everything you can to hold me down." He throws me an accusing look, his eyes burning with his thoughts. "You're selfish, Kate."

I reel back in my chair, shocked. Selfish? All I ever think about is him. I grasp for answers in my mind until the idea comes. In a moment I know what to do.

I get up and skirt past Kevin, into the kitchen. He doesn't follow. I pull out the town phone book and flip through the pages. I find what I'm looking for and dial. Kevin comes into the kitchen, but I turn my back to him and scribble down the information I hear on a piece of paper. I answer a few questions—surprisingly few. Then I hang up.

I face Kevin and hold out the piece of paper I've written on. He eyes it, like it could be some kind of a trick, but he takes it, reads it, then looks up with questioning eyes.

I point at the paper. "I'm not trying to trap you. I love you, Kevin. I always have and I always will. I want you here with me because you love me—and for no other reason. And I will prove it."

Kevin passes the paper back to me, but I fold my hands behind my back. "Keep it." I'm strangely calm. "A memento of how much I love you."

He looks down at it again. "Are you sure?"

I look him in the eye. "I'm sure."

"You're off to a bad start, Kate." Dr. Alexander tapped his pen in time to a rhythm only he could hear. We were in the center's therapy room.

I glared at him, unblinking. I'd spent the night and most of the morning in confinement, waiting for him to arrive. Everything I'd tried to communicate since I'd landed in this forsaken place had gotten garbled. Nothing I said made sense; I'd lost my ability to communicate. No matter what words I used, none of them worked anymore—none meant what they had when I lived on the other side of these walls.

"Can you tell me what happened? Why a guard and an orderly were forced to physically remove you from the lounge?" he'd asked.

"I don't want to have this conversation." I was perched on the very edge of the couch.

He scratched his toupee. "We aren't having a conversation," he said calmly. "You haven't said more than two words since I arrived twenty minutes ago."

I glared at my fingernails. "I've been having it in my head." And I fell into silence. This was a game I wasn't proud of, but I couldn't seem to stop. I tried to provoke Dr. Alexander into asking me to explain myself. To be clear, say what I mean. He never did. And I always gave in to his waiting game and started talking. As much as I wanted this time to be different, it wasn't.

I blurted out my fear. "I'm crazy, aren't I? I never really believed it before now, but locked up here …" I held my hands open, words once again failing me. "I must be. Or else why would I be here?" I was breaking the rules. I wasn't supposed to ask him questions, I was supposed to answer them. At one of my first sessions with Dr. Alexander, he had told me, "The only thing that matters, Kate, is what you think. You live your life by what you think."

But, to my great surprise, Dr. Alexander responded. "The mind is a powerful thing. It's capable of a great deal more than we recognize."

Not exactly a clear yes or no, but I knew him well enough, after nearly three months of weekly therapy, to know he was saying more than it seemed. "So I'm not crazy, I just have a powerful mind?" It struck me as funny, but I didn't laugh. Nothing about my life so far suggested my brain, or any other part of me, was powerful.

He didn't laugh either. "Consider your memory loss." He leaned forward, his eyes bright with knowledge. "Memory is automatic. We collect and file information about our lives every moment of every day." He licked his lips, warming to the subject. "Recall—the process of remembering—is complex, that's true, but for the most part, it happens smoothly, without much effort." He sat back, regarding me with a wry look. "But you don't want to talk today."

I glared at him. "No, I do. Keep talking."

He tapped his forehead. "Sometimes information gets stuck and we have to work at retrieving it, but for the most part, we recall things easily. But you"—he pointed at me as if needing to clarify who he meant—"you've forgotten large chunks of your recent information—the bits and pieces that make up your life. And recalling it is no easy task."

"Amnesia," I said. But he flicked a wrist, dismissing the idea.

"Forgetting on purpose is more like it. Your memory is coming to you in fits and bursts, yes?"

I nodded. Did he think I'd purposely erased my memories? Impossible.

"Which is exactly how you experienced Kevin's voice. In a seemingly unpredictable pattern. He would speak to you at random times, about everyday things."

A nerve twitched near my left eye. "Except that one time …"

Dr. Alexander nodded. "Yes, except then." He sat back and was silent for a long while, tapping his fingertips together and looking at the far wall. "The first time you heard Kevin's voice was—"

I interrupted. "The day after his funeral."

He gave a quick nod. "Yes, and when did you first realize your memories were gone?"

"The same day. I was talking to Blair and I realized—"

This time Dr. Alexander interrupted, "Both symptoms happened simultaneously, on the same day."

"I guess so. Yes."

He looked thoughtful. "Would you be willing to try something new, Kate?"

I had been doing things my way for months, and it had landed me in a psychiatric assessment center facing possible assault charges. Yeah, I was willing to try something new.

He dropped the pad of paper and pen and scooted his chair over to the side of the couch. "Lie down and close your eyes."

I did.

"I'm going to count backward from ten."

I popped one eye open. "Is this hypnosis?"

He gave his head a crisp shake. "Not exactly. I'm going to assist you into a relaxed state, and together we will try to pull out your missing memories." He said this with a smile.

"How is that not hypnosis?" I said.

His raised eyebrow held me in place. "Are you comfortable?"

I closed my eye. "Yes."

"Relax your body." He cleared his throat, as if warming up for an aria. "Your brain remembers everything. It's a remarkable thing.

It captures information of all kinds, organizes the data, and then stores it in different places in your brain." I kept quiet, breathing in and out. His voice came from above me. "It's the retrieval aspect of your brain function that you're having trouble with. Normally your brain can remember details by collecting them from various sources throughout your mind. For some reason you aren't able to gain access to your memories. Something is blocking them."

I thought of Eliza Campbell telling me that my spiritual pipes were stopped up—blocked.

Dr. Alexander went on, "Along with your lost memories, you began to hear Kevin's voice—auditory hallucination. We've always understood them as two separate symptoms, but it occurs to me that they are actually related."

"Related how?" I mumbled. My body was loose, relaxed, the sound of his smooth voice like water over stones. I hadn't slept well since the incident at the bank. His calm voice and technical talk made me sleepy.

"That is what I hope to discover. Let's try this and see what answers it holds. Then we can discuss more when we're finished. Are you ready?"

"Yes."

He counted down from ten. After he reached one, he said, "Picture your memory as a giant cookie jar. Can you see the cookie jar?"

A cookie jar appeared. "Yes." It was the ceramic one my mother had kept in the kitchen all the years I was growing up. It was shaped like a chubby chef in a white apron and floppy chef's hat. His cheeks full and round, his oversized Betty Boop eyes crinkled in a perpetual smile. It floated in darkness, alone, unconnected.

"I want you to reach into the cookie jar with your right hand. Inside are all of your memories. Are you reaching inside the cookie jar, Kate?"

My hand reached deep into the jar. "It's empty."

"Your memories are folded pieces of paper at the bottom of the jar. Can you feel them?"

I wiggled my fingers and felt the smooth bottom of the ceramic jar. I touched something. Paper. Then another one. And another. "Yes. Little pieces of paper."

"Very good. Now pick up one of the pieces of paper, and pull it out of the jar."

I felt around inside my cookie jar, stirring the papers, then I pulled one out.

"Read the piece of paper, Kate."

I swallowed hard. "I can't."

He waited a moment, then asked, "Is there writing on the paper?"

I started crying.

"Kate, truth can't hurt you. The truth sets you free. Read the piece of paper."

"I can't." Tears ran down the sides of my head onto my hair.

"You can see the words clearly, Kate. They are neatly typed, easy to read."

A long keening sound filled the room, like a wolf. It hurt my ears. I wanted it to stop, but it kept going. Louder. I clamped my hands over my ears, trying to drown out the sound. Then I realized the sound was coming from me.

38

Maggie slapped her cards on the recreation room card table. "Gin!"

I tossed my hand down. "You win again."

She gathered the cards and shuffled, her purple fingernails flashing, her lips frozen in a kind but wary smile. Her eyes flitted around the lounge, not stopping on any one thing for any length of time.

After two weeks incarcerated in the assessment center, I'd grown accustomed to the bars on the windows, the utilitarian furniture, the constant blare from the TV that no one watched. Well, maybe more resigned than accustomed. There was nothing to like about being here, but I was in no position to pack up and go. The more cooperation I showed toward the assessment process, the better my chances of avoiding charges.

Maggie and I had been playing cards for almost an hour, pretending to be normal. She acted as if she regularly visited places like this, and I acted as if being locked up wasn't the worst thing I could think of. Every few minutes she glanced at the security guard stationed by the door, his arms crossed, a baton tucked into a belt loop, watching the smattering of patients scattered around the room. I, conversely, avoided looking at him.

Maggie set the playing cards to one side of the small table and sat back in her chair. "I'd like to say you look well, Kate, but you don't." She softened the words with a wink. "In fact you look much the same as you did when I visited you in your home after the funeral."

I tucked a heavy strand of hair behind my ear. The noise from the TV across the room—a talk show discussing hairstyles for dogs—fought for my attention.

Since I had come to the center, I had shared a washroom with my suicidal anorexic roommate, who spent most of her day locked inside, counting ribs in the mirror and pinching bits of skin. Whenever I knocked, she turned the shower on and hummed. But it was better than her other habit of going through everyone's belongings looking for something fatal to swallow.

Maggie was right; I was unwashed, unkempt. I acknowledged this fact with a sweeping wave of my hand.

Maggie leaned in and spoke with a soft voice. "It's a matter of choices, dear girl."

I gestured to the room, taking in the entire situation. "I'm fresh out of choices at the moment."

Her face lit up. "That's a choice too. Deciding you're out of choices."

A shard of defensiveness stabbed at my back. Who was she to tell me my reality? No matter how good of a friend she'd been, I didn't need someone yipping cryptic, Yoda-like sayings at me.

Maggie blew a raspberry. "All this," Maggie continued, waving a hand above her head, "can be changed at a moment's notice. Don't pay any attention to it. You need to decide to get well, dear."

More of the same advice she'd given me the first time she visited me. "I decided that months ago."

She just looked at me.

I closed my eyes, exhausted by the possibility that I'd walked a thousand miles only to find myself in the same place I thought I'd left. So much had happened to me since Kevin died, but inside I was the same kind of confused. Dr. Alexander had pushed me to the brink, the very edge of where I was willing to go. The border of my sanity, howling like a wounded animal.

"Things got a whole lot worse," I mumbled, thinking of the warning Maggie had given me three months ago.

She gave my hand a soft rub of sympathy. "It breaks my heart to see you here, duck." Then she poked my hand with two quick fingers. "But you can get out, start your life anew."

"That's what I've been trying to do, Maggie. All this time I've been trying to start my life over, and look where I've ended up."

Maggie rested her chin on the knuckles of her right fist. "I've been chatting with your mother and sister. They've told me about the terrible time you've had. And I agree, you're in a bad place." She paused, and for a moment she looked like the matronly aunt of the famous sculpture *The Thinker*. "But you didn't get to this place by trying to create a new life for yourself."

I looked at her, startled.

She gave a sad smile. "No, dear, you got here by trying to wrestle with the past. Trying to change what *was* into something else."

A static-filled voice on the intercom filled the room. Visiting hours were over. Maggie pushed up from her chair and stretched her back. "I'm praying for you, Kate."

I knew I was supposed to say thank you. But I wanted to say, "Save your breath." The mention of God conjured the image of The Reverend towering, glacial, smothering, hollering about my sin and filth. I wondered what Maggie would think about him. But I nodded and watched her as she left, dipping her head as she nudged past the security guard.

I brooded about choices well into the evening. My future stretched out like a hallway lined with closed doors, each a possibility, leading somewhere. But which door to walk through? Which one would open for me, and which would slam in my face?

Choices. What choices had I made? I'd been in therapy for months, but always a reluctant participant. I had talked in the hallowed privacy of Dr. Alexander's sumptuous office, but had refused all other treatment methods he prescribed. I had attended group therapy, but never shared my story, never shared myself with the others. Fear had held me back from participating.

And Jack. I'd gotten more from the time spent with him than all the others combined. His calm presence and easy manner always set me at ease. But I turned my back on him too. For all my talk of moving on with my life, all I'd managed was to drive everyone away.

The next day, I lay on the nubby couch of the center's therapy room, and Dr. Alexander counted backward from ten. When he got to five, he stopped counting and said, "Are you certain you want to try this today?"

I didn't move. "Yes, why?"

"You're gripping the edge of the cushion so hard your knuckles are white."

I loosened my hold and pulled in a long breath. "I'm fine. Really. I want to do this."

"Good, good," Dr. Alexander murmured. "Let's begin again, starting at ten." He counted, I breathed. In moments I was looking at my mother's cookie jar, floating in darkness.

"Are you ready to reach into the jar, Kate?" Dr. Alexander's voice came from far away, a pinpoint on the ceiling.

"It's just floating; I don't like it hanging in space."

"Where would you like to take your jar? Take it somewhere pleasant."

The space around the jar opened, and bright sunlight poured in from every angle. The dark turned shimmering blue. Warmth surged and surrounded me and my cookie jar.

I dangled my feet in the cool water of the outdoor pool my family visited every summer until I was seventeen. I was alone and the surface of the pool glistened with stillness. I held the jar on my lap and gazed into its murky interior. "Okay," I said, my voice undulating like the ripples on the water. "I'm ready."

"Put your hand in the jar and feel the pieces of paper at the bottom."

I pushed my hand inside and instantly felt bits of paper brush against my hand. I stirred them around, then scooped a handful and let the bits of paper fall through my fingers like sand. "There are so many," I said.

"Choose one and read what you see on the paper."

I grabbed the smallest piece I could find, a tiny scrap that couldn't hold many words. I pulled it out, so small it was a dot in my hand. I smiled at it, smiled at this harmless thing. Too minute to carry consequence. "I have one."

Dr. Alexander cleared his throat, and the sound floated down from his distant cloud. "When you're ready, read the words on the paper."

I unfolded the bit of paper only to find it was folded again, then again. I kept unfolding, but the paper grew and grew. "I can't find the words." Each time I opened one fold, I found another. I moved my hands quickly over the paper, flipping and turning it until it was the size of a road map. Fear squeezed my heart. "They aren't here," I said, my voice high like a bird singing. "No words."

"You are calm, Kate. As you look at the paper, feel safe and peaceful."

I turned and lay down in the water, floating on my back. I held the paper above me, straight-armed to keep it dry. The warm water lapped around me, held me up as if I were made of cork. I looked at the paper above me as the words arranged themselves into neat rows. "It's not mine," I said.

"All the memories in the jar are your memories, Kate." Dr. Alexander's voice reached my wet ears. He was below me now, a shadow at the bottom of the pool, like my father waiting to grab my ankles and toss me into the sky.

I shook my head, water sloshing into my ears. "It's not my memory. I don't want this one."

His silence told me he would wait.

I opened my hands and the paper floated away, a kite with no string. It drifted above me. Dipped and swayed. I crossed my arms over my chest and lay as a corpse in a casket, tears flowing from my eyes into the pool. "I didn't mean for it to happen." My heart pulsed against my palm. "I should have never—" I stopped.

"Let the truth set you free, Kate," he said, his words floating up in a bubble from the bottom of the pool. Then, another voice, soft and feminine. I couldn't make out the words. She spoke to someone, not me, someone else. Who were they?

They speak to each other in hushed tones. When they walk, their shoes make no noise. Everything is white and clean. An unsmiling woman speaks to me, only to me. They never look at Kevin or acknowledge him in any way. One woman, wearing nurse's white, touches my arm and says, "Scared? You'll be fine."

She leads me down a hall to another room. Kevin follows at a distance. If she notices him, she never lets on. She hands me a dressing gown and tells me to change, then I'm to lie down on the table.

I fumble with the buttons on my blouse and the woman, the nurse, not Kevin, helps me. I cry softly as she pulls the blouse off my shoulders. "Can you do the rest yourself?"

I nod.

She looks out the window. "It's snowing. Almost Christmastime. Do you like the snow?"

I don't know; I can't answer. She leaves the room while I finish changing.

I lie on the table and turn my head so I can watch the snow fall. I think about it covering the earth, the universe, until all of humanity is covered in a blanket of clean white snow. Kevin stands silent beside me. I'm glad he is here. Glad he is silent.

The door opens and I hear voices. I squeeze my eyes shut.

"I'm done after this," one voice says. "Off for two weeks. Me and my sweetie are heading west. Taking in some skiing." It's the nurse who helped me undress.

I'm cold.

Another voice. "I can't ski worth beans. Oh, she's crying again."

A pat on my arm. "That's okay, hon. Everybody cries sometimes."

They stop talking; I hear them move around the room, preparing for what will happen.

I keep my eyes shut tight. I'm sobbing, my body jerking and hiccupping. I pray, "I'm so sorry." But I think what I mean is, "Please don't blame me."

The door opens again. A male voice. "Ready?"

Everything is white.

"Everything's ready, doctor."

A click, like a switch turned on, and the air fills with the roar of a machine. "Just relax," the doctor says. "Spread your knees a bit more." The machine roars like the ocean. Then the sound changes, a slurping sound. I feel pressure—terrible pressure. I scream, a long keening sound, like a wolf.

39

My name blared over the intercom. I sighed and kicked the bedcovers off my stocking feet. It was too early for medication, so it meant someone was here to see me. Probably Mom, who had visited every day since my arrival at the psychiatric facility more than two weeks ago. I pulled on my jeans and threw a sweater over my T-shirt.

I came around the corner and stopped short in front of the reception desk. Jack Slater stood, head bent, speaking to the woman behind the desk. He hadn't seen me yet. He signed the visitor sheet and handed it back.

If I turned and hustled back to my room, he wouldn't see me, wouldn't know I'd been there. Then he would leave and I would tell them I hadn't heard the page, was in the shower, something. Jack looked up and gave a flat smile, the kind where you arrange your lips in the posture of a smile when you know it isn't appropriate to be happy.

I pushed my greasy hair away from my face, wishing I actually had taken a shower. I pulled at my loose-knit clothes and shuffled up to the desk. He reached for my hand, squeezed it, and let go, his hand warm and familiar. I didn't know what to say, so I said nothing. And he simply watched, unhurried.

Finally I said, "Want to walk the grounds?"

"Sounds good."

We waited for a nurse to buzz us through the locked door. When it clicked open, I pushed the door hard and ran to the middle of the patio, as if they might change their mind and pull me back inside.

Jack called, "Wait for me." He smiled.

We walked across the stone patio, down a grassy slope, and onto a sports field built so patients could play football or soccer, but I'd never seen anyone do anything but walk on it. We were silent and I was glad. I needed time to adjust to Jack being in this place, witnessing the worst of me. Obviously he'd tracked me down. How, I didn't know, didn't need to know. But I was glad he was here.

"Have you ever had a time in your life when everything went wrong at once?" I said suddenly.

Jack didn't hesitate. "Yes."

I studied his profile. "Oh?"

"Sometimes I think my whole life is just everything going wrong at once."

My thoughts exactly. "But you're a pastor." *And not locked in a nuthouse.*

Jack smiled. "I'm a pastor so I have everything figured out? Not even close." He glanced at me. "Life is complex. People are complex." He said it calmly; no need to get upset, kick up a fuss. Just accept it.

"People," I said. "I'd be perfectly happy in my life if it weren't for other people."

He didn't laugh. "There are days I think the same thing." We walked on, our faces cooled by the October wind. "But, truth is, most people aren't really evil. Most of us are just scared."

I thought of Donna, her cool matter-of-factness. "Evil isn't scared of anything."

Jack looked at me for a moment then spoke slowly, as if each word was being measured and weighed out. "Sometimes evil comes through the front door, robs you blind, and laughs when you cry."

"But?"

He looked straight ahead, squinting into the wind. "I don't have a 'but' for you."

We fell into silence and I studied the grass with each step. "You're handling yourself very well."

"Am I?"

"Yes. I walked out on you at the restaurant, but you still came here to see me." I half turned to him, not quite able to look into his face. "And you don't even seem nervous about being alone with someone who is being held here because she attacked a banker."

"I'm a pastor. I deal with crazy all the time," Jack said. "And I know a lot of people who fantasize about attacking bankers."

I laughed. The sound, strange in my throat, was music in my ears. Despite my misgivings I'd missed him. "Can I buy you a coffee, Pastor Jack?"

He grinned. "I'd love one." We turned and made our way back to the center.

I tapped the rim of Jack's mug. "Actually the coffee here is free."

He took a sip. "Good. I'll have two."

The dining room was much like you'd expect to see in a school

or old-folks home. Rows of tables and chairs, floors waxed to maximum shine. We had scheduled hours for meals, but coffee and other
beverages were always available. A homey touch in the middle of
institutional hell. Jack and I were alone, two people in a sea of dining furniture. From the kitchen, sounds of food being prepared
chimed.

Jack ran a hand through his dark hair. "Can we talk about what
happened with my father?"

I pushed my spine into the back of my chair. A strange topic of
conversation considering he'd come to visit me in a mental institu-
tion. Not that I wanted to talk about mental institutions either. "I
don't want to go through all of that again, Jack. I'm trying to move
on."

He reached over the table, as if to grab my hands, but he stopped
short. "Of course not. I don't mean the details of what he did. I
mean the fact that he's my father and what that means—" he paused,
"to ... our friendship."

My heart pounded a heavy thud, then began to race. "I
don't—"

He interrupted. "What my father did to you left you justifi-
ably angry. And maybe turned you off of God completely." He drew
swirls on the table with his finger. "And the way you looked at me the
last time we talked ..."

"I know you're not like your father. It's just—"

"I'm nothing like him." He punctuated this with a beseeching
look, a sort of pleading. I wanted to smooth it from his face with my
hands. He shouldn't have felt the need to convince me he was different from his father. His kindness over the past months had proven

that a hundredfold. It wasn't Jack I questioned, it was God. I cast my eyes to the floor. "You say I'm loved by a holy God; your father calls me a filthy sinner." I pulled my chair closer to the table. "Both of you believe you're speaking for the same God. How can that be? How can one God be saying such opposite things?"

Jack said, "My father did teach me about God, but over the years I've come to reject the way my father understands God." He took another sip of coffee. "I don't agree with the way he lives out what he believes. For him life is black and white, right and wrong."

"But not for you?"

He shook his head. "My experiences have taught me to see shades of gray."

That caught my attention. "What experiences?"

He spread his hands. "My story, like so many, begins with a girl."

Huh? I felt a pang, like a pinch. "A girl?"

He leaned back and looked over my head, into his past, I assumed. "I had a girlfriend a few years ago. Fiancée, actually."

In my head I heard the sound that in the comics is spelled "Zonk." I had only thought of Jack as just Jack. Alone. Virginal. Like Bambi's dad in the movie, strong and distant and waiting on a cliff top. Unattached, as if he'd just appeared one day, new, unwritten. Now I tried to picture him with someone, holding her, kissing her, loving her. I shook my head. Better not to try to picture it.

"She broke it off." His fingers played around his mouth. "I had a hard time getting over it."

"I know what that's like." I arranged my face in what I hoped was a nonchalant expression. I had no idea what this had to do with God, but I didn't care. I wanted to hear this story. "Tell me about her." I lifted a casual hand.

He fixed me with a long gaze that was like waiting for the click from a reluctant photographer, *Take the picture already.* "It was ten years ago." He shook his head, as if surprised by the number. "I was twenty, she was twenty-two. She was new to the city and to our church. The first time I saw her—" His eyes glistened at the memory. "Boom."

Boom? *Oh, please.* "You mean she was nice looking? Sort of attractive?"

Jack fixed his gaze on the wall behind me as if his favorite movie was playing there. "Gorgeous, long blonde hair, these big brown eyes, and all smiles." He smiled too, as if she'd just walked in the room.

"How nice." *If you like that type.* Blonde isn't a real color, it was invented by Hollywood. Everyone knew that. I was surprised by my jealous thoughts. Why should I be affected by a woman from Jack's past? It had nothing to do with me.

Jack continued, "And, like all gorgeous blondes, she was responsible for my utter downfall." He chuckled at his joke.

I grimaced. Utter downfall? An overstatement I was sure. "You don't look 'downfallen' to me."

He looked at me, eyebrows pulled close as if surprised to see me there. "By the time that woman finished making a run through my life, I'd lost everything. Her, my church, my family, everything."

Lost everything. Jack had lost everything once. I glanced down at my open, empty hands. "How?"

"Helene got pregnant." He looked into my eyes, a man facing facts. "It wasn't my baby. We hadn't slept together." He laughed again, a short sound that seemed to say, "Sucker."

"She betrayed you." My voice hushed like a revelation. *You're betrayed, like me.* "You must have been furious."

He rubbed his hand across his jaw and chin. "I was way more pathetic than that." He spoke quickly, as if wanting to get the words out and be done with them. "I told her I wanted to marry her anyway. Raise the baby as my own." He tossed out a snort. "She didn't want any of it. Said she wanted out, that she couldn't face people in the church. Said she didn't love me the way I loved her." He slapped a hand on his leg. "And that was it. She took off—I haven't seen her since."

Took off. Just left, a clean cut, taking everything with her, Jack's future, the baby, everything. I stared at my shoes, suddenly shy to look at him. *Lost everything.* "I'm sorry. But it doesn't explain—"

"My father," he finished.

I nodded.

"I was in seminary at the time all this happened. A guy in seminary with a pregnant fiancée—" he looked wide-eyed, "—not good."

"But it wasn't your baby. And she left you."

He didn't seem to hear me. "My Dad ... Wow. I thought he would have a heart attack." An easily envisioned event for a man his size, I thought, but kept it to myself. Jack grabbed the front of his own shirt and shook it, an imitation of his father's hand. "'Admit your sin like a man,' Dad said."

I slapped my hand on the table. "That's not fair. You hadn't done anything wrong. How could he not believe you?" What was the matter with that man? It was as if he were part bulldozer.

Jack frowned. "Like I said, Dad's world is black and white. Helene was a beautiful woman; there was never any doubt in my father's mind that the child was mine. He said he'd always suspected I was morally weak."

I'd never met anyone more upright than Jack Slater Jr.

I pictured my father's face, no minister of the gospel, no church-going man, but I couldn't imagine him saying anything so cruel to me—or anyone else. I reached across the table and laid my hand over Jack's. He placed his other hand over top of mine.

"We argued," Jack said, "more than once. Then one Sunday morning, Dad stood in the pulpit and announced my 'sin' to the church." Jack fell silent for several seconds, then, "I was beyond shocked. As soon as the words left his mouth, people turned in their seats to look at me, craning their necks to get a good look at the disgraced pastor's son sitting in the back." He rapped his knuckles on the table. "And I saw my father and his church for what they were."

"Your father is a beast," I said, horrified by the story.

Jack nodded, but said, "I can't say that. He's just a man who cares more about his image than anything else."

The intercom crackled to life and, for the second time that day, my name was paged. I checked my watch. It was time for medica-tion, a process I didn't want Jack to witness. "I have to go."

I walked him toward the public exit, the boundary that separated me from the rest of society, for their protection. "Your life was like a soap opera," I said on the way.

A grin flashed then faded. "Everyone's life is a soap opera some-times. No one is exempt—not you, not me, not even my father. It's taken me a long time to untangle the mess left by that time, but through it I came to understand God was with me in the middle of my chaos. He was there, helping me make sense out of it."

"That's not what your father would think. He'd say you were being punished for your sins."

He nodded. "I know. But over the last ten years I've come to realize that I'm not responsible for my dad's relationship with God. Or for how it plays out in his life. I pray for him and trust God is with him just like I believe God is with me."

I stared hard at the gold sign that read *Reception*, thinking about his words. All I knew was that if I were God, I would have abandoned The Reverend years ago. "I have to go," I said, my voice tight.

"I'll come again?" he said, seeking permission.

I nodded. "Yes." Then added, "Thank you."

I told the receptionist to buzz Jack out. She pushed a button and the locked door clicked open. Jack pulled it open.

I stepped toward him. "How did you forgive him?"

He chewed his lip. "I'm still working on it."

I had entered that place an expectant mother.

I left empty, body and soul.

I'd proven beyond all doubt that my marriage—Kevin—is the only thing that matters. I'm a hallowed saint in the tabernacle of our marriage. A martyr in the church of Kevin.

I had stayed overnight, an expensive precautionary step, but Kevin had insisted. He said he wanted to be certain there was no infection or side effects. Now I'm home, and it's two days before Christmas.

Kevin speaks into the phone. "Kate has the flu. We'll still have Christmas morning here, she insists, but we'll need to scale it back." He listens, making "uh-huh" sounds every few moments. "Sounds great. See you then." He hangs up and turns to me. "Your mom said she'll make the waffles Christmas morning so you won't have to." He pauses. "She said she wants to have as normal a Christmas as possible."

I wrap my arms around myself, shivering. Normal. Dad gone, taken by a swollen river—this is our first Christmas without him. I feel his absence like a heartbeat. I'm wearing a warm red sweater, so soft it feels like a hug. I nod, but say nothing. Everything hurts. I look at my husband, marveling at how easily he lied to my mother just moments ago. The lies dropped from his mouth with such ease, it was like an art form.

But who am I to judge? I don't want my mother to know— not now, not ever. "I'm going upstairs," I say, and make a slow getaway on unsteady legs.

I awake in the middle of the night. It's dark, but the blind hasn't been drawn. Kevin's side of the bed is smooth and empty. I'm sweating. My body feels like it's on fire. I go into the bathroom and run cold water, splashing my face again and again. I look down and see blood. On my clothes, on the floor between my feet. Without thought or feeling, I strip my clothes off and rinse them in the tub.

After I dress in clean nightclothes, I go downstairs in search of Kevin. It's dark, and for a moment I think Kevin must not be home. But where would he be in the middle of the night, with his wife bleeding and feverish upstairs? I turn down the hall and see light peering out from his closed den. I walk over and press my ear to the door. Kevin's voice. He's on the phone.

"I don't know," he says in response to a question I can't hear. "She's weak, lost a lot of blood. But she'll be fine in a few days."

I silently panic. Who is he talking to? Who else knows what I've done? I clutch the walls for support.

Kevin says, "She needs me here. There's no one else. Everyone thinks she had the flu. I don't know when I'll be able to call you again. I'll do my best." There is a long pause, then, "I love you too."

I hear the click as Kevin hangs up the phone. I hear his breath, a long sigh, like a man with problems, a man who has decisions to make. I pad up the stairs and go back to bed.

The room was dark around me. The shower was running; my room-mate's loud humming filled the space. Flat on my back in bed, I watched the pictures of my past swirl around me. They were outside of me, but close, nearly touching. They dipped and pulsed, danced and swayed like lovers. I watched them, feeling calm.

The images linked, creating a chain I could follow from start to finish. Soon they were whole, spelling out my life in crisp detail. I wanted to close my eyes against the glare of them, but instead I watched, unblinking. Soon I would invite them in, collect them, let them return inside my skin. But for a moment I held them at bay.

"Kevin?" Where was he now? Heaven or hell, or some other

place? Was he with our child? The question burned, so fresh was the knowledge that I'd lost her (a girl, yes, I was sure, a brown-haired girl).

"Kevin, I need to know," I whispered. I couldn't let go of him. I saw his face in every memory, every hope, everything I'd tried to accomplish. I had gone through with the abortion to prove not just my love, but that my life was in his hands. So when he died, I'd lost everything: Kevin, our child, and all my reasons for doing what I had done. All my striving had come to nothing.

"What did I do to make you leave me?" His face danced before me, moving in time with my memories. How does something go so wrong?

"I loved you so much, Kevin. I don't even want to know if you are sorry anymore." My stomach knotted in a dry heave. "Just tell me what I did to make you stop loving me."

The shower turned off, the humming stopped. Anger rose up in me, bent and fruitless. The memories washed me in truth. My truth. I could deny them no longer. I cried as my body filled with the pictures of my past, and the self-loathing they brought with them.

40

"Why do you keep coming here?" I said to Jack. I'd been in the assessment center nearly three weeks and Jack had visited nearly every day for the past week. We would walk the grounds, taking the same route as the first time he'd come.

I didn't mean to sound blunt, but the events of the past months had stripped away my ability to engage in polite conversation.

"I like the coffee," he said, his tone teasing, conversational. Then he said, "We're friends. It matters to me if you're okay."

I watched his profile as we walked. He'd recently had a haircut, a dark semicircle of hair rimmed his ear. Friends? He barely knew me. And what he did know of me he'd discovered by sheer determined effort on his part. How had I come to matter to him? Why had he decided to care about me? I didn't know the answer to that question any more than I knew why Kevin had decided to stop caring about me. Maybe Jack just didn't know enough about me to scare him off. Maybe he needed to know.

"I'm going to tell you the whole story. Then you can decide for yourself," I said.

"Decide what?"

"If we're friends or not."

He was quiet, then said, "Okay."

I started with the day of the funeral and I told him everything—Kevin's voice, Blair, my lost memories, Donna, Heather, and lastly the recovered knowledge of my abortion. It was a confession, a purging. When I finished, I was in tears. I kept my head down, stared at the grass, waiting for Jack to say something. He was a pastor, and for all his caring, I felt certain that some part of my story would disturb him—like hearing Kevin's voice. Or disgust him—like my abortion. I couldn't be certain.

He was quiet for a long, long while. Then he wrapped his arms around me and held me.

His comfort felt like a homecoming. He stood very still, like a tree with deep roots, unmovable. His arms were tethers, holding fast so I couldn't fly away. His silence filled the empty spaces with acceptance. He didn't shush me, didn't tell me everything would be okay, didn't ask me to explain myself. He simply held me up.

"We're friends," he whispered in my hair.

Dr. Alexander's face was a painful red. He said he'd gone sailing the day before and gotten windburned. That was putting it lightly. His entire face was burned except for the glimmering white flesh that had been shaded by his sunglasses. His nose was already peeling. He looked tired and feverish as he sat across from me in the therapy room and scribbled in his notebook. "I'm sure you're anxious to hear what the judge had to say."

I hadn't attended the hearing that had taken place that morning. Dr. Alexander felt it was in my best interest to stay away. And since my presence wasn't required, I was happy to wait it out at the assessment center rather than sitting stiff and helpless on the hard bench of a courtroom. Better to be helpless far from that place where I couldn't hear the debate over my life.

But looking at Dr. Alexander's bright red face, my bravado failed. What had they said about me? What decisions had been made? Where was I going from here? I managed a warbling smile. "Well, I haven't accosted anyone lately, so that must have counted in my favor."

The corners of Dr. Alexander's mouth twitched in a near smile, but he pushed his lips together. "Indeed. Based on my reports to the court, and my recommendations, the judge ordered your release from the psychiatric hospital." He held up a cautionary hand, as if I'd leaped off the couch and shouted *Hallelujah*. "The severity of the offense, however, warrants disciplinary action."

I closed my eyes, waiting.

"One year probation, including community service."

I let out a long breath, sat back, and let the news wash over me. "I can go home?"

He nodded. "But there are a few more conditions. You must keep all scheduled appointments with me—and I'm requiring that we meet twice a week for the next month or so. And you must return to group therapy until the group disbands in December."

A small price, one I should have paid before ever coming here. But that was in the past. Now I could go home, start again, get on with my life.

His eyes fluttered closed, then opened slowly. "There's the matter of where you'll serve your community service. They have provided a list of approved programs, or, you can submit a request to serve your time at a suitable program not on the list."

One name jumped to mind: Jack. "Actually … I know a pastor—Jack Slater—who runs a center in the city. Youth programs and Sunday services."

"That may work fine," he mumbled, scribbling notes.

"And I've made a decision." I clasped my hands on my lap, waiting for him to ask *What is it?*, but his red face just looked at me with the professional patience that I had grown accustomed to. I thought of offering him the cream I had in my purse for his face. It was expensive and made from the essence of some rare tropical fruit that only grew on one tiny island off the coast of Samoa. Instead I kept my hands in my lap.

"I've decided to sell my house in Greenfield and move to the city," I said.

He tapped his pad of paper with his pen, but otherwise didn't move. "That's a big move. I wonder if you're ready for such a drastic change."

I held my empty hands out to Dr. Alexander. "I know it's big, but I'm ready. And I'm not running away, either. I'm going to take my time, put the house up for sale, clean it up."

He doodled in his notebook and muttered, "Good, good."

"I'll find a small place, a condo maybe."

He closed his eyes in a long blink. "Go slow, Kate. You have your probation to fulfill, community service, and appointments. That's enough to keep you occupied for a long while."

I nodded an enthusiastic agreement. "Yes, all here in the city. Moving means I'll be closer to all of my obligations."

He touched two fingers to his forehead. "Yes, well, go slow."

I reached in my purse and handed him my lotion and two aspirin. He took them both without comment.

The next morning my mother picked me up in front of the psychiatric center. For once I hadn't called Heather to come to my aid. I didn't know when I'd be able to talk to her again.

Mom and I hugged in silence, neither of us sure what to say.

Once we were out of the maze of the city, she said, "Am I taking you home?" She threw me a quick sideways glance. "I mean, do you want to go home, or would you like to come to my house for a while?" She chewed her lip. I could see she was agitated, hesitant.

I shifted until I faced her. "Home would be good. Thanks, Mom." She looked older somehow, the skin under her chin wrinkled and loose. A year of grief had gathered on her face.

It was October. Dad had gone into the river a year ago. She and I had walked such different paths in the past year. She had absorbed the swift loss of her husband. Grieved hard, and yet, in time began to live a little too. I had gone in as much of an opposite direction from her as possible. Down a rough path and straight into the rabbit's hole. But I'd been given a second chance.

I watched the countryside whirl by. "Things are going to be better. Dr. Alexander thinks I've turned a corner."

Mom patted my knee. "I'm so glad, Kate. You have a whole life ahead of you."

Greenfield looked smaller somehow. We drove past the same

homes, business, and shops that had always been there, but Main Street seemed shorter, the storefronts tiny. When we stopped at a red light beside the bank, I looked away.

At home I invited Mom in for tea, but she said she'd come by later after I'd gotten settled.

I unlocked the door, but didn't go in. I put my suitcase down on the stoop and walked around the house. I examined the siding, noticed a crack in the downspout and that the flowers had dried and withered. *Not too bad, considering ...*

Finally I went inside. Just like the town, it seemed as if the house had shrunk. The rooms I had roamed through for weeks now looked cramped, cloistering. I had some work ahead of me if I wanted to get this place in shape to sell. But that would have to wait a while. In my bag I had a stack of paperwork to fill out, all related to my release from the center and my obligations. I had to call my probation officer, arrange appointments with Dr. Alexander, file for permission to serve my community service time at Glen Hills—and then there were the insurance forms.

I plunked the kettle on the stove. The forms could wait for one day. Maybe I would call Maggie, or go for a walk—I certainly needed to pick up some food. And a new set of sheets for the bed. I would sleep in my own bed tonight. I smiled, then a giggle jumped from my mouth. I was free to do whatever I pleased.

41

The following Wednesday, my first day of community service at Glen Hills, I stood in the gym of Glen Hills Community Center, transfixed by a huge banner hanging on the wall. Big Tim's smiling face looked down at me. Under his picture were the dates of his birth and death and the slogan: Let No More Children Die.

In the picture he looked more like a child than I remembered. His face was rounded by lingering baby fat, his hair expertly combed. Freckles I'd never noticed dotted his nose and cheeks. And Tim's smile, expansive, without a trace of self-consciousness. He looked larger than life, vibrant. *And now he's gone.*

All around the fringes of the banner, people had written messages.

Jack came up and stood beside me. Together we silently read the observances to a gunned-down boy; hopeful, sorrowful, angry, even vengeful. People from all over the community—friends, family, strangers—signed their names, their sorrow in indelible ink. My tears flowed freely at the impact of the banner. It was painfully beautiful.

Jack spoke first. "It was Sekeena's idea. She raised the money to have the banner made. We hosted a day here where people could come and remember Big Tim, sign the banner, and talk about how to reclaim our neighborhoods from violence."

Still looking at the banner, I said, "What did you write?"

Jack pointed to the bottom right corner. He had written: *I'll see you again, my friend.*

He looked at me and put a warm hand on my shoulder. "I called my father."

I should have been startled by the abrupt change of topic, the mention of The Reverend, but I wasn't. Looking at Big Tim's broad smile, I was blanketed by a sad calm. "What did he say?"

He took his hand from my shoulder and ran it through his hair. "He was polite. Distant. But it was a start." We studied the banner in silence for a moment, then he said, "You're the reason I called him."

"You talked about me?"

"No, not yet ... I mean, when I visited you the first time at the—" He jerked his thumb at the door, a vague gesture I understood to mean the psychiatric assessment center. "You asked me how I forgave him. It got me thinking."

"You said you were still working on forgiving him." I'd thought of his statement many times since. It had made me realize that perhaps forgiveness wasn't a singular event, but a progression, or better, a dance that took some figuring before you could perform the steps.

Jack stuck his hands into his front pockets. "I decided I was ready to take another stab at it. So I called him. We talked for about ten minutes." He shrugged. "We didn't say anything about the past, or the fact we haven't spoken in years—" He sighed. "I asked how my mom was, how the church was. That sort of thing."

"It's funny, isn't it? When there's so much to say, you don't know how to start."

He tipped his head down and nodded. "Exactly. But I plan to call again. I need to talk to him about what he did to you."

My heart fluttered. "Don't, Jack, there's no need—"

He interrupted. "He needs to be accountable for hurting you, Kate. It's as simple as that."

I smiled. "Thank you for saying so." I turned back to the banner and read more of the messages. Jack handed me a black marker. "Take your time, and when you're ready, we'll talk about your new career at Glen Hills." He winked and then walked across the gym.

"Career" was an exaggeration, but today was my first day serving the three hundred hours of community service portion of my one-year probation. The judge also allowed a continuation of the restraining order Donna Walsh had against me. Apparently I needed to take a tape measure everywhere I went in case I bumped into her. One hundred fifty feet, and no closer. She hardly needed to worry. I had no desire to go anywhere near her.

I fiddled with the marker, wondering what I could add to the banner, what I could say that hadn't already been expressed. When we met, he went out of his way to invite me, include me in the game. His smile was constant and infectious. He was one of those rare people who never gave a thought about who you were, what you had done, or if you fit in. He simply wanted you to join in, to be included.

I pulled the cap off the pen and wrote not a message to Big Tim, but a prayer to whomever might read it: *Let me live as he did—loving others, connected.*

Later that evening I arrived ten minutes early to group therapy. I switched on the lights and felt butterflies spasming in my stomach. It had been more than a month since I'd last been there, and while I was there partly because the conditions of my probation required me to attend, I was glad to be back, to have a second chance with them. I'd spent so much time with this group, listening, watching, but not reaching out. Tonight I planned to change that.

I stood by the door pulling at my red cotton shirt and craning my neck to see if anyone was coming down the hall.

Janice was the first to arrive, and I smiled and waved at her in greeting. She gave me a blank look and then said, "Oh, it's you. Back again, I see." She brushed by me and took a seat in the circle of chairs in the middle of the room. Mimi arrived next, with Bobby hot on her heels.

Mimi danced around me in greeting. "I'm so thrilled you've taken such a positive step by returning to our little group," she said, sounding like a shrill imitation of Laura-Lea. Bobby stood so close to her, it was hard to tell where she ended and he began. He touched her every few seconds as if he was afraid she might fly away if left unattended. Clearly I had missed something while I had been away. I wondered what else had changed. Bobby and Mimi sailed across the room in a sort of bizarre two-headed waltz and chose chairs next to each other, across from Janice who was busy ignoring them.

Laura-Lea flew into the room ranting about traffic and how it was enough to cause anyone to develop an emotional imbalance. She patted me on the arm in a distracted, adorable sort of way. She didn't

seem surprised to see me. I supposed Dr. Alexander must have called
her and told her I was coming tonight. That I was mandated, forced
to attend. I pushed the thought from my mind. No, tonight I was
going to focus on sharing my story, on contributing to the group, not
isolating myself from them with fear.

Laura-Lea leaned in close and purred, "I'm going to have to
really, really insist you open tonight's session by telling your story."
She pouted, letting me know she was really, really serious. I nodded
and she squeezed my arm.

Moments later Grace flitted into the room and threw her arms
around my neck. I had to bend down to hug her, she was so short.
"The prodigal has returned," she said, beaming.

I was genuinely happy to see her. "Yes, I'm back."

Grace took my hand. "Good. Come sit by me."

Richard and Malcolm arrived moments later. Richard's arm
draped around Malcolm's shoulders in a sort of aggressive buddy hold;
he was in the middle of what seemed to be a complicated story about
the ethics of fine dining. "I never eat anywhere that doesn't insist on
a tie," Richard was telling Malcolm. "Takeout is for suckers."

Malcolm vacillated between seeming engrossed in Richard's
monologue and looking desperate, a reluctant disciple at the feet
of a self-appointed master. He nodded and murmured, "Yes, I see, of
course."

Richard removed his hand from Malcolm's shoulder, and
Malcolm scurried over to the empty chair between Janice and Grace.
Richard frowned at the two women, then took the remaining empty
chair across the circle from Malcolm.

Laura-Lea cleared her throat, a signal the session was to begin.

Richard flashed Malcolm two thumbs up. "At the break I'll tell you how to order the right wine with your meal. There's an art to it, you know." He kept his thumbs raised until Malcolm returned the gesture.

I was amazed by what had changed since the last time I'd been here. The group was like a living thing, shifting, growing, rearranging itself. Moving apart and coming together again in a new way as each member grew comfortable, familiar. I felt a pang of regret, and a longing to be a part of them. I was even more determined to share my story with the group.

Laura-Lea scooched back in her chair and clapped her hands twice. Everyone else did the same. I threw Grace a puzzled glance, but she was looking at Laura-Lea. Then, without prompting, they all took a long breath in through their noses, and let it out through their mouths. In unison. Like a breathing band, an airy orchestra. *This is new too.* I breathed with them.

Laura-Lea threw an arm out toward me. "Everyone, let's welcome Kate back to the group. She's agreed to begin the session tonight with her story."

Richard raised a finger in the air. "Here, here. About time." Seemed he'd forgotten the first time I shared my story. He hadn't exactly been a pillar of support then. I hoped he had reined in his big mouth.

I glanced at Grace for support, and she patted my knee. "Go on, dear. I did it, and you can too."

I took another of those long breaths through my nose and blew it out hard through my mouth. "You're right, Grace. I can do this." I shifted in my chair until I was comfortable and began to talk.

⌒⌒

When I finished speaking, the room was quiet. No one, not even Richard, spoke or looked at me. I shifted in my chair, chanting a silent mantra, *Please, please, please someone say something.*

After a moment Grace—who had held my hand for much of my storytelling—stood and spread her arms open to me. Relieved, I stood and stepped into her embrace. She patted my back, and then held me at arm's length looking me in the eye. "I can understand why it was difficult for you to share your story."

"I'll say," I heard Mimi murmur to Bobby. Bobby just giggled and held Mimi's hand.

Grace let me go and I sat down, gripping the edge of my chair. Janice was looking everywhere in the room except at me. Laura-Lea looked around the group, clearly expecting everyone to chime in. Bobby and Mimi fussed with each other, while Malcolm stared at his feet.

Richard waved his hand, making small circles in the air. "You do realize that Kevin's voice wasn't really him at all. It was you. You made it up," he tapped his temple.

A spark of anger flashed. What made him the expert? Who was he to tell me anything? I mean, he wasn't completely off base, but he was certainly no expert. I struggled to maintain my cool. I shared my story because I wanted to connect with the group and he was part of the group. I spoke slowly. "Thank you for your ideas, Richard."

Laura-Lea's face split into a grin and she waggled her eyebrows in a way that said, Good girl!

Malcolm piped up. "I think he means you invented it in your mind."

I turned toward Malcolm. "I know what he meant."

Janice flicked a hand toward me. "It's not so strange, if you think about it. Young girl like you loses her husband, well, I'd go a bit batty too, I suppose."

"Uh, thanks Janice." *I think.* I ducked my head, suddenly shy. "Listen. I know I haven't contributed much to the group before now. But I promise I'll do better." I glanced around the room. "I'm just like everyone here. I'm simply trying to get my life on track—trying to find normal."

Normal. That's what I had wanted for so long.

I'm curled like a cat on the sofa, knees bent, feet tucked under me. I reach out to take the hot tea Kevin hands me. The cup burns my fingers and I set it down fast on the table beside me.

"Sorry, sorry," Kevin says. I don't look at him. Instead I snuggle deeper into my red sweater, letting the softness of the cushions ease my ache. My body aches and I try not to move too much. Moving makes the blood gush. Everything hurts.

Kevin hovers over me for a long moment, but I won't look up. I stretch for a book, a novel, on the table, but I can't quite reach. Kevin snaps it up and hands it to me. I open it to page one. The words are a blur. My head pounds.

Kevin walks over to the Christmas tree and examines it as if he'd never seen it before. The lights are on even though it is the middle of the day. The opened gifts are arranged under the tree, looking ordinary after the display of colored paper.

"Would you get me an Advil?" My question makes him jump.

He spins around to face me, but he shakes his head. "You have to wait another hour or so."

I furrow my brows. "Why? I hurt."

He sighs and fidgets with his shirt cuff. He looks lost, out of place somehow. As if he has no idea how he got here, or what to do now that he's arrived. "That's what it says on the bottle. Every six hours. You took one five hours ago."

"Oh." I close my eyes and let out a long breath. I pull my feet out from under me and give a soft moan as I stretch them out on the sofa. Kevin bends and cups my heels with his hands, easing my feet to the cushion.

"I can do it," I snap at him. "I'm not an invalid."

He jerks back, hands at his sides, but his face is stony. "I'm just trying to help." He spits the words like bits of sand.

"You've helped enough," I say, wanting only to end this meaningless exchange, this fussing over something as inconsequential as a pill. I just want to be still and quiet.

His hands ball to fists at his side, then he opens them wide. "You'll be fine in a few days. Everything will be back to normal."

I look at him, from his rumpled dress pants to the open collar of his silk shirt. He's far too sophisticated for these humble surroundings. He's a GQ model set down in the middle of a rural community.

"What's normal?" I ask. And he just looks back at me.

42

The dollar value for my house, on the seller's agreement, was more than I'd expected for a two-bedroom house in a small town, but the realtor, Rose, had explained that asking prices were just that—asking. We'd lower the price if the house didn't sell in two months. Glancing out the front window, I saw Rose pounding a *For Sale* sign into the front lawn. The woman came prepared.

Two months. It would be mid-December by then. I hoped to be in a new home before Christmas, to put this house and all that had happened in it behind me. Like Maggie had said, I needed to stop wrestling with the past.

I watched Rose drive off, then turned to survey my house.

But maybe I also needed to face it. I climbed the stairs and went into the guest room, which over the years had become a catchall space in the house. It was a storeroom of memories.

I opened the closet and shuffled through the junk at the bottom. Dust danced around my head and into my nose as I rummaged through the room, uncovering collections of discarded clothing, random pieces of paper, bizarre collections of mateless shoes, furniture polish, a broken tennis racket, and ice skates I hadn't worn since high school.

I pushed through all these things, tossing them out of the closet without much more than a glance. It was almost as if I was looking for something. As if some part of me knew what I'd find.

In the back of the closet, I spied it—a large shoe box that had once contained a pair of men's winter boots, size twelve. I picked it up and held it at arm's length, as if it might contain a poisonous snake.

Just look inside.

I pulled off the lid. A bright red sweater had been stuffed into the box, and it swelled up, pushing its way out. I pulled it out and held it to my face. It smelled dull and neglected. I picked up the shoe box and the sweater and carried them into my bedroom. I crawled onto the bare mattress and let the memories rise up and speak.

Inside the shoe box were letters and a few postcards sent from friends traveling to faraway places. And random photos, blurry shots that didn't make the photo album, but were never thrown out either.

I found a picture of a campground where Kevin and I had spent a weekend, and an unfocused picture of my sister, mouth full of potato salad, at a family picnic.

There were several from last Christmas. Kevin sitting by the tree, looking miserable. Heather and her boyfriend, long gone now, smooching under the mistletoe. My mother waving as she walked in the door. Of me, sitting on the couch, propped up with pillows, a blanket over my legs. I'm wearing the red sweater, unsmiling, pale and thin, like a Siberian famine victim. I tore the photo into pieces.

It's early morning, barely seven, and the sun tries to break the dark. The trees, bright with new leaves, reach into the sky, licking up the first rays. I curl my legs under me and stare out the window. Kevin, holding a coffee cup, stands over me.

"How long, Kate?" He pauses, waiting for me to respond, but I have no answers. He tries again. "How long are you planning to live like this? Moping inside this house? It's been six months."

I pull my red sweater tight against my body and stare out the window. How long does it take to turn the world around?

Kevin holds out a piece of paper. "Are you coming?" he says.

It's an invitation to a party. Black tie, it says, eight p.m., it says, celebrate Donna Walsh's promotion, it says.

I'm so tired. If I close my eyes, I dream; if I keep them open, life continues around me as if nothing has changed. I'm not sure which is worse.

Kevin drops the invitation onto my knees. "I'm going."

I nod. I know what he means. He's going. To the party, to the city, to the bed of his mentor, his lover, Donna Walsh. He's going, going, gone.

He pokes at the invitation. "I've waited a long time for you to heal, to get back to yourself." He shakes his head, a disappointed parent at wits' end with his dopey child. "It's time to get on with life, Kate."

I turn to him and look into his deep brown eyes. "Then go. Get on with life."

His eyes widen, then narrow with the shock.

I wave a hand toward the door.

"Don't wait for me," he says.

43

Red and gold hovered like halos atop green trees as Dr. Alexander and I walked through the downtown park. The wind blew, but the sun still warmed us.

Upon arriving at his office for this, my third appointment since I'd been released, I eyed the couch, the somber walls, the soothing carpet and said, "Can we walk and talk instead?"

Dr. Alexander had looked out the window and agreed. Ten minutes later we had entered the winding paths of a riverside park only two blocks from his office. He walked with hands clasped in front, making a V of his arms. I was surprised to note he wasn't carrying his usual notepad and pen. A jogger passed us on the right, then a lean man on a bicycle zipped by, looking serious in black spandex. All around us were people who walked, picnicked, chatted to one another—none paying any attention to this commonplace duo: a father and daughter, or work colleagues, a mentor and his protégé.

As usual he was silent, waiting for me to begin. The past four months since Kevin's funeral tumbled through my mind, and as I walked beside the river, I felt like a survivor of some terrible calamity, an earthquake or fire or flood. After being released from the psychiatric center, it was as if I'd been handed my life back, and that somehow the worst was over. "Could all of this happen to me again?"

He frowned at the swiftly moving water. "Yes."

I took a moment to absorb the word. I'd wanted him to smile and shake my hand, say *Congratulations* and send me on my way with a certificate of sanity. I wanted him to pooh-pooh my fears of relapse, assure me I'd reached my quota of mental illness. "Oh."

He turned to me in a quick, almost startled manner. "It probably wouldn't happen exactly the same way, with the same symptoms. But psychosis could reoccur in the future." As an afterthought he said, "Not that you're completely recovered from this episode."

I stopped walking and watched the wide river rushing to wherever it was going. In places the water roiled and churned, making it appear white. Farther out, where the water was deepest, it looked flat, nearly motionless, as if a sheet of glass had been laid on top. I wanted to lie on the smooth surface and look up into the endless clear sky. I imagined lying on my back, spread-eagle, buoyed by still water, while the rest of the river rushed beside me, beneath me, but could not budge my clear, still island.

"Better," I said, but the word stuck in my throat and came out garbled, indistinct. I cleared my throat. "I'm better."

"Give yourself some time, Kate." He looked at me. "Your mental state is better—improved—but give it time."

I started walking again. "Okay."

He didn't fall into step, but stood. "You're at an important juncture. Your symptoms, the voice, missing memories have largely dissipated. You've regained the bulk of your memory, if not all of it. But there's more to recovery than an absence of symptoms."

I turned to look at him. We stood several feet apart, facing each other on the path, his voice raised slightly to cover the distance.

"You must decide what to do with the truth you've recovered. The events of your recent past were traumatic enough to cause your mind to bury them. Now that you know your whole story, you're going to have to do something with it." He took slow steps until he was only a few feet in front of me.

He motioned his head toward the path, indicating we should keep walking.

I said, "So if something bad happens in the future, a death, or something like that, I could—" I snapped my fingers.

"Perhaps. Or it could be something much smaller that triggers another episode. Or nothing at all." He gave me a steady look. "The key is what I said before: You need to decide what to do with the truth of your past, Kate."

We walked beside a stand of trees that obscured the river, blocking it from view. The early autumn wind rustled the leaves and swirled around us. I listened for the sound of the rushing, churning river just beyond the trees. "And if I do what you say, if I deal with my past—will I be okay after that?"

The wind rustled through the leaves. "Let's begin by tapering you off your medication, and we'll take it one step at a time."

The kitchen was filled with oven-cleaner fumes. I coughed and pushed the window above the sink wide open. I'd spent the last two days cleaning house—scrubbing it of all personal effects.

"No personal items should be in sight in any room of the house," Rose the realtor had said. So I threw most of my personal items in garbage bags and heaped them in the backyard.

I hadn't just cleaned the house—I didn't want to simply pack my things. I needed to expunge the house, so I had walked from room to room, garbage bag in hand, sweeping framed photos, porcelain figurines, even books, into the bag and tossing them into the backyard as if everything in the house was contaminated and I was trying to scrub it clean.

The doorbell rang, and I groaned. Who could it be? I kept scrubbing the crusty mess inside the oven that I'd been working on for over an hour. I didn't want company.

After a second ring I walked to the door and pulled it open.

Blair stood on the stoop and flung an arm toward the front yard. "For sale? What does that mean?"

I rolled my eyes. "It means the house is for sale. Interested?"

Blair ran his hands through his hair. He took a half step toward me, expecting me to let him in the house.

I crossed my arms. "Not interested in buying the house? Fine. Then you can go."

"Kate." That's all he said. Just that. He was unshaven. His skin looked sallow and gray, as if he'd been pouring ashes on his head. "Kate. Please, Kate."

I stood my ground. "Why are you here? Did you honestly believe I would want to talk to you?"

His face flushed red. "Let me tell you how sorry I am. Let me explain."

Explain? There was no explanation for how he had betrayed me.

Just like Heather, he'd befriended Donna. But worse, he'd been a part of their affair, a friend to their infidelity. Kevin's relationship confidant. I was disgusted. "I've known you forever, Blair. You've always been a part of my life. I've trusted you for so long. And what you did—"

"Kate—"

"And not just you," I cut him off. "Heather, too. I'm drowning in lies. That's why 'For Sale.' That's why I'm leaving. I can't stand to be here anymore."

Tears fell down his cheeks, splotching onto his light blue T-shirt. "I loved Kevin. He was like a brother to me." He looked miserable, like a large, hesitant child. "I wish I'd never known about the affair."

"You didn't just know, you approved. "

"I know," he whispered over and over. He shut his eyes and tipped his head back until I was eyeing his Adam's apple. I watched it bob as he swallowed rapidly.

"Just leave, Blair."

Blair held up two hands in an I-surrender gesture. "I know what I did was wrong," he said, voice rising with emotion. "I know it. But do you know why I did it?" He jammed his hands on his hips, defying me to guess. "Because I'm in love with you, Kate. I always have been."

I stared at him.

"I've been in love with you since the moment we met, back in high school. But you were with Kevin, my best friend." He gave me an imploring look, eyes wide, brows high on his forehead. "Don't you see? I've had to lie to you from that moment on."

I wanted to scream. Throw things. I squeezed my eyes shut and spoke very slowly. "I don't see. I'm sure you believe you're making all kinds of sense." I opened my eyes. "And maybe you are. But I'm done talking about this." I waved my hand, ordering him to go. "I don't need that kind of love, Blair."

He stood for a long moment, shoulders slumped, defeated. He'd said what he came to say, but it made no difference. He turned and walked, but after a few steps, stopped to pinch back a petunia. With a bolt I realized he was the one who'd been tending to my lawn and watering the flowers in the backyard. It had to have been him. Even after I threw him out, after the things I'd said to him, he was still tending to my yard. But it didn't matter.

I called to him. "Blair, wait."

He sprinted up the steps. "What?"

I held my hand out. "Give me your key to my house."

The doorbell rang again and I rolled my eyes. I imagined myself punching Blair in the face if he returned, then realized that I should probably resign from the punching business.

I pulled off the rubber gloves I'd been wearing while still trying to finish scrubbing the oven. On my way to the door, I caught a glance of myself in the mirror. My face was smeared with what I assumed was oven grunge. My hair was disheveled and a thin sheen of sweat clung to my brow.

A knock. "Kate?"

Jack.

I pulled the door open without hesitation and stepped back to make room for him. I smiled, genuinely happy to see him.

He entered the house, and I had to take another pace back. The foyer seemed to shrink as he filled it with his presence. I had a surreal sensation of two worlds clanging together. My city life had come to town.

Jack stood by the door, looking around. He gave me a shy look. "Nice place." I backed up farther still, staring at him like he was a ghost. What was he doing here? He stepped into the living room, looking around. "I see a *For Sale* sign on the front lawn."

I nodded. "Yep. It's time." I skirted around him and closed the door. "Why are you here? I mean, I'm surprised to see you." Surprised didn't even cover it. He didn't even own a car. "How did you get here?"

"I borrowed Lester's car. You met Lester, he stands at the back of the gym on Sunday mornings and hands out coffee." I remembered Lester as a crumpled old man with the shakes and ragged clothing. He'd struck me more as a homeless person than a guy who owned a car.

Jack rubbed his hands together. "Speaking of coffee, where does a guy go for a cup in this town?"

"He goes to my kitchen," I said, leading the way.

He grinned. "Talk about convenient." He followed me into the kitchen. He had to step over the cleaning supplies strewn across the floor. "Can I make an observation?"

I fumbled with the coffeemaker. The smell of oven cleaner over-powered the aroma of the coffee grounds. "Knock yourself out."

"You're a mess." He stood at the sink, so close if I lifted my arm I'd touch him. He grinned.

My hands moved to my hair and face. I felt heat rush to my

cheeks. "I've been cleaning house, not preening for a beauty pag-
eant." I smiled back. I clicked the *On* button of the coffeemaker,
then grabbed a paper towel and ran it across my face. I wondered if
I could excuse myself long enough to have a fast shower, freshen up
a bit.

He tipped his head toward the open oven door. "I see that."
Something about Jack kept me off balance. His deep voice and boyish
charm combined to make him appear both masculine and youthful.
I curved my lips into a self-conscious smile.

He peered closer at my face. "Your smile is sad."

I didn't know what to say, so I said nothing.

"I'd love to see those brown eyes of yours light up," he said
quietly.

I dropped my gaze to the floor, unable to meet his look.

"I'd like to see you happy, Kate. Really happy. Dancing for joy
kind of happy."

I nodded. I tried to picture myself, arms over my head, body
twisting with enjoyment, feet tapping out their pleasure. A yearning
rose up in my chest. What would it take to feel that way?

He reached up and put the flat of his hand against my cheek. "I
wish I knew how to make that happen." His voice was thick.

His hand was a blanket over my cheek. "Me, too," I whispered.

His thumb ran along my jawline and back again. Without moving my head, I looked up at him. His eyes were focused on his hand.
His roving thumb touched the corner of my mouth and his blue eyes
met mine for a long moment. He dropped his hand suddenly and
looked around the kitchen. He noticed the to-do list on the table
next to the realtor's agreement, and picked up the list. He let out a

low whistle. "You've got a pile of work to do here. Painting, drywall repair, replace bedroom door frame, steam cleaning. Who is going to help you?"

Who would help me? *Hmm, let me think …* Who hadn't I run off, lied to, kicked out of my life? I blew out a hard breath. "Pathetically enough, I've got no help."

He glanced down at the list. "Well, that's why I came today. When you told me you were moving, I figured you might need some manpower."

I opened my mouth, ready to interrupt him.

He held up a hand. "Just with the big stuff. Things too heavy or too difficult for you to do by yourself. I'm pretty handy for a pastor. And movers don't help with things like painting and repairs."

I poured him a cup of coffee. "Actually I'm not hiring movers. I'm selling the house furnished." There was nothing in the house I wanted anymore. I handed him the cup. "You must think I'm a loser. I've lived in this town my whole life, and I can't think of a single person who would come and help me."

He stood close to me, holding the cup. "Loser is the last thing I'd ever think about you." He touched my shoulder, and then let his hand drop. "You've been through so much. It blows my mind when I think about everything you've been through." He frowned deeply. "Just let me help you. Please?"

"Yeah, of course. I want help. I need help," I said, as if that fact weren't perfectly obvious to both of us.

"Great." He sat down at the table. "Let's make a game plan. What have you started already?"

I sat across from him. "Decluttering, mostly. I've just started cleaning. But most of these repairs are beyond me. I've never been very handy."

He took a sip of the coffee, made a face, and then poured an outrageous amount of sugar into it from the bowl on the table. He took another sip, seemingly satisfied. "What about the exterior?"

I stared dumbly at the list. I hadn't given the exterior much thought aside from the lawn and gardens. "It's in pretty good shape, I think."

Jack nodded. "From what I saw when I came in, I agree, but when you start looking close, it's amazing how many little things can show up." He stood and moved to the back door. "Leaking eaves, cracked downspouts, loose bricks." He looked like a boy listing his favorite toys. "I could have a look around out there—see what's what." His hand was on the doorknob.

"Yes, thank you, Jack," I said, but he was already out the door.

I snapped the rubber gloves on and resumed scrubbing the oven. Most of the fumes from the cleaner had dissipated through the open window. I stuck my head in the oven and scrubbed out the last of the crud on the bottom. Knowing Jack was outside tackling the jobs I couldn't do myself made my task feel lighter. I had help, a friend. I hummed as I worked.

Afterward I filled the sink with warm, soapy water in order to wash the racks. I glanced at the fridge. Might as well clean the refrigerator shelves at the same time, I thought. The act of cleaning brought me great satisfaction, as if I were accomplishing more than just squeaky-clean surfaces. I was setting the stage for a new phase in my life. I began emptying the contents of the fridge, tossing expired bottles of salad dressing and humming to myself. I sniffed a dubious-looking tub of strawberry yogurt.

"Kate?" Kevin's voice called. It sounded muffled, as if from far away.

I dropped the yogurt, blots of thick pink sprayed across the floor. My heart hammered in my chest. *Kevin's calling me.* The kitchen slanted left like an amusement park ride, then righted itself again. For a moment I thought I would be sick.

The rubber gloves suddenly felt hot and smothering against my skin. I stripped them off and dropped them on the floor. I took a step, then another until I was in the living room. I heard nothing.

I moved to the stairs and climbed, my throat so dry I couldn't swallow. Upstairs I leaned hard on the wall and listened, but heard nothing. *The bedroom.* I walked to the doorway.

Inside the room Kevin stood looking out the window, his back to me. He wore faded jeans, like the ones he wore around the house when we were first married, before the designer suits. His simple, black cotton shirt rippled and stretched over his broad shoulders as he raised both hands and placed them on the frame of the window. His dark hair looked slightly shaggy, long enough to brush his collar. A painful yearning pierced my stomach. He was beautiful.

He touched the wall at the bottom of the window, running a finger along a long gouge in the drywall made when I had hoisted the chest of drawers out the window. I wanted to touch him, to run my fingers across the cliffs and valleys of his face and body. He studied the marks on the wall. "Kate?" he called again.

A million pinpricks ran across my scalp and down my spine. Nearly breathless I said, "I'm here."

He turned slowly, fingering the marks on the wall as if they were braille. My heart roared in my ears, the room swam, his profile blurred. Then he faced me.

Jack.

The tension flooded from my body and I leaned against the doorjamb for support. "I thought you were outside," I said, panting as if I'd just run the hundred-yard dash.

Jack said, "I was. I noticed this window looked different from the rest, so I came in through the front door and up here—are you all right? You look very pale."

I pressed my hand to my collarbone. "Breathed in too many oven cleaner fumes, I guess."

He frowned. "Maybe you should take a break."

I turned and walked back down the stairs, mumbling, "Yes, I need a break."

44

At six thirty that evening the doorbell rang. I opened the door and there stood Maggie wearing a purple pantsuit the exact shade of her new PT Cruiser parked on the street, and a pink Doris Day hat that sat slightly too far forward on her head and wobbled when she spoke. "I'm just bursting in uninvited, dearest."

And she did, shouldering her way into the house before I could step aside for her. She waved two hands at me, her vinyl white purse swinging dangerously close to my face. "I've tried calling, I've tried leaving messages." She glared at me, one eye bulging larger than the other. "Nothing. So I decided to drop in unannounced. Imagine my surprise at seeing a *For Sale* sign on your front lawn. It's rude, you know—"

She caught sight of Jack, who'd sauntered in from the kitchen, a questioning look on his face.

"Well, hello there," Maggie purred, extending her hand to him so that he could not shake it, but kiss it. Which he did, adding a clipped bow. Maggie turned to me, eyebrows waggling. "My goodness, he's lovely. Wherever did you find him?"

"Maggie, meet Jack. Pastor Jack. He's helping me with some house repairs."

Jack held up a plumber's wrench as if offering proof. "A pleasure to meet you, Maggie."

She clapped her hands twice. "A man of the cloth. How exciting." She stomped a foot, commanding our full attention. "Naturally I want to hear all about this love affair from both of you, but first—"

I interrupted, my face burning. I couldn't bear to look at Jack. "It's not a love aff—"

Maggie held up her hand. "But first! There is a *For Sale* sign on your lawn, and I want to know what's going on." She grabbed my arm and pulled me down the hall into the den. She looked over her shoulder at Jack. "I need a tête-à-tête with our mutual friend. You carry on doing what you were doing." She marched me into the den and closed the door behind her. "Goodness, Kate, he's what the young people call a hunk."

I shook my head. "You've misunderstood—"

"I understand perfectly, dear. And I approve. It's one thing for a withered up old lady like me to go on being single. I can pull off eccentric." She motioned for me to take a seat in the desk chair. "You're too young for eccentric. You need a man in your life, and that Jack Slater fellow is just the sort to paint your wagon."

I sat and gaped bug-eyed at her, but I couldn't help but smile a little. "There's so much wrong with that sentence, I don't even know where to begin."

Maggie dragged a second chair beside me and sat. "Wrong? You're a fine one to talk about wrong. You've got your house for sale, a hunk in your kitchen adjusting your taps, and all without saying a word to me."

"I know I should have called you after I was released from the assessment center. I've been meaning to, it's just things have been busy …" I trailed off. My excuses were lame. I hadn't called Maggie, or anyone else for that matter, because I didn't want anyone trying to talk me out of moving to the city, of getting on with my life. Or maybe because I just didn't want to talk, period.

She sighed in an exaggerated way. "Good intentions pave the road to—well, never mind." She looked up at the ceiling, beseeching the heavens. "Bygones and all that stuff. Tell me about that *For Sale* sign."

"I'm moving to the city."

To my surprise Maggie jumped up and applauded. "Well done, Kate." She clasped her hands over her breast. "Oh, I remember this so well."

Remembered? "What do you mean?"

She sat again. "After Jeremy left, I sulked and stalled for a long time, then one day I knew it was time to move on. It was all of a sudden, all at once. One day I didn't know what to do, the next I did." She patted my leg. "Was it like that for you? All at once?"

I thought about it for a moment. "I guess it was." Why had I avoided Maggie? She was a breath of fresh air, always encouraging me. Guilt poked at me. I'd treated her badly, unfairly. She'd been nothing but a true friend to me.

She winked. "Except it took me three years to come to that sensible conclusion, and it only took you a few months." She nodded, approving the timeline. "Now let's dish about that Handsome Harry in your kitchen." Maggie let out a long, low whistle. "My, my."

"Oh, Maggie …"

She put a finger on her chin. "I wonder what it would be like to kiss him."

"Oy. He's just a friend, Maggie. I met him at the community center, and he's been helping me out—"

"Uh-huh. Big guy like that, you'd have to bend your head back like this." She tilted her head, showing me her throat. "Don't you think?"

I shook my head. "I don't know, Mag—"

"How tall are you?" She stood and waved for me to do the same.

"Seriously, cut it out—"

"He looks strong, too." She ran a hand up her arm from elbow to shoulder.

"You've lost your mind." I was laughing now.

She raised an eyebrow. "Have I? I don't think so. I saw the look on his face when he looked at you."

"What look?" The words were out of my mouth before I could think. Like some Pavlovian dog, my interest piqued at the hint of a man's attentions.

Maggie's face split into a wider grin. "Ah, I thought you were just friends?" She nudged me with her elbow.

I grabbed her by the shoulders and turned her toward the door. "We are. And this conversation is getting ridiculous." I shoved her lightly, moving her out of the den.

"Fine, fine," she said, clearly delighted. "I'm your friend too, and I'm officially volunteering to help you with the fix-ups." She turned and gave me a broad wink. "Unless you'd rather I leave you alone with Mr. Friend."

I was smiling wide. Maggie's perky tenacity, her stubborn optimism touched a chord in me. "I'd love it if you stayed. Thank you for offering."

Her eyes sparkled with impish delight. "Happy to. I'll start in the upstairs bathroom." She walked off down the hall. "I'm simply a whiz with bathroom fixtures. Where would I find a clean rag?"

"Under the sink," I called after her. I turned back into the room. Across from me was a full-length mirror. I walked toward myself carefully, taking full account of my reflection. My face was pale, making my brown eyes look large. I ran a hand over my loose cotton shirt and track pants. I inched close to the mirror until my nose nearly touched the glass. I closed my eyes and bent my head back. But only for a moment. I opened my eyes, saw the longing reflected in the image before me. I shivered.

"Stop it," I told myself. *You're a grown woman, not a hormonal teenager.* I turned and hurried from the room.

45

I slumped in the corner of the gym, exhausted. My life had been a mad dash since I'd been released from the psychiatric assessment center more than two weeks before. Keeping up my appointments with Dr. Alexander, group therapy, my probation officer, and logging in hours of community service had me burning up the asphalt of the highway between Greenfield and the city.

When I was home, I cleaned, preparing the final touches on the house before Rose opened it for showings in just two days. And I'd had no time to look for a place to live in the city.

I leaned against the gym wall and closed my eyes. The sounds of basketball filled my ears. There were more teenagers than usual; the numbers had been steadily increasing since Big Tim's death. The news of his murder seemed to act as a magnet, drawing in youth from the streets. The banner that bore his image still hung in the gym. I'd noticed several new messages had been added.

"Hey! Take off, loser." Sekeena's distressed voice rose above the din of bouncing balls. I opened my eyes. Sekeena stood on the far side of the gym, her arms wrapped around her torso. She was wearing a baggy tracksuit, the hood pulled up over her head.

Creeper, a popular boy with an unfortunate nickname, stood near her, tossing a basketball up in the air. I had watched him and Sekeena try to outdo each other on the court the first time I'd visited the gym. He was tall and lean, and he and Sekeena were always in each other's face. Jack had told me that the boy's real name was Terrance, but he earned his nickname in junior high when a growth spurt shot him to six feet tall and he compensated by slouching, his spine curving into a near-perfect *C*.

Sekeena threw Creeper a violent look and skulked away from him, toward me. She threw herself down on the floor beside me. She used her sleeve to wipe the tears from her cheeks.

"Sekeena, what happened?"

She stuck her chin out, putting on her tough-girl act. "Nuthin."

I turned and watched the basketball game, pretending interest. "Oh, good. For a second there I thought your crying meant there was something wrong. Thanks for clearing that up."

She gave a half laugh, half sob, and leaned on my shoulder. I put one arm around her and patted the pocket of my pants, looking for a tissue. When would I learn to stuff them with tissue like my mother always had? No matter the season or the crisis, if you needed a tissue, my mother could produce a variety to choose from. I came up empty-handed.

Sekeena sat up, pushing the tears off her face with her palms. "I'm pregnant."

I tried not to look shocked. She was a tomboy, an in-your-face, play-hard girl who never gave a guy an inch. At least on the basketball court. Obviously she'd been giving one guy plenty of room. Or maybe not.

"Creeper?" I asked, taking an educated guess.

She didn't seem to think it was a dumb question. She wiped her face with the back of her hand. "Yep."

"Was it … your choice?" The world was a different place than the one I had spent my teens in just a decade ago. And the city was far removed from the sleepy town I'd grown up in. Working with teenagers had taught me I couldn't take even the simplest thing for granted.

She tossed her head back. "Creeper doesn't force girls." She gave a bitter laugh. "He doesn't have to."

I looked over to the game. Creeper took control of the ball and dribbled it in for an easy layup. "Does he know?"

She fiddled with the drawstring of her track pants. "No," she said in a flat, sort of disgusted way that teenagers speak when they don't want to talk. The she threw me a startled look. "Don't tell him, either."

"If that's what you want." I stood and offered a hand to hoist her up off the floor. "Let's go talk in Jack's office."

She stood, but pulled away. "Nothing to talk about," she mumbled. "And I have to go look for a place to live."

"Your parents kicked you out?" I pictured an overtaxed mother, young children tugging at her leg, an unemployed father clad in a white undershirt, sitting at the kitchen table waving a furious fist in the air and hollering, *Get outta here!*

Sekeena's lip curled in a sneer. "No, they didn't throw me out. At least not yet." She crossed her arms, head bent so far down she looked like a rag doll. "My mom said to just get an abortion." She snapped her fingers.

I felt a sharp pain, like someone pinched my breastbone. "Is that what you're going to do?"

"Quick fix. My mom's style, not mine." She pointed to her flat abdomen. "And don't bother her about it, she's busy with her own problems."

She took two tiny steps backward. "Anyway, I'm going to split, see where I can hole up until I decide what to do about ..." She shrugged.

I reached out a hand. "Did Jack have some suggestions for where you can live?"

She chewed her lip. "I haven't told Jack. Telling him is worse than telling my parents, ya know?"

Some perverse part of me felt proud that Sekeena had confided in me before Jack, as if it somehow justified my being there with those teenagers. But I also knew that Jack wouldn't react as Sekeena suspected. "He'll understand. And he'll be able to help, too." He'd done nothing but help me from the day I met him; I knew he would bend over backward to help Sekeena.

She tucked her chin to her chest. "He's such a straight shooter. He'll be disappointed in me." Her voice dropped to a whisper. "I don't know how to tell him."

Creeper had played a part in the problem as well and could shoulder some of the blame, I thought. But I held my tongue, no use adding fuel to the fire. "Would you like me to talk to Jack for you?"

She was silent for so long I wasn't sure she'd heard me. Then a quiet peep, "Yeah. Thanks."

She turned, but I stopped her with a touch. "Are you certain you need to leave home right now? I mean, do you have to?"

She frowned. "My mom is on my case to get an abortion. My dad yells at her to shut up, then yells at me."

"I'm sorry."

"Yesterday my mom told me, basically, that I have to get an abortion or move out. She doesn't want the burden. Like she would do all the work?" She snorted. "She acts like I don't have a brain." She was quiet for a moment, then said, "I don't know what to do. I just need to get out of there so I can think straight." She jogged away a few steps, turned and waved, the conversation over. She headed for the exit.

I watched her go, wondering what choice she would make. And how could I help her to make it? She had no idea I'd had an abortion, and I wasn't sure I wanted to share that information with the kids who gathered. What could I do to help her?

I checked my watch. Three fifteen. I was due for my appointment with Dr. Alexander.

I drove, deep in thought about Sekeena. She was so young, too young to be a mother. Too young to have to make such huge decisions about life and death. I idled at a stop sign and looked around. Where was I?

I had driven blindly, without thinking, for at least fifteen minutes and found myself in a neighborhood I'd never seen before. Tree-shaded boulevards were trimmed with winding walkways. Rows of large, Victorian-era houses lined the street. It was reminiscent of a 1950s TV show, where the world seemed honest and clean.

I inched the car forward, drinking in the sites of the pastel-colored houses, greener-than-green lawns with giant oak trees shading oversized lots. At the end of the street, I noticed a corner house with a sign out front that said *For Sale by Owner.* I slowed my car.

I stopped in front of the lot. Painted in buttery yellow with white trim, the two-story house seemed to smile and bend and bow. I glanced at the time. I was late for my appointment with Dr. Alexander. And I was on probation, required to keep all appointments with him. But I turned the engine off and climbed out of the car. I pulled out my phone and called Dr. Alexander's office. "Sorry, but I'll be late for my appointment," I told his receptionist. We rescheduled for the next day.

I walked up the curved sidewalk just as a woman, whom I would have pegged at about sixty, maybe sixty-five, came out onto the veranda. She waved, as if she'd been expecting me.

I returned the wave. "I noticed the *For Sale* sign."

She stuck her hand out. "I'm Georgia." She pushed a strand of salt-and-pepper hair back up into the twist on her head. "Are you looking to buy a house?"

"I suppose I am," I said.

"Come in, then."

It was one of those hold-your-breath moments, walking into the house. Like entering a cool breeze, a calm river, a soothing sunrise. The small rooms of a traditional Victorian had been pushed aside and opened up so that the broad foyer flowed into what could correctly be called a *great room.* The rounded archways, crown molding, and restored ancient flooring worked together to provide a sense of

stepping back to a gentler time. Across the room a large-scale fireplace warmed the room. The walls had been painted a soft dove gray,
trimmed in the same crisp white as the veranda. It was a room that
made you say "Oh." And nothing more.

When we walked into the kitchen, I was temporarily dazed by
the size of it. Georgia seemed chagrined. "Harry always said the
kitchen is the heartbeat of the home. We wanted it nice in here."

Nice was an understatement. Four chefs could work here
without interfering with each other. Windows ran horizontally
across one full wall, giving a full—nearly panoramic—view of
the backyard. I peered out, half expecting to see children playing.
Instead there was only green grass and fruit trees. And a boxwood
hedge that seemed to act as a barrier or fence. "What's beyond
the hedge?"

Georgia didn't even look out the window. "The garden. Well,
mostly weeds now, I admit. I haven't had time for babying tomatoes
since Harry turned sick."

I turned to her, feeling a prick of guilt. "I'm sorry. Is he better?"

She smiled. "*Better* like only God could make him. He died five
months ago, just after we finished the renovation on this place." She
let out a laugh. "But, bear in mind, the renovations have lasted nearly
twenty-five years." Her eyes drifted out to the backyard. "We raised
our children here, five of them, and over the years, we tinkered—
fixing a room up here, wallpapering there. Harry called it his burden
of love."

Her eyes sparkled bright, perhaps from tears. I felt a lump grow
in my chest. Like a fist. "I'm sorry."

Georgia jerked, as if suddenly waking. "No, don't be. I'm going to live with my middle daughter and her children. Three sweet babies for me to hold and spoil." She ran a hand along the countertop. "It's time."

Upstairs were five bedrooms, each one sunnier than the last, and four bathrooms. After the tour we sat on the back porch and sipped the iced tea Georgia had made. The silence between us stretched out like a homecoming. I was completely at ease with this place, this woman—a complete stranger. I caught her staring at me. "I'm sorry. I'm just amazed. You look—"

"What?"

She shook her head. "You're going to think I'm trying to sell you a bill of goods, but you look just as if you were home." She held up her glass to the house. "This place suits you."

"I'll take it."

Iced tea spilled from her glass as she nearly lost her grip on it. "Oh, Kate, I didn't mean—"

"I know you didn't. And I know it's impractical, ridiculous really, for a single woman to buy a house like this. But ..." I could neither explain nor deny the impression; that's how best to describe it— nothing but an impression, a notion more than a thought or idea, that I was to live here. A wordless imprint on my heart that spoke to me: Yes, here.

I looked around. "You said you're moving in with your daughter. Would you consider selling the house furnished?"

Her hand fluttered near her throat. "Well, I don't know. There are a few pieces of furniture that are heirlooms. My children would never want me to part with them. But—"

"But the rest of the furniture?"

"I suppose so. I don't see why not." She fanned her face with her hand. "

"Good. Should I write the check out to you?"

Georgia stood up too, shaking her head and smiling. "You're certainly not one to waste any time."

"I've wasted too much time already."

46

Every surface in my Greenfield house gleamed. After only two weeks on the market, it had sold. The walls were freshly painted, the furniture arranged just so. It hardly looked like the house I had lived in for the past five years. With Jack and Maggie's help, I'd managed to complete the long to-do list and now it was time for me to go. But I lingered, walking through the rooms, as if I'd forgotten something.

The new owners would take possession in a few days and I now had a new, furnished home in the city.

In the cleaned-out kitchen I sighed. I didn't feel a connection with this sparkling-clean room. The sound of the refrigerator humming seemed loud. How had I not heard such a loud sound all those years?

I opened the back door and stepped outside. I had raked the last of the autumn leaves only a few days ago. The air was crisp with the promise of winter. I had wanted to be in my new home before Christmas, and I'd managed that, with six weeks to spare.

So much change, so quickly. Dr. Alexander had told me to take things slowly, not to rush. Once again I hadn't listened. But it wasn't rebellion. I was simply doing what I knew had to be done.

I couldn't stay in Greenfield any longer. Couldn't wrestle my past anymore. With one last look at the yard, I headed back into the house.

In the kitchen I picked up the sponge and bucket, planning to put them in my car, when I remembered I hadn't pulled out the stove and washed behind it.

Would the new owners even think to look behind the stove? Would it really matter if I left it dirty? I pulled the stove out and leaned forward, looking at the floor. It was disgusting.

I filled the bucket with water, added a cap of yellow cleaner, and got down on my knees. I started with the sides of the stove, then ran a sponge over the floor, and grazed something as I wiped. I thought it was a dried shard of pasta, or a shriveled pea, but, upon examination, I saw it was a pill. A painkiller from the bottle I'd spilled on the floor when Kevin's voice had screamed at me.

I held it up, rolling it between my fingers, remembering that horrible day, the day I spiraled into full-blown mental health crisis. The hinge on which my mental health had swung.

I sat on the floor, behind the stove, and rested my head against the wall. *Kevin's voice.* The answer seemed to be that I had manufactured it, created in my grieving mind—not to haunt me, but in an effort to save myself—to reassemble the pieces of my past, burying the terrible truth and creating instead the life I had wanted to live. That was the official explanation, the one Dr. Alexander and I had put together over the past weeks. And it seemed to fit, seemed to make sense—only …

If I had made Kevin's voice up in my own mind, that meant that I had been speaking for him—using my words and his voice. So why would I have screamed at myself? Why would I have called myself names, said hateful things, berated and abused myself?

I rolled the white pill between two fingers. And what about the more recent event, when I mistook Jack for Kevin? It would have been obvious to anyone that it was Jack who had been standing there in his jeans and black shirt. But I had seen Kevin—not just seen him, but yearned for him. For a moment I had been completely convinced it was him standing there. What did that mean to my mental health? A simple mistake? A ... what had Dr. Alexander called it? A psychotic break?

I pushed myself up and stepped out from behind the stove. No guarantees—that's another thing Dr. Alexander had said.

I finished cleaning the floor, pushed the stove against the wall, and gathered up the cleaning supplies. I felt oddly self-conscious in the spotless, picture-perfect house, an intruder. I laid a set of house keys on the small table by the door.

Tears streamed down my face as I stood, hand on the doorknob, ready to leave, but not ready to leave. I walked back into the living room and sat on the floor, my back to the sofa. I let the grief of the past pour out of me onto the floor.

Random images began to drift through my exhausted mind, just like they had when I was still in the psychiatric ward. But these were different, more complete; they spanned my whole life, from my earliest childhood memory forward. Words, memories, hopes floated together through my consciousness: strange images, unrelated to anything, even to each other. Just pictures and words, fragments of thoughts, shards of ideas. The dress I'd worn to senior prom; my mother baking cookies on a rainy day; Jack's face; my father's funeral; Christmas presents.

I hugged my knees to my chest. "Kevin?" I didn't expect him to answer, knew he wouldn't—couldn't—but I had to speak to him one last time. I pushed myself up from the floor and stood in the middle of the living room. "I'm leaving this place. Going to the city just like you wanted to. And I think I understand now how you felt suffocated in this house." My throat burned and clenched as emotion rose and I pushed it down again. "I understand the desire to move on, to reach for something bigger than this town." I turned a slow circle and spoke to the ceiling as if he might be floating there. "But what you did was horrible, Kevin. You didn't just reach for a new life, you ruined the one you had. And we didn't deserve that. Not me, and not our child." I moved to the front door. "I'm still grieving my baby," I whispered. "But I can no longer grieve for her father. Good-bye, Kevin."

I knew he wouldn't answer.

47

"I'm so glad you called." I could hear the relief in Heather's voice.

I gripped the handset, wondering if it was a good idea to have phoned her. I'd just taken possession of my new house, and the sprawling space and airy, open rooms filled me with possibilities for the future. As the cool of winter approached, and with it the promise of Christmas coming in a matter of weeks, I'd been thinking about the future more and more.

Dr. Alexander had said I needed to decide what to do with my past, and if I was going to have any hope of moving on, I needed to make peace with it. I had no idea what that would look like. My past still seemed so unwieldy, so difficult. A yawning chasm of loss too large for me to explore and understand.

But Jack's struggle to forgive his father had inspired me. Maybe I was ready to begin working on forgiving too. Not because I had a burning desire to absolve the villains in my life, but because I'd already lived through the worst of what *not* forgiving could do to me. I knew what it was like to carry hatred.

So I had picked up the phone, determined to reach out, for my own sanity's sake. Heather seemed like a logical place to start. She was my sister, after all. We'd grown up together, shared secrets, and swapped clothes. And, despite her friendship with Donna, she had supported me over the past several months, coming to the rescue more than once.

Perhaps if I spoke to Heather, I'd be able to forgive her, be able to remember the best parts of our relationship.

But hearing her voice on the phone made me doubt my plan. The last time I'd seen her had been at the psychiatric center when I had been hauled out of the recreation room and put in confinement. Partly because of her.

I squeezed the receiver. "I've moved."

She sighed. "I know. Mom told me." She fell silent. Was she hoping for an invitation? *Come on over and see my silk drapes?* Was I willing to extend one to her? I glanced around the house. Its bright walls and open spaces felt large enough to hold the whole world. But was there room in my heart for Heather, after her betrayal? My sister—friend of Donna the Destroyer, the angel of death. Death to marriage. Death to Kevin. Death to my unborn child.

"Are you still in touch with Donna?"

"Kate—"

"Just asking."

Her breath came in noisy puffs over the line. "We're still friends, yes."

I thought of hanging up. What was there to say? But the roiling of my stomach told me there was at least one more thing to say to her. One more thing I needed to know. "Remember last Christmas, when I was so sick with the flu?"

"Huh? Yeah, I remember."

I squeezed my eyes shut. "Did Donna say anything to you about that?

"What are you talking about? No, she never said anything about your being sick. Why would she?"

Relief flooded my body and I was struck with ironic gratitude. Donna hadn't told my secret. She knew I'd had an abortion; I had overheard Kevin talking to her about it on the phone. But she'd kept my secret.

The day may come when I would be able to tell Heather about my abortion, but I wasn't ready. Didn't know when I would be. But I didn't want Donna telling her, either. "Nothing. No reason. Just forget it."

Heather spoke quickly. "She's never said anything bad about you, Kate. Not once."

"How kind of her," my voice dripped sarcasm. Donna had wrapped my husband around her finger, swayed Heather's loyalties, and ruined my life, but she was too much a lady to speak ill of her conquered opponent. She would draw blood when it suited her, but drew the line at rubbing salt in the wound. A true lady.

Heather said, "I know it's difficult for you to understand. But try to see it from my perspective. I literally had no one to talk to. Mom was a mess still from losing Dad, and you were in crisis—" Her breath warbled across the line, but when she spoke her voice was normal. "I know it sounds twisted. But when Donna spoke to me the day of the funeral, she was so open. She listened to me." She made a sound of frustration, an *argh*. "I can't explain it. It just ... happened." Her voice sounded small. "Please, Kate. I didn't mean to hurt you. I'm sorry."

Sorry. The word was a gauntlet thrown down, it couldn't be ignored. She'd said the word and I was forced to either accept or reject it. "Will you stop seeing her?"

She was quiet for a moment. Then, "If you want me to."

I held the receiver away from my ear and shook my head at the heavens. What kind of reluctant regret was this? If I wanted her to? "Shouldn't *you* want to stop seeing her? Shouldn't the idea of befriending that woman make you feel—"

She interrupted, "Okay. I'll stop seeing her. Okay?" Her words were clipped, terse, but her voice was soft.

I stood, tight-lipped, staring out the window into the backyard. The sky was white with clouds and the promise of snow. I had choices. That's what Maggie had said. I always have choices. I closed my eyes and pictured my sister. She had been the one I turned to after I'd smashed my car, the one I had called after Kevin's voice screamed. Each time I needed her, she'd been there.

"Okay," I said. "Okay." It was a start, something I could cling to as I worked at forgiving her. Our shared roots were deep; they intertwined through time and family. But it would be a long road. "I'm having a party next weekend."

She was silent.

"A sort of housewarming, early Christmas party," I explained. I paused. Did I want to include her? Could I face her? I made a choice. "Why don't you bring Mom?"

The house crackled with energy. From my vantage point, sitting on the top stair looking down onto the living room and foyer, I watched my guests mingle and sway through the rooms of my new house. Outside the first snow of December sprinkled down, causing everyone inside to brighten and hum with anticipation of winter, Christmas, and a new year. From my perch I watched my mother, in a high-backed chair in one corner of the living room, as she leaned forward to hear whatever it was Grace said to her. The two women had met tonight for the first time, and found an instant connection— two women who had thought this time of their lives would be about retirement and travel, but instead found themselves suddenly alone. After a few minutes of circulating with the other partygoers, they drifted to a quiet corner.

Across the room Heather stood, back against the wall laughing, a group of gangly and admiring teenage boys gathered around her. She looked flushed and happy to be the center of attention, even if it was the attention of high school boys from Glen Hills. I couldn't hear what they were saying, but Heather's eyes sparkled and she would blare out an occasional "Oh, stop it!" when it was obvious she didn't want them to stop.

When Heather had arrived with Mom, I had greeted her briefly before turning to hug Mom and hustle them in away from the cold air. The distraction of the ongoing party was a buffer between Heather and me. Every once in a while our eyes met briefly, but I always looked away. Maybe we would find a quiet moment later in the evening to talk. Or maybe not. Perhaps it was enough for now that I had invited her and she had come.

Sekeena and Creeper sat side by side on the floor in another corner of the living room. They passed a cell phone back and forth, each pushing buttons, texting, I supposed, and occasionally Sekeena reached out to give Creeper a playful swat in reaction to something he said. I wondered if she had told him the news. At least they were talking.

Creeper leaned in close to see what she had written, their heads close together. They looked like children, without a care in the world. Deceptive. Even now they had a difficult burden to carry. Choices to make. I wanted very much to help Sekeena, and planned to talk to her about an idea I had that might suit her, help her, but not tonight. Tonight she was having fun, smiling and giggling. It was a party, a time to relax and pretend there were no difficult decisions to be made, no bad things at all.

At that moment Maggie—decked out in a Santa dress, complete with a red, fur-trimmed hat—wandered in from kitchen. She spoke loudly so that the group of women who followed her—Janice, Mimi, and three teenage girls from Glen Hills—could hear her. She was like a queen in her court, or perhaps Mrs. Claus giving a tour of the North Pole. Her outfit would have been adorable on a child of five. But the women loved her, ate up her homegrown wisdom, laughed, asked questions, followed her like a row of ducks, and devoured an enormous amount of veggies and dip.

Malcolm, Richard, and Bobby stood near the door, a triangle of manhood, murmuring about whatever it is men talk about at parties like this: golf, or baseball, prostates, or politics. Maybe fine dining. They stood far apart and leaned their heads in close, and from where I sat above on the stairs, they resembled synchronized swimmers from a 1940s musical.

The doorbell chimed. Mom looked around and then got up to answer it. I stayed where I was, watching from above. At the door Jack entered, followed by Lester. I was surprised to see Lester, but I shouldn't have been. It was Jack's nature to want to share a good time with as many people as possible.

Lester looked bright and freshly scrubbed. His clean-shaven face gleamed pink and childlike, his hair slicked back. Jack looked around—for me, I supposed—and then handed Mom a bouquet of flowers wrapped in brown paper and said something that made her smile and then laugh. She turned to Lester and he ducked his head in a semi-bow.

Mom stepped away toward the kitchen, no doubt to find something to put the flowers in. The boys from Glen Hills sauntered over to Jack and Lester, abandoning Heather, who now looked strange and forsaken, still leaning against the wall like a forgotten statue. The boys slapped high fives with Jack, calls of "Dude!" all around. Then Jack looked straight up at me, as if he knew he'd find me lurking high above the party.

He excused himself from the group and made his way up the stairs, a smile playing around his lips. It struck me how handsome he was—his angular face, broad shoulders, the combination of dark hair and blue eyes. The image of me, head tipped back, neck stretched, ready to receive an imaginary kiss from him, filled my mind. My face flushed hot.

He sat beside me on the step. "Hiding out, I see."

I shook my head, smiling but embarrassed, as if he could read my thoughts. "Nope. I just came up to get a sweater and got caught up with the view." I pointed to the party below.

He looked down. "You'll have to introduce me to everyone. I met your mom." He nudged me. "And I plan on having a long talk with her tonight—so many questions about her daughter." His grin spread across his face and he stood. "I'm going to find me some punch. This party does have punch, right?" He clumped down the stairs, not waiting for a response.

"In the kitchen," I said, calling after him.

Before his foot hit the bottom step, Maggie appeared from nowhere and wrapped him in a bear hug. "Hello, handsome," she exclaimed. She turned to the gaggle of women gathered behind her. "Everyone, this is Pastor Jack, Kate's dear friend and plumber." The three girls from Glen Hills squirreled up their faces and laughed at Maggie, or Jack, or both. Maggie hitched her arm through Jack's and paraded him through the room like a long-lost son. "Look at him," she hollered to the room. "Isn't he lovely?"

Jack posed iron-man style, hamming it up for the crowd. The women erupted with laughter. I stood and looked down for one last moment before joining the party. I'd finally decided what to do with my past. For the first time, I'd chosen to throw open the doors of my life and allow all the pieces to mingle together. No hiding, no avoiding people. I had introduced the parts of myself to each other with this party. From above they almost resembled one large organism, pulsing with life, combining parts to create one whole living thing. Even the walls of the house itself seemed to breathe, to expand, and make room for everyone.

I skipped down the stairs. Maggie came up beside me. She had abandoned Jack and now had Lester hooked by the arm. "You must introduce us, dear."

"Uh, Maggie, this is Lester."

Maggie spun around and offered her hand for him to kiss. "Charmed."

Lester looked addled. He took hold of her dangling fingers and gave them a little shake. "Pleased to meet you."

Maggie wrapped an arm around his shoulders. "Come sit and tell me all about yourself." She threw me a Groucho Marx look, eyebrows wagging, as she led him to the sofa.

Across the room Jack was holed up with Mom, talking quietly. He glanced up and caught me staring. He grinned and flapped his hand, stay away. Mom laughed and shooed me away too.

Sekeena tapped my shoulder. "Creeper and I are going for a walk. Is it okay if we come back later?"

"It's getting cold," I said, then bit my tongue. Creeper stood by the door, pulling on his jacket. I smoothed Sekeena's long hair. "Yes, do come back after your walk."

"He and I got things to talk about." She smiled.

I put my hand on her back. "Before you go, I wanted to ask you—have you found a place to move yet?"

She shook her head. "Not yet."

"In that case, would you consider moving in here, with me?"

She gave me a wide-eyed look. "Seriously?"

I nodded. "I'd love the company." I turned her toward Creeper. "Add it to your list of things to talk about on your walk, okay?"

"Okay." I could hear the happiness in her voice. She joined Creeper and they slipped out the front door.

Maggie breezed by on her way to the kitchen; for once the gaggle of women weren't following. She stopped a few feet past me and then backed up. "Getting Lester a cup of tea. You have good tea, don't you, dear?" She rushed on before I could answer. Moments later she returned. "I plunked the kettle on. I need to get back. He's just the

nicest man. Why haven't you introduced us before?" She laughed
and scurried over to Lester, patting his leg as she sat.

Grace called to me from the foyer, "Kate, come tell me about
these amazing watercolors you have."

The party hummed and surrounded me. And as I joined Grace,
I felt a sense of belonging. Everyone here knew my struggle—or at
least some parts of it. They knew I had problems, but they were here
anyway, celebrating with me. Accepting me.

48

I ran my finger over the calendar. It had been one year ago today, just four days before Christmas, since my abortion.

I gazed out the window at the fresh blanket of snow and felt vaguely annoyed by its brilliance. This was not a day to celebrate, nor a day that represented freshness. Not only was it the anniversary of an event I had tried to forget—drove myself over the edge of sanity in order to forget—but it was Sunday, and I had no desire to go to church.

I'd attended a few services since moving to the city, and Jack had always made it clear that I was under no obligation to attend. Which suited me. Still, Jack had done so much for me, and I felt more than a small duty to support him.

I sipped my coffee and sighed, a stone of discontent lodged in my belly. I didn't know what I wanted, to be alone or to be with people. To stay or go. Restless, I snatched up the TV remote and clicked on the set. A flat-screen TV, mounted near the top cupboards, swelled to life. I swallowed more coffee, feeling the warmth of it seep into the rock in my gut. I flipped through the channels; a showcase of religious programming, infomercials, and sports programs. Just when I decided to turn it off, a familiar face filled the screen and my breath caught in my throat.

I froze, remote still pointed at the television, as the Reverend J. D. Slater hollered, red-faced, from his pulpit into the camera. "God is not mocked!" he shouted. "The Bible tells us He knows what's been done in the dark places. He *sees* what's done in the secret places." Rev. Slater pointed an accusing finger at the camera, at me. "You think you can do as you please and go unpunished?" He paused for dramatic effect, I supposed. It affected me dramatically and I held my breath, waiting for my punishment to fall from the heavens. "God is a heavenly spotlight, blasting rays of truth into the dark corners of your life. He'll expose your sin, and in the light of His high beams of holiness, you'll have nowhere to run." His chins wagged in fury. "No more excuses. You'll be face-to-face with your wretchedness."

With a trembling finger, I clicked off the TV and stared at the blank screen. I'd already been face-to-face with my wretchedness. I'd walked down that path. Maybe I was still walking it. My memories were intact, but my heart was still a box of shattered glass. And I had serious doubts that God could put it back together. Or would care to. At least not the God I saw reflected in The Reverend. His was an angry God. A black-and-white, right-and-wrong sort of God, much like The Reverend himself. A God who'd condemned me with his "high beams of holiness."

But then there was the God I saw reflected in Jack. A God of seemingly endless patience. One who befriended people, walked beside them. A God whom Jack believed loved me. I used to assume I knew what love was.

But what kind of love could God have for someone like me? The love demonstrated by The Reverend or the kind demonstrated by Jack? Which one was the real God?

A small thought formed in my mind. *Ask Him.* I pushed it away. It struck me as the height of irony that hearing from dead people was mental illness, while millions believed it was sane as a Sunday drive to hear the voice of God.

I pushed my hands through my hair. What would I say to God, anyway? And what would He say to me?

Ask Him.

A tremble rippled across my lower back and up my spine. My body shook as if cold.

I spoke into the open space. "Who are you?"

I am the One who made you.

A sensation like a hand, warm as liquid honey, touched me, permeating my skin. Firm and soothing, yet light and calm, it caressed me, cradled me.

I whispered, "Oh, God."

I am the One who knows you.

I was overcome with immediate intimacy. I felt a sensation like the deep searching of a hand, tender as it moved over the scar tissue slashed across my life. It massaged my mind and stroked the welted wounds of my spirit. I reached back with longing. A reunion of lovers lost to each other over time, now free to explore. The hand slid over my womb and lay like a blanket, and I cried out as our sorrow mingled together there.

Then warm honey flowed over the base of my spine, and my trembling stopped. An image of a hot, spinning marble lodged between my vertebrae filled my mind. It contained all of my anger, compressed into a tiny ball and hidden from my view.

The honey stopped just short of reaching the ball. I understood instinctively what was being asked of me; the One who knew me would not force His way into my anger; He only waited. My anger, my hatred, was justified. I'd been betrayed and had suffered because of it. Still, He waited.

I breathed my permission with one word, "Yes." In an instant that place was invaded with warmth and I heard the crack of marble breaking open, shattering. I went down to my knees. A groan, deeper than words, poured out from my mouth.

God bathed me with His presence and my mind called out to Him, "I am known by You."

And He sang back to me, *My love, my love.*

49

I sank into the sumptuous couch in Dr. Alexander's office. Two days before Christmas, and not a holly leaf or jingle bell in sight. Maybe psychiatrists don't celebrate Christmas, I thought. Or maybe Christmas decorations didn't look professional for a man whose patients must include people from every sort of religion or nonreligion there was. Not that I could talk; my own house wasn't exactly lit up for the holidays. But I would rectify that after the appointment by going shopping. For the first time in a long while, I wanted to celebrate.

Dr. Alexander raised his eyes from my file he'd been reading. "Tell me about your week."

There were no words for what had happened in my kitchen two days ago. Certainly terms existed, phrases that could explain it—but no words could express my experience. I looked at Dr. Alexander's crooked toupee and patient face, and knew it was best to hold my tongue. "There's a teenage girl at Glen Hills, Sekeena, and she's pregnant. She needs a place to live." I bit my lip. He waited, said nothing. I cleared my throat as if about to proclaim a public announcement. "I've invited her to live with me." I rushed on before he had a chance to say anything. "My house is so big, and I wondered, even when I bought it, what I would do with all the space. But this is a perfect solution. She needs a place to live, and I have all this space to fill."

He frowned. "You should bring this up in group therapy."

"Huh? Why?"

He raised his eyebrows high on his forehead and his toupee wobbled, then settled again. "To get feedback from people who know you." He sat forward. "Taking a pregnant teen into your home is a huge responsibility for anyone. For someone with your history …" He sat back again, his eyes flicking over the file on his lap. "By connecting with other points of view about an issue, you'll see things from different angles. Your group therapy members will come up with questions you wouldn't think of yourself."

It was my turn to frown. "It's my decision."

His face brightened into something approaching a smile. "Of course. Heaven knows you dislike following orders." *Heaven certainly did know.* He tossed the file onto the small table beside him. "Many of the choices you made in the past were so difficult to live with that you tried to wipe them from your mind." He gave me a pointed look. "The decision is yours, but I suggest you take advantage of the support you have around you."

I chewed the inside of my cheek. "Are you afraid after I come off the meds completely I might relapse—fall apart?"

He pressed his fingertips together. "You have a great deal of anger to deal with yet, Kate."

"I know." The sound of marble cracking resounded through my mind. I was willing to begin to let go of my anger. God had somehow entered into that burning, furious part of my mind and begun to cool it. I shivered at the memory. Of the collaboration of God's and my desire to heal the wounds. It gave me hope that I could continue toward forgiving Kevin, Blair, and Heather. Even Donna Walsh. Someday. Not today. I didn't have to do it today. But I could choose, just as Maggie had said. I had choices. It was a start.

"It was a good week," was all I said.

His eyebrows arched, as if impressed, as he reached for my file. "We've been weaning you off the medication for a few weeks now." His pen poised above the file, he said, "How have things been going for you at the lower doses?"

I smiled. "Fine."

"Uh-huh. Racing thoughts? Dry mouth? Voices?"

Voices? Yes, one voice, but this time it was a voice of healing, of new beginnings. But what would a psychiatrist say to news that I'd heard the voice of God?

I recalled the first question the on-call doctor at the hospital psychiatric ward had asked me, "Have you been talking to God?" It was a diagnostic question, designed to see how far gone I was. Now, as of two days ago, God had spoken to me.

"I'm not hearing Kevin's voice," I said, a note of honesty ringing clear and sharp. Maybe too sharp. Dr. Alexander gave me a withering glance. Trying to keep things from a psychiatrist is like playing hide-and-seek behind a water hose. "I mean, it's different," I mumbled.

"Different? You're hearing a voice?"

I took a deep breath. "No. I've started talking to God. Praying. And, well, it's not like we sit around and chat. It's just that He sort of … communicates with me." Even to my ears I sounded crazy. Maybe spiritual things were a little bit crazy.

"And you believe God speaks to you?" There was a hint of weariness in his voice, as if he were plodding past scenery he'd seen before.

I waved both hands at him. "I'm just praying, that's all."

His eyebrow went up, but otherwise he didn't move a muscle. "Do you consider yourself a spiritual person?"

Eliza Campbell had asked me the same question nearly six months ago. Then, I was plugged up, she had said. Now a fissure of joy ran up my spine. "Yes," I said. "I'm a spiritual person."

He made a sweeping gesture with his hand. "Yes, well, prayer and meditation are considered by many to be a vital part of good mental health." He tapped the pad of paper with his pen. "And you haven't heard Kevin's voice?"

I straightened my shoulders. "I'm done talking to the dead. I'm ready to talk to the living God."

EPILOGUE

The doorbell chimes. I jump up from the game of Uno I'm playing with Sekeena and Creeper and go to answer it. I glance at the clock; Jack is right on time. I pull the door open and the cool March air touches my face and arms. "We just started playing. We'll deal you in next hand." I wave him in, but he doesn't move.

He stands under the porch light in his loose-fit jeans and denim shirt over a white T-shirt even though it's still cool enough to warrant a jacket. His dark hair is tousled, his face clean-shaven. He stands like an actor who's forgotten his lines. His blue eyes dart here and there, settling nowhere. He jerks his head to the right; he wants me to join him on the porch.

I grab a sweater and step out, closing the door behind me just as a burst of laughter erupts from inside, and Sekeena calls "Uno!" Jack looks past me, through the glass of the front door, into the house and smiles.

He looks back at me, and I gesture to two wicker rockers in the corner, but he shakes his head. I'm disconcerted by his uncharacteristic silence and a nervous giggle burbles up from my throat.

"What is it, Jack?"

He searches my face. Finally he says, "You know how you think about something for a long time? You play it out in your head over and over, how you think it's going to go, but when the time comes it's nothing like you thought it would be?"

I laugh in earnest. "That, as you well know, explains the last year of my life."

He rubs his hands down the front of his jeans. "I'm having one of those moments right now."

I'm puzzled by his words, but I wait. I know he'll make it clear. Still, I wish he would agree to sit down.

Hands on his hips, he looks handsome, and flustered. I try to hide a smile. He looks up, blue eyes shining in the porch light. "I don't know if I should say anything." He turns toward the dark front yard. When he turns back, he says, "I've imagined what I would say. What you would say. Especially what you would say." He presses his lips together hard and looks up at the porch ceiling. "I sound like a dope."

I shake my head. I want to say no, he doesn't sound like a dope, that I very much want to hear what he will say next.

He presses his hands together and points them at me, like directing a prayer my way. "You've been through so much. Since before I met you, your life has been this runaway train, and even though things have been better—" He interrupts himself, raising his eyebrows, asking me to confirm his observation.

And in a rush, I know what he's going to say. My skin tingles with the knowledge. I nod. "Things are better for me." I pause, searching for the right words. "I've come a long way." I tap my temple. "I've found some peace of mind."

"I know." He smiles. "The thing is, I never knew— You are the most—" He stares down at his feet. "I've never met anyone like you."

He takes two slow steps toward me. "I've wrestled with this for a long time, Kate. Whether it's the right time to tell you. But I think we both know ..."

My heart ricochets around my rib cage. "Tell me."

He presses his lips together hard, then says, "I love you." He blurts it out, the sounds running together, making them a single word.

Once again I am wrapped in the sensation of liquid honey pouring down my body. I'm known by him. His presence surrounds me, reaches out to me. Tears blur my vision. "Say it again."

He laughs, his face open, relieved, happy. "I'm completely, stupidly in love with you."

I beam at him. "I'm so glad."

Then I'm in his arms and it is as if the fabric of his waiting is torn asunder, shredded by the moment of fulfillment. There are no tender touches, no soft exploration, no tentative parting of gentle lips. Instead his kiss is a bold declaration: I belong to him, and he to me. Connected by something larger than both of us.

He pulls back. "I don't want to rush, Kate. I understand we need to go slow." His hands run over my hair, my face, down my back to my hips, up again.

I touch his face. I nod yes, we'll go slow. Take our time, whatever you say. "I love you, Jack."

Tears well in his eyes, his voice is like gravel. "My love."

My heart thrums in my ears. I pull back a little, so I can read his eyes. "Dr. Alexander says there are no guarantees. I'm making progress, but the future—"

He puts a finger to my lips. "The future belongs to God." His finger trails from my mouth down my chin and rests in the small valley of my collarbone. "I love the living, breathing part of you, Kate. That will never change." And his mouth presses down again.

Behind me the door opens. I turn.

Sekeena stands there, bug-eyed at the sight of Jack and me. "Whoa."

We grin at her, arms around each other. To Jack I say, "Let's play some Uno."

He looks deep into my eyes. "I. Love. Uno."

I laugh as we step inside and close the door.

... a little more ...

When a delightful concert comes to an end,

the orchestra might offer an encore.

When a fine meal comes to an end,

it's always nice to savor a bit of dessert.

When a great story comes to an end,

we think you may want to linger.

And so, we offer ...

AfterWords—just a little something more after you

have finished a David C. Cook novel.

We invite you to stay awhile in the story.

Thanks for reading!

Turn the page for ...

- **An Interview with Bonnie Grove**
  - **Group Discussion Topics**

An AfterWords (AW) Interview
with Bonnie Grove

In a charming outdoor bistro in Italy, a smiling woman sighs over the perfect espresso and gazes out toward the Mediterranean. Unfortunately, this isn't Bonnie Grove, who has never visited Italy nor laid eyes on the Mediterranean. In order to chat with Bonnie we must zip our down-filled parkas to the chin and trudge headlong into the northern winds to Canada. We find her huddled near the fireplace inside a Starbucks gulping a mochaccino and waving a pen high above her head. "Anyone have a rhyme for 'igloo'?" she hollers into the crowd. She tosses the pen down. "Yeah, me neither. This is why I don't write poetry."

AfterWords Interviewer: So you're no Sylvia Plath wannabe. We can live with that. Tell us, why do you write?

Bonnie Grove: Oh man. I KNEW you'd ask that. I keep thinking I need to come up with a really good answer for that question. It's on my to-do list.

AW: Uh … so you don't know why you write?

BG: Oh sure I do. I just don't know the exact words to explain it. It's complicated. I didn't start out to be a writer. I meant to be a psychologist. That's the road I was on when I started writing. What drew me to psychology were the stories behind the human experiences. And what drew me to writing is the human experiences inside the stories. So, I don't know if I'm a successful writer or a failed psychologist.

AW: *That's tough. No wonder you write about mental breakdowns.*

BG: Tell me about it.

AW: *Still, your background in psychology must have come in handy while writing* Talking to the Dead.

BG: Yes. I have a great deal of respect for the field. I've been privileged to sit with individuals, couples, and families while they try to put their lives into words; try to voice their experiences. In those sacred moments, I have felt God's presence so near, so immediate it literally caused me to fall silent. And it's that story—the story of God present in our immediate turmoil that I wanted to tell.

AW: *That's why the tagline on your Web site is "Life is messy, God is love"?*

BG: Exactly. Hey, if you order the pumpkin muffin, I'll share it with you.

AW: *Uh, okay. Thanks, I guess.*

BG: Anyway, yes. My life is messy (picks several pumpkin muffin crumbs off her shirt). I bet you've had moments of mess in your life too.

AW: Sure. We all have.

BG: Yep, we all have. I've left behind the notion that life should be something else, something, I don't know … perfect? Or neat, or whatever it is. I've given myself full permission to shift through the truth of my life. I tromp around in it, knowing God is there beside me.

AW: So, is Talking to the Dead *a work of fiction, or is it a fictionalized autobiography?*

BG: It's trickier to talk about than it seems. Kate's story is a work of fiction. I haven't lived through any of the actual circumstances Kate went through. So the short answer is: Kate is not me, and this is not my story. But, on another level, we have all lived her experiences. We've all lived through loss, grief, shame. It's the journey toward making sense of our lives, making sense of the bad. Is there such a thing as an emotional autobiography? If so, I guess that's what I've written. Including the good parts, like forgiveness and love.

AW: Let's talk about love. The romantic scenes in this novel are deeply affecting, without resorting to clichés or sentimentality. What's your secret for handling the romance element in your novels?

BG: Love is lived out in the everyday. Sweaty palms and thrumming hearts can only get you so far and while they are fun, they aren't the hallmarks of mature love. It's important, when talking about love, to get beyond the gooseflesh rush of passion and talk about long-haul love. Kate and Kevin's dysfunctional love had moments of brilliance. It had to, or why would he hold such sway over Kate? And Jack's love, well, that's love of a different kind, isn't it? Steady, honest, transparent. He is in my mind a model of a man of integrity in love. When God is the center and source of your love, it can't help but transcend cliché and sentimentality.

AW: Where did the character of Kate Davis come from?

BG: Like most of this book, she came in bits and pieces at first. I began with attributes I wanted to explore through story. Her feistiness, her confusion, and her strong sense of irony were the first three characteristics I knew she had going for her. In time, thank God, she moved out of that two-dimensional world and became a three-dimensional character. Her feistiness morphed and developed into emotional intelligence, survival, and, ultimately, hope. Her sense of irony brought moments of light and relief, and then, again led to hope. It was her confusion that was most fun to work with. She keeps having conversations she doesn't mean to have. She goes into something thinking she knows what she wants to say and what needs to be discussed, but somewhere in the course of the conversation she loses track of things and is left wondering, *What just happened?* It was in writing the scenes involving Kate's confusion that she came fully alive.

AW: Alive? I've heard authors say sometimes their characters talk to them. Did that happen to you?

BG: Yes. It's a bit strange, but I've come to understand it as two parts of my brain talking to each other—a way to resolve dissidence using picture and sound. But it's fun. Kate was the character who spoke to me most often. But Kevin and I had some difficulties too. Dead people aren't especially chatty—so getting into his head and writing him as a fully alive person took effort. I was struggling with a scene and I demanded, "Say something, Kevin!" and he said, "I'm too good for this scene. Write a better one." That's when I truly understood him. And yes, I wrote him a better scene. It was the only way to get him to talk.

AW: What do you hope readers take away from the story?

BG: A great reading experience—that may sound like "a given," but it was important to me to try to write a book people would want to read—enjoy on several levels, so that is a huge hope. On top of that, I hope the reader will let her imagination drift, allow herself to ask questions of herself, her life, and in doing so discover just how immediately close God is to her in that moment. That is where clarity comes from.

AW: In her endorsement, Francine Rivers says, "It takes a gifted and intuitive writer like Bonnie to bring humor into the middle of such a serious story. She made me laugh in several of her scenes with 'counselors' and their philosophies." How did you manage to bring humor into the story?

BG: First off, let me say I'm honored that Francine Rivers enjoyed the book. I am a massive fan of hers and it is more than an honor that she read the book and offered such a generous endorsement. But, to answer your question about humor: Did you know there is an entire field of psychology that looks at humor? How it works, what it does for us, why we use it?

AW: Get out!

BG: True. Fascinating stuff. Two keys to the use of humor: type and timing. You must use the appropriate type of humor that fits with the situation. And your timing must be bang-on. You can't fudge timing. In this novel, I used humor to take the pressure off the reader, to help her take a deep breath and relax before plunging in further. (Stuffs more muffin in her mouth.) And that's all I have to say about that.

AW: How do you write a novel?

BG: (between bites of pumpkin muffin) How do I write a novel? I don't think I've written enough novels to answer that question. I know how I wrote *Talking to the Dead*, but I'm at work on a new novel and the process is completely different. Maybe that's the answer—it's different every time. Or, maybe after a few more, I'll have some concrete notion of how I write a novel. Truthfully, I hope it's the former.

AW: Did you say new book? What can you tell us about it?

BG: At the moment it is untitled but I fondly refer to it as *Gabby Wells: The Musical.*

AW: It's a musical?

BG: Ah, no. But it's all the fun drama of a musical, without the singing, or dancing. Or music. It's the story of a women who finds Jesus, begins reading the "red words" (words of Jesus) in the Bible, and then is framed for murder.

AW: Oh my! That sounds—hey, you ate the entire muffin!

BG: Oh. I did, too … Sorry about that. If we get another one, I'll for sure share that one with you.

Group Discussion Topics

Here are some themes to consider:

1. Friendship. Maggie thrust hers onto Kate, Heather forged an inappropriate one. Kate offers her friendship to Sekeena. Examine the role friendship played in Kate's unfolding drama.

2. Loss. Loss comes in many forms in Kate's story. There are the obvious losses brought by death, but there are many more. Examine the levels of loss Kate experienced.

3. Mental health. Kate's grief and guilt expressed itself in many different ways. Examine the evidence that suggests Kate was mentally ill, and the evidence that suggests she was mentally healthy.

4. Love. Kate's understanding of love changes throughout the book. Love is expressed and rebuffed and rejoiced in at different times. Examine the different kinds of love in the book.

5. Humor. Even in the throes of her sorrow and grief, Kate experienced moments of quirkiness, of lightness, and even humor. How was this accomplished in the book?

6. Therapy. Kate underwent several types of therapy. How did each help her? In what ways did they fail to help her?

7. Faith. Kate wrestles with God. Jack's faith inspires her, and The Reverend's faith frightens her. Explore Kate's journey toward faith—its small but important beginnings, to the end of the book. What do you think about Kate's faith experience?

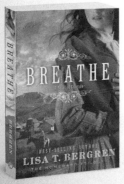
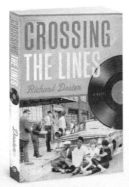